Also by Karyn Monk

My FAVORITE THIEF

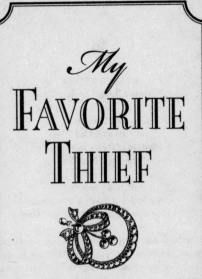

KARYN MONK

Bantam Books
New York Toronto London Sydney Auckland

MY FAVORITE THIEF
A Bantam Book / January 2004

Published by
Bantam Dell
A Division of Random House, Inc.
New York, New York

Bantam Books and the rooster colophon are registered trademarks of
Random House, Inc.

ISBN 0-553-58441-3

Manufactured in the United States of America
Published simultaneously in Canada

OPM   10   9   8   7   6   5   4   3   2   1

For

Philip

My hero

My
FAVORITE THIEF

Chapter One

H E HOISTED HIS LEG OVER THE WINDOW SASH AND
dropped heavily into the dark chamber, barely stifling a
groan.

I am getting too goddamn old for this.

Cursing silently, he rubbed the muscle spasm gripping his shoulder. He should have known better than to
climb that tree. Since when had they started growing
with so few bloody branches? He had thought he would
ascend it with the agility of an acrobat, easily shifting
from branch to branch. Instead he had dangled from it
like a frantic puppy, legs swinging and scrambling, arms
quivering. At one point he had lost his grip and nearly
crashed to the ground. That would have been fine entertainment for the ladies and gentlemen attending Lord
and Lady Chadwick's dinner party on the main floor, he
reflected darkly. Nothing like having a masked man
plummet from the sky just outside your dining room
window as the servants are heaping your plate with
stringy mutton and greasy peas.

He stood unmoving, giving his eyes a chance to
adjust to the dark. It was quickly apparent that Lady

Chadwick liked gold. Everything within her bedchamber fairly shimmered, from the heavy brocade coverlet upon her gilded bed to the garishly carved commode that towered like a throne beside it. No doubt in her private moments she imagined herself the consort of a magnificent prince or duke, instead of the bloated, sniveling fop she had elected to marry. He supposed every woman was entitled to some fantasy in her life. His gaze shifted to the bureau at the opposite end of the chamber, which boasted a profusion of richly decorated bottles and jars. Stealing silently across the shadows, he reached for the jewelry chest rising amidst the clutter.

Locked.

He eased open the uppermost drawer of the bureau and rifled through the layers of undergarments folded within. The key lay nestled beneath the armor of Lady Chadwick's formidable corsets. Why did women always presume thieves would never think to look there? he wondered. He supposed they preferred to believe that most men were either too modest or too gentlemanly to rummage through a woman's lingerie.

As it happened, he was neither.

Carefully inserting the key into the jewelry case's tiny lock, he turned it once, then raised the lid.

A glittering collection of precious stones lay gleaming upon the dark velvet within. In addition to her penchant for gold, Lady Chadwick also enjoyed the sensation of large diamonds, rubies, and emeralds against her skin. He supposed that was fair compensation for enduring the tedium of marriage to Lord Chadwick for so many years. He lifted a magnificent emerald necklace to the thin moonbeam filtering through the window, watching in fascination as its color shifted from near-black to the clear green hue of the river he had played in for so many years as a lad.

The chamber door opened suddenly, flooding him in a wash of light.

"Oh, I beg your pardon," the young woman standing in the threshold quickly apologized. "I didn't realize anyone was in here—"

Harrison watched with grim resignation as understanding swept through her. Ultimately, he had no choice. Even so, guilt weighed heavy in his chest as he grabbed the girl and jerked her toward him. She stumbled forward and he caught her, then kicked the door shut. He clamped a gloved hand against her mouth and twisted her around, imprisoning her slender form against him. Her fear was palpable, he could feel it in the rapid pounding of her heart against his arm, could hear it in her soft, desperate little pants of breath. Self-loathing welled within him.

For God's sake, focus.

"If you scream, I will kill you," he whispered harshly into her ear. "Do you understand?"

Her body stiffened. He was acutely aware of the scent of her as he held her close. Not roses or lavender, or any of the other sickly-sweet perfumes he was accustomed to women wearing. The girl pinned against him had an unusually light, clean fragrance, like the essence of a meadow just after a summer rain.

"I'm going to take my hand away from your mouth now. If you swear to me that you won't scream or try to run away, I give you my word that you won't be harmed. Do I have your promise?"

She nodded.

Harrison warily removed his hand from the girl's lips. He didn't know whether he could trust her. Her evening gown suggested she was one of Lady Chadwick's dinner guests. Whatever her reasons for quitting the dining room, it likely wouldn't be long before some dutiful maid was sent to find out what was detaining her.

The girl's delicate rib cage continued to rise and fall against his arm. Her breathing had slowed a little, and he was grateful for that, even though he supposed it would have been better for both of them had she swooned. Then he could have simply laid her on the bed and climbed back out the window. As it was, he was going to have to tie her up so she couldn't go screaming out of the room the moment he left, compromising his escape.

"Please." Her voice was small, hesitant. "You're holding me so tight I can't breathe."

She was Scottish, he realized, the sweetly refined cadence of her voice pleasing to him.

"Forgive me." He instantly released her.

She faltered slightly, as if she had not expected him to free her quite so abruptly. He instinctively reached out to catch her, but this time his hold was gentle. She glanced at him over her shoulder, surprised.

"Thank you."

Moonlight spilled across her face, illuminating her features. She was not as young as he had thought, for there were fine lines around her enormous dark eyes and across the paleness of her forehead, suggesting her age to be at least twenty-five years or more. Her cheekbones were high and pronounced, emphasizing the elegant fragility that seemed to surround her. Her finely shaped brows were drawn together and her mouth was set in a sober line as she studied him, her expression hovering somewhere between fear and something else, an emotion that looked almost like empathy. That was ridiculous, he told himself impatiently.

No woman of gentle breeding would sympathize with a common jewel thief—especially one who had just threatened to kill her.

"You dropped your necklace." She pointed to the sparkling pool of emerald and diamonds upon the carpet.

Harrison regarded her incredulously.

"It might be better to leave that one, and take a few smaller pieces instead," she suggested. "Lady Chadwick is sure to notice that her precious emerald necklace is missing the minute she goes to put her jewelry away tonight. If you take some of her less important pieces, she is unlikely to realize right away that they are gone, which means you will have an easier time selling them. Once their theft has been reported to the police and the newspapers, your sources might be reluctant to buy them."

He raised a bemused brow. "Are you always this helpful during a robbery?"

She colored slightly, embarrassed. "I just thought you might consider the advantages of selecting quality pieces which are more modest in appearance. The larger, more opulent stones are not always the most valuable—they can be flawed within."

"I realize that."

"Forgive me—of course you do." Her gaze became curious. "You're the Dark Shadow, aren't you?"

Harrison stalked over to the bureau and began to ransack Lady Chadwick's intimate apparel, searching for something with which he could tie up his quizzical young guest.

"When do you think you will have stolen enough?"

He paused to look at her. "I beg your pardon?"

"The newspapers have been filled with stories of your robberies for months now," she explained. "I'm wondering when you think you will have stolen enough that you will be able to resign from a life of crime and apply your talents toward a more law-abiding profession. Ultimately, sir, I'm sure you will find the rewards are much greater in leading a respectable, productive life."

Anger pulsed through him. In his experience,

women who spewed sanctimonious advice about the path of righteousness had invariably lived sheltered lives. They didn't know the first goddamn thing about life beyond their own smug existence.

"It is something you should consider," she continued seriously. "If you are caught you will be sent to prison. I can assure you that is not a very pleasant place to be."

"I'll bear that in mind." He yanked a stocking from the drawer. "I regret having to do this, but I'm going to have to tie you to that chair over there. I'll try not to make the bindings too tight—"

"Miss Kent?" There was a cursory rap upon the chamber door before it swung open.

"Help!" shrieked a horrified maid, appalled by the sight of Harrison in his dark clothes and mask stalking toward the girl with a twisted stocking in his hands. *"Murder!"* She tore down the corridor, screaming loud enough to wake the dead.

"Quick—go out the window!" exclaimed the girl. "Hurry!"

Swearing furiously, Harrison threw down the stocking and sprinted toward the window. Shouting and screaming split the night air, causing the coachmen and the curious on the previously sedate street to surge toward the house. He was relatively certain he could scrabble down that godforsaken tree in less than a minute without breaking any significant bones.

The distinct possibility that some earnest champion from the mob might shoot him down from the branches like a giant, hapless bird gave him pause.

"What are you waiting for—go!" The girl waved her arms at him as if she were shooing an errant child out the door.

Realizing he had little choice, he heaved one leg

over the window sash and stretched his aching arms toward the tree.

A shot streaked through the darkness, clipping the branch where his fingers had brushed.

"I got him!" roared an excited voice from below. "Stop, thief!"

"Come back!" pleaded the girl, grabbing him by his coat. "You can't go that way!"

"I realize that," Harrison agreed tautly.

"You'll have to leave from Lord Chadwick's chamber across the hall—hopefully there won't be anyone waiting for you on the other side of the house." She went to the doorway and peered into the corridor.

"Come out with your hands in the air!"

Harrison joined the girl at the doorway to see a scrawny young groom trudging warily up the stairs, balancing a battered old rifle unsteadily before him.

"I warn you," he bleated nervously, "I've killed before an' I ain't afraid to do it again."

Harrison thought that unlikely, unless the lad was referring to killing rodents in the stable. At that moment, however, the prospect of being shot by a terrified youth with an ancient firearm struck him as highly undesirable—especially given that the boy might miss and hit the pretty young stranger who was so gallantly trying to assist him instead. With no hope of racing across the hallway to another chamber, his only chance for escape had disintegrated. How ironic, he reflected bitterly, to be caught and arrested for his crimes at this late stage.

He exhaled in disgust and raised his hands.

"He has a pistol!" screamed the girl suddenly at the groom. "Don't shoot or he'll kill me!"

Harrison stared at her in disbelief. "What in the name of God are you doing?"

"We have no choice," she whispered fiercely. "You've got to use me to get out of here!"

"Let her go!" The groom sounded as if he was going to be sick. "I told you, I ain't afraid to shoot!"

"For Christ's sake, Dick, don't threaten him!" barked a footman, venturing up the stairs behind him.

"He's liable to murder the whole bloody lot of us!" the butler added, joining them.

"Fine, then!" squealed the groom, thoroughly agitated. "Maybe you'd like to have this instead!" He shoved his weapon at him.

"Don't give it to me, you idiot," snapped the butler, pushing it back. "I don't know how to fire it!"

"Silence, all of you!" Breathless and sweating profusely, Lord Chadwick struggled to affect an air of dignified authority as he reached the top of the staircase. "This is Lord Chadwick speaking." He paused to dab his brow with a linen handkerchief, letting the import of his presence sink in.

"Lord Chadwick, thank goodness you're here." The girl pretended to sound relieved. "Please tell everyone to clear the staircase and let us come down—he won't shoot anyone as long as no one tries to stop him—"

"Everyone in the house has exactly two minutes to go down to the kitchen and lock the door behind them," snapped Harrison. Since this girl had just added abduction to his litany of crimes, he supposed he might as well play some actual part in it.

"Go into the kitchen?" Lord Chadwick sounded outraged by the idea. "Look here, sir, I don't know who you are or what you mean by breaking into my home, but I assure you that I am not moving from this spot until you release my guest safely into my custody, do you hear? Miss Kent's well-being is my responsibility, and I have no intention of abandoning her to your foul, despicable ways—"

"The first person I see upon leaving this room will

be shot dead, Lord Chadwick," Harrison vowed darkly, "and that includes you. Now *move* before I—"

A deafening blast suddenly tore through the house, cutting short Harrison's threat.

"Run for your lives!" His bulging eyes nearly bursting from their sockets, Lord Chadwick knocked his startled servants aside as he fought to beat them down the stairs. *"Run before he murders all of us!!"*

The entire household instantly exploded into a maelstrom of fleeing bodies, the distinctions of sex and class obliterated as servants and aristocrats crashed into one another in their desperate bid for safety.

"I told them to go into the kitchen," muttered Harrison, exasperated. "Now I've got an even bigger crowd to contend with once I get outside."

"If you keep me in front of you, they won't shoot," the girl suggested.

"I'm not taking you with me—that idiot groom is liable to kill you in his attempt to save you."

"I think he dropped his rifle." She glanced around the door and saw the clumsy firearm lying abandoned on the carpet. "There, you see? He must have thrown it down after it went off."

"It's Miss Kent, is it?" Harrison's tone was bland.

"It's Charlotte, actually. Miss Kent always sounds so terribly formal—"

"It may surprise you to learn, Miss Kent, that I'm not in the habit of abducting helpless women and using them as a shield. I don't intend to start now." A dull throbbing had started to pound at the base of Harrison's skull. He was beginning to wish he had stayed home that night.

"You're not actually abducting me—I'm offering to help you," Charlotte pointed out. "Unless you are prepared to be arrested and spend the rest of your days in a prison cell, you have to let me help you get out of here."

Her eyes were large and earnest. It was impossible
to determine their color in the soft veil of light spilling
into the room, but it struck Harrison that they were unlike any he had ever seen. There was a singular strength
emanating from the strange young woman standing before him, a unique resolve that was as bewildering as it
was captivating.

"Are you carrying a pistol?" she demanded.

"No."

She frowned. "What about a dirk?"

Reluctantly, he nodded. "I have a dagger in my
boot."

"A dagger is fine for threatening to cut my throat,"
she allowed matter-of-factly, "but if someone decides to
try to wrestle it from your hand, we're going to have a
problem."

He didn't know what to make of her. Any normal
gentle-born woman would have been drowning in tears
by now, begging him to release her unharmed. Instead
this strange girl was scanning the room, apparently trying to come up with another weapon for him. He went
to the window and glanced at the crowd still gathered
on the street below. The hammering in his head was
spreading now, sending deep tentacles of pain streaking
across his forehead and into his temples.

"I know!" she exclaimed suddenly. "You can hold
Lady Chadwick's hairbrush in your pocket and press it
against my ribs as we go out, giving everyone the impression that you have a firearm."

She grabbed a heavy silver brush from the bureau
and held it out to him. As if she actually believed he was
a man of great daring, who was easily capable of outwitting an irate mob on the strength of a mere hairbrush.
For some strange reason, he was loath to disillusion her.
When was the last time a woman had looked at him
with such pure, untainted trust in her eyes? he won-

dered bleakly. The pain in his head was getting worse now. He knew in a few minutes it would be excruciating, and then he would be unable to think at all. If there was any chance of escape, however small, this was his only moment to grasp it.

"And what do we do when we get outside?" he asked.

"Don't you have a carriage waiting for you?"

"No."

She frowned again, as if she found it incomprehensible that a thief could attempt a robbery so poorly prepared. "Then we'll have to take mine," she decided, moving toward the doorway.

"Are you hurt?"

She regarded him in confusion. "No—why?"

"Your leg—you seem to be having trouble walking."

"It's nothing," she assured him shortly. "I'm fine."

Shoving Lady Chadwick's hairbrush into his coat, he wrapped his arm around her.

"I don't need your help to walk," she protested, trying to push him away. "I'm quite capable of—"

"I'm only doing as you suggested and pretending that I am using you as a shield."

"Oh." She stopped fighting him, but her body was rigid beneath his arm. It was obvious he had touched a raw nerve when he mentioned her leg.

"Once we are outside, if anyone decides to overtake me, I want you to get the hell away from me so you are out of harm's way." Harrison regarded her seriously. "Is that clear?"

She shook her head. "No one is going to attack you as long as I stay in front—"

"Is that clear?"

"If I move away from you, someone might shoot you."

"We're not leaving, Miss Kent, until you say yes."

She sighed, reluctant. "Yes."

"Fine, then. Let's go."

They moved awkwardly down the staircase together. By the time they had reached the main floor, his accomplice was breathing heavily, and despite her assurances that she was fine, Harrison knew her gait was painfully stiff. He had little time to reflect upon this, however, as they stepped up to the front door and into the view of the crowd awaiting them outside.

"Everyone move back," Harrison commanded, holding fast to his partner, "and send Miss Kent's carriage over."

The terrified horde obediently took a few steps backward. The carriage, however, was not forthcoming.

"Send Miss Kent's carriage over," repeated Harrison heatedly. *"Now!"*

"I heard ye the first time, ye soddin' piece o' scum," barked a furious voice. "An' if ye so much as bend a wee hair on the lass's head while I'm bringin' it to ye, I'll be scrapin' yer cowardly flesh from yer thievin' bones and choppin' it fine afore I grind ye into haggis!"

Harrison watched in astonishment as an ancient little man scuttled as fast as his skinny legs would carry him toward the line of carriages on the street. Displaying a remarkable agility for his advanced years, he hauled himself up into the driver's seat of one vehicle, snapped his reins against the horse's hindquarters, and sent the carriage lurching forward.

"That's Oliver," Charlotte whispered to Harrison as the carriage barreled toward them. "He is very protective of me."

"Wonderful," drawled Harrison.

The carriage clattered to a stop directly in front of the entrance. Oliver cast Harrison a murderous look before regarding Charlotte with concern. "Are ye hurt, lass?"

"No, Oliver," Charlotte assured him gently. "I'm fine."

"Ye'd best make sure she stays that way, ye spineless cur," he warned Harrison, "if ye're thinkin' ye'd like to keep yerself in one fine piece."

The idea of the wiry little Scotsman fighting him was preposterous. But Harrison recognized the old man's overwhelming fear for the girl pinned against him, and he knew better than to trifle with the elder's emotions.

He had learned that strength born of fear and frustration could be far more dangerous than that of mere youth and muscle.

"I give you my word that Miss Kent will not come to any harm as long as you do exactly as I say," he told him.

Oliver snorted in disgust. "Canna trust the word of a rogue who'd snatch a helpless young lass an' push a pistol to her ribs," he spat contemptuously. "Ye thieves today have nae honor, an' that's the sad truth o' the matter. Now in my day, ye'd nae see me wavin' a gun about—"

"Please, Oliver," interrupted Charlotte. "We have to go *now*."

Oliver glowered at Harrison. "All right then, ye wicked rascal, see if ye've enough manners in ye to help Miss Charlotte into the carriage, an' we'll be off."

Relaxing his hold upon her slightly, Harrison reached up to open the carriage door.

"*No!*" cried Charlotte suddenly.

Harrison turned just in time to see a nattily attired gentleman clutching a pistol in front of the doorway from which he and Miss Kent had just emerged. One of Lord Chadwick's guests had not abandoned the house after all, he realized numbly. Instead he had hidden in-

side, waiting for the perfect moment to race out and
shoot the infamous Dark Shadow in the back. The man's
beefy hands were trembling visibly, his brow jeweled
with perspiration as he leveled the pistol at Harrison.

Harrison wrapped himself around Charlotte, enveloping her in the hard shield of his body just as the
weapon exploded. Pain ripped into him, burning a path
through flesh and bone. Holding Charlotte fast, he
jerked open the carriage door.

"Stop, thief!" roared his assailant. "Or I'll shoot
again!"

His shoulder on fire, Harrison whipped around,
shoving Charlotte behind his back. He brandished Lady
Chadwick's hairbrush menacingly through the fabric of
his coat. "Throw down your weapon or I'll shoot your
bloody—"

Another shot exploded through the darkness.

Harrison froze, knowing if he flinched the bullet
would strike his protective young charge instead.

For a moment no one moved, anxiously waiting to
see if the infamous Dark Shadow had been killed.

"Thomas!" screamed a woman suddenly. "Oh, dear
God—Thomas!"

Confused, Harrison raised his gaze to the front
doorway.

The fashionably attired guest lay sprawled upon the
stairs, his arms and legs spread out upon the polished
stone steps. At first it looked as if he had merely slipped
and fallen. But something was leaking across the pale
surface of the step beneath him and weeping onto the
next in a grotesque river of crimson.

"Saint Columba—ye've killed him, ye filthy
swine!" blazed Oliver, appalled.

Harrison stared in bewilderment at the limp, bleeding form of the man on the stairs, his hand still gripping
Lady Chadwick's hairbrush.

"Get in the carriage!" urged Charlotte. "Now!"

"I'm nae takin' him anywhere," Oliver raged, "the bastartin' devil! He can bloody well hang—"

"He didn't do it!" Charlotte was trying desperately to get Harrison to move. "He couldn't have, Oliver—he doesn't have a pistol!"

Oliver scowled, confused. "He doesna?"

"Please, you can't stay here!" Charlotte pulled hard on Harrison's arm, trying to get him into the carriage.

The night was filled with screams now. Men and women were running away, disappearing down laneways and into neighboring mansions, wildly trying to escape the murdering Dark Shadow. There was nothing he could do for the poor bastard bleeding on Lord Chadwick's steps, Harrison realized bleakly. Surrendering to Miss Kent's pleas, he helped her into the carriage. Then he hauled himself up and banged the door shut as the vehicle flew forward.

Pain was everywhere now—blinding in ferocity. Its talons had sunk deep into his brain and eyes and ears, while the fire streaking through his shoulder was radiating to the tips of his fingers. His coat sleeve was sodden with blood, and his mouth was nauseatingly dry. He was alive, and so was the strange young woman who had interrupted his disastrous escapade.

Everything else was lost.

Chapter Two

I KNOW YE'RE THERE, ANNIE, SO YE NEEDN'T BE SNEAK-in' up the back stairs like a ghost, hopin' I willna notice." Eunice banged her rolling pin against a crumbly ball of dough, throwing her considerable weight against the recalcitrant mound as she flattened it into submission.

"I didn't want to disturb ye." Annie adjusted the damp, thin hood of her cloak and stared guiltily down at her boots. "I didn't think anyone would still be in the kitchen."

"Miss Charlotte hasn't returned from her dinner at Lord and Lady Chadwick's, so we're makin' oatcakes while we wait for her, Oliver, and Flynn to come in," Doreen explained, slapping several rounds of dough onto a hot griddle. "Why don't ye come have one with a nice cup of tea?"

Annie shook her head. "I'm dead tired." She hunched further into the depths of her cape. "I'll just be off to bed."

Doreen narrowed her eyes. Her aging vision had weakened in the past few years, but she was still canny enough to recognize when someone was trying to hide something from her.

"Why don't ye let me take yer cloak and hang it up for ye by the stove?" she offered kindly. " 'Tis wet from the rain that's started—nae point in draggin' it all the way up to yer room."

"No." Annie's pale hand clutched the garment closed at her throat. "I'd rather keep it with me—I'm cold."

Doreen dropped the last oat circle onto the griddle and sighed. "All right, lass, keep it with ye. But if ye've a problem, ye needn't be afraid to tell me and Eunice, or Miss Charlotte, if ye'd prefer. That's what we're here for—to help ye."

Eunice looked up from her dough, baffled. "What problem?"

"There ain't no problem," Annie quickly assured her. "I'm fine."

Doreen fisted her blue-veined hands on her narrow hips, unconvinced. "Then why are ye tryin' so hard to hide yer face?"

"I ain't." The girl's voice was small and tight.

"Did someone hurt you?" Eunice demanded.

Annie vehemently shook her head. "It's just a little bruise." Her voice began to break. "It'll be all but gone come mornin'—"

"All right then, my duck, let's have a look," soothed Eunice, wiping the flour from her strong, plump fingers as she moved toward the cowering girl. "There's nae to fear, lass—I'm just goin' to take a wee look and see what can be done for it." She gently slipped Annie's hood off her head. "Sweet Saint Columba—who did this to ye?"

"He didn't mean to hit me," Annie insisted, raising her hand to the ugly plum-colored stain blooming around her left eye. "I made Jimmy mad, is all, an' he swung his fist before I had a chance to dodge it. He'll be

awful sorry about it the next time he sees me—I know
he will."

"If I catch the filthy devil, I'll make him more than
sorry!" raged Doreen, her little walnut-colored eyes
blazing with fury. "I'll crown him with a pot and put a
boot to his arse afore I throw him in the street!"

"Oh, please, Doreen, you mustn't hurt Jimmy." Annie regarded her imploringly. "He's just havin' a hard
time bein' without me, is all." Her voice was soft with
regret. "He misses me."

"He misses the brass ye used to make for him by
sellin' yerself on the street to any piece of scum who fancied ye, more like," fumed Doreen. "He misses feelin'
like he owns ye."

"Here now, lass, sit down and let's get a cool cloth
on that eye and see if we canna keep the swellin' down."
Eunice poured cold water from a chipped jug onto a
cloth and pressed it gently against Annie's bruised face.
"Does it hurt much?"

Annie winced. "I've had worse."

"I wish I had a leech to put on it," Eunice lamented,
shaking her head. "That takes the swellin' down nice
and quick. After this I'll put a little of my rose-and-
rotten-apple conserve on it, and by tomorrow morn'
ye'll be good as new."

"Thank ye." Annie was silent a moment before hesitantly asking, "Ye ain't goin' to tell Miss Kent, will ye?
She'll be dreadful disappointed in me if she knows I
went and saw my Jimmy. When she asked me to come
stay here, she said she believed I could make somethin'
fine of myself, as long as I was willin' to give up whorin'.
I didn't know that meant givin' up Jimmy, too." She bit
her lip. "He thinks whorin' is all I'm good for."

"We'll leave ye to tell Miss Charlotte about yer eye
yerself. But if she asks us if we know how it happened,

we'll nae lie to her," Doreen warned sternly, "and neither should you."

" 'Tis always best to tell the truth and shame the
devil." Eunice folded her cloth over so a cooler part lay
against Annie's bruised eye. "Even though the truth may
sting a wee bit."

"I don't want Miss Kent to think I've disobeyed
her." Panic tightened Annie's thin, sharp features. "Then
she'll make me leave."

"Miss Charlotte would nae make ye leave as long as
she thought ye was willin' to honestly try for another
life," Doreen assured her. "She lived on the streets herself, once, when she was just a lass. She's even spent time
in prison."

Annie's eyes widened. "Really? For what?"

"For stealin', when she was nae much younger than
you."

"She doesna judge people for havin' a bad start,"
continued Eunice, "as she knows most bairns with a
hard start have nae hope of makin' a decent life for
themselves. That's why she opened up this refuge
house—because she wanted to help."

"Sounds like they're home already," remarked
Doreen as the clatter of horses' hooves came to a stop in
front of the house.

Alarm spread across Annie's face. "I'm off, then,"
she said, leaping up from her chair. "I'll tell her about
Jimmy in the mornin'—when my eye don't look so
bad."

"It canna be Miss Charlotte—it's too early," Doreen
argued, patting her shoulder. "Ye just let Eunice take
care of ye, lass, an' I'll go see—"

"Eunice! Doreen!" Charlotte's voice was anxious as
she called to them from the main floor above the
kitchen. "Come quick!"

"Somethin's amiss," hissed Doreen, snatching up a heavy iron skillet.

"Aye." Eunice grabbed her rolling pin. "Ye stay here, Annie, and dinna move till we tell ye 'tis safe."

"And pull those oatcakes off the griddle afore they burn," added Doreen, heading up the stairs. "They're all but done."

C HARLOTTE STOOD IN THE ENTRANCE HALL, DESPER-ately struggling to hold up her half of the Dark Shadow. Her small friend, Flynn, who claimed to be twelve but struck Charlotte as more the size of a ten-year-old, was valiantly trying to support the enormous thief's other half.

"Let's toss him on the supper table," Flynn suggested, fighting to keep from dropping his heavy, rain-soaked burden.

"I think he should be put to bed," Charlotte countered. "He's very weak."

"Stand back or I'll smash yer scurvy skull in!" Doreen exploded through the doors from the kitchen, waving a heavy black skillet before her.

Eunice burst into the hallway behind her, a floury rolling pin poised above her like a truncheon. "Sweet Saint Columba!" she gasped, taking in the sight of Charlotte and Flynn holding up the bleeding Dark Shadow between them.

"Flynn and I need your help." Charlotte felt a little better at the sight of the two white-haired women flailing their makeshift weapons about. No matter how desperate the circumstances, she could always count on Eunice and Doreen to be ready to fight. "This man is injured and cannot walk."

"I can manage," grunted Flynn, his little freckled face twisted with exertion. "He ain't that heavy."

"Ye may find him light, lad," agreed Doreen, taking hold of Harrison's arm, "but Miss Charlotte's nae so young and swack as you."

"Shall we take him to the kitchen?" asked Eunice, grabbing Harrison's other arm.

"No, let's take him to the empty chamber upstairs." Charlotte clenched her jaw, trying to ignore the painful throbbing in her leg. She was not accustomed to bearing any weight on the injured limb other than her own. Most days even that was difficult for her. "He has been shot and needs to be attended to."

Eunice regarded her with concern. "I'm hopin' that's his blood on yer dress, lass, and not yers."

"I'm fine, Eunice."

"Oh, dear Lord in Heaven, Miss Kent!" squealed Annie, emerging from the doorway to the kitchen. "I'm awful sorry—I told him to keep away!"

Charlotte regarded her in confusion, taking in her bruised eye. "Do you know him?"

"Of course I know that stinkin' piece of dung—how dare he think he can go about frightenin' a fine lady like yerself!" Trembling with fury, Annie marched over to Harrison. "Bastin' me is one thing, Jimmy, but scarin' Miss Kent here makes ye lower than scum—do ye hear? An' don't try to hide from me behind some pissin' mask!" She reached up to jerk his disguise off.

Harrison's hand snaked around her wrist with bruising strength.

"Don't touch me," he ground out softly, twisting her hand away from his face. "Or my mask."

"You ain't Jimmy!" Annie gasped, stunned.

"No," he agreed. "I ain't." He released her.

"He's the Dark Shadow." Flynn regarded her with great superiority, pleased to know something she didn't. "Miss Kent found him tryin' to nick some jewels from Lord Chadwick's house, but instead of turnin' him over she decided to help him. Then some gotch-gutted nob tried to shoot him an' got shot instead, only the Shadow here didn't do it, 'cause he only had a hairbrush in his pocket. I was in the carriage an' I seen the whole thing."

Doreen blinked, confounded. "A hairbrush?"

"Aye—he's schooled in the old ways." Oliver nodded with approval as he shuffled in through the front door. "Although I must say, laddie, speakin' strictly from one professional to another, next time ye might consider a dirk instead."

"Thank you," Harrison managed, his teeth clenched with pain. "I'll bear that in mind."

"We have to get him upstairs, quickly tend his wound, and try to get him safely out of here." Despite Charlotte's concern for the Dark Shadow, she knew she could not possibly hide him in her refuge house for any length of time. "Everyone believes he has taken me hostage. Even though Oliver drove fast and we got away swiftly, the authorities are looking for us."

"It willna be long afore they decide to come here, either hopin' to find the Shadow, or at least find that Miss Charlotte was released safe an' just went home," finished Oliver.

"Right then—let's set a stout heart to a steep hillside." Eunice tightened her grip on Harrison's arm. "Ye push him up from behind, Ollie."

Breathing heavily, Charlotte did her best to support some of the Dark Shadow's substantial weight as the little group awkwardly climbed to the top floor of the modest house.

"Someone new movin' in?"

Harrison turned his head to see a pretty, sleepy-eyed girl of twenty-three or so peering around a chamber door, the brilliant red of her hair pouring over her simple white nightgown like flames.

"Who's this, then?" she wondered, staring at him with interest.

"We got the Dark Shadow, Ruby!" exclaimed Flynn, excited. "Come see!"

Ruby's eyes grew round. "Really?"

"Has he decided to stop thievin'?" demanded a younger girl, appearing behind Ruby. With her flat little nose and her sharp chin she was not quite pretty, but there was a sweetly youthful quality to her that made her somewhat attractive nonetheless. Harrison didn't think she could have been more than fifteen.

"I'm thinkin' he will, Violet," Oliver interjected, before Harrison could answer. "If tonight counts for anythin', the lad's losin' his touch."

"I'm not losing a damn thing." The pain in Harrison's head was nearly blinding now, and his shoulder felt as if it was being slowly ground into pulp. If he didn't lie down soon, he was certain he would just collapse where he stood.

"If ye ain't givin' up yer criminal ways, then what are ye doin' here?" demanded Violet testily. "Only them that's willin' to make somethin' better of themselves can stay at Miss Kent's house. That's the rule."

"Right now I'm not overly concerned about his future plans, Violet," Charlotte explained. "I'm more concerned that he not bleed to death before we can do something to help him. Perhaps you and Ruby would run downstairs and fetch us some warm water and clean rags for binding."

"And go into the medicine chest in the kitchen cupboard and bring me extract of lead, a lancet, a needle, a probe, and some thread," added Eunice, huffing as they awkwardly eased their injured guest onto a narrow iron bedstead.

"And whiskey." Harrison closed his eyes. "Lots of it."

"I'm afraid I don't keep spirits in the house,"

Charlotte told him, apologetic. "If you like, Ruby will make you a nice cup of tea."

He raised his lids to glare at her. He had a bullet in his shoulder and an excruciating headache that was making him feel cold and nauseated. Did this sanctimonious young girl really believe all he needed was a goddamn cup of tea? "Wine, then."

"No wine, either, I'm afraid." She seemed utterly unmoved by his glower. Clearly his mask was protecting her from its full impact.

"I've some nice, sweet cooking sherry in the larder," Eunice offered, taking pity on him. "Ye can have that."

The thought of ingesting some sickly-sweet cheap cooking swill made Harrison's stomach lurch. "No." Then, realizing that the elderly woman was offering him something that she probably believed was precious, he added, "Thank you."

"Tea it is, then, Ruby," declared Doreen, who had set to work with Oliver trying to remove Harrison's gloves, blood-soaked coat, and shirt. "There's hot water in the kettle on the stove."

"I don't want anything." An overwhelming weariness was seeping through him, which combined with the crushing pain in his head made him want to retreat from the world. Sleep was what he needed. If he could sleep, the pain just might be gone when he wakened. He would worry about the bullet, and the police, and his disastrous visit to Lord Chadwick's house, in the morning.

"Ye'll be drinkin' it anyway," she informed him briskly. "By the looks of yer clothes ye've lost enough blood to float a wee ship, an' ye need to have somethin' to drink to help ye make more. I'll nae have ye turnin' yer toes up on my sheets—'tis bad luck."

" 'Twas hard enough gettin' ye up the stairs while ye

were alive, lad," said Oliver, chuckling. "I'm nae of a mind to drag ye down again when ye're dead."

"Ye could always tie a rope around him and toss him out the window," suggested Annie helpfully. "That'd be quicker than bangin' him down the stairs."

"He ain't goin' to snuff it, is he?" Flynn looked disappointed. "I want to hear about his fleecin'."

"Nae from a wee scratch like this." Having peeled the sodden layers of fabric off Harrison's torso and mopped away most of the blood, Doreen was finally able to survey the actual damage to his shoulder. "The ball bit through and come out the other side, nice and clean. Me and Eunice will stitch him up, and in a week or so he'll be fit an' fine." She firmly pressed a wadded up cloth against the oozing wound.

"Why is he trembling like that?" asked Charlotte, concerned. "It's not cold in here."

"He's probably got a chill from losin' so much blood," Eunice speculated. "Annie, run and gather up every blanket ye can find—we'll pile them on him an' see if we canna get him warm again."

"It's not the blood," Harrison managed, his teeth chattering as Annie left to do Eunice's bidding. "It's the pain—in my head."

"If ye've a pain in yer head, ye'd best let me take yer mask an' cap off so I can give ye my soothing saline-and-vinegar wash," Eunice told him. " 'Tis good for inflammation of the brain, an aching tooth, an' if ye drink a wee bit it rinses yer insides as clean as a—"

"Laudanum." The word was barely a whisper.

Charlotte looked at Eunice uncertainly.

"He's used it before or he wouldna be askin' for it," Eunice reflected. "His headaches must be a battle he's fought and lost afore."

"Best ye give him some, Eunice," said Oliver,

frowning. "Must be a terrible pain to make a big lad like him shiver an' shake like that."

"I'll just go an' fetch it." Eunice picked up her skirts and bustled out the door.

"I'm goin' downstairs to clean up the mess we made as we came in from the rain," Oliver decided. "Nae point in leavin' tracks for the police to wonder about when they come."

"We've got everythin' you wanted," declared Ruby, racing through the door.

"Is this enough rags?" Violet appeared behind her carrying an armful of shredded linen and a basin of water.

"It'll do." Doreen wet a clean rag in the water and began to gently swab the Dark Shadow's shoulder.

"Here are some blankets!" Annie hurried into the room, her small frame all but hidden behind the mountain of cheap plaids and quilts she had stripped from the other beds.

"Right then, Annie, ye and Miss Charlotte lay them over him nice an' warm while I stitch up this shoulder of his," directed Doreen.

Charlotte took one side of the first blanket Annie offered and laid it carefully over the Dark Shadow, covering him from the waist down. More covers followed, but with his chest and bleeding shoulder exposed, it was impossible to get him warm. After a few minutes Eunice returned with a small brown bottle, from which she carefully dispensed a series of drops into a glass of water.

"Easy now, lad, let's have ye up a wee bit while I pour this down yer throat," she clucked, wrapping one soft, fleshy arm beneath his neck.

Harrison blindly opened his mouth, too overwhelmed with pain to care what the hell he was drinking. If these old Scottish ladies were trying to poison him, so much the better. At least in death there would be some escape from this excruciating torment. The moment the familiar taste of the laudanum hit his tongue, he nearly whimpered with relief. It would take time for the drug to work, but at least there was a reprieve somewhere in front of him, if only he could hang on. He drained the glass, then collapsed against the narrow little bed, wholly uninterested in the matter of his shoulder.

"It looks nasty at the moment," Doreen told Harrison as she bandaged him, "but if ye keep it clean an' change the linens several times a day, it should close up fine. Ye can take the stitches out in a few days—dinna leave them too long, or they'll grow into yer flesh." She knotted a final strip of linen around his arm, then nodded with satisfaction. "Now Ruby and me will fetch yer tea."

"I'm goin' to take yer shirt and coat an' see if there's any hope of washin' this blood out and mendin' the tear," added Eunice. "If not, dinna worry—we'll find ye somethin' else to wear when ye're leavin'."

"Thank you." Harrison's tongue felt thick in his mouth, making the words clumsy.

"Polite, ain't he?" observed Violet after Eunice and Doreen were gone. "Talks like a real swell, he does."

"The Dark Shadow ain't no swell," objected Flynn, clearly interpreting this as an insult. "He's one of us."

"He may have started as one of us, but he talks too fine to be one of us anymore," Annie argued.

"He's a thief, ain't he?" Violet looked to Charlotte to settle the matter. "Didn't Flynn say ye found him nickin' Lord Chadwick's jewels?"

"He was in the process of stealing when I came upon him." Charlotte gently laid a blanket over the Dark Shadow's body. Now that the laudanum was starting to take effect, his shivering had subsided, but she was worried that he might still be cold. She tucked the blanket securely beneath the feather mattress, covering the hard, muscled contours of chest and belly. His black mask and cap remained in place, safely concealing his identity for the moment. His breathing had slowed and deepened and his eyes were closed, suggesting he had fallen asleep.

"Then that makes him one of us," Violet decided.

"Whatever he is, I'm bettin' he's rare handsome beneath that mask," said Ruby, entering the chamber carrying a tray of tea and oatcakes.

"How can ye tell?" wondered Violet.

"Look at his hands," she instructed. "They're lovely clean—not all rough and stained, but they ain't sickly white and soft neither, the way some nobs' hands are. So he works with his hands, but then takes time to wash 'em, an' file his nails short. That's a prime man that does that."

"I like a man who bathes," Annie agreed. "An' scrubs his teeth now and again, too."

"I know some girls won't let chaps kiss 'em if their mouths is all rotten an' stinkin'," said Ruby. "They say they're more like to get diseased from that than from puttin' their pricks between their—"

"Here now, that's enough blather!" interrupted Oliver sternly, appearing suddenly in the doorway. "That's nae way to speak when Flynn and Miss Charlotte is about."

Flynn shrugged his shoulders. "I've heard worse."

"It's all right, Oliver." Charlotte was always touched by Oliver's gruff protectiveness. "Annie, Ruby, and Violet were just talking about the life they knew before coming here. They should feel comfortable talking about it. That's part of healing from the past and moving on from it."

"I'm sorry, Miss Kent," Ruby apologized, chastened. "Sometimes I forget to speak proper when ye're about."

"A fine lady like you ain't supposed to know about such things," Violet agreed. "It ain't right."

Charlotte adjusted the blankets covering the Dark Shadow, who appeared to be sleeping, and said nothing. Years had passed since the ugly, violent part of her early life. Years in which Haydon and Genevieve had lovingly raised her and done their utmost to protect her. But the penchant for malevolent gossip in the aristocratic circles of Scotland and London had made it clear from the beginning that she would never be permitted to escape the sordidness of her beginnings. Even so, she said nothing to contradict Violet's assumption that she was a fine lady.

She made no secret of her past, she told herself, swallowing thickly.

She simply preferred not to discuss it.

A sudden banging on the front door interrupted her thoughts.

"That'll be the peelers, most like," Oliver said, referring to the police. He regarded her soberly. "Ye'd best go downstairs, lass, and let them know ye're home safe. We'll tell them the Shadow jumped from the carriage at Waterloo Bridge, an' we just made for home as fast as we could."

"What'll we do with him if they decide to search the house?" Ruby tilted her head at the dozing form of the Dark Shadow.

"I won't let them," said Charlotte.

"Ye may have nae choice," Oliver told her. "Ye listen from the stairs, lad," he instructed Flynn, "an' tell the lasses if the bobbies are fixin' to search."

"But how will we move him?" Violet cast a worried look at the Dark Shadow. "He looks bloody heavy."

"We'll just heave him to the floor and shove him under the bedstead," Annie decided. "If Ruby climbs onto the mattress and we toss some blankets over her, they'll never know he's there."

"Dinna fret, lass," Oliver said gently, sensing the fear that was starting to take hold of Charlotte. "He took ye hostage, remember? Ye've done nae wrong, an' the bobbies will be pleased to see ye're safe. After that, they'll be on their way." He reached out and gave her hand a reassuring squeeze.

Charlotte managed a small smile. *Get hold of yourself,* she ordered silently. *You're safe.*

"We'll be back in a few minutes," she told Flynn and the girls. Trying hard to affect a calm she didn't feel, she straightened her shoulders and moved awkwardly down the stairs to face the police.

Chapter Three

GOOD EVENING, GENTLEMEN. I AM MISS CHARLOTTE Kent, and I am sorry to have kept you waiting."

Charlotte smiled at the two men standing in the drawing room. The younger man was a police constable, who could not have been on the force overly long since he looked to be no more than nineteen or twenty. His rain-soaked, ill-fitting uniform caused alarm to flare within her, as it always did when she saw a policeman. Fighting the sensation, she limped past him with as much dignity as she could muster. She could feel his surprise as he observed her labored movement, and knew the exact moment when it turned to a kind of sickened pity.

She inhaled a steadying breath, reminding herself that he could not be blamed for his reaction to her. When she was a young girl Genevieve had suggested she try to ignore the stares of others, but that had proven impossible. Over the years she had grown accustomed to the embarrassed glances of the world, those startled expressions of horror, curiosity, and, at their most brutally honest, revulsion.

"Please, sit down." She gestured to the faded chairs and sofa as she seated herself.

The second man nodded at the young police constable, giving him permission to be seated. Charlotte turned her attention to this gentleman, because he was obviously of greater authority than the policeman, and because he was not wearing a uniform and was therefore less intimidating to her. He appeared to be about thirty-seven or so, and she supposed his face was handsome enough, although at that moment it was far too sober to be considered pleasant. He was dressed in a plain brown coat of fairly good quality, dark trousers, and wet, worn shoes—suggesting that his means were adequate but by no means vast, and he was either in the habit of walking a great deal, or did not think it necessary to waste money on new footwear when there were still a few miles to be squeezed from his current pair.

"Miss Kent, permit me to introduce myself," he began. "I am Inspector Turner of Scotland Yard, and this is Police Constable Wilkins. First let me say that I am greatly relieved to find you here—at this moment there are scores of policemen and concerned citizens searching the streets of London for both you and the Dark Shadow. I realize you have suffered a very difficult ordeal this evening, but I hope you won't mind answering a few questions?"

Charlotte shook her head. "I would be pleased to, Inspector Turner."

"How did you manage to escape the Dark Shadow and make it back to your home?"

"It all happened rather quickly, actually," she replied. "We drove off as fast as we could, because the Dark Shadow ordered Oliver—who is my coachman and butler—to drive away, and, fearing both for my life and his own, he obeyed. After we had been driving for a while, he suddenly said 'Turn here!' and Oliver did, and then he—the Dark Shadow, that is—threw open the door and jumped out, and I told Oliver to just keep driving as fast as he could for home, and that is how we came here."

"I see." Lewis Turner nodded, as if he believed her tale was completely plausible. He always found it best when questioning people to first let them tell their story exactly as they wanted him to hear it. The time for pointing out the inconsistencies came later. "And where was it, exactly, that he jumped from the carriage?"

"I—I'm not sure. I think it was somewhere near Charing Cross. Or—no, actually, it was by Waterloo Bridge," she corrected herself, suddenly remembering Oliver's instructions. "Yes, that's right. He jumped out by the bridge, and we just kept on."

"And did you happen to see in which direction he was going, after he leapt out?"

"I'm afraid not, Inspector."

He frowned. "You didn't make note of whether he was going north or south? Did he appear to go down to the river, or head for an alley?"

"I'm sorry—I was rather frightened at the time, and didn't think to look out of the carriage after him. I was just very relieved that he was gone, and that he hadn't harmed us."

"Of course. Is there anything else you can tell us about what you noticed? Is it possible for you to give us a description of him?"

"Unfortunately, no. He was wearing a mask."

"How tall would you judge him to be?"

"I'm not sure. We were seated in the carriage."

"What about before you were in the carriage, when he was using you as a shield in Lord Chadwick's home? Surely you must have some impression of his height."

"Well, he was certainly a good deal taller than me, Inspector. Beyond that I'm not sure how to describe—"

"Was he taller than me?" He rose from his chair, trying to give her some measurement for comparison. "Or was he more the height of Wilkins?" He gestured for the police constable to stand as well.

Charlotte studied the two men, feeling slightly flustered. She did not want to give them any more information than was absolutely necessary. "Unfortunately, it was quite dark, and for the greater part of my ordeal he was behind me—"

"I'm only asking for your impression, Miss Kent," Lewis assured her. "Just tell me what you remember."

"I believe he was closer to Constable Wilkins's height."

"Was he close to his height, or taller?" he persisted.

Charlotte pretended to think a moment, knowing full well that the Dark Shadow was a good deal taller than the constable. "Close to his height—or perhaps a little taller. I'm sorry, Inspector, that I cannot be more precise."

"Every piece of information is of great help in this investigation, Miss Kent," he assured her. "What more can you tell me about him? Can you give me a description of his face?"

"No—he was wearing a mask."

"Did you notice his eye color?"

"As I have said, it was very dark—"

"It was dark in the carriage, but what about when you were coming down the stairs with him in Lord Chadwick's home and making your way to the front door? Lord Chadwick keeps his home relatively well lit, does he not?"

"He—the Dark Shadow—was always behind me, Inspector. As you may recall, he was using me as a shield."

"And there was no moment, throughout the entire duration of your being in his company, in which you had an opportunity to see his eyes?" The lines between his brows deepened a little, suggesting he found this rather unlikely.

"I'm not saying I didn't see them, Inspector. I'm saying it was too dark for me to take note of their color."

"Did you happen to notice anything else about him? Did he have any distinguishing marks on his hands or wrists, or did he wear a ring of any kind?"

"I'm afraid I don't know—he was wearing gloves."

"What kind of gloves?"

"Dark ones."

"Were they leather? Wool? Cotton?"

"Leather, I believe."

"Expensively made, or second-rate?"

"I'm really not sure."

"What about his weapon? Can you describe it for me?"

"Actually, I'm afraid not. He kept it concealed in his coat the entire time."

He regarded her skeptically. "Are you certain?"

"Yes—why does that surprise you?"

"Generally, most thieves don't make an effort to conceal their weapons once they are found out—unless they are trying to remain anonymous in a crowd, which clearly he was not. Further, a number of witnesses who saw him have said that they also saw his firearm, which they describe as a very large pistol with a light-colored handle. The only thing that varies in their statements is the actual size of the weapon, which ranges from approximately nine inches to a foot or more."

"I'm afraid they are mistaken, Inspector. I was with him the entire time, and I can assure you that he kept his weapon hidden in his coat."

"Even when he shot and killed Lord Haywood?"

She regarded him with dismay. "Lord Haywood died?" Although she had seen the poor man sprawled upon the staircase bleeding, she had desperately prayed that he had only been wounded.

"You did see the Dark Shadow shoot him before he forced you into the carriage, didn't you?"

"The Dark Shadow didn't shoot him," she informed him. "Lord Haywood was shot by someone else."

Lewis kept his expression contained. "Why do you say that?"

"Because I was there—I was right beside him. He never fired at Lord Haywood. He never fired at anyone."

"Of course he did," Constable Wilkins countered. "Everyone saw him do it."

"They did not see him do it," Charlotte retorted, "because he didn't do it."

"Some fifty people have said that they saw the Dark Shadow point his pistol directly at Lord Haywood and shoot him dead," Lewis argued. "Are you saying that all fifty of those witnesses are lying?"

"I am saying that they are mistaken."

"All fifty of them?"

"It was dark, Inspector, and they were a good distance from him. I was right beside him, and I know without a doubt that he never withdrew his pistol from his coat."

"According to my reports, at the time Lord Haywood was shot, you were actually behind the Dark Shadow—is that correct?"

"Yes."

"Then I fail to see how you could know whether his firearm was drawn from his coat at that point or not."

"I know," Charlotte insisted.

"How?"

"Because it was still in his coat when he climbed into the carriage."

"Perhaps he put it back into his coat after he fired the shot."

"He didn't."

"The witnesses have also said that the Shadow was struck by one of Lord Haywood's bullets—is that also incorrect?"

"No," she admitted. "He was shot."

"Where?"

"I'm not entirely sure—it was very dark—"

"Of course, you've mentioned that numerous times." His tone remained pleasant, but he allowed her to see that he was finding some elements of her story rather dubious. "If he was able to leap from your carriage and run off into the night, it would be fair to say it was not a very serious injury, would you agree?"

"I suppose not."

"Could you give me some idea as to where you think he might have been struck?"

"I believe he was struck either in the arm or in the shoulder. I'm not really sure which."

"Left or right arm or shoulder?"

"I believe it was the left."

"Was he bleeding badly?"

"I'm not sure."

"And were you also injured?"

"No, I was not."

"And so I take it, Miss Kent, that the blood on your gown is his?"

Charlotte glanced uneasily down at her gown. She had forgotten entirely about the bloodstains she had acquired while helping the Dark Shadow into her house. "Yes." Her mouth suddenly felt dry. "That is his blood."

"If you don't mind my asking, Miss Kent, how is it that you got so much of his blood upon you?"

"I suppose it happened as he was holding me—or maybe in the carriage—he must have been thrown against me at some point as we raced away."

He regarded her thoughtfully a moment, evaluating everything she had told him. "With your permission, Miss Kent, Constable Wilkins and I would like to make an inspection of your carriage, to see if there is any more blood there, or any other evidence which might help us to solve the mystery of the Shadow's identity."

"Of course. Oliver will be pleased to show it to you."

"And so after the Shadow leapt from your carriage, your coachman drove you home," he continued, picking up the thread of her story. "Approximately what time was it when you arrived?"

"I don't know."

"Well, then, how long would you estimate you have been home?"

"I'm not sure—an hour, perhaps."

"And how far a distance would you say it is from your home to Waterloo Bridge?"

"I don't know—I suppose it is approximately a fifteen- or twenty-minute drive."

"It is a fifteen- or twenty-minute drive if one is traveling in no great hurry, but you have indicated that you told your coachman to drive as fast as he could. How long do you recall it taking before you arrived home?"

"I really don't recall, Inspector Turner," she told him, feeling slightly agitated. "As you can imagine, I was greatly distressed by what I had just been through. Are you almost finished with your questions?"

"I apologize for having to take you through what certainly must have been a terrible ordeal for you, Miss Kent. Now that the Dark Shadow has killed Lord Haywood, the pressure for the police to find this criminal and see him tried for murder will be enormous. Any piece of information, however slight or insignificant it may seem to you, can only help us to solve this case."

"I'm afraid I cannot think of anything else."

"If I may, Miss Kent, I would like to speak with your coachman a moment, to ask him what he recalls about the incident."

"Certainly."

"But first, Constable Wilkins and I would like to make an inspection of your house and the surrounding grounds."

Panic streaked up her spine. "Search my house? Why?"

"It's just a formality, really," he assured her. "It's just that one of your neighbors claims to have watched as you arrived home. She said she saw three people disembark from the carriage—which is perplexing, given that you have indicated that the Shadow left your carriage near Waterloo Bridge. I just want to be certain he did indeed leave your carriage, and did not merely get out and then perhaps travel here hanging onto the back of it—without your knowledge, of course."

"I'm so sorry, Inspector," Charlotte apologized, thinking quickly. "In all the excitement, I forgot to mention that Flynn was with us."

"Who is Flynn?"

"He is a young boy who is staying with me. As you may be aware, this is a refuge house for unfortunate women and children who are trying to escape the harshness of their past and make a better life for themselves. Flynn had come along with Oliver for the ride—he likes to go out driving at night, and he is good company for Oliver while I am visiting. Whoever saw the three of us must have seen me, Oliver, and Flynn get out of the carriage and go into the house."

"That is most likely the case," he agreed. "Nevertheless,

I'm sure you won't object if Constable Wilkins and I make a quick search, just to ensure your safety. I promise we won't disturb your household for long." Without waiting for her permission he rose and strode down the stairs to the dining room with Constable Wilkins following.

"I can assure you that is entirely unnecessary." Charlotte limped after them as best she could. "Why on earth would the Dark Shadow want to come here?" She raised her voice slightly as she added, "There are no jewels of any value in this house." Oliver was nowhere to be seen, which Charlotte desperately hoped meant that he had gone upstairs to help Flynn and the girls hide their guest.

"If he were here, it would not be with the intention of stealing." Lewis went into the main floor study, appraised it for a moment, then walked out and headed for the stairs leading down to the kitchen. "Because of the amount of time you spent with him this evening, it is possible he may have sensed your generous nature. If it turns out that his wounds are severe, he may try to appeal to you for help. It would not be the first time a criminal has sought assistance from one of his victims. Sometimes they mistake their victims' frightened compliance for a kind of empathy."

"After you are gone, Inspector, I shall see to it that all the doors and windows are locked for the night, and I will instruct everyone not to answer the door."

"That would be wise. However, as we know, the Dark Shadow is adept at breaking into homes. Constable Wilkins and I will make certain he isn't here before you lock up." He went into the kitchen, where Eunice and Doreen were busily working. "Good evening, ladies."

"Eunice and Doreen, this is Inspector Turner and Police Constable Wilkins," said Charlotte. "They are conducting a search of the house, to ensure that the

Shadow didn't decide to follow me here and perhaps break in."

"That's a fine idea," Eunice said, calmly drying a plate. " 'Twas a terrible thing ye suffered tonight, lass. If the police here can make ye feel a wee bit safer, I'm sure we'll all sleep sounder for it."

"Aye." Doreen poked violently at the flames burning brightly within the stove. " 'Tis bad enough the streets are crawlin' with vermin, but 'tis a sad state when ye canna feel safe even in yer own home. That's the way of things today, Inspector, isn't it?"

"Unfortunately, yes." Lewis poked his head into the pantry and the scullery. He then turned his gaze to Doreen and frowned. "If you don't mind my asking, why have you got the stove burning so hot at this late hour?"

"Me and Eunice likes to do some cookin' in the evenin' when Miss Kent is out," Doreen explained.

"But you're finished now, are you not?" he enquired, approaching the stove.

"Aye—but with all the fuss goin' on tonight, neither of us could go to bed, an' when I saw how lovely an' hot the coals were, I knew they were just perfect for burnin' some old rags." She pushed the last fragment of the Dark Shadow's bloodstained shirt into the orange embers, then banged the iron burner plate back into place. "There now, mind ye dinna get too close—ye'd nae want to scorch that handsome coat of yers."

"Will ye take some tea while ye're here, Inspector?" offered Eunice sweetly. "I've just made a fresh pot, an' there's warm ginger biscuits to go with it."

"No, thank you."

"How about you, Constable?" Eunice held the plate of fragrant biscuits up to Constable Wilkins. "They're lovely an' crisp—"

"We don't have time for refreshments," Lewis said firmly.

Constable Wilkins regarded the plate mournfully.

"Did either of you ladies see or hear anything unusual after Miss Kent returned home?" Lewis asked. "Any strange noises in the house, for instance?"

"Nae more strange than usual," said Doreen. "With the lasses an' young Flynn traipsin' about, there's always some clamorin' somewhere."

"I see. And where might they be?"

"At this hour they're most probably in bed," Eunice told him.

"Thank you. Please don't feel you need to accompany me, Miss Kent," he told Charlotte. "Constable Wilkins and I can manage on our own."

"I appreciate that, Inspector." Charlotte fought to remain calm as she laboriously started up the stairs in front of him. "It's just that the girls staying here might feel a little unnerved by your presence, and particularly that of Police Constable Wilkins. I want to be there to reassure them."

"As you wish."

He made a quick perusal of the bedrooms that belonged to Charlotte, Eunice, Doreen, and Oliver. Finding nothing amiss, he proceeded to the top floor.

"Don't be frightened, Violet," Charlotte soothed when she saw the young girl peering at them from behind her chamber door. "This is Inspector Turner and Constable Wilkins. They are just taking a look at the house to make sure that we are safe."

Violet eyed the two men in wary silence. Lewis speculated the poor girl had learned long ago that when it came to policemen, the less one spoke the better.

"Who is in there?" he demanded, indicating the closed door of the room in which Charlotte had left the Dark Shadow.

"That's Ruby's chamber," Charlotte told him.

"She's sleepin'." Flynn rubbed his eyes as he emerged from his own tiny room.

"Unfortunately, Miss Kent, we shall have to waken her."

"I understand, Inspector." Charlotte went over to the door and rapped firmly upon it. "Ruby? It's Miss Kent. I'm sorry to disturb you, but there is a detective and a policeman here and they need to take a quick look inside your room. Is that all right?"

"I ain't decent," Ruby mumbled sleepily. "Give me a minute."

Lewis waited impatiently, listening to the sounds of a bed creaking, a wardrobe door being opened and shut, and then a most unladylike oath as some part of Ruby's body thudded against something hard. Finally, the door opened and she appeared, looking grumpy and disheveled, with her brilliant copper hair spilling wildly over the rumpled blanket she had retrieved to drape around herself.

"I ain't done nothin'," she spat defensively at Constable Wilkins.

"The police aren't here for you, Ruby," Charlotte explained. "They are looking for any sign that the Dark Shadow may have tried to break into the house."

Ruby yawned and scratched herself. "He ain't in here."

"If you don't mind, I'd like to take a look for myself. Wilkins, you go check the boy's room." Lewis walked into the dark chamber, pushing the door wide until it was softly bathed in the light spilling from the oil lamps in the corridor.

Charlotte watched nervously as he stood in the center of the room. For what seemed an eternity he did not move, but merely stood there, his eyes searching. He studied the tousled bedclothes upon the narrow bed, the empty glass upon the dressing table, the slightly ajar door of the wardrobe. Although Charlotte didn't think there was anything unusual there, she sensed that something about the chamber bothered him. He stood almost frozen, waiting. And then it occurred to Charlotte that he was not merely looking.

He was listening.

Please God, she prayed fervently, wondering what she would do when he looked beneath the tent of art-fully draped blankets the girls had arranged over the bed. *Please make him turn around and come out.*

Instead, Lewis moved toward the bed, slowly, like a cat inching its way toward a wounded bird. He studied the pillow a moment, assessing the size of the hollow pressed into its feathery depths, and looking to see if there were any hairs against its pale linen other than Ruby's brilliant red ones.

They had underestimated him, Charlotte realized, feeling as if she was going to be sick. Constable Wilkins might have been easy to fool or distract, but the inspector's instincts were far more keenly honed. Something was suspicious to him, whether it was a scent in the air, some barely visible thread or hair upon the carpet or linens, or the all but imperceptible pulse of the Dark Shadow's breathing.

Lewis grasped the edge of the blankets suddenly and whipped them up.

And looked in stunned surprise at the emptiness beneath the bedstead.

"I told you he ain't here," Ruby said.

He glared around the room, angry now, convinced that he had been deceived. He strode to the wardrobe and threw the doors open. There was nothing inside but a couple of shabby gowns and an old pair of boots.

"I didn't find anything in the boy's room," Constable Wilkins reported as he entered. "Do you want me to look in the—"

"Silence!" Lewis commanded.

The sound of a carriage door slamming shut caught his attention. By the time he crossed the room and leaned out of the small window, the vehicle was already speeding away.

"Stop!" he shouted. "Come back!"

The carriage rounded a corner and disappeared.

Cursing, he ran from the room and down the stairs, with a startled Constable Wilkins at his heels. As they reached the landing for the second floor they nearly collided with Oliver, who was shuffling up bearing an enormous tea tray.

"Here now, lads, what's amiss?"

"Get out of my way, you old fool!" Lewis snapped. "I'm after the Dark Shadow!"

"Are ye now?" Oliver marveled, suitably impressed. "Funny, I didna see him—but nae matter, let me help ye with the door." He turned with his tray and began to slowly trudge down the stairs, still obstructing their path.

"I don't need your help with the bloody door!"

"All right, then, lad, nae need to get cross," Oliver scolded. "I'm nae so spry as I used to be, an' when ye get to be my age ye'll find 'tis nae easy for you, either."

Lewis barely heard him as he heaved open the front door and burst out onto the street.

"Where was he going?" he demanded, seeing a woman standing outside gazing forlornly after the carriage. "Did you hear what directions he gave the driver?"

"He's off to the Rose an' Crown most like, or maybe the Rats' Castle in St. Giles—an' when ye find him, I want ye to tell him I hope he rots in hell!" Annie's battered face was trembling with rage. "Just look what he did to me—he ain't nothin' but a filthy brute, an' I'll be glad when ye arrest him for beatin' on women!"

Lewis looked at her in confusion. "He beat you?"

"He'll tell you I was askin' for it—well, I'm tellin' you I didn't ask for it, an' while I may live with him now an' again I ain't his wife, an' now that I'm stayin' with Miss Kent he ain't got no right to baste me an' I want him charged with attempted murder!"

"You live with the Dark Shadow?" Contable Wilkins, who had finally managed to make it past Oliver, looked utterly astonished.

Annie stared at him incredulously. "Ye think my Jimmy is the Dark Shadow?" She exploded with laughter.

"Who was in that carriage?" demanded Lewis.

"That was my Jimmy," she managed, nearly breathless with hilarity. "Black Jimmy, they call him, on account of his black temper, and I've the marks to prove it—but Jimmy ain't no Dark Shadow! If he was, he'd be drinkin' in some gin palace in Oxford Street, not chokin' on the piss they pour at the Rats' Castle!"

"Is everything all right, Annie?" Charlotte had donned a cloak to protect her from the rain and was now making her way down the front steps. "Oh, my, what happened to your face?"

"My Jimmy hit me," she told her honestly, "an' I know ye told me he was no good and I shouldn't see him no more, but he came here tonight an' said I had to go back with him, an' when I told him no, he punched me, but these peelers here is goin' to arrest him now, an' make sure he learns the law says he can't just pitch into me whenever he likes." She looked at Lewis expectantly.

"Actually we are presently working on another case," he told her, infuriated by the fact that he had already wasted so much time there.

"Ye men are all the same," Annie observed acidly. "Ye talk the high and mighty when it suits you, but deep down ye all believe we women is good for nothin' but beddin' and beatin'—'specially a poor girl like me."

Lewis clenched his jaw, frustrated. What the hell did she expect him to do? he wondered angrily. Head down to some criminal-infested den in St. Giles and try to arrest every man who had ever laid a hand on his wife or girlfriend? The prisons of London would be overflowing before the hour was out. Even so, he felt strangely awkward as he stared into Annie's pretty, battered face. The thought of some filthy bastard using the girl for his pleasure and then beating her filled him with impotent fury.

"I can assure you that isn't true," he told her.

Annie snorted contemptuously. "Course it is."

"Come inside out of the rain, Annie, and let's get you warm and dry and see to that eye of yours." Charlotte wrapped a protective arm around her. "I believe Inspector Turner and Constable Wilkins are finished with their questions." She regarded him coolly, letting him know that she disapproved of his apparent lack of interest in what had befallen poor Annie. "Is there anything further you require, Inspector?"

"I just wanted to have a word with your coachman, and take a look at your carriage."

"I'll have Oliver meet you around the back so he can show you the carriage, and answer any further questions you may have."

"Thank you, Miss Kent. My apologies for disturbing you. Good night."

Charlotte's heart was pounding anxiously as she

shepherded Annie back into the house. Once the door was closed behind her and she was certain Inspector Turner and Constable Wilkins were headed to the stable, she regarded her household of former thieves and prostitutes in confusion.

"Where is he?" Her voice was barely a whisper.

"He's gone, lass," Oliver told her, cramming an old battered hat on his head as he prepared to go outside to meet the inspector and Constable Wilkins.

"Once we knew the bobbies was fixin' to search the house, we had to get him out of here right quick," Ruby explained. "So while they was dawdlin' in the kitchen an' such, we woke the Shadow, threw a shirt an' coat on him, plopped a hat on his head, an' dragged him down the back stairs."

"Then we heaved him in a carriage an' paid the driver to take him wherever he wanted to go," added Violet.

Flynn nodded. "He was awake by then, an' knew what was about."

"I told the lad I didna need to know where he was headed, but said he should take his mask off afore he got there, so the driver wouldna take notice of him," Oliver continued.

"We was hopin' he'd get away nice an' quiet, but I stayed out an' pretended it was my Jimmy who left when the peelers saw the carriage leavin'." Annie shook her head with irritation. "That one peeler got a bit touchy when I told him he was just like all the others, but I knew he'd never actually try to find Jimmy. None of 'em care when a whore gets a beatin', an' that's the hard truth of it."

"You aren't a whore anymore, Annie," Charlotte reminded her. "And if Jimmy or anyone else ever lays a hand on you again, I shall insist that the police find them and lay charges."

"Ye're most kind, Miss Kent." Annie smiled fondly at her. "But the bobbies don't care about what happens to a girl like me."

"Well, we care about ye, lass," Eunice informed her flatly.

"Aye, and I've told ye if Jimmy dares show his face around here, I'm puttin' my boot to his ass an' makin' sure he doesna come after ye again," added Doreen. "Come on then, lass," she continued, turning her attention to Charlotte. "Ye look as if ye're about to fall over. Let's get ye into yer bed."

"Dinna worry about the peelers," Oliver added, heading toward the door. "I'll show them the carriage and send them on their way."

"Thank you, Oliver." The throbbing in Charlotte's leg told her that she had been walking and standing for far too long. "I suppose there's nothing more we can do now."

"Let me help ye upstairs, lass," said Doreen.

"No, thank you, Doreen. I can manage. Good night, everyone."

She limped slowly up the stairs. After entering her room she closed the door, then collapsed wearily onto the bed, heedless of the blood on her evening gown or the uncomfortable constriction of her corset. She had not wanted any of them to know how exhausted she was, or how profound an effect Inspector Turner's interrogation had had upon her. She inhaled a shallow breath and rolled onto her side, fighting to endure the pain now streaking from her thigh to her toes.

Thanks to the efforts of her fiercely loyal household, the Dark Shadow had made it safely out of her home. With luck, he would make it back to wherever it was he lived that night. If he decided to reform his ways and stop stealing, he might even avoid being found and arrested for the murder of Lord Haywood. Her efforts to help him had been successful.

She closed her eyes, confused by the powerful sense of loss that had gripped her on learning the Dark Shadow was gone.

Chapter Four

"SOD IT, ARCHIE, I'M STARVIN'. CAN WE GO, NOW?" The woman glared sulkily at the enormous man beside her.

"Shut yer bloody gob, Sal, unless ye want to feel me fist in it," Archie warned. "I'll tell ye when it's time to go."

"We've been here all night," Sal pointed out, too cross and tired to be intimidated by his threat. "I'm hungry an' I need to take a piss."

"Then piss," he said, glowering. "Who the hell is stoppin' ye?"

"What—right here on the street?"

"Why not? It's cleaner than the privies or pots ye're used to."

"I ain't pissin' on no street," she informed him tartly. "It ain't proper."

A bark of laugher escaped him. "Oh, so ye're all high an' proper now, are ye? For a bit o' brass ye'd piss in a church in front of Jesus Christ himself, an' ye know it."

"Archie!" Sal smacked his shoulder. "Don't talk blasphemy!"

"If ye're suddenly shy, go behind one of them

houses," he suggested, weary of her constant complaining. "No one will see ye if ye're quick."

"An' what if someone catches me an' yells for a peeler?" she demanded. "Then what?"

"Then I guess ye'll be sleepin' in a cell tonight." He shrugged.

"Would you come after me?"

"What for?"

"To try to get me out!"

"Why? Ye'd only be in a night or two. Ye've stayed longer."

"An' after the last time I made up my mind I ain't goin' back."

"Fine, then—don't piss. Just quit yer squawkin'—I'm sick o' listenin' to ye."

Sally crossed her arms defiantly over her ample breasts and squeezed her thighs together, trying to quell the mounting pressure in her bladder. "What are we waitin' for here, anyway?" she demanded sourly. "She ain't goin' nowhere today—not after what happened last night. Why don't we just come back tomorrow?"

"Why don't ye shut up, Sal, afore I break yer bloody jaw?"

"Fuck you, Archie." She turned and began to march furiously down the street.

Archie rolled his eyes. He knew he had gone too far. "Sal," he called, his voice low and irritated. "Sal!"

She stopped and regarded him definatly. "What?"

"Come back."

"Why?"

"Because I want ye to."

"Well, maybe I don't want to. Did ye ever think of that?"

"Fine, then," he snarled, sick of her mood. "Bugger off, then."

She glared at him, pretending to debate whether or

not he was worth returning to. Finally she gave a mighty huff, annoyed by the feelings that kept dragging her back to him. Somewhere deep down, in a place he was afraid for her to see, Archie Buchan actually cared for her, she told herself fiercely. He wasn't rich or handsome, but he was strong and smart and good with his fists, which made him a good protector—at least when he wasn't throwing punches her way. Most of all, he was hers.

With nothing else to call her own, that had to be enough.

"I ain't stayin' long," she informed him as she walked back. "Just a few more minutes, an' then I'm off to find some tea an' a privy."

Archie kept his gaze on the modest little house across the street and said nothing. He didn't really give a damn whether Sal waited with him or not. He had just wanted to see how long it would take for her to back down. If she hadn't been smart and returned right quick, he'd have made her sorry for it later. That was the way of it with women, he'd learned.

You had to make them sorry, or they'd never show you any respect.

"Ye can go when ye like," he told her. "Just bring me a meat pie and some ale when ye come back."

"How long are you goin' to stay, then?"

He shrugged. "Till I leave."

"But what are ye waitin' for?" she persisted, trying to understand. "Now that ye know where she lives, why don't ye just squeeze her for a few quid an' be done with it?"

"That's what's wrong with ye, Sal—ye think too small. Do ye honestly think she's only worth a few quid?"

"She ain't rich, that's for sure," Sal returned, scratching under her armpit. "Her house ain't much, an' her togs ain't fancy. Even last night when she went to that swell's house, I didn't see no jewels on her."

"There's more than a few quid in her, Sal," Archie assured her. "She may live with whores and thieves, but she's the ward of a bloody marquess." His expression was dark as he finished softly, "I ain't about to let her get by for just a few goddamn quid."

Pain PIERCED HER SENSES LONG BEFORE THE SUNLIGHT did. It stole up her leg slowly, almost delicately, like a spider creeping along the stem of a flower. It paused a moment at her knee, weaving its intricate web of throbbing through the stiff joint, then proceeded up her thigh, silently rousing the nerves from their dormant state. The pain began to intensify, swiftly now, coursing through flesh and bone, tightening and twisting the muscles until they began to spasm in protest. Charlotte gasped suddenly and sat up, fighting the urge to cry out as she grabbed her calf and began to desperately knead the tightly braided muscles.

Please, please, please, she chanted silently, her teeth clenched together and her brow shimmering with sweat as she struggled to break the cramp that had seized her. Her hands moved desperately over the battered, misshapen limb, squeezing and pressing, trying to pummel the treacherous muscles back into their previous state. She knew she should get up and try to walk upon it, or grab her toes and pull them back in an attempt to stretch the contracted muscles, but the pain was too overwhelming for her find the courage to risk even more. *Please, please,* she continued desperately, focusing on the word, trying to draw strength from the possibility that God might actually be listening. There were tears in her eyes now, of pain and desperation and the terrible helplessness that gripped her whenever she found herself in this hideous state. *Please,* she wept, the word falling from her lips in a small, broken whisper, a promise and a plea, for in that moment she would have vowed almost anything in exchange for relief.

Gradually, the cramp began to lessen.

She continued to massage her aching leg, knowing that if she quit too soon, the spasm would find the strength to attack once more. Little by little it eased its terrible grip upon her, until finally she was able to whimper and fall back against the mattress, her chest heaving, her cheeks wet with tears.

"Miss Kent?" Annie called hesitantly through the door. "Are ye all right?"

Brushing her hands against her face, Charlotte sat up. "I'm fine, Annie."

Annie remained in the hallway, unconvinced. "Can I come in, then?"

Charlotte was dismayed to see that she was still wearing her bloodstained gown from the previous night. "Just a minute." She limped over to her wardrobe, retrieved a simple dressing gown, and hastily covered herself. Then she went to the door and opened it. "Good morning, Annie. Is everything all right?"

"I thought I heard cryin'." Annie regarded her curiously, taking in the pale sheen of her skin and the telltale droplets upon her lashes. "Are ye sick?"

"No." Charlotte managed a small, forced smile. "I'm fine, Annie. What about you—is your eye paining you today?"

"Not much. Eunice did a good job of keepin' the swellin' down, and that apple mush of hers kept it from gettin' too blue." She looked past Charlotte into the room. "Did ye sleep on yer bed last night?"

Charlotte glanced over at the rumpled bed. "I was so tired after everything that happened last night, I thought I'd lie down for a minute, and instead fell sound—"

"Where is she, Oliver?" demanded a worried voice from the main floor. "Charlotte!"

"I'm here, Annabelle." Charlotte could hear concern in her sister's voice. "In my room—come on upstairs."

A small army of feet raced up the narrow staircase and four of Charlotte's five siblings charged into her bedchamber.

"Oh, Charlotte," burst out Annabelle, "thank goodness you're here!"

Annie stared in fascination at the beautiful young woman who rushed over and threw her arms around Charlotte. Her features were remarkably lovely, and although her pale blond hair was falling down from beneath an elegant green and ivory hat, its disarray could not detract from its magnificent thickness and shine.

"We heard that you were abducted by the Dark Shadow last night—are you all right?" A second young woman also wrapped her arms protectively around Charlotte. She struck Annie as unusually pretty as well, with enormous dark eyes and coffee-colored hair that had been hurriedly pinned into place.

"I'm fine, Grace," Charlotte assured her, drawing comfort from the hugs of her sisters. "Really."

"Are you certain?" A handsome young man with red hair and blue eyes regarded her doubtfully.

"Yes, Simon."

"Is that blood on your dress?" With his strawberry-blond waves and earnest expression the other man struck Annie as younger than the rest—perhaps as old as twenty-two, but no more. Annie liked his sweetly unsophisticated air.

Charlotte self-consciously closed the neckline of her dressing gown, trying to hide the bloodstained gown underneath. "Yes, Jamie, but it isn't mine—it's from the Dark Shadow. Everyone, this is Miss Clarke," she continued, indicating Annie. "Annie, let me introduce you to my sisters and brothers: Annabelle, Lady Harding; Grace, Lady Maitland; Mr. Simon Kent; and Mr. James Kent."

"Ye don't look nothin' alike," Annie observed candidly.

Grace laughed. "You're right, we don't."

"But we are alike in many other ways," Annabelle assured her.

Annie regarded her doubtfully, noting her elegant hat, expensively tailored dress, and glossy pearls. Charlotte did not exhibit even a fraction of the confidence or poise that her two sisters possessed.

"You look awful, Charlotte," Jamie announced, laying his hand against her forehead. "Pale and drawn, and your skin is cold. Have you eaten anything today?"

"I'm fine Jamie, just a little tired. Jamie is studying medicine at Edinburgh University," she explained to Annie, smiling. "Which means he likes to practice being a doctor with everyone he meets."

"It's good to have a doctor in the family." Annie nodded with approval. "Ye never know when someone's goin' to snuff it."

"Hopefully, once I've graduated, I'll be able to keep some people from snuffing it," Jamie joked.

"However did you manage to escape the Dark Shadow?" asked Annabelle, still holding fast to her sister.

"I didn't, actually," Charlotte admitted. "I was trying to help him get away and then he was shot by Lord Haywood, and so we came here. Eunice and Doreen dressed his wound, then everyone worked together to sneak him out of the house as the police were searching for him."

"You helped him escape after he shot poor Lord

Haywood?" Grace regarded her in astonishment. "Why?"

"Because he didn't shoot Lord Haywood. He only had Lady Chadwick's hairbrush in his pocket. He never hurt anyone."

"The newspapers said he tried to strangle you, then dragged you down the stairs against your will, using you as a shield," Simon informed her.

Charlotte regarded him in dismay. "It's in the newspapers?"

"Of course—it's on the front page of this morning's *Daily Telegraph*."

"When they were printing it last night no one realized you had returned home safely, so the headline read: *Dark Shadow Murders Lord Haywood, Abducts Lord Redmond's Ward*. We were all horrified when Beaton brought it to us this morning."

"Do ye all live together, then?" asked Annie curiously.

"Grace and I are both married and live in Scotland, but we come to London for a visit in the summer every year," Annabelle explained. "While we're here we usually stay together at our parents' home."

"And since I'm on a break from my studies at the moment, I convinced Simon that we should go with them, so we could see how Charlotte was making out with her new refuge house," Jamie added.

"This dreadful attention is sure to hurt us," Charlotte lamented. "It's been hard enough to get people to donate their money to keep the house going."

Annie frowned. "But ye're rich, ain't ye? I mean, what with your father bein' a marquess an' all."

"My parents have some wealth," Charlotte allowed, "and they have been extremely generous in helping me set up this house. They paid for the lease and gave me money to buy furnishings, but I assured them that I could raise the funds to run it myself, so I wouldn't forever be relying on their charity. I thought if I could just make the wealthy aware of the terrible suffering of London's poor women and children, they would gladly want to help them."

"Then ye found out most rich folk would flay a flea for his skin," Eunice observed contemptuously, entering the room bearing an enormous tray of tea, cheese, and oatcakes.

"They dinna mind spendin' on themselves," Doreen snorted, carrying another tray filled with cups and saucers. "'Tis only when it comes to others that they suddenly canna recall where they put their wallets."

"Never mind, lass, there's as good fish in the sea as ever come out of it," Oliver finished philosophically. "We just need to get ye tossin' yer net out more."

"I had hoped to get some support at Lord Chadwick's dinner last night," Charlotte reflected. "I thought it would be a good opportunity to talk about the work we are doing here, and entice people to donate their money. Unfortunately, I never got the chance."

"Maybe you got something better out of it then just a couple of donations," Annabelle mused. "After all, last night most of London had no idea who you are."

"You're right, Annabelle," agreed Grace. "After reading the papers this morning, almost everyone in London knows that Miss Charlotte Kent was abducted last night by the infamous Dark Shadow."

"And until this evening's papers are printed, everyone will be speculating whether you're going to be found alive or dead," added Simon, helping himself to one of Eunice's oatcakes. "You're a celebrity."

"Not just to the nobs, neither," Annie pointed out. "My friends can't read, but they can sure talk, an' nothin' takes their fancy better than a good sneak job or murder."

"I don't see how my sudden celebrity is going to help us." Charlotte disliked intensely the idea that so much attention was suddenly upon her. "Society doesn't like to hear about the problems of the poor, unless you're asking them to give to something safe and respectable and established, like a church or a hospital. When I ask people to make a donation so I can help unfortunate women and children get off the streets and make a new life, they lecture me on how those women and children are born lacking morality, and say I shouldn't be associating with such people."

"It's them that ye shouldna be associatin' with," Eunice huffed angrily.

"I know those swells." Annie's cheeks were flushed with indignation. "All high and mighty in their fine traps, lookin' down at ye like ye was some nasty bug what crawled out from under a rock—but give 'em half a chance and they is more than willin' to grab a feel or have a snatch—"

"Here now!" Oliver scowled, but his voice was gentle as he reminded her, "That's nae way to be talkin', lass."

Annie sighed. "Beg pardon—I forgot."

"You just have to keep asking them, Charlotte," Annabelle told her. "Keep asking, until finally they are too ashamed to keep refusing you."

"But most of them never even give me the chance to ask. I sent more than two dozen letters last month asking a number of wealthy people for a meeting so I could tell them about my house, and so far all of them have eluded my request. They claim to be too busy to see me."

"Which is why you have to get out and attend a few balls and parties," Grace suggested. "Get them to commit some funds while they are surrounded by others and don't want to appear stingy or unsympathetic to the problems of the poor."

"Hook 'em when they're a wee bit wellied," Oliver advised. "That's when they'll be dippin' deepest into their pockets."

Charlotte sighed. "I don't really like going to parties. I only went to Lord and Lady Chadwick's house for dinner because Lady Chadwick had promised Haydon and Genevieve that they would have me over occasionally while I'm in London. I was concerned they might be insulted if I refused their invitation."

"I know you don't care much for those affairs, Charlotte." Grace regarded her sympathetically. "But if you really care about this house and providing help to those who need it, and you don't want to keep going to Genevieve and Haydon for money, I'm afraid you're going to have to overcome your distaste for them."

"And tomorrow night is the perfect time to start," Annabelle decided. "Lord and Lady Marston are throwing their spectacular annual summer ball, which is sure to be one of the grandest affairs of the season. Didn't you receive an invitation? They always make a point of sending one to all of us."

"I sent them a note telling them I wouldn't be attending," Charlotte told her. "I know they only invite me out of respect for Haydon. They don't really want me to go."

"Well, you are going to attend," Annabelle decided. "And you needn't be afraid, because Jamie, Simon, Grace, and I will all be going with you. It will be fun," she insisted, seeing a look of despair cloud her sister's face. "Everyone will be thrilled to see that you are safe and well."

"I'm sure they will all want to talk to you, to find out how you escaped the Dark Shadow," Grace added.

"And while they're crowding about, you can talk

about your house and ask them to donate money," Jamie finished. "All you have to do is get one person to commit, and the others will follow, just so they won't appear tightfisted. You'll see."

Charlotte shook her head. "I can't go, Annabelle."

"Why not?"

Because I hate everyone staring at me, she thought desperately. *Because I'm not charming or beautiful or gay like the other women there will be. Because everyone will pretend not to look at me when I limp across the room, but I'll know that they are. Because if I stand for too long my leg will throb and go into spasm, but if I sit down everyone will whisper that I'm a cripple. Because I can't bear their pity. And I can't bear their contempt. It weakens me too much, and I can't afford to be weak.*

"I haven't anything to wear."

Annabelle laughed. "That doesn't matter. Between Grace's gowns and mine, I'm sure we can find something wonderful for you to wear."

"They won't fit," Charlotte protested. "I'm smaller than both of you."

"Not by much," countered Doreen. "With a wee nip here an' a tuck there, Eunice and me can have any gown lookin' like it was made for ye."

"I don't have any evening slippers," Charlotte added. Why couldn't they just see that she couldn't go? "The ones I wore last night were ruined in the rain, and I haven't any others."

"But ye've time to buy new ones," Annie pointed out, excited by the prospect of Charlotte attending an actual ball. "The shop windows is fully of lovely shoes— ye could get somethin' really prime—with bows on 'em an' such."

"Annie is right," Simon agreed. "And don't worry about the cost—you know Haydon and Genevieve are very happy to pay for your personal effects."

"Why don't you get dressed, and then we'll get

Oliver to drive us over to Bond Street and we'll buy you some shoes. Then we'll go back to the house and you can try on a few gowns, to see which one you like best."

"I can't go, Annabelle." Charlotte's voice was small as she quietly admitted, "I don't want all those people staring at me."

"What's this?" demanded Oliver, frowning. "Is this the wee lass who faced the Dark Shadow just last night, an' brought him down in front of a mob?"

"The lass who helped him walk when he was all weak an' bleedin', an' near dragged him up the stairs?" Doreen added.

"The lass who faced both a police inspector and a constable as cool as ye please, without givin' either of them a hint o' who was lyin' in bed just above their heads?" finished Eunice.

Oliver reached out and squeezed her hand. "Seems to me if ye're strong enough for that, then ye're strong enough to blather with a few rich nobs at a party."

"You don't have to stay long, Charlotte," Jamie assured her. "Just tell us when you want to leave and we'll take you home. I promise."

"Then you can tell me an' Ruby an' Violet all about it," said Annie eagerly. "I'm sure it'll be prime."

Charlotte was sure it wouldn't be prime at all—at least not for her. But there was no denying that it would be a good opportunity for her to try to elicit donations.

"Very well," she said, fighting the dread tightening her chest. "I'll go."

Harrison buried his face into the carpet and groaned.

A trickle of sunlight had slipped through the crack between the heavy velvet draperies and was spilling onto his face. He squeezed his eyes tight and shifted away from it, his mind too clouded to judge if he was ready to tolerate it. *Slowly,* he reminded himself, inhaling a shallow, steadying breath. He waited a moment, trying to assess the level of pain in his head. He felt weary and his brain was foggy, but experience had taught him that was probably just the aftereffect of the laudanum. No more headache, he decided. Relieved, he rolled onto his side.

And swore fiercely at the explosion of pain in his shoulder.

He eased himself up off his bedroom floor, dazed and confused. The moment he saw the worn fabric of the cheaply tailored coat he was wearing, his fragmented memory began to fall into place. He shrugged out of the garment and opened the shirt he wore beneath, then stared in bewilderment at the swath of bloody bandages wrapped around his shoulder. A milky image of two elderly Scottish women came to his mind, dismissing it as only a flesh wound. There had been others there, too, he realized, struggling to remember. A few pretty young girls with rough speech. An old man. A young boy.

And a strangely attractive young woman who had done her best to protect him after she stumbled upon him in Lady Chadwick's chamber.

"Harry? Are you up yet?"

Harrison hastily closed his shirt and threw on the coat again, covering his injury. "Come in, Tony."

The door opened and a lean, golden-haired young man rushed excitedly into the gloom of the chamber, carrying a newspaper.

"Have you heard? The Dark Shadow has struck again, only this time he's gone and killed Lord Haywood."

"My apologies, your lordship," managed Harrison's butler, hurrying breathlessly into the room. "I told Mr. Poole you were not yet available to receive visitors, but he was most insistent that he see you immediately, and raced up the stairs before I could—"

"That's all right, Telford," Harrison managed. His tongue felt thick and clumsy. "Thank you."

"There, Telford, you see? I told you Harry wouldn't mind." Tony regarded the hapless butler with amusement. Telford shot him a disapproving look and headed back down the corridor. "Shot him clean in the chest, poor bastard," Tony continued excitedly, shifting his attention back to Harrison, "then left him to bleed to death while he made off with some terrified young girl—and no one knows what's become of her. Jesus, Harry, you look bloody awful," he remarked, frowning. "What the hell were you up to last night?"

"Not much." Harrison staggered to the washstand and splashed some cold water on his face.

"Did you go out?"

"I went to the club for a while. Had a drink."

"By the look of you this morning, I'd say it was more than one," Tony observed wryly.

Harrison shrugged, then clenched his jaw as his wounded shoulder throbbed in protest. "What brings you here this morning, Tony?" he asked, changing the subject.

"Don't you remember? We're having lunch today. You told me to pick you up at eleven o'clock." He regarded Harrison curiously. "You do remember, Harry, don't you?"

Harrison was careful to keep his expression bland. In fact he had no memory whatsoever of arranging to have lunch with Tony. *Yet another incident,* he realized, fighting the sick sensation uncoiling within him. This was how it began. An inability to recall small, ordinary things, like agreeing to have lunch with a friend, or where he left a book he was reading, or the name of someone he had met just the previous week. Each incident on its own easily dismissed as nothing, or the fact that he had too much on his mind, or that he had been suffering too many headaches lately. But strung together into a chain, they pointed to something quite different.

A dull pounding sensation began to creep up the back of his skull, warning him another headache could be imminent.

"Of course I remember," he lied.

"Good." Tony smiled. "Why don't I leave you to get dressed, then, and I'll meet you in your study downstairs?"

"Meet me in the drawing room. My study is a mess."

"I don't mind," Tony assured him cheerfully. "I'm more comfortable amidst disorder."

"The drawing room is better, Tony," Harrison asserted, a little more forcefully. "I'd prefer it if you waited for me there."

Tony cast him an exasperated look. "Fine, Harry, I'll go wait in your bloody stuffy drawing room. Just don't take too long—I'm anxious to get to your club and find out if anyone has heard anything more about the Dark Shadow, or if Lord Redmond's ward has turned up yet."

"Who?"

"The girl the Shadow abducted," Tony explained. "She's one of those urchins the Marquess of Redmond took on when he married his wife years ago. Of course she's grown up now, but she's a cripple so Redmond hasn't been able to marry her off—not that she'd make much of a match, given her background. Apparently she came to London last year to set up some sort of refuge house for whores and urchins."

Another image pierced the veil obscuring his memory. The face of a pretty girl staring down at him with concern, her enormous eyes shadowed with fear and something more, an emotion Harrison could not readily identify.

"And they haven't found her yet?" he asked, confused.

"Well, they hadn't at the time they printed this paper, but that was last night," Tony allowed. "Once we get to the club, we should be able to find out if she has turned up—alive or dead."

"It's highly unlikely that she'll be dead. The Dark Shadow is a jewel thief, not a murderer."

"That changed last night, I'm afraid. Once he shot Lord Haywood he became a murderer, which means the authorities will have to intensify their efforts to find him. If he kills Redmond's ward, they'll be under even greater pressure to bring him to justice. The Shadow's days are numbered now, mark my words. I'll see you downstairs, Harry," he finished, tucking his newspaper under his arm. "Don't be long."

Harrison waited until the door had closed behind Tony. Only then did he raise his hands to his head and squeeze.

He would not take any more laudanum. He had to keep his mind sharp. He wouldn't have any wine with his lunch, either, so he could be alert to what everyone was saying about the Dark Shadow. If he was to avoid being captured, he needed to remember what they knew. And he could remember, he told himself adamantly.

He shoved the memory of his father away, focused on overcoming the pain looming in his head.

I will not give in to you, he vowed harshly. *I will not.*

· · ·

"THERE NOW," SAID ANNABELLE, BREATHLESS AS SHE piled three more packages into Oliver's quivering arms. "That's seven pairs of evening shoes, four shawls, and a half dozen new pairs of gloves. All we need now are some stockings and undergarments, and we can go home and have Charlotte try on some gowns."

"Why don't you take all these things back to the carriage, Oliver," Grace suggested, "and then meet us up at the end of the street? That way we can go into a few more shops along the way without you constantly trying to find a good place to stop the carriage."

Oliver peered over the mountain of boxes heaped in his arms at Charlotte. "Are ye fit to walk a wee bit more, lass?" he asked, concerned. "Or would ye like to leave yer sisters to finish the rest and come back to the carriage?"

"I'm fine, Oliver."

In fact her leg was stiff and aching, but she was not about to admit that to either him or her sisters. From the moment she had disembarked from the carriage and begun shopping with Annabelle and Grace, all of her senses had told her that she was being followed. At first she had told herself she was being ridiculous. Who could possibly be interested in following her? Yet the sensation continued, a nagging awareness that had been honed in her from the time she was a child living on the streets. Of course more people in the shops were staring at her than usual, because the moment they realized who she was the shopkeepers began exclaiming how relieved they were that she was alive. But it wasn't the public's fascinated gawking that was making the hairs prickle along the back of her neck. Someone was watching her.

And she was convinced that someone had to be the Dark Shadow.

"You go back to the carriage, Oliver," she instructed, smiling at him. "We'll be along shortly."

Oliver regarded her doubtfully. He had spent too many years battling his own aches and pains to not recognize the signs in others. "Are ye sure, lass?"

"I promise to return to the carriage the moment I get tired," Charlotte solemnly vowed.

"We won't be much longer, Oliver," Annabelle added. "Just a few more stores."

He huffed impatiently. "That's what ye said an hour ago."

"But this time we really mean it," Grace assured him. "And we won't let Charlotte overdo it—we promise."

"See that ye don't. The lass is nae accustomed to traipsin' all over London in search of a pair o' shoes." With that he turned and headed back to the carriage.

"You are all right to continue, aren't you, Charlotte?" It suddenly occurred to Annabelle that she was not being sensitive to her sister's infirmity. "If you like, Grace and I can finish buying what you need without you."

"Actually, I was thinking I might just stop for a bit," Charlotte admitted. "Why don't you and Grace go into this store and I'll just stay outside and look in some windows until you're finished. I do find standing in the shops much harder than being outside where I can move around a little."

"I'll wait with you," Grace offered, disliking the idea of leaving her sister alone.

"No, that isn't necessary," Charlotte hastily assured her. "You'll only be a few minutes, and Annabelle may require your opinion on something. I'm sure we can finish up quicker if you are there to help her make a decision—otherwise, Annabelle is liable to just buy everything in the store."

"I'm not quite that bad," Annabelle protested, laughing.

"You are when you're left on your own," Grace teased. "Very well, Charlotte. We promise not to be long."

"Take as much time as you need." Charlotte smiled. "I'll be fine."

She waited a moment for them to go in the shop. Then she casually glanced down the street, searching for the tall, broadly built figure of the Dark Shadow. There were dozens of people crowding the narrow sidewalk, but none of the men struck her as commanding enough to be the infamous thief who had held her so tightly the night before. She began to limp along, enduring the fleeting stares of surprise or pity that she always elicited. *Ignore them.* On and on she walked, trying not to feel humiliated as others passed her. She had not gone far, but it was sufficient to make her realize that her leg would not take her much further. Frustrated and discouraged, she stopped and turned around.

And saw a tall, heavyset man dart into one of the alleys leading off the fashionable thoroughfare.

Her heart pounding against her ribs, she moved toward the alley, trying not to draw any attention. The tide of people walking on the street had become thick and fast, and it was a struggle for her to make her way through it. *Wait for me,* she pleaded silently, a flame of anticipation flaring within her. She had thought the Dark Shadow had disappeared from her life forever. But she had been wrong. It would have been easy for him to return to her house that morning, waiting for her to emerge. Understandably, he did not want to approach her while she was in the company of her sisters. That explained why he was clandestinely following her. He was waiting for a moment where he might find her alone, no doubt so he could thank her for helping him.

While she was enormously pleased to see him again, she had to make it clear that no thanks were necessary. She would reassure him that she was happy to have been able to help him when he so desperately needed it. And then, in what scant minutes remained, she would plead with him to abandon his life of crime. She would encourage him to try to build something honest and pure with his abilities, which she was certain were considerable, so that he could make a decent life for himself without the constant fear of being imprisoned, or worse.

The alley was dank and sour with the stench of sewage and rotting garbage. She forced herself to inhale shallow breaths as she limped along the refuse-strewn path. The Dark Shadow had crept quickly down the passage and disappeared behind a pile of decrepit crates.

"You don't need to be alarmed," Charlotte called softly. "It's only me."

He didn't answer.

"No one knows you are following me," she added, trying to put him at ease. "I slipped away. If my sisters start looking for me, they'll likely begin by going into a few shops. They'll never think to search for me here."

No response.

She bit her lip, wondering why he didn't answer her. "Are you all right?"

He emerged slightly from the shadows and nodded. The rough cap pulled low over his forehead masked his features, and his manner was wary. Clearly he was not certain she could be trusted.

"I'm glad to see you're feeling better," she told him. "I was very worried about you last night. When they told me you were gone, I feared you might not have had the strength to make it safely home." She took a few tentative steps. She didn't know whether he trusted her enough to permit her to see his face, obscured though it might be.

"It is dangerous for you to be following me," she continued. "A police detective came to my house last night looking for you. I'm afraid he may not have been satisfied with my story of how you released me. After you leave here, you must be careful not to seek me out again. Do you understand?"

She had nearly reached him. She paused, waiting for him to instruct her not to come any further.

Silence.

"Was there something you wanted to tell me?" Her voice was gentle, almost coaxing.

He said nothing.

"Do you want me to go, then?"

He shook his head.

"Shall I come closer?"

He hesitated. Finally, he nodded.

Nervous excitement was pouring through her now, making her feel both elated and just a little afraid. She took a step toward him, and another, until she was close enough to reach out and touch him.

His head was bowed and the light dim, but she could still make out the grizzled gray upon his lined, weathered cheek. She stared at it, surprised. She had not expected the Dark Shadow to be quite that old. Her gaze shifted from the roughly cut line of his jaw to his mouth. It no longer struck her as full and sensual as it had been the night before. The mouth she was staring at was thin and spare and hard, its corners barely lifted in a harsh smile. And then her eyes fell upon the thick white scar that branched out from the lower lip.

Sick, paralyzing dread suddenly gripped her, rendering her unable to speak.

"Hello, Lottie," drawled a low, amused voice. "I'm guessin' ye didna expect to find me here, did ye?"

Archie raised his head as he stepped out of the shadows, giving her the full benefit of his face. "What's the matter?" he asked sarcastically, taking perverse pleasure in her terrified shock. "Ye'd think yer old man was come back from the dead."

No, thought Charlotte, feeling as if she was going to be sick. *He can't be here. He can't.*

"I must say, ye dinna look too happy to see me," he remarked, frowning. "Why don't ye come over and give us a kiss? Or do ye think ye're too fine to touch a filthy dip like me?" He snorted with laughter.

"What do you want?" she managed, her voice barely a whisper. She was not a little girl anymore, she reminded herself desperately. He had no power over her anymore.

She glanced wildly about the alley, feeling dangerously alone and vulnerable.

"Why, I just wanted to see ye," he declared innocently. "Surely a da's got the right to see his own flesh an' blood, don't he? Especially after spendin' four long years doin' hard labor in prison. Gives a man a lot of time to think, hard labor does. Do ye know about the crank machine, Lottie?" His gaze narrowed. "Do ye know how many times a man has to turn it in a day, or suffer the cut o' the lash?"

Charlotte numbly shook her head.

"Ten thousand," he told her. "Sounds impossible, don't it? An' some days it is—especially when the warder makes the screw so tight ye have to heave yer whole body against the fuckin' thing just to get it to turn once. First to go is yer hands—the skin on 'em blisters an' rots, but ye scarce notice because the bones get so cramped ye feel like ye'll ne'er be able to open yer fingers again. An' then it's the rest of ye that's ruined, from yer wrists right down to yer feet. But ye canna think o' that. By the time ye've finished ye're all but dead, but then they're draggin' ye to it the next day, an' there's nae ye can do but start over, an' hope it doesna kill ye afore yer time is up. But o' course it didna kill me, as ye can plainly see." He smiled at her, exposing a jagged row of yellow, rotting teeth. "I'm a survivor, Lottie, like you. Although, I must say, I didna expect ye to survive near as well as ye have. I mean, just look at ye with yer fancy togs, ridin' about in a carriage. Ye've come long way from the dirty wee lass who used to pick pockets and raise her skirts for a bit o' brass in Devil's Den, that's for sure." He spat on the ground.

"How did you find me?" she whispered, still struggling to accept that the man standing before her was real, and not some dreadful nightmare.

"Well, it weren't easy," he admitted. "After I got out I moved 'round a bit and stayed clear of Inveraray. I figured ye was probably dead. Ye always was weak and sickly, and I thought if prison didna kill ye straight off, reform school would. But after a few years I found myself near Inveraray, an' thought I'd try to find out what happened to ye. Imagine my surprise when I heard some spinster who married some sod from the prison had sprung ye from jail. The prison governor wouldna tell me no more, but I figured if those people wanted ye, they could have ye. Ye'd have been grown by then anyway, an' it weren't as if I could look after ye. So I shoved on.

"Then a few months ago I comes to London, an' as I'm goin' about St. Giles an' Seven Dials, I hears about some crippled lass who has set up a home for whores and such—a lass who comes from money, on account of her bein' the ward of the Marquess of Redmond, who lives in the north o' Scotland. I asks around a bit, an' find out they call her Miss Charlotte Kent. An' I thinks to myself, a crippled Scottish lass named Charlotte, goin' 'round with doxies and priggers? So I finds out where yer house is, an' the minute I see ye limpin' out of it, I know 'tis my own Lottie, all grown up." He picked at his teeth with a grimy nail. "So I'm thinkin', since ye've done so well for yerself all these years while I was rottin' in prison, 'tis high time ye shared a wee bit o' yer good fortune with yer da. After all, I'm the one who brought ye to the world. If nae for me, ye'd have nothin'."

Charlotte bit the side of her mouth until blood leaked onto her tongue. All the fear she had suffered as a child was surging through her, rendering her unable to answer him. It was hopeless to argue anyway, she realized bleakly. Her father had never tolerated disrespect from her. Any fledgling signs of spirit or disobedience had always been swiftly quashed with either his belt or his fists.

Her leg was throbbing violently now. She had to get back to the carriage soon, before it collapsed in spasm.

"What do you want from me?"

"Why, nae more than my due," he assured her. "After all, I'm the one who had to look after ye all those years, after yer ma died. Had to keep bread in yer mouth and togs on yer back, an' a roof over yer head, too, when I could. Some chaps would've said sod it, an' let ye make yer own way, but not Boney Buchan. Yer mother swore on her deathbed that ye was my flesh and blood, an' even though she was a lyin' thievin' bitch, I decided to treat ye as if ye were."

His ugly description of her mother had no effect on Charlotte. She didn't remember her well enough to feel anything for her except a detached pity for the torment she must have endured while living with her father. That and a complete bewilderment as to what had drawn her mother to him in the first place. It amazed Charlotte that the man standing before her actually thought he had looked after her. In some twisted corner of his mind, he believed that all those hideous, terrifying years, filled with drunkenness and ranting and violence, could be equated with care. But she didn't argue.

She had learned long ago that defiance would only be answered with brutality.

"How much?" she whispered.

"Five thousand pounds."

She stared at him in shock.

"Ye heard me right," he assured her, amused by the startled look on her face. "Five thousand pounds, an' that's bloody cheap when ye consider all I had to suffer on account of ye. If nae for ye I'd have nae been caught that day, Lottie. I'd nae have spent eight years in some shithole prison, wonderin' if I'd live long enough to be a free man again. An' all the while I was breakin' my back an' gettin' beat by the warders, ye was livin' in the bloody lap o' luxury, with some goddamn marquess payin' to have ye sit on velvet an' lick sweets all day." He raised a leering brow. "Or was there somethin' else ye was lickin' for him that made him so willin' to keep ye?"

His crudeness revolted her. Everything about him revolted her. She swallowed thickly, fighting the nausea churning within her.

"I don't have five thousand pounds," she told him helplessly. "I don't have that kind of money."

"Do ye take me for a fool?" His face twisted with fury. "I know about yer precious marquess, Lottie. I been to Mayfair, an' I seen his fine house. So dinna be thinkin' ye can toss me a few quid and be done with it. I wants my money, an' I wants it quick."

"I'm not lying to you," Charlotte told him desperately. "I don't live in Mayfair, and the house I live in is leased. Lord Redmond pays for that directly, but our agreement is that I have to raise the funds to keep it running through donations. When I need anything else, I sign for it and the bills are sent to him. I don't have five thousand pounds."

He spat on the ground in disgust. "Then ye'll just have to get it, won't ye?"

"I can't—Lord Redmond would never just give me that kind of money, and I haven't received any large donations—"

His enormous hands shot forward suddenly, grabbing her.

"Dinna tell me ye canna get it, Lottie," he warned harshly, his breath hot and foul against her cheek. "I know where ye live, and I know where those other shits of his lordship live, too. If ye dinna want to see somethin' happen to yer precious new family, ye'll get me my money. Understand?"

He crushed her arms with bruising strength, reminding her of what he was capable. And suddenly she was seven years old again. Tears sprang to her eyes and her body began to quiver with an overwhelming mixture of fear and desperation and hatred.

"Yes," she managed raggedly, fighting to keep her tears from falling. If he saw her cry, it would only make it worse. He always slapped her harder when she cried. "I'll get it."

He glowered at her, his dark eyes burning with menace. "Ye've got four days. I'll come for it after that. And dinna be thinkin' of tellin' no one about this, Lottie," he warned. "If I catch the peelers or anyone else sniffin' about for me, I'll make ye and yer precious family of swells sorry ye was ever born. Got it?"

"Yes," she whispered.

"Good." Abruptly, he released her. "I'll see ye in four days." He turned and sprinted away.

Charlotte pressed the heels of her hands against her eyes. Annabelle and Grace were probably searching for her by now. Breathing hard, she fought to regain some modicum of composure as she began to slowly limp back toward the elegant world that gleamed at the end of the alley.

"There you are!" called Annabelle, noticing her after she had emerged onto the street. "Where on earth have you been?"

"I just went into this shop," Charlotte lied, pointing to the nearest store.

"We were worried about you." Grace regarded her with concern. "Are you all right? You look terribly pale."

"I'm a little tired. Can we go now?"

"Of course we can." Grace took her arm and wrapped it around her own. "You just lean against me while we walk up to meet Oliver."

"I'm so sorry we took so long. We should have realized it would be too much for you," Annabelle apologized.

"Did you get something nice?" Charlotte asked, trying to shift their attention away from her.

"We got the most beautiful silk stockings for you—they're so light and sheer you'd almost think you were wearing nothing," Annabelle said enthusiastically. "And then we saw the most gorgeous corset, and we knew you'd never buy such a fancy one for yourself, but Grace and I decided you really had to have it . . ."

Charlotte smiled and nodded, pretending to listen as her sisters chattered happily about all the lovely things they had bought for her.

She was trapped, she realized frantically as she limped toward Oliver and their waiting carriage.

Boney Buchan had found her. Until she paid him what he wanted, she was completely at his mercy.

Chapter Five

IT WAS A PERFECT NIGHT FOR A JEWEL THIEF.

Diamonds, rubies, and emeralds glittered upon the milky breasts and sagging earlobes of nearly every woman in the ballroom, while the men accompanying them boasted sparkling stones in their cuffs and shirt studs. The air was laden with the scent of heavy perfume and richly spiced food, and eager gossip over the Dark Shadow's disastrous robbery attempt of two nights earlier was all but drowning out the lively strains of the orchestra. Everyone had an opinion on the mysterious jewel thief's identity, the severity of the wound he had suffered, and the extraordinary step he had taken by murdering Lord Haywood and abducting Lord Redmond's spinster ward. Harrison gripped the stem of his untouched wine glass as he studied the room, only half listening to the vigorous debates raging around him. His shoulder was throbbing and the sickly-sweet odors wafting through the air were threatening to trigger a headache.

If not for the brilliant jewelry circling around him, he would have stayed home and nursed his aching shoulder with a bottle of good French brandy.

"...then he jumps out of the carriage and disappears, just like that," finished Lord Chadwick, his great, bloated chest puffed up with importance as he surveyed his fascinated audience.

"She's lucky he didn't kill her," observed Lord Shelton, shaking his little balding head in disbelief.

"Why would he want to do a thing like that?" Lord Reynolds frowned. "Miss Kent is a cripple. She would hardly have been any threat to him."

"No one has been as close to the Dark Shadow as she has," Lord Shelton explained, as if it were obvious. "Given the chance, she might be able to identify him. Killing her would ensure that never happened."

"The newspapers reported that she never saw his face—he kept his mask on the entire time," pointed out Tony.

"Doesn't matter," Lord Shelton insisted. "She might be able to spot some mannerism he has, or perhaps recognize the sound of his voice."

"Can't imagine charging someone with murder based on their voice," scoffed Lord Beckett dismissively, stroking the wiry gray point of his beard. "He could have disguised it while he was with her."

"At any rate, he damned well got away." Lord Chadwick took a hefty swallow of his wine, unnerved by the fact that he had come so close to death. "Now all the police can do is wait until he strikes again."

"I doubt Miss Kent was much help to them." Lord Reynolds's voice was laden with disapproval. "After all, she's well known for her sympathies toward criminals."

"That's what comes from having bad blood," complained Lord Shelton. "You can try to cover it up, but you can't change it, no matter how much money you throw at it."

"You think Miss Kent has bad blood because she

wants to help the less fortunate?" Harrison's tone was mild.

"Of course not," Lord Shelton assured him. "Lots of ladies work to help the less fortunate—my own wife included. But there are reputable, well-established charities for these causes, which only ask that respectable women help to raise funds for them, by making handicrafts to sell at their bazaars, for instance, or getting their husbands to donate money."

"Miss Kent lives with thieves and whores," Lord Reynolds added. "No decent woman would permit herself to sleep under the same roof with the scum of society. It's shocking. I'm surprised Lord Redmond allows it."

"She lives with them because she's one of them." Lord Beckett's lip curled with disdain. "All of Redmond's wards came from thieves and whores—and every one of them was jailed at one time or another for their filthy, criminal ways. Redmond has done his best to clean them up, but you can't turn pigs into horses, and he's been a bloody fool to try."

Harrison casually studied his wine, maintaining a demeanor of complete indifference. It had never occurred to him that Miss Kent had sprung from a criminal background herself as she primly lectured him on the unpleasantness of prison and the merits of leading a respectable life. The idea of her being jailed as a child bothered him. Although he was well aware that British jails regularly incarcerated urchins, somehow he always imagined that they were invariably a tough lot. Miss Kent scarcely fit his profile of a common street urchin.

"I believe she was working with the Dark Shadow to rob Chadwick that night," Lord Shelton theorized. "If that maid hadn't come upon the two of them in Lady Chadwick's chamber, they'd have made away with all her jewels."

"That's ridiculous," objected Lord Chadwick. "Let's not forget that Miss Kent was an invited guest in my home, and that she is the ward of Lord Redmond."

"Don't you think it strange Miss Kent just happened to come upon the Dark Shadow in your wife's chamber while everyone else was down at dinner?"

"But the Shadow is well known for breaking into houses while the owners are there," Tony pointed out. "He likes to slip in and out with no one noticing."

"But why was she upstairs when everyone else was dining?" Lord Beckett's eyes narrowed cryptically. "Seems suspect, if you ask me."

"Miss Kent told my wife she wasn't feeling well and asked if she could be excused for a few minutes," Lord Chadwick explained. "Since all of the guest chambers had been assigned to overnight guests, my wife quite sensibly told her to use her own chamber."

"And then she just happens upon the Dark Shadow?" Lord Shelton shook his head, unconvinced. "She was going up to meet him, I say, and help him rob you blind."

"But why on earth would she need to steal jewels from Chadwick?" wondered Lord Beckett. "After all, Redmond has money. He takes care of her, just as he does all his children."

"The urge to steal is in the blood," Lord Shelton explained authoritatively, "just like the urge toward violence or depravity. Can't be helped. That's why the only answer is to lock criminals up. Miss Kent's refuge house is just a place for the scum of society to fatten up on beef and cake while they trade tricks amongst each other before going out to take advantage of the rest of us lawabiding citizens. If I ever meet Miss Kent, I'll damn well tell her so."

"It seems you're going to have your chance," Lord

Reynolds mused. "I believe that's she on the other side of the ballroom."

Harrison raised his gaze in astonishment. A crowd of people was swarming around someone at the opposite end of the room, forming a glittering vortex of jewels and evening wear that prevented him from seeing the object of their attention.

And then suddenly someone moved, and he found himself staring at the lovely young woman who had saved his life.

She seemed fragile and uncertain to him amidst the curious crowd, which was showering her with excited questions. Her delicately structured face was pale and grave, although every now and then one of the tall young men standing on either side of her would make some comment that would elicit a forced smile from her. He did not know who her two young escorts were, but it was immediately apparent to him that they were extremely protective of her. One was supporting her by holding her hand upon his arm, while the other was effectively shielding her from the people clamoring around her. There were two women standing close to her as well, a stunningly beautiful blond woman who was answering the group's questions with easy charm, and a lovely dark-haired woman who smiled and nodded. Thrust into the glare of the enormous ballroom, Charlotte seemed smaller to him, smaller and shyer and afraid. He could almost feel her distress as she stood there, could feel the awkwardness and embarrassment gripping her as she endured the relentless scrutiny of the curious mob around her.

What the hell was she doing there, when it was so obvious she was finding the attention excruciating?

"Come on, Harry, let's go talk to her," suggested Tony eagerly.

"No."

"Don't you want to find out more about her encounter with the Dark Shadow?"

"Not really."

Harrison swirled his wine around his glass as he studied her, affecting a cursory, almost bored inspection. She shouldn't be there, he thought as she valiantly tried to answer a question. Not because he feared she might reveal something about him that would lead to his capture. She had already proven her determination to protect him, even though he could not understand why. She probably assumed he was just another criminal who needed saving. A misguided victim of an unjust society, who only required a hot meal and a few words of wisdom and prayer to realize the error of his ways. And why shouldn't she think that? He had not given her any reason to think otherwise.

"I'm going out to get some air." He set his untouched glass down on a table and strode toward the doors leading to the garden, leaving Tony free to join the crowd fawning around the newly renowned Miss Kent.

". . . AND THAT IS WHY THESE POOR WOMEN AND CHIL-dren must be helped, not by sending them to workhouses, which only break their bodies and their spirits, but by creating a safe home for them where they can receive food and shelter and decent clothes, and where they are taught to read and learn a trade. It is only by equipping them to earn a decent wage that we help them to change their lives for the better."

Charlotte clenched her fists and swallowed, trying not to let her audience see how nervous she was. She knew they were not really interested in what she was saying. They wanted to hear about her being held hostage by the Dark Shadow, not to be lectured on their moral obligation to help the poor. But Annabelle and Grace had advised her to take control of the conversation from the outset to try to elicit donations, and that was what she was doing.

"It is a noble cause you have taken upon yourself, Miss Kent," Lord Reynolds remarked.

Yes, she thought, relief trickling through her. *If I can get just one of you to understand and support my work, then surely others will follow.* "Thank you, Lord Reynolds. May I count upon you to make a donation?"

"Regrettably, I am unable to contribute to every new charity that comes along, and as I'm sure you are aware, there are hundreds of them. My wife is most active on behalf of the Church Pastoral-Aid Society and the Anti-Gambling League, to name but two. There are also a number of asylums currently operating in London which provide shelter and assistance to the poor, are there not?"

"They are always full and have to turn countless people away, so the streets remain filled with children and women who desperately need help," Charlotte told him. "We need more institutions to aid these people, especially as thousands come to London in the hope of finding a better life, and instead are reduced to stealing in order to survive."

"No one needs to steal," objected Lord Beckett with a sanctimonious sniff. "There is always work to be had somewhere, providing they are able and willing. The problem is, they aren't willing."

"Stealing is in their blood," Lord Shelton added. "Can't be helped. You can take them in, Miss Kent, but I'll warrant they'll just be out preying upon innocent people the moment the mood strikes them. They're better off in jail. At least there they will learn that there are consequences for their actions."

"Some of these children are put onto the streets by

their parents at the age of six or seven," Charlotte countered, trying to help them understand. "They sell bruised fruit or scraps of ribbon or cloth if they can find some, but if they can't, their parents force them to steal. If they come home with nothing, they are cruelly beaten and sent out again."

She gripped the cool silk of her gown, trying not to think of Boney Buchan. This wasn't stealing, she told herself desperately. She would simply borrow whatever money she raised for her asylum and give it to him. Then she would find a way to pay it back. She had no idea how she would do that, but she couldn't focus on that. Her father had to be paid first. Her family had to be protected by whatever means necessary.

"My house of refuge is small," she conceded, "but I believe if we can save even a few more children and young women from the streets, that will make an enormous difference. Our society will be better for it."

"Indeed." Lord Shelton sounded utterly unconvinced.

"Tell us about the Dark Shadow, Miss Kent," said Lord Reynolds, bored with the discussion about her charity. "Did he threaten to kill you?"

Charlotte hesitated, reluctant to shift the conversation. She was losing them, she realized. Perhaps she should just answer a question or two about the Dark Shadow, just to keep their attention. "I don't think he ever said those exact words—"

"Did you think you were going to die when he took you hostage?"

"I was afraid, but I never believed he would actually kill me—"

"What about after he shot and killed poor Lord Haywood?" demanded Lord Beckett. "Weren't you terrified?"

"The Dark Shadow didn't kill Lord Haywood," she said emphatically. "The shot was fired by someone else."

"That's ridiculous," objected Lord Shelton. "The Dark Shadow killed him. Everyone saw it."

"They are mistaken," Charlotte countered. "I was right beside him. He never fired his weapon."

"So you're saying the Dark Shadow had an accomplice?"

"Of course, he must have," Lord Reynolds interjected before she could answer. "Lord Haywood was killed while threatening to shoot the Dark Shadow, so if the Shadow didn't shoot him, he must have had an accomplice protecting him."

"I don't know who shot Lord Haywood," said Charlotte, "but I don't think—"

"That must have been the same person who picked him up after he got out of Miss Kent's carriage," added another man.

The crowd murmured with excitement at this new possibility as questions and answers began to be tossed back and forth amongst them.

"How do you know someone picked him up?"

"He was wounded, so he had to have had help getting away."

"Miss Kent, did he ever indicate to you that he had someone waiting for him?"

"Did you have the sense that you were being followed?"

"You are the only person who has ever actually spoken with him at length," Tony shouted above the din. "What did he sound like?"

Charlotte regarded the crowd uncertainly. She did not want to reveal any more information about the Dark Shadow, but she realized people would think it strange if she refused to answer. She could not afford to give them the impression that she was trying to protect him, as that would only hinder her attempts to raise money. "I'm not sure what you mean—"

"Would you say he was an educated man, or someone of a less privileged background?" Tony elaborated.

She hesitated. "I believe he was probably educated."

"Are you suggesting he spoke like a gentleman?" Lord Shelton looked outraged by the possibility.

"I suppose so," Charlotte conceded, "but other than that I don't really recall—"

"Would you recognize his voice if you heard it again?"

Charlotte stared at the tall, dark-haired man who had asked the question. His face was obscured by the fact that he was apparently preoccupied with the task of removing some obstinate piece of lint from his otherwise meticulous evening coat.

"No," she answered. "He spoke only a few words."

The recalcitrant wisp of fluff removed, he raised his head to meet her gaze. His eyes were penetrating, but his tone was light as he continued, "Then it would seem that the Dark Shadow could be anywhere—even in attendance at this ball tonight—and you would be unable to identify him."

"That's correct."

"A pity." His mouth curved as his gaze swept over the women around him. "Given the magnificent trinkets on display here this evening, this would be an excellent place for him to peruse some of London's finest jewelry. I know if I were he, I would be quite taken by that dazzling necklace resting so comfortably against Lady Pembroke's lovely throat."

"Really, Lord Bryden, how you jest!" Lady Pembroke flitted her fan with feigned modesty over the mountainous expanse of her ruby-and-diamond-dotted bosom.

"I believe my sister has answered enough questions

for now," said Simon, aware that Charlotte had endured as much attention as she could.

"Besides, I'm sure there are lots of you who would rather be dancing than standing around talking about the Dark Shadow," added Jamie jokingly.

The people in the crowd murmured their assent and began to disperse, eager to discuss the deliciously frightening possibility that the Dark Shadow was there amongst them, and to evaluate whose jewels might be significant enough to attract his attention.

"Why don't you sit down over here, Charlotte, while Simon and I fetch you something to eat?"

"I'm not hungry," she said, grateful for the chair Jamie offered her.

"You should eat something, Charlotte," Grace told her. "You haven't had much today."

"Are you feeling all right?" Annabelle regarded her worriedly. "You seem pale to me."

"I'm fine," Charlotte assured her. "I just hate having everyone stare at me."

In fact her stomach had been roiling since her meeting with her father. Standing before those people and enduring their questions about the Dark Shadow and their disparaging comments about her work had only increased her distress. She had found the experience profoundly upsetting and humiliating. They all pitied her because of her leg, and despised her because of her past—two things that she could never change. Worse, she had failed to obtain even one donation.

How on earth was she to come up with the money her father had demanded?

"We should never have made you come here," Simon muttered, angered by the way the crowd had dismissed her appeal for help. "If you want to leave, I'll take you home."

"She can't leave just yet," Annabelle protested.

"Then everyone will gossip about the fact that she got upset after all their questions and left."

"Who cares?" Jamie cast a scathing look around the room. "Let them say whatever they want."

"It matters because Charlotte is trying to establish credibility amongst these people so that she can turn to them for donations and make a success of her refuge house," Annabelle explained. "I know it's hard for you, Charlotte, but I really think you should try to stay and at least pretend you are having a good time, even if it's only for half an hour. There could be some people here who didn't want to pledge a donation in front of everyone, but might well approach you later. You don't want them to think that you are easily flustered by a few pointed comments."

Charlotte realized that her sister was probably right. "Very well."

"Shall Simon and I get you some refreshments?"

She managed a small smile. "That would be nice."

"And if you think you're all right resting here for a moment, Grace and I will go over and say good evening to Lord and Lady Chadwick. We won't be long."

"I'll be fine, Annabelle. I'll just sit here and rest a little."

She sat perfectly straight in her chair, her hands clenched upon her lap as she watched her brothers and sisters leave. Her leg was throbbing beneath the heavy layers of her skirts. She wanted to stretch it out to ease the clench of its aching muscles, but such a movement would have been considered unladylike. And so she kept her leg bent in its socially acceptable position and tried to distract herself by watching the elegant men and women who were gliding effortlessly around the ballroom.

She had always loved dancing. It seemed to her such a wondrous, joyful activity, with the men in their immaculately dark suits and crisp white shirts leading beautifully gowned women in sweeping circles to the strains of music. The precise, measured grace of their movements enchanted her, from the moment the man extended his gloved hand and escorted his smiling partner onto the floor. She could not remember what it was like to move with ease. Her leg had been brutally shattered when she was only nine. Any recollections she might have had of running or skipping or even just walking evenly had been vanquished beneath the years of crushing pain that followed. But no shard of envy invaded her breast as she watched the dancers move. Instead she closed her eyes and retreated inward, feeling the music filter through her as she imagined herself gliding around the floor, on beautiful straight legs that were strong and supple and free of pain.

"Miss Kent?"

Her eyes flew open. Embarrassment heated her cheeks as she looked at the handsome blond man standing before her. How long had he been watching her?

"Forgive me, I didn't mean to startle you," he apologized. "I'm Tony Poole. I just wanted to tell you how horrified I was to hear about what happened to you at the hands of the Dark Shadow. Like everyone else in London, I'll be greatly relieved when he is finally captured and hanged. I hope Lord Bryden didn't upset you too much by suggesting that the rogue might actually be here this evening. Bryden was just making a foolish joke without stopping to consider the effect it might have on you, given the ordeal you suffered. I can assure you he didn't mean anything by it."

His eyes were large and toffee-colored, and they appeared to be genuinely earnest. Charlotte regarded him uncertainly, wondering what had prompted him to walk over and tell her this. A lifetime of being stared at and talked about had left her guarded with strangers.

"Thank you, Mr. Poole, for your concern, but you needn't worry. I'm fine."

"If you will permit me, I'll bring Bryden over and introduce him to you, and then you'll see he really isn't such a bad sort," Tony offered. "He might even be willing to help that refuge house of yours with a donation."

The prospect of a donation eased her initial wariness. "Do you really think so?"

"I'll make sure of it." He flashed her a conspiratorial smile. "I'll make him feel so guilty for his remark, he'll have no choice but to make an enormous donation just to get me be quiet. If you'll just give me a minute, I'll fetch him."

"Why don't you take me to him instead?"

"Are you sure you wouldn't prefer me to bring him to you?" His tone was chivalrous, but it was obvious to her that he was concerned about her ability to walk.

"I'm fine, Mr. Poole," she assured him. She hated the idea of sitting in the chair like some aged matron, patiently waiting for people to be presented to her. It only perpetuated everyone's view of her as a helpless cripple—which she wasn't. "I was only sitting for a moment because I found myself a little tired. I'm quite rested now."

"Wonderful." Tony extended his hand to help her up from her seat, then gave her a wink. "Let's go find Bryden and see if we can't get him to give you a nice fat sum."

OH, COME NOW, LORD BRYDEN, YOU CAN'T POSSIBLY say no to me!"

Lady Elizabeth Collins blinked her long lashes at him, her sultry little mouth drawn up in a pout. It was a mouth made for pleasure, Harrison reflected, watching as she provocatively caressed the edge of her glass with her pink tongue before sipping her drink. A few years ago he might have enjoyed contemplating the soft slickness of that velvety little mouth. Might have spent an hour or two exchanging heated glances and verbal jousts with her, watching as the champagne flushed her skin and the gradual ripening of the evening eroded her defenses. Might have artfully woven a net of yearning around her, waiting for the exact moment when he would lead her out into the warm dark green of the garden. There he would have kissed her and touched her and pleasured her, teaching her all the things she could do with that greedy little mouth. It would have been a pleasant diversion for both of them, nothing more. But as he watched her lapping up the gold bubbles in her glass, the thought of expending so much effort on some fleeting sexual encounter failed to arouse him. He was tired, his shoulder hurt like the devil, and he was badly in need of a drink. But he couldn't drink—he had to keep his mind sharp. And so he tilted his head to one side and said in a tone edged with self-mockery, "Tonight you are all the drink I need, Lady Elizabeth."

"Now there's a gallant line," quipped Tony, slipping between the two of them. "Honestly, Harry, I had no idea you were such a romantic. I can see I arrived just in time to save poor Lady Elizabeth from falling victim to your charms. Miss Kent, may I present to you the fatally charming Harrison Payne, Earl of Bryden, and Lady Elizabeth Collins. Harry, I don't believe you have been formally introduced to Miss Kent, who is the ward of the Marquess of Redmond, and more recently, a reluctant acquaintance of the Dark Shadow."

Harrison stared in surprise at Charlotte. Although she had given no indication that she knew who he was when he had stood at the back of the crowd, he knew better than to test her at such a close range. Perhaps some sliver of male vanity made him believe he had made more of an impression on her than could be hidden behind a mask or dark coat. There was also the possibility that at some point as he lay barely conscious in her home, she or one of the others who had tended him had taken the liberty of peering beneath his mask.

What the hell would he do if she recognized him?

"Good evening, Lord Bryden." Charlotte wished they had not come upon Lord Bryden at such a painfully inopportune moment. From the way he was staring at her, she felt certain he was annoyed with her sudden intrusion.

"Now, Harry, I believe your little jest about the Dark Shadow possibly being in attendance this evening was rather disturbing for Miss Kent," scolded Tony. "Knowing that you would be most upset to learn that you had disturbed her peace of mind, I thought you might want to apologize."

Harrison raised a brow, feigning polite concern. "Forgive me, Miss Kent, if I said anything that may have caused you distress. I can assure you that was not my intent. Will you accept my apology?"

Lord Bryden was an exceptionally handsome man, Charlotte decided, from the chiseled line of his jaw to the sensual curve of his faintly smiling mouth. His hair was the glossy black of a raven's wing, and he wore it slightly longer than was fashionable, suggesting that either he didn't care for trends, or he was too preoccupied with other matters to worry about the details of his appearance. Yet his evening clothes were well cut and well fitted, further emphasizing both his considerable height and the solid expanse of his chest and shoulders. It was his eyes, however, that captivated her attention. They were a combination of smoke and sea, like a darkening sky just before a summer storm. They regarded her with only the politest of interest, asking nothing, revealing nothing.

A strange unease began to well within her.

"Of course I accept your apology, Lord Bryden," she said. "I understand that the subject of the Dark Shadow is of enormous interest to nearly everyone in London, and consequently I must learn to expect that people are going to want to question me on him."

"I assured Miss Kent that you would be pleased to make a donation to her asylum—as a way of making amends," Tony added helpfully.

"Of course," Harrison agreed. "I would be pleased to contribute to your very fine charity, Miss Kent. Tomorrow I shall send over a bank note for one hundred pounds."

It was a very generous donation. A day earlier, Charlotte would have been elated by such a contribution, especially by someone whose acquaintance she had only just made. But she needed five thousand pounds within three days' time. One hundred pounds was nothing to her anymore. "Thank you."

Harrison was surprised by her obvious lack of enthusiasm. He was not well versed in the costs of feeding and clothing a half dozen or so whores and urchins, but he imagined a hundred pounds, managed carefully, could be made to last a reasonable amount of time. Why was she not more pleased?

"Why don't we say two hundred pounds?" he amended. Perhaps she had incurred some expenses that needed to be paid off. "I imagine running an asylum in the middle of London can be rather expensive."

"Thank you, Lord Bryden." Two hundred pounds still wouldn't begin to address the amount her father had demanded of her, but it was a start. "You are most kind."

"Oh, I absolutely adore this music," exclaimed Lady Elizabeth suddenly, deciding she had tolerated Charlotte and Tony's intrusion long enough. "Lord Bryden, I insist that you dance this waltz with me—I won't take no for an answer!" Emboldened by the champagne she had consumed and the certainty that Harrison was not unaffected by her considerable charms, she reached out and took his hand. "You will forgive us, Miss Kent, if we take our leave of you?"

"Of course," murmured Charlotte, wondering what it was about Lord Bryden that was bothering her. "Please enjoy yourselves."

"It was a pleasure to meet you, Miss Kent." Although he didn't feel like dancing, Harrison was relieved to have a reason to excuse himself from Miss Kent's presence. He was satisfied that she did not recognize him, but to stay in her company any longer was risky. "I wish you and the members of your household the very best."

"Thank you."

Charlotte watched as Lord Bryden dutifully led Lady Elizabeth onto the crowded dance floor. He walked with the grace of a panther, his stride fluid and sure. She was quite certain he would be an accomplished dancer.

"If you like, I shall escort you back to where I found you, Miss Kent," Tony offered. "Your family is probably wondering what has happened to you."

"Thank you, Mr. Poole." Charlotte's gaze remained fastened upon Lord Bryden. He gave a small, courtly bow to Lady Elizabeth, the movement easy and elegant. Then he raised his arms to take hold of his lovely young partner.

And winced.

The pained contortion of his face was abrupt. In the next instant he had completely mastered it, to the extent that had Charlotte blinked, she would have missed it altogether. He had now assumed an expression of polite enjoyment, which he maintained perfectly as he led Lady Elizabeth in expert circles around the floor.

It can't be, thought Charlotte, shocked by the certainty that it was his shoulder that had caused him to wince. Lord Bryden was an esteemed member of London society. It was preposterous to think he could possibly be a common jewel thief. She stared at him as he swept Lady Elizabeth around, swiftly comparing his height and build with that of the Dark Shadow. Both were tall and solidly built. Both moved with fluid grace. That meant nothing, she told herself impatiently. The same could be said of nearly a third of the men in the ballroom. She swiftly began to contrast the details of Lord Bryden's face, hair, and voice to what she could recall of the Dark Shadow. The jewel thief's mask had kept her from seeing any of his features, and the cap he had worn had effectively covered his hair. As for his voice—

"Miss Kent?" Tony was looking at her in confusion. "Is everything all right?"

She snapped her attention back to her escort. "Yes, I'm fine."

She laid her hand upon his offered arm and began to limp back to the area where Simon and Jamie were waiting for her, her mind fervently evaluating Lord Bryden. The Dark Shadow's voice had been low and rich, but the same could be said of many men. At that moment she could not recall it well enough to draw an accurate comparison. What was it, then, that was causing alarm to race up her spine?

His eyes.

"There you are!" exclaimed Jamie, moving forward to greet her. "We wondered what had become of you." He regarded Tony with friendly interest. "I don't believe we have met."

"Mr. Poole, permit me to introduce my brothers, Mr. James Kent and Mr. Simon Kent," said Charlotte. "Jamie and Simon, this is Mr. Poole."

"A pleasure to meet both of you," said Tony, bowing slightly. "I do hope you don't mind that I stole your sister away for a short time. I wanted to introduce her to a friend of mine—which I hope you found worthwhile, Miss Kent." He gave Charlotte a teasing smile. "I knew if we put Bryden on the spot he would have no choice but to pay you."

Simon frowned. "Pay her?"

"I encouraged Lord Bryden to make a substantial donation to your sister's asylum, as a way of making amends for his rather thoughtless joke that the Dark Shadow might actually be here amongst us this evening," Tony explained. "Miss Kent quite wisely showed no emotion when he made his initial pledge, which caused poor Bryden to double his original offer!" He laughed. "No matter, he can afford it. Had she continued to play it cool with him, I think we could have got him to go even higher."

"That's wonderful, Charlotte," said Jamie.

Charlotte nodded, barely listening. Lord Bryden was the Dark Shadow? But that made no sense. He was an earl, after all. His background would have been filled with the trappings of wealth and privilege. What on earth would make him take such enormous risks to steal from the very people with whom he socialized?

"What can you tell me of Lord Bryden?" She tried to sound only casually interested as she smiled at Tony. "Have you known him very long?"

"We've been friends a good while," Tony answered. "He may make the odd joke here and there, but basically Bryden's a serious sort. He became earl when he was just twenty-four—his father died rather suddenly, and Bryden had to step in and take over the estate and holdings, which were in something of a mess, I'm afraid. He's done an astonishing job of building it all up again, though. Everyone was amazed by what he managed to accomplish in a short period of time. He has a natural talent for business, it seems. I keep hoping if I stay around him long enough, some of that talent will rub off on me!" He laughed. "It was a pleasure to meet you, Miss Kent," he finished, bowing. "And both of you, also," he added, nodding at Simon and Jamie. "Enjoy the rest of your evening."

"How much did Lord Bryden agree to donate?" asked Simon after he was gone.

"Two hundred pounds."

Jamie grinned. "Two hundred pounds will keep you going for months, and once word gets out that Lord Bryden has contributed to your asylum, surely there will be others willing to follow his lead."

"You look pale, Charlotte." Simon regarded her worriedly. "Would you like to leave?"

She shook her head. "I don't believe I thanked Lord Bryden properly for his generous bequest. If you don't mind staying a little longer, I'll just go and have a quick word with him."

"I'll come with you," Jamie offered.

"No, thank you. I think it would be better if I spoke with him alone."

"Are you sure?"

"Quite sure."

HARRISON LIFTED A GLASS OF BRANDY FROM THE SIL-ver tray a footman was offering him and took a hefty swallow. Given the close call he had just experienced with Miss Kent, his resolve to refrain from drinking for the evening had been abandoned. As far as he was concerned, the evening was over. One drink, and then he was going to summon his carriage and go home. He was invited to several other balls over the next few days. Perhaps one of them would prove more profitable.

He turned to see Miss Kent limping toward him, alone.

Jesus bloody Christ.

Gone was the reticent, faintly perplexed air she had when Tony had dragged her over to meet him earlier. Harrison had sensed then that something about him bothered her. He had tried to be careful not to say or do anything that might remind her of the Dark Shadow. Clearly, he had failed. Maybe he had some telltale mannerism of which he was unaware. Or perhaps the timbre of his voice was more distinctive than he realized. Whatever it was, Charlotte Kent had made the connection between him and the jewel thief she had stumbled upon two nights earlier.

Now that he was not in imminent danger of either bleeding to death or being arrested, she no doubt wanted to reform his blackened soul and set him firmly on the path to righteousness.

"Forgive me, Lord Bryden, but I would like to speak with you further about your donation," she began, her voice loud enough to be heard by those immediately around them. "Perhaps we could find a quiet place to talk."

Harrison regarded her calmly. "Of course, Miss Kent. Why don't we step out onto the terrace? I hear that Lady Marston's roses are not to be missed." He set his brandy glass on a table and politely offered her his arm.

A flush of heat pulsed through Charlotte as she laid her gloved fingers against the hard warmth of his sleeve. She knew that arm. She had seen it stripped bare, had known the supple contours of its muscles, lean and firm and filled with power. She had felt it wrapped tight around her, holding her a prisoner against the Dark Shadow's body, and later, clinging to her for support as she and Flynn struggled to help him into her house.

It seemed strange to lay her hand upon it with such polite restraint.

"Shall we?" enquired Lord Bryden.

She began to limp toward the doors leading to the terrace, uncomfortably aware that everyone was staring at her.

"Would you like to go down into the gardens, or do you prefer the terrace?" Lord Bryden asked politely.

Charlotte looked at the multitude of steps cascading down into the gardens and bit her lip. "I think I would prefer to stay up on the terrace, if that is all right with you."

"Of course." Harrison felt like an idiot for having suggested the gardens. Of course she didn't want to go tramping up and down all those steps with her injured leg. He scanned the grounds below one corner of the terrace, making sure no one was there to overhear their conversation. Then he glanced at the balconies above. Empty. "Would this area over here suit you? There is a bench where you can sit down, if you like."

"Thank you."

He led her over to the stone bench and seated her. "A very pleasant evening, don't you think, Miss Kent?"

"I know who you are," Charlotte said in a strained whisper.

He leaned against the balustrade and folded his arms across his chest, feigning bemusement. "Really?"

"I'm not going to try to change you, if that's what you're thinking," she added quickly. She didn't have much time before one of her brothers or sisters came looking for her.

"That's a relief," he observed wryly. "And, may I add, somewhat refreshing. In my experience, most women usually can't wait to change me."

"I know about your background, Lord Bryden," Charlotte continued, flustered by his calm. The fact that he did not find her to be a threat only made her feel more guilty about what she was going to do. "How your father died and left your estate in such a terrible state. I suppose you started stealing then, perhaps thinking you would take only enough to give you the money you needed to make some investments and get things going again. But stealing is not always a matter of need. I understand that. After a while, if you haven't been caught, it means you're either very lucky, or very good. Either way, it gets into your blood. You find you can't help yourself. And there is always something more that you want."

"This really is fascinating, Miss Kent. Have you considered writing an article on this subject? I'm sure it would be well received—"

"I need more money from you."

Harrison stared at her. This was not what he had expected. "Are you trying to blackmail me?" he asked, incredulous.

"It isn't for me," she swiftly assured him.

"Then whom, may I ask, is it for?"

"It's for my refuge house," she lied. "To help pay for expenses."

"Two hundred pounds wasn't generous enough?"

"Two hundred pounds was very generous. But I'm afraid I need quite a bit more than that."

"I see. Just how much more are we talking about?"

"I need five thousand pounds."

Harrison had the grace not to laugh, but that was the limit of his restraint. "Forgive me, Miss Kent, but have you gone completely mad?"

"I realize it's a lot of money."

"It is more money than your entire house and all its furnishings are worth," Harrison pointed out. "Were you thinking of setting up a refuge house in the middle of Mayfair? Or perhaps leasing an estate in the country for all your charming friends?"

"No."

"Then what, may I ask, is it that compels you to ask me for such an exorbitant sum?"

"That is not your concern, Lord Bryden. I need five thousand pounds, and I need it quickly."

"Then I suggest you ask your father for it. I'm sure Lord Redmond has never let you want for anything. It's a enormous amount of money, but if he doesn't have the funds, I'm certain the bank will grant him a loan."

"I cannot ask my father for it."

"Why not?"

"Because he would want to know what it is for, and I can't tell him."

"Why not?"

"That really isn't your concern, Lord Bryden."

"You're right, it isn't. Unfortunately, Miss Kent, I am unable to help you, as I don't happen to have five thousand pounds at my disposal."

She looked at him in dismay. "In the past several months you have stolen jewels that have been valued at thousands of pounds," she pointed out. "It was detailed in the newspapers. Are you saying you have already spent the money?"

"Unfortunately, the figures reported in the newspapers are greatly exaggerated," Harrison objected. "Secondly, stolen jewels never fetch their appraised value on the black market. That is part of their appeal. The dealers who buy them like to feel they are getting a rather spectacular deal, given the risks involved in purchasing them."

"If you don't have the money, then I suppose you will have to steal it." Charlotte shifted uncomfortably on the bench. She didn't like the idea of forcing him to steal, but it seemed there was no choice.

"I must confess, I find your attitude bewildering, given that you have devoted your life to reforming black-souled criminals like me. Do you believe I am completely beyond salvation?"

"I'm not interested in reforming you, Lord Brydon," she informed him stiffly. He was toying with her, and she did not like to be mocked. "You are not a desperate child or a starving woman. You have not been forced to steal out of deprivation, in order to have a crust of bread to eat or decent boots for your filthy, blistered feet, or to provide food and shelter for your loved ones. You are an intelligent, educated man from a privileged background, who has made the decision to steal. No doubt when you started you had some reason that you felt was compelling enough, but I don't believe that after all these years those reasons still exist. You steal now either because you are addicted to the thrill of stealing, or because you live beyond your means and have to supplement your income. I don't know which it is, and unfortunately, I don't have time to care. I need five thousand pounds within three days' time, and I'm asking you if you will get it for me."

"And just why, precisely, do you think I should do that?"

She bit her lip. There was only one reason she could give him that would be persuasive enough to make him give her the money. Even so, she hated having to resort to it.

"I helped you the other night, when you were trapped at Lord Chadwick's," she pointed out. "Without my assistance you would have been arrested. Don't you think you owe me something for that?"

"Absolutely," Harrison agreed. "I would think that I owe you something in the amount of a few hundred pounds, which I have already offered to give you. But five thousand pounds really does amount to blackmail. You do realize that, don't you?"

She regarded him miserably. "I suppose I do."

"So, Miss Kent, if you are blackmailing me, you're going to have to tell me what it is you're going to do if I refuse to give you this money. I don't have much experience with this sort of thing, you understand, but I believe that is how it works."

She lowered her gaze to her skirts, unable to look at him. "Unfortunately, I will be forced to go to the police and tell them that you are the Dark Shadow."

She hated saying it. Harrison could see that. She had hoped he would just give her a bank note for five thousand pounds and that would be that. He studied her a moment, watching as her hands clutched nervously at the emerald silk of her gown. What in the name of God would require her to need such an enormous amount of money in such a short period of time? He didn't believe any bank would be demanding such a payment from her. First of all, the expenses of running that modest little house of hers could only amount to about five hundred pounds a year—a thousand pounds at the very most. Since she had only opened it recently, he did not see how she could be in any significant debt. Secondly, all the finances concerning her house would undoubtedly have been in Lord Redmond's name, which meant that any unpaid mortgages or loans would have been directed to him, not her.

What, then, had driven her to such a desperate act?

"Has someone threatened you?" he asked.

Charlotte avoided his gaze. Her father had been clear about what would happen if she told anyone about him. He would hurt her family. Her leg began to throb, reminding her that Boney Buchan was a man capable of inflicting great pain.

"No."

She was lying. He could see it in the forced calm of her face. Anger began to uncoil within him.

"You're lying, Miss Kent. You're afraid of something—if not for your own welfare, then for the welfare of someone you care about. Has someone threatened one of the girls staying at your house? That one with the black eye—Annie—or the red-haired one—what the devil was her name?"

"You don't need to know why I need the money, Lord Bryden," Charlotte told him. "All that matters is that I have to have it."

"If someone is intimidating a member of your household, Miss Kent, you should contact the police. They can help you."

"The police cannot help me in this matter."

"But you believe I can."

"I believe five thousand pounds can."

"I don't know which I find more flattering—the fact that you thought I would have such an amount of money, or that you think I can easily steal it. Given my rather pathetic performance the other night, in which I not only failed to take anything of value, but also managed to attract a mob, be accused of murder, and get shot before being helplessly dragged away on the floor of your carriage, I'm actually surprised you think I can do this. To what do I owe this stirring expression of faith?"

"Until the other night, you were renowned for your thefts. All of London has been astonished by your ability to slip in and out of people's homes without being detected. If I hadn't interrupted you, the night would have ended very differently."

"You're right. And if our paths had not crossed, just how, exactly, would you get the five thousand pounds you claim to so desperately need?"

"I don't know. I suppose I would have been forced to steal it on my own."

She was serious, he realized, looking at her in amazement.

"You must know that I have stolen before—that I have even been jailed for it." Her gaze fell to the mess of wrinkles she had inflicted upon her skirts and she gave a small, self-conscious laugh. "Surely you haven't managed to miss all of the furtive whispers about me and my tawdry background this evening, Lord Bryden. Our encounter at Lord Chadwick's has had the unfortunate effect of thrusting me into forefront of London's gossip."

"I don't pay any attention to gossip, Miss Kent," Harrison told her. "It is a vile sport that doesn't interest me."

His eyes were dark and filled with emotion. There was anger swirling within their depths, and something more, a deeper, rawer sentiment she could not readily identify.

"Besides," he added, shrugging, "whatever they say about you cannot be nearly as bad as what they are now saying about me. That is, unless I missed the part where you committed theft, abduction, and murder all on the same night."

"You didn't murder anyone."

"You are the only one who knows that."

"Oliver knows as well. So does Flynn."

"I can't tell you how comforting I find that. I am sure that if I am ever captured, the courts will find the testimony of a decrepit old man who probably can't see past his nose and an urchin thief most compelling."

"Oliver is not decrepit, and Flynn is no longer a thief. And I would also testify on your behalf."

"Forgive me if I find that less than reassuring, given that you are the one who is threatening to expose me."

"I don't want to expose you, Lord Bryden. I just need the money."

"Blackmail is an ugly practice, Miss Kent, whatever

instigates it. And I'm afraid I don't respond well to being threatened."

"There you are!" Annabelle's voice cut through the tension between them like a silvery bell, startling Charlotte. "We've been looking everywhere for you, Charlotte."

Harrison adopted an air of polite amusement as he watched her sisters cross the terrace toward them in a rustling swish of silk and satin.

"Annabelle and Grace, may I present to you Lord Bryden," Charlotte said, feeling guilty as she awkwardly rose from the bench. "Lord Bryden, these are my sisters, Lady Harding and Lady Maitland," she added to Harrison, feeling hopelessly ill at ease.

"A pleasure to meet you, Lord Bryden," said Annabelle, smiling.

"And for me also," added Grace.

"Forgive me for stealing your lovely sister away from the ballroom, but I thought she might prefer the cool quiet of the garden while she talked to me about the important work of her refuge house," explained Harrison smoothly. "I had no idea that running an asylum for the unfortunate could be so costly."

"You can rest assured that whatever amount you donate, Charlotte will be sure to put to good use." Annabelle smiled at her sister.

Grace nodded in agreement. "She has always been very careful when it comes to money—much more so than anyone else in our family."

Harrison cast a faintly skeptical look at Charlotte. "Indeed."

"Are you ready to leave yet, Charlotte?" asked Annabelle. "I don't mean to interrupt your conversation with Lord Bryden, but Jamie has summoned the carriage—"

"Actually, your sister and I had just finished our discussion, and I was about to escort her back into the ball-room," Harrison interjected. He gallantly offered Charlotte his arm. "Shall we, Miss Kent?"

Reluctantly, Charlotte took his arm and permitted him to walk her and her sisters slowly back into the oppressively perfumed heat of the ballroom.

"It was a pleasure to meet you and hear all about the noble work you are doing, Miss Kent," Harrison said, holding her hand against his arm. "I cannot help but be inspired by your commitment to helping the less fortunate, and by the extraordinary lengths to which you are willing to go to ensure that those who so desperately need your assistance are able to get it. It is really quite moving."

He was mocking her again, Charlotte realized, feeling angry and desperate. She tried to extract her hand from his grip.

"In fact, I am so moved by your concern for the poor that I would like to do whatever I can to help you," Harrison continued, keeping her hand firmly upon his arm. "If you give me a few days, I shall arrange for that donation we discussed. Hopefully it will be sufficient to take care of all your immediate expenses."

Charlotte eyed him uncertainly. Had Lord Bryden just agreed to give her the entire five thousand pounds?

His expression was maddeningly contained, making it impossible for her to discern whether he was being truthful or merely toying with her.

"Thank you, Lord Bryden," she said stiffly, trying to pull her hand away. "I am most grateful."

"It is I who am grateful to you," he assured her, still holding her fast. "After all, if you are able to reform even the most hardened and lost of souls at your house of refuge, it would seem there is hope for all us."

His gaze was dark and unfathomable. But Charlotte knew he was mocking her. After all, she had just revealed herself to be no better than he, or any of the others who threatened and stole to get what they wanted.

"You're too kind," she managed tautly, finally jerking her hand free from his grasp.

"It was also a pleasure to meet you, Lady Harding and Lady Maitland," continued Harrison, bowing slightly to Annabelle and Grace. "I do hope I have the honor of seeing you both again." He smiled at them and turned away, retreating back toward the doors leading to the terrace.

"Lord Bryden seemed very nice," remarked Annabelle later as they drove home in their carriage.

"And it seems he is going to make a rather large donation," Grace added, excited for Charlotte.

"That's splendid," declared Jamie. "So you see, Charlotte, it was worth it for us to drag you to this affair after all."

"Maybe now you'll be encouraged and attend more of them," Simon suggested.

Charlotte nodded and sank back against her seat, exhausted.

She had only done what was necessary to protect her family, she told herself as the carriage rattled through the night. It was wrong—she understood that.

Unfortunately, sometimes the line between right and wrong was difficult to distinguish.

Chapter Six

HE EXHALED A LONG, HOT BREATH AND HESITATED before taking another, knowing it would be stale and reeking of camphor.

He wished to hell Lady Pembroke's maid had not been quite so diligent in her application of the foul-smelling compound, which was supposed to keep moths from attacking the woolen clothes and furs that had been relegated to that wardrobe for the summer. He began to count, timing how long he could go without air. Boredom had driven him to practice this trick while he waited, and he was actually becoming quite good at it. He flexed his fingers a half dozen times, fanning and rippling the appendages like a pianist. Then he slowly rotated his wrists, his shoulders, his neck, encouraging the flow of blood to the stiff, aching muscles. After his upper body had been sufficiently exercised he focused his attention on the lower, flexing the complex structure of bones in his feet and ankles, tightening and releasing the muscles of his calves and thighs, shifting his weight from one hip to the other in an effort to ease the tension that had mounted over the hours in his back. He wanted to crack the wardrobe door open to let in a hint of cooler air, but his unyielding discipline would not permit it.

Victory was in the details.

It was a lesson his father had taught him, and it was a lesson he had learned well. The door to the guest room he had chosen could open any time, as Miss Kent had so aptly demonstrated several nights earlier, revealing some earnest maid or footman who had been directed to fetch something, or to prepare the chamber for an unexpected guest, or to open the window to create more ventilation in the night's stifling summer heat. If a servant noticed the door to the wardrobe was ajar, that might entice him or her to walk over and inspect it.

Better to endure the heat.

His lungs were burning now, protesting their lack of oxygen. A painful band of pressure cinched his body, creating a pounding of hot blood in his face and skull as he fought the impulse to breathe. He could feel the veins of his neck swell and pulse in protest, the ramming of his heart against the muscled wall of his chest, the painful pleas of his rib cage as it struggled to fill itself. *Breathe,* his body urged, begging him to succumb to his weakness. His head was pounding and his ears rang with the sick, dizzying pressure of his lungs and veins and arteries. The darkness was getting heavier and he could no longer hear anything beyond a distant roar.

Just a few more seconds. Just a few more...

His body contorted like the lash of a whip and his mouth flew open, greedily inhaling a long draft of the wardrobe's sweltering air. He sucked it in quickly, efficiently, silently. After a moment, his lungs sufficiently sated, he sat back once again, no longer focused on the musty heat or the uncomfortable lack of space. He had managed to push himself beyond his previous limit without taking a breath.

It was a good sign.

He shifted his head from side to side, releasing the tension in his neck and upper spine, then held himself perfectly still, listening. It had been at least an hour since Lord and Lady Pembroke had departed in their carriage. In that time the servants had relegated themselves to the tasks that were required of them before their employers returned. Lady Pembroke's maid had likely tidied her mistress's bedchamber, straightening up and putting away all the brushes and pins and pots of cosmetics that had been pulled out to make her ladyship presentable. She had then probably arranged Lady Pembroke's dresser, emptied the slops from her washbasin and chamber pot, turned down her bed, laid out her night clothes, and put out the lamps. The evening was sufficiently hot that a fire would not be needed, so that had ended her responsibilities for the evening—at least until her ladyship returned. She would be summoned again at three or four in the morning to light the lamps, help her ladyship take off her gown, hoops, and corset, unpin her hair, remove and put away her jewelry, bring her fresh water for washing, and once again remove any slops. Until then, she would join the other members of the household downstairs in the kitchen, where they would share a meal, drink a little ale or gin, and gossip voraciously about their employers.

It was time for him to go to work.

He silently pushed open the wardrobe door, listening carefully. He heard nothing except the distant sound of raucous laughter. Obviously the servants had opened the gin. Good. He extracted himself from the wardrobe and stood a moment, letting his body adjust to the sudden profusion of space. Once he was certain he could move without stumbling, he stole along the richly patterned carpet and went to the door. He turned the handle slowly, carefully, preparing for a squeaking protest from either the knob itself or from the hinges on which the door rested. But some diligent servant had kept the hardware well oiled, and the door swung open in cooperative quiet.

He crept along the hallway to Lady Pembroke's bedchamber and pressed his ear against the door. Silence. He glanced down at the narrow strip of space beneath the door and the floor. Darkness. He laid his hand on the door handle and carefully eased the door open, hoping that the same conscientious servant had doused the hinges of this one with oil as well. They had.

He slipped into the room and shut the door behind him. Once his eyes had adjusted to the gloom he went directly to the window drapes, opened them, unlocked the window, then quietly eased it open. Because of the Dark Shadow's activities many of the wealthiest households in London had recently taken to locking their windows at night, despite the oppressive summer heat, as a way of protecting themselves. But the days were long and stifling, and since it would be unendurable to do otherwise, the windows remained open then. That gave him ample opportunity to slip inside before evening fell, and find some out-of-the-way niche in which he could hide. No one suspected the Dark Shadow might actually be lurking within their home for hours before he actually stole anything.

He glanced down at the narrow balcony below the window with its handsome stone balustrade, and the one after that, quickly assessing how he would creep along them to get to the Corinthian column that rose along the side of the front entrance. Once he reached it he would climb down, then jump below the street level to the area just in front of the kitchen door. Hidden from view he would remove his mask and cap and don the expensive hat and coat he had left wrapped in a bundle in the corner. Then he would light a cigar and calmly walk home, looking like nothing more than a perfectly respectable gentleman out for a stroll on a hot summer evening.

He moved to Lady Pembroke's dressing table, which was now bathed in the faint wash of moonlight streaming in through the window. An elegant arrangement of crystal jars and bottles were neatly grouped beside an engraved sterling silver brush, mirror, and comb set. No jewelry chest. Unperturbed, he began to methodically search each of her drawers.

Nothing.

Growing slightly irritated, he looked about the room. It wasn't on her night table, or on the elegantly carved writing desk situated in one corner of the boudoir. Obviously his thefts were having an effect on how the rich ladies of London stored their precious baubles. He stalked over to the bed, lifted the edge of the silk embroidered coverlet and felt under the mattress. Nothing.

He dropped to his knees and swept his arm beneath the bedstead, searching. It wasn't there.

He stood and gazed about the room, trying to think where else Lady Pembroke might have hidden her jewelry chest before going out. The excessively carved doors of her wardrobe caught his attention. *Of course.* She probably thought no one would think to search for jewelry in that ornate monstrosity. He moved toward it swiftly, eager to find the magnificent ruby-and-diamond necklace she had been wearing the previous night at the Marstons' ball. He knew she and her husband were only attending a small dinner party on this particular evening. He was counting on her vanity to have kept her from wearing the very same jewelry. No self-respecting woman of affluence wanted people to think her husband could only afford to give her one decent necklace. He grasped the handle of the wardrobe and silently eased it open.

A pair of booted feet rammed into his stomach, sending him flying back like an arrow.

"Good evening," drawled his attacker. "I was beginning to worry that maybe you weren't coming after all."

He inhaled a deep breath, fighting to master the pain in his gut, and looked up to see a veritable duplicate of himself standing over him. The man's face and hair were completely hidden by a black mask and cap. The rest of his clothes were dark, making him barely a shadow in the thinly lit room.

"I believe you are looking for this." His attacker reached into his own pocket and withdrew Lady Pembroke's glittering ruby necklace. "And no wonder—it really is a spectacular piece. As someone who also appreciates the splendor of fine jewelry, I must commend you on your exceptional taste. I imagine it was at the Marstons' ball that you first noticed it, wasn't it?"

He regarded his assailant warily, saying nothing. He was not about to reveal himself because this reflection of him felt like chatting.

"You've been rather busy these past few months, haven't you?" the man continued. "Breaking into houses all over London, slipping in and out like a ghost. It's really been quite impressive. Unfortunately, however, your career as a jewel thief is over." He dropped the necklace into his pocket, then pulled a length of rope from the other one. "Now be a good burglar and give me your hands."

He sat up slowly, obligingly holding his fists together at the wrists. His captor bent to secure them with a rope.

Enabling him to smash both his fists into the arrogant prick's face.

The blow was hard, but so was his assailant. His head snapped back as his hands shot forward, grabbing him by his shoulders. A fist drove into his jaw, cracking his teeth together which such force he staggered into Lady Pembroke's writing desk. The delicately carved piece collapsed, smashing everything upon it. The acrid smell of kerosene from a shattered oil lamp filled the room. He knew in a moment or two the servants would come running. His assailant was on him again, growling with rage. He fought him hard, but his attacker was powerful and equally determined. They both went crashing to the floor, each scrambling to gain the advantage. Agitated voices were in the corridor now. He clawed ferociously at his would-be captor, tearing off his black cap and mask in the process.

"Bryden!" The word escaped his mouth before he could stop it.

Harrison's hand clamped around the Dark Shadow's wrist like a manacle, refusing to let him escape. "You can't get away," he grated out furiously. "It ends here."

The Dark Shadow relaxed slightly, his shoulders slumped in apparent defeat. He finally had him, Harrison thought, triumphant. It was over. The rush of adrenaline that had filled him a moment earlier began to seep away, making him acutely aware of every aching muscle and bone. He really was getting too goddamn old for this. Now he had to somehow explain his presence to the servants...

A blade whipped across his hand, slicing open his glove and the skin beneath. His hand contracted in a spasm of pain, causing him to let go.

"It's over for you, Bryden," the man snarled. "Not me." He drove his knee with savage force into Harrison's testicles.

Stars exploded all around him. For a moment he thought he would vomit. Instead he collapsed to the floor beside the bed, curled up like an infant and equally helpless.

The Dark Shadow pulled Lady Pembroke's necklace from Harrison's pocket and flew to the window.

"Stop, thief!" roared a servant from the doorway, unable to see Harrison as he pointed a quivering pistol at the figure in the window.

The escaping thief did not hesitate. He hurled his blade at the man, sending the speeding shaft directly into the poor servant's chest.

The pistol fired and a shower of plaster rained from the ceiling as the injured servant crumpled to the floor.

The Dark Shadow did not look back. With the agile grace of a cat he leapt over the windowsill and disappeared from Harrison's sight.

Harrison looked over to see the groaning man lying upon the floor, a scarlet stain weeping through the white of his shirt. There was nothing he could do for him, he realized bleakly, except pray the other servants would be able to fetch a doctor quickly. He had to get the hell out of there himself, before he was arrested for murder.

He dragged himself off the floor and staggered to the window, then heaved a leg over the sill.

"Oh, my God—*help!*" shrieked a voice behind him as another servant ventured fearfully into the room. *"Murder!! Murder!!"*

Harrison did not look back. He moved clumsily along the narrow stone balcony in front of the window, then grunted as he shifted to the next one. He awkwardly made his way down part of the column beside the door, then gave up on the thing and jumped. His body crashed to the ground with a heavy thud, sending a streak of pain up one knee. He forced himself to get up and quickly limped down the street, then rounded a corner.

He did not know which direction the Dark Shadow had taken, and at that point, he didn't give a damn. He began to thread his way through the dimly lit streets, listening as the agitated shouting and screaming behind him grew fainter.

He would head toward Drury Lane, he decided, breathing heavily. It was always noisy and crowded at that time with dozens of people spilling in and out of taverns. No one would notice him there, not even in his current unkempt, staggering condition. If anything, he would fit right in. He would buy a drink and wait a while before hiring a carriage to take him home. The driver would give him at least some semblance of an alibi for part of the evening, should the need arise.

He thought it unlikely that either of the two servants who had burst into the room had seen his face clearly, but prudence demanded that he take precautions just the same. He had to be careful. The Dark Shadow had recognized him, which meant the bastard had the advantage.

Now he was the one who would be hunted.

Chapter Seven

"... AN' THEN HE LEAPS OUT THE WINDOW, LEAVING poor Mr. Beale drownin' in his own blood."

Inspector Lewis Turner stared grimly at the enormous reddish-brown stain that had saturated the intricately woven Persian carpet of Lady Pembroke's bedchamber. "Go on."

"Well, it was awful dark in the room, but I could see Mr. Beale was done for," the young footman continued excitedly. " 'Hang on, Mr. Beale,' I says, just thinkin' to give him a bit of a lift—I mean, there's no sense in thinkin' ye're a croaker just because ye are—' 'tis only a scratch!'—an' he looks at me an' says, 'I don't think so, Tom, my boy—I think I'm right done for.' So I kneels down beside him an' wonders what should I do for him—I mean, if I pulls out the blade, will that make him feel better, or snuff him quick?

"An' while I'm thinkin' on that, he groans a little, not much, mind ye, no more than if ye had the collywobbles, an' then he grabs my hand and says 'This is it, Tom, I know it, and there's somethin' ye must make right for me.' 'Anythin',' I says, and I'm feeling right sad now, because Mr. Beale was always fair to me since I come here, and I liked him well enough, even though some of the other servants used to laugh about him behind 'is back and call him an old lobcock. 'I'll do anythin' for ye, sir,' I says, and I means it. An' he's lookin' at me real close now, his eyes all wide and not blinkin' like them dolls you can buy up in Cheapside—the little girls go mad for 'em on account of their eyes bein' so big an' all, but I think they look horrible, like some sort of mad thing, an' who wants eyes that's always lookin' at ye anyway, even when ye're stark-ballock naked?"

Lewis struggled for patience, reminding himself that the footman had just held a dying, brutally injured man in his arms. It was to be expected that such a horrific experience might make him ramble a little. "What did Mr. Beale say?" he asked, trying to guide Tom back to the relevant part of his story.

"He says, 'Make sure they catch the Dark Shadow and hang him for me,' and his hand is all tight and clammy now, an' them eyes of his are big as beets, an' I know he's goin' to kick it soon, so I says, 'I will, Mr. Beale, you just worry about stayin' alive till the doctor comes.' 'No doctor can fix me,' he says, an' I say, 'it ain't all that bad,' an' he says, 'Ye're a good boy Tom, but a bad liar,' an' I kind of smile at that, because even though he's bleedin' to death he's still makin' a joke, an' I'm thinkin' maybe I'm wrong, maybe he's goin' to be all right after all. I've heard about people who was layin' in their coffin, dead as a herring, an' just as they're about to be dropped in the ground they sit up all of a sudden and say 'Here now, what's this about?' "

"What else did Mr. Beale say about the Dark Shadow?" Lewis decided if he let the young man ramble any more, he'd never get on with his investigation.

He had been dragged from his bed at two o'clock in the morning to investigate this latest crime scene of the

Dark Shadow. It was now nearly dawn. He was tired, he was hungry, and he was infuriated that the Dark Shadow had managed yet another robbery and murder while he had been lying in bed dreaming, for God's sake. It made him and the entire Metropolitan Police Force look like fools.

That was a perception he did not tolerate well.

"Why, nothin'." Tom frowned, somewhat miffed at having his colorful account interrupted. "He just said to make sure that they got him and hanged him."

"Did he describe him for you?"

He vigorously scratched his head, thinking. "No."

"Did he tell you anything about him that might give us some clue as to his identity?"

He shrugged his skinny shoulders. "Not that I remember."

"Thank you, Tom." Lewis was suddenly anxious to be rid of the stale-smelling servant, with his blood-stained shirt and his talk of beet-sized eyes and strange-looking dolls. "I'll let you know if I need to speak with you again."

"Don't ye want to hear the rest of my story?"

"I presume that then Mr. Beale took his last breath and died. Isn't that right?"

"He just kept starin' at me, an' I kept tryin' to tell him it was goin' to be fine, an' then he got all quiet. But his eyes never closed. They just kept lookin' at me." Tom's voice was hushed as he finished fearfully, "Like he was tryin' to tell me somethin' from beyond this world."

"Often when people die their eyes don't close," Lewis assured him. "It is entirely normal."

The young footman glanced nervously at the enormous bloodstain on the carpet. "Do ye think he's still here—watchin' us? Especially since he died so violent. Do you think his spirit is waitin' to see if I'll do like I said?"

"There's no such thing as ghosts, Tom." Lewis felt as if he were talking to a child. "The best thing we can do for Mr. Beale is to find the Dark Shadow and bring him to justice, so that his untimely death can be avenged. Is there anything more you can tell me that you think might be of help in this case?"

Tom shrugged. "I didn't get a very good look at him."

"Was he tall or short?" Maybe there was one small additional piece of information he could extract from the servant that might help. "Thin or fat? Moving quickly and easily like a young man, or slower and more stiffly?"

"He was tall enough, I guess—bit hard to tell, really, since he was kind of hunched over to get through the window. I wouldn't say he was thin, really, but I wouldn't say he was fat, neither. More middlin' like. I didn't take no notice of how he was movin', on account of the fact that I was more concerned with poor Mr. Beale."

"Of course. Thank you, Tom. If you think of anything else, I would appreciate it if you would contact me." Lewis handed him his card.

Tom nodded glumly as he took the small white rectangle, clearly disappointed that his interview was over. "Yes, sir, Inspector Turner, sir. I will."

Lewis turned his attention back to the overturned writing desk and the litter of broken glass, papers, pen, and ink surrounding it. It was not characteristic of the Dark Shadow to ransack a room. Typically the thief worked silently and left everything in perfect order, so that the owners of a home had no idea they had even been robbed until the next time the wife went searching through her jewelry box. This meant days often went by before anyone realized a crime had occurred. What the devil had caused him to start heaving over furniture?

"His hair was black."

Lewis turned around, surprised to see that young Tom had not yet left the room. "Pardon me?"

"His hair was black—or real dark, anyway. It might have been dark brown—like dirt."

"The Dark Shadow always wears a cap to cover his hair," Lewis pointed out. Obviously the young man was embellishing his story to gain a few more minutes of his attention.

"He wasn't wearin' a cap."

Lewis regarded him skeptically. "Are you sure?"

He nodded. "Sure as I'm standin' here."

"Was he wearing a mask?"

"I ain't sure," Tom admitted. "It was dark, and he was already climbin' out the window when I come runnin' in. I didn't see his face. But I did see his head, an' the hair on it looked black."

Lewis considered this a moment. The Dark Shadow always wore a cap and mask—they were vital to concealing his identity. If it were, indeed, the Dark Shadow who had visited Lord Pembroke's house that night and murdered poor Mr. Beale, why on earth would he not be wearing a cap?

By the time Lewis had arrived at the house, Mr. Beale's body had already been moved to his bed by the servants, who felt it wasn't decent to leave him lying sprawled upon Lady Pembroke's bedchamber floor. This well-meaning gesture had unfortunately meant that Lewis was unable to see for himself exactly where and how Mr. Beale had fallen. But it was clear from the bloodstain that he had been injured and died near the door; there was no trail of blood to suggest that he had been stabbed somewhere else in the room and then staggered back to the door in an attempt to escape. Was there an altercation between the butler and the Dark Shadow before Mr. Beale was stabbed? That would explain the overturned furniture. But the other servants had described hearing a loud commotion in Lady Pembroke's bedchamber, which was what had instigated Mr. Beale to fetch his pistol and go upstairs in the first place. Tom had said he had heard Mr. Beale yelling at the thief to stop just before his pistol went off. The damage to the ceiling and the plaster showered across the floor indicated that Mr. Beale had completely missed his mark, suggesting that the weapon had discharged after he had been stabbed. The Dark Shadow had then apparently climbed out the window and disappeared.

Leaving the question: What had happened that had caused him to heave over the desk and make so much noise in the first place?

A scrap of something dark peeking out from beneath Lady Pembroke's bedstead suddenly caught his eye. He walked over and studied it, memorizing its location and arrangement before he actually picked it up. It was a black woolen cap. Plain, of common make, without any label inside to indicate either where it had been manufactured or purchased.

"Godamighty—that's his, ain't it?" Tom stared at the cap in horror, as if he thought the Dark Shadow might somehow be hiding inside it.

Lewis dropped to his knees and lifted the skirt of the heavy damask cover on Lady Pembroke's bed. There, just by the edge of the bed frame, lay a black ripple of fabric. He pulled it out and stared at the two small eyeholes cut into the center of a silk scarf.

"An' his mask, too!" Tom's face was chalk white. "Do ye think Mr. Beale's ghost put 'em there, as a message?"

"I can assure you, whoever left these was of flesh and blood." Lewis studied the two articles, wondering just what the hell he had found. It didn't make any sense.

Why on earth would the Dark Shadow remove his mask and cap and leave them lying there to be found?

"We've got him!" Police Constable Wilkins's burst through the door, his expression jubilant.

Lewis stared at the young officer, stunned. "You caught the Dark Shadow?"

"No, but we found something that's going to lead us to him," Constable Wilkins amended, nearly quivering with excitement. "We found this on the ground outside. He must have dropped it while he was making his escape."

Lewis set down the mask and cap on Lady Pembroke's bed and took the white linen square from Constable Wilkins's hand. It was of an expensive make, precisely woven with an elegant trim of fine hemstitching around the edges. Clearly a gentleman's handkerchief.

Carefully embroidered into one corner in white thread was the single initial *B*.

"All we have to do is find the man whose initial matches that, and we've got him!" declared Constable Wilkins, ecstatic.

"The last time I checked, Constable Wilkins, the law does not permit us to charge a man with murder based on the fact that we found a handkerchief bearing his initial somewhere in the vicinity of the crime scene," Lewis pointed out. "It is merely another clue in our case, which may or may not be of significance."

"It's his handkerchief," Constable Wilkins insisted. "It hasn't been there long—it's too clean."

"It may be his," Lewis allowed, "or it may belong to someone who simply shares the same initial. It may have been mistakenly dropped by the Dark Shadow, or it may have been planted there by him in an attempt to confuse us." He studied the snowy piece of fabric, thinking. "It has been my observation over the years that criminals generally assume a method that follows a certain pattern. Sometimes it takes them a while to perfect their technique, but once they do, they tend to adhere to it. This is especially true in the case of criminals who achieve a degree of notoriety. They enjoy the public interest in them, and therefore they want to make sure the public knows that they are the ones who have committed a crime, and not someone else.

"Until recently, the Dark Shadow has always been meticulously careful during his break-ins, slipping in and out undetected, never leaving so much as a pin out of place. Now, suddenly, he is taking young women hostage, heaving furniture about, dropping personal articles, and murdering people. Don't you find that rather odd?"

"He's getting bolder, and that has made him sloppier," Constable Wilkins argued. "He probably took off his mask and cap on account of the room being so hot and dark—he wanted to see better. Lady Pembroke said that her jewelry box was hidden in the back of the wardrobe beneath a pile of clothes, while the key to it was hidden under her pillow. He probably got his dander up trying to find the key, and that's why he tossed her desk over once he realized it wasn't there."

"Perhaps," allowed Lewis, unconvinced. "He also only took one item from her jewelry chest: a diamond-and-ruby necklace. But Lord Pembroke has attested that there were many other significant pieces of jewelry stored in the chest. Why didn't he take any of those as well?"

"He never takes everything," Constable Wilkinson reminded him. "That's part of how his thefts go undetected for so long. At first glance, it doesn't seem like anything is missing."

"But if he was already throwing over furniture and making a great deal of noise looking for either the chest or the key, then he knew once he found the chest that there was no possibility of his visit going unnoticed. He might as well have emptied the entire box and tossed it on the floor. Instead he closed it up and carefully placed it back in the wardrobe, with all of Lady Pembroke's garments neatly folded on top of it once more. Why go to such trouble—especially when he knows the servants are coming and he has to hurry and get out?"

"Maybe he'd already nicked the necklace and put the box back, and then he knocked over the desk when Mr. Beale came with his pistol," supplied Tom. "Maybe they had a bit of a scuffle before he stabbed him."

"All of the servants have said that they first knew the house was being robbed because of a loud crashing sound coming from the upstairs. That was long before Mr. Beale arrived waving his pistol. Also, Mr. Beale was stabbed in the chest, and when you came in, which you say was just a moment after the pistol was fired, you found him lying on his back, by the doorway. If Mr. Beale came into the room and wrestled with the Dark Shadow over here, where the desk is, and then got stabbed, how did he come to be lying way over there by the doorway?"

"Maybe he got stabbed as he was trying to run away," Constable Wilkins suggested.

"Then logic suggests he would have fallen on his front," argued Lewis, "not his back."

"Maybe he was staggerin' backward with the knife in him, an' then just fell back as well," theorized Tom.

"There is no blood in any other part of the room other than by the doorway."

"It's possible the blood hadn't leaked out enough to land on the floor until he got over there," Constable Wilkins reflected.

Lewis clenched his jaw, resisting the impulse to raise his hands and massage his aching temples. It was either ridiculously late or ungodly early, depending on how one wanted to look at it. He was exhausted, and he wanted nothing more than to go home, collapse on his bed, and get a couple of hours sleep. But the Dark Shadow had killed again, which meant sleep was out of the question. After he had finished his inspection there he would go directly to Scotland Yard and report to Chief Inspector Holloway, his superior officer.

Chief Inspector Holloway would not be pleased.

Until the murder of Lord Haywood several nights earlier, the newspapers had taken great pleasure in writing about the Dark Shadow as if he were some kind of romantic, almost heroic figure. They had delighted in his every move, reporting on his daring break-ins as if he were a character to be celebrated instead of reviled. They emphasized the fact that he only robbed the extravagantly wealthy. Some even suggested that he might actually use his stolen proceeds to help the poor, although there was no evidence to support this theory. That idea had immediately won over London's lower classes, who always enjoyed the antics of a good thief. They despised the rich anyway, so if someone was nipping a gaudy piece of jewelry here and there from them, that was fine entertainment. They also enjoyed the fact that the police seemed blatantly helpless to catch this exceptionally clever criminal.

All that had changed the night Lord Haywood was shot.

"Thank you for your time, Tom," Lewis said, dismissing him again. "You know how to reach me if you think of anything else that might be helpful in this case."

"Yes, sir." Tom cast the room one last glance, shuddered, then hurried out the door.

"Constable Wilkins, I would like you and the other police officers here to finish searching every room in the house. Once you have done that, I want you to start knocking on doors. Ask every neighbor on the street if they saw or heard anything suspicious last night. Check all their windows and doors for signs of forced entry. It's possible he broke into another house near here and hid there a while after fleeing this home. Have a team of officers search the back gardens, laneways, and carriage houses of the surrounding area, looking for any signs of disturbance. I want to know about anything unusual, even if it's just a single crushed flower in a garden. Understand?"

"Yes, sir, Inspector. What shall I tell Lady Pembroke about her bedchamber? She is most upset about its condition, and has been asking when she can send up the servants to clean it."

"Tell her I expect to be just a few more minutes. I'll come down and speak to her and his lordship once I have finished here."

"Very good, sir."

Lewis closed the door after him. Then he moved to the center of the room. His gaze swept slowly over the havoc-stricken bedchamber, methodically taking note of everything he saw. He stared at the shattered kerosene lamp lying amidst a clutter of kerosene-soaked writing paper, a ruined assortment of pens, jars, a broken ceramic figurine, and a spilled bottle of black ink. His gaze moved to the open window, where the Dark Shadow had escaped into the night without the benefit of either a mask or a cap. He studied the enormous, magnificently carved wardrobe, its two massive doors still yawning open. Then he stared at the mask, cap, and neatly embroidered handkerchief he had laid out on Lady Pembroke's bed. Finally, he looked at the ugly, rust-colored stain on the carpet.

He clenched his jaw, frustrated by the inconsistencies around him. This was the case that would make or break his career, he realized grimly. Since abduction and

murder had become involved, the public was being
whipped into a terrified frenzy by the newspapers, while
the police force was being castigated as a bunch of buf-
foons. If he failed to capture the Dark Shadow quickly,
he would be relegated to spending the rest of his career
investigating linen thefts up in Camden Town. He had
to find the bastard before he killed again.

He frowned as he looked at Lady Pembroke's immaculately arranged bed.

Lord Pembroke had told him that she had hidden
the key to her jewelry chest beneath her pillow. The
chest had been opened without force, so obviously the
Dark Shadow had managed to find it. Yet the bed
showed no sign of having been touched. If the Dark
Shadow was heaving over furniture in frustration, why
would he have been so careful as he searched Lady Pembroke's bed? Perhaps he had found the key, opened the
chest, then returned the key to its hiding place and carefully arranged the covers once more. But that made no
sense if he had already broken the desk. Confused by
this, Lewis drew down the heavy crimson coverlet and
lifted up the pillows, searching for the key.

It wasn't there.

Bemused, he pulled up the covers from the rest of
the bed. Then he looked under the bed, beneath the
mattress, and through the debris upon the carpet. He
searched every surface and every drawer. He rifled
through her wardrobe. Finally he turned to the jewelry
box, which was now sitting upon the bureau.

Lord Pembroke had reported that he had found the
box at the back of the wardrobe, exactly where Lady
Pembroke had hidden it. The only difference was that it
was unlocked.

Lewis knew the Dark Shadow typically left everything exactly as he had found it. But on that night he
had knocked a desk over, either before or after he had

found the key. Knowing servants were coming, he had not bothered to lock the chest as he returned it to the cupboard. He had, however, taken the time to cover it neatly beneath the garments that had been on it before.

That struck Lewis as odd.

What was more bizarre was that after rummaging through the bed and retrieving the key, he had proceeded to neatly make the bed up again.

If he hadn't yet knocked over the desk, why bother rearranging the bed when he knew he was going to momentarily return the key to its hiding place? And if he had knocked over the desk before finding the key, then why start fussing about arranging coverlets when he knew the servants were on their way?

Unable to make any sense of it, he picked up the handkerchief Wilkins had found. Could the Dark Shadow really have been so careless as to leave his monogrammed handkerchief lying on the ground? Lewis doubted it, but at that point, he had little else to go on.

He would begin by asking Lady Pembroke on what occasions she had recently worn her ruby necklace. Then he would contact the hosts of those parties and request their guest lists. That would enable him to determine if anyone bearing the last initial *B* had recently had the opportunity to admire Lady Pembroke's necklace.

He might not be able to arrest a man on the strength of a handkerchief, but he could certainly have him watched.

HARRISON STARED OUT THE WINDOW OF HIS STUDY into the rain-drenched night, fighting the silken threads of pain filtering through his head. *Not tonight,* he commanded silently. He needed to think, and he couldn't think if he was sprawled on his bed in the dark, immobilized with pain. He raised his palms to his forehead and pressed hard, trying to squeeze the advancing pain out, or at least hold it at bay for a while. It wavered, not retreating, but not getting any worse either. He closed his eyes and breathed deeply. No dizziness. No nausea. That was good. Maybe it wouldn't progress beyond a dull ache.

He could tolerate that.

He went to his desk and poured himself a brandy. He knew it might cloud his mind a little, but it would also dull the pain in his head, and at that moment that seemed more important. Besides, he wasn't going out anywhere. His scuffle with the Dark Shadow the previous evening and his subsequent crash to the ground as he escaped had left him stiff and sore. That, combined with the cut to his left hand and his throbbing, stitched-up shoulder, was making him feel every wretched minute of his forty years. He had thought he was getting too old for this sort of thing. Until his fight with the Shadow, he had not realized just how old he really was.

He took a swallow of brandy, disgusted with himself.

There was a hesitant rap upon his study door.

"Come in."

"Forgive me, your lordship, for disturbing you," apologized Telford, his butler, his expression sober. "But there is a young woman here to see you. A Miss Kent. She says it is a matter of some urgency."

Harrison had wondered whether or not she would come. By early that evening all of London had had a chance to read about the Dark Shadow's latest robbery and murder in grisly detail. Miss Kent would have been horrified to learn how Lord Pembroke's butler had been killed as he bravely tried to protect Lady Pembroke's precious jewels from the infamous Dark Shadow. Harrison was amazed that Miss Kent had still sought him out, believing him to be a cold-blooded murderer.

Either she was extraordinarily stupid, or her need for five thousand pounds was even more desperate than he realized.

"Send Miss Kent to the drawing room, Telford," Harrison instructed. "I'll see her there."

"Unfortunately, Lady Bryden is using the drawing room at the moment." Telford shifted uneasily on his feet before delicately adding: "I don't believe she is feeling well enough to receive Miss Kent."

"What is she doing?"

"She believes she is having an argument with Lord Bryden, your father, my lord. At times she is rather loud."

"I see. Did she eat anything this evening, Telford?"

"No, my lord. I set her place in the dining room, as usual, and as you have instructed, I also set one for your father. Lady Bryden appeared to be in fine spirits until I served the first course."

"What happened?"

"She began to imagine she was having a disagreement with your father. Apparently, she believed he was refusing to eat, because he didn't like what was being served. Lady Bryden accused him of being far too set in his ways, and worried he might be insulting Mrs. Griffin. I tried to calm her by saying I would bring Lord Bryden something else more to his liking, but Lady Bryden would not hear of it and left the room. She has been alone in the drawing room arguing with him ever since."

"What did you serve her, Telford?"

"Boiled breast of mutton and caper sauce. Mrs. Griffin assured me it was one of her specialties."

"My father disliked mutton."

Telford's expression fell. "Forgive me, sir. Had I

known, I could have advised Mrs. Griffin to prepare something else. Mrs. Griffin is most anxious to please you, sir, and she thought she was making something that Lady Bryden would enjoy."

"It's all right, Telford, neither you nor Mrs. Griffin could possibly have known. Kindly show Miss Kent in here, then go and ask Mrs. Griffin to prepare a tray for my mother of tea, toast, cheese, fruit, and a few slices of cold chicken or beef. Then tell my mother I will be up to see her shortly, and say that I'll be most displeased if she and my father are still arguing when I get there."

"Yes, my lord." He gave Harrison a small bow and hurried from the room.

He turned to the window and took another swallow of brandy, feeling unbearably tired. When his father died and Harrison had first inherited his title and the crushing responsibility that went with it, he had believed that if he could just hold on for a year or two, eventually it would get easier. But it never had. There were a few fleeting moments where things had seemed more bearable, at least from a financial point of view. But the exhausting weight of responsibility had never abated.

He had just come to accept there was no choice but to carry it.

"Miss Kent, my lord," announced Telford, interrupting Harrison's thoughts as he ushered Charlotte into the study.

"Thank you, Telford. That will be all."

His butler bowed and closed the door.

Charlotte seemed smaller and more fragile to Harrison as he turned to look at her. Her face was grave and pale, her green-and-gold eyes wide and haunted. There was an almost ethereal quality to her, like a lovely wisp of snow that would disintegrate the instant it touched anything of substance. Fear of him had reduced her to this condition, he realized. On the night she had stumbled upon him in Lord Chadwick's home, she had exuded an extraordinary strength and will as she had helped him to escape. Now she was all but trembling in his presence. He had hoped that with what little she knew of him, she might have held some fragment of faith that he was not a murderer. But the dread in her eyes told him otherwise.

A bitter taste filled his mouth. He washed it away by draining his glass.

"Good evening, Miss Kent," he said. "I trust you have come for your money?"

"I'm so sorry." Her voice was small and raw. "Can you ever forgive me?"

"That depends." Jesus, had the foolish girl reported him to the police? His mind began to race. He could not stay here if the authorities were on their way to arrest him. He knew they wouldn't believe anything he had to say. But if he suddenly disappeared and left his mother in the care of the servants, he knew the effect on her would be devastating. "What, exactly, Miss Kent, have you done that warrants my forgiveness?"

Charlotte stared at him helplessly. His expression was composed, but she wasn't fooled by it. She had known too much anguish in her own life to not be able to recognize it in others. He was haunted by the atrocity of his crime, just as she had known he would be. But in her mind, she was as much responsible for the death of Lord Pembroke's butler as he was.

She was the one who had forced Lord Bryden to steal that night.

"I never should have asked you for money," she began haltingly. "But I was desperate, and I thought you would be able to help me. It never occurred to me that you wouldn't be able to easily afford it."

He raised a brow and said nothing.

"Once you told me you didn't have the money, I shouldn't have suggested that you steal it. I don't think I thought it through—or maybe I just thought that you were so skilled at stealing, that it would be easy for you. I was being foolish, of course, and selfish. Now, because of me, you have been forced to kill a man." Her expression was haunted. "Can you ever forgive me?"

He stared at her, dumbfounded. This was not what he had expected. But then, Miss Kent never seemed to do or say what he expected. He exhaled a tense breath, permitting himself to relax slightly.

Apparently he did not have to flee his home just yet.

"I know you didn't intend to kill that man, Lord Bryden." Charlotte wished he would say something. "If anyone is to be held responsible, it is I. I should never have forced you into a situation where you had no recourse but to defend yourself." She looked away.

Harrison clenched his jaw in frustration. How much could he explain to her? She already believed that he was the Dark Shadow. He could not tell her the truth without exposing all the sordid details of his past. He had fought too long and hard to raise himself above his mistakes to start unveiling them to some woman he barely knew. Besides, she had no reason to believe anything he told her.

"Am I correct, then, in assuming that you are not going to turn me over to the authorities?" he enquired dryly.

Charlotte looked at him in surprise. "Do you really think that I would do that?"

"Forgive me if I offended you. It's just that the other night you indicated that unless I paid you five thousand pounds, you would report me to the police."

"I have no desire to see you sent to prison—or worse, tried for murder. But after last night, surely you must realize that you cannot continue to steal. Either someone else will be harmed, or you will be caught. No jewels are worth such a terrible price."

"Thank you, Miss Kent, for your advice."

His tone was mocking, the chiseled lines of his face hard. He didn't think she understood, she realized. While Lord Bryden knew some of the details of her past, he didn't have any inkling of what that past meant. He had spent his entire life safely ensconced in the silk-covered walls of his elegant home, and undoubtedly also within the grand halls and endless corridors of some magnificent ancestral estate. According to his friend Mr. Poole, he had experienced some financial problems after his father's death, but evidently not enough to destroy his family's wealth. He had probably started stealing out of what he deemed necessity.

As Charlotte stared at him, looking every bit the arrogant aristocrat in his elegantly tailored clothes, with his richly appointed furnishings and his perfectly deferential servants bowing around him, anger began to pulse through her. He had no comprehension of what necessity was. Necessity was being so hungry that you felt weak and sick. It was being forced to eat a moldy crust of bread or a rotten, half-eaten apple you found lying in the gutter, and be grateful there was something in your stomach. Necessity was being terrified to go back to your filthy dark flat because you hadn't managed to beg or steal anything of consequence that day, and you knew your father was going to beat you until you could barely move. Necessity was being forced to stand before a gaping, jeering crowd and slowly lift your skirts—

"Miss Kent? Are you all right?"

She blinked and looked at him. Everything was suddenly very white.

"Jesus Christ, sit down." He wrapped a strong arm around her and helped her over to the sofa. "Here, put your head down—you look like you're going to faint."

Charlotte permitted him to seat her, to lay his gentle hands across her shoulders and ease her forward, until her face was staring at the simple gray pleats of her tailored skirt. Her mind reeling, she fought to separate the past from the present. She focused on the warmth of his touch across her shoulders, the steady sound of his breathing as he leaned into her, the highly polished sheen of his expensive black boots. His scent was all around her, a wonderfully clean, masculine smell, soap and leather and a hint of brandy. Suddenly he released her and walked away, and she felt chilled and alone. But he was back a moment later, kneeling beside her, holding a glass of something fragrant to her lips.

"Take a sip of this," he urged, helping her to slowly sit up again. "Not too fast, though. It's strong."

She didn't flinch as the brandy burned a path down her throat. She took another swallow, then raised her gaze to him.

"Feel better?" he asked, setting the glass on a table.

She nodded, embarrassed. "Yes. Thank you."

Harrison stayed kneeling beside her. The sun-washed fragrance of her was intoxicating his senses, a light, crisp scent of wildflowers and orange. She struck him as exceptionally lovely in the honeyed light of his study, with her creamy silk skin and those wide, jade eyes flecked with amber. A few coppery strands of hair had escaped the confines of her hat to play teasingly against the paleness of her neck, giving her a sweetly disheveled look. He found himself recalling the feel of her slender form pressing against him on the first night they met, her rib cage rising and falling within his embrace, the soft swell of her breasts grazing his arm, her firm buttocks pressed against his thighs.

Desire surged through him, hot and hard.

He rose abruptly and went to his desk, distancing himself from her. What the hell was the matter with him, for God's sake? He poured himself a brandy, trying to focus. He recalled that on the night they had met he had expected her to swoon—in fact, he had even hoped for it. But she hadn't. Instead she had tried to help him, demonstrating a remarkable strength and courage. Nothing about her had struck him as fragile or weak on that night, even after he finally noticed her disability.

Yet soon after, she had been frightened enough to resort to blackmail, an act which she obviously found completely abhorrent.

"Tell me why you need the money, Charlotte."

She regarded him warily. "I told you, it's for my refuge house."

"Don't play games with me. You are desperate for money, but you won't turn to your own family for it. Someone is threatening you, and I want to know who."

She looked away. "I can't tell you."

"Then I won't help you."

His reluctance to help her was understandable, Charlotte realized. After all, he barely knew her, and she was asking for an enormous sum of money. But she hadn't gone there expecting him to suddenly hand her five thousand pounds. She had only wanted to apologize for her actions, and to ensure that he was not hurt.

"I understand," she said quietly. "Then we don't have anything more to discuss." She started to rise, acutely aware that her time was running out.

Harrison crossed to her in two strides and sat her down again, forcing her to look at him.

"Listen to me," he began firmly. "I know those girls who have come to you for help have all kinds of filthy scum in their lives—vicious brutes who think women are nothing but a piece of property, to be used and tossed aside when they're of no more use to them. What you're doing to help those young women is admirable, Charlotte, but it's also dangerous. Those men don't like having their women taken from them—even if it's the girl's choice. If you or one of the girls is being threatened, you have to go to the police, *now*—do you hear?"

"You don't understand—"

"Then tell me, damn it!"

His eyes were dark and filled with concern. She looked down at his enormous hands. They were strong hands, clean and smooth and well cared for, not rough and blackened and dirty like her father's. She stared in confusion at the pale bandage wrapped around his left hand. Blood had started to seep from the wound hidden beneath, its bright red essence suggesting that the injury was still fresh. He was just a man, she reflected, and a coddled aristocrat at that. He might have had great success playing the role of an elite jewel thief, but he was a world apart from the brutal forces that had bred and shaped her. He could be injured. He could be killed.

He was no match for a vicious street fighter like Boney Buchan.

And neither was she.

"I cannot tell you," she said in a pained whisper. "I can't."

Harrison regarded her incredulously. She was unbelievable. She limped about in her modest little outfits, all shy and reticent and looking like a strong gust of wind might blow her away. But when she decided to be stubborn, she called upon some hidden inner strength and held fast. It was incomprehensible that she was refusing to let him help her—or at least go to the bloody police. But she was.

Whoever was demanding five thousand pounds had obviously terrified her into silence.

He cursed silently. He didn't need this. He had enough problems of his own. At any moment he could be arrested, or even murdered if whoever was running about playing the Dark Shadow decided he had become too great a nuisance to ignore. His mother had almost completely lost her grip on reality, and needed constant monitoring and protection. His brother and sister required his financial support. And his incapacitating headaches were stripping away the precious time he needed to fortify his investments before his own mind finally disintegrated. He glared at Charlotte, wishing to hell she had never stumbled into his life.

Had he not already assumed enough responsibility, for Christ's sake?

"There you are!" exclaimed his mother suddenly, bursting into the room. "I've been looking everywhere for you, Harry. Wherever have you been hiding?"

Harrison abruptly moved away from Charlotte and stood. "I've been right here, Mother. Didn't Telford inform you I would come up to see you shortly?"

"Telford said that you were most upset to hear that your father and I had been arguing, and that's when I knew I had to find you and make you feel better."

Charlotte watched in wonder as the slight, silvery-haired woman lifted a pale hand to tenderly brush a lock of hair off Harrison's forehead. She appeared to be in her late fifties, and she moved with the graceful confidence of a woman who had spent her entire life knowing she was both beautiful and treasured. She wore a magnificent evening gown of sapphire silk, which was a little loose and too wide in the skirts to be deemed fashionable, suggesting it had been in Lady Bryden's wardrobe for many years. A spectacular sapphire-and-diamond necklace was draped around her neck, and heavy matching earrings sparkled from her ears. Her hands glittered with a profusion of rings, and an enormous diamond pin radiated from one shoulder. She looked as if she were dressed to attend the most extravagant of balls, and had decided to pile on as much of her jewelry as possible.

Was she the reason Lord Bryden crept about London at night stealing jewels? Charlotte wondered, astonished.

"Poor, sweet Harry," Lady Bryden cooed, "you mustn't worry when your father and I argue. That's what adults do, every now and then, when they are having a disagreement. It doesn't mean anything, dear. Your father and I care far too much for each other to let a little argument come between us. Besides," she added, her gray eyes twinkling with mischief, "eventually the poor man always comes to realize that I am right." She turned to Charlotte and gasped.

"Oh, Harry, you haven't introduced me to your little friend. What a pretty thing she is, too, why, just look at all that lovely chestnut-colored hair. Reminds me of a beautiful horse I had when I was a girl. Timmy, I called him, although my father said that was a terrible name for a horse, and insisted upon calling him Apollo instead. Animals are so sensitive—I always tell your father we have much to learn from them, but he still refuses to let me bring the dogs up on the bed. Honestly, the man can be so stubborn sometimes. If it weren't for me, he'd still be eating poached eggs and jellied tongue every night for dinner. What's your name, dear?"

"Forgive me, mother," interjected Harrison, "this is Lady Charlotte Kent, the daughter of the Marquess of Redmond." He prayed Charlotte wouldn't correct him and tell his mother she was actually Lord Redmond's ward, which would instigate a flurry of questions.

"I'm delighted to meet you, child." Lady Bryden smiled warmly at Charlotte. "It has been quite some time since my Harry has had a little friend over. I always tell him we should throw a party and invite all his friends, but poor Harry is a bit shy, and he won't let me do it. But one day I'm going to surprise you, young man," she teased, gazing adoringly at him, "and you'll come home to find the house filled with all your lovely playmates, and we can play games on the lawn and have tea and lemonade and little iced cakes and candied fruit—won't that be nice?" She turned her attention back to Charlotte. "You'll have to come too, dear. I'm sure Harry would like that."

"Thank you so much, Lady Bryden." Charlotte smiled at the woman, liking her immensely for the obvious affection she felt toward her son. "I would be delighted to attend."

"Excellent. I'll just go and have a word with Lord Bryden, and we'll see if we can agree upon a date. He pretends to be too old to enjoy such childish activities, but the truth of the matter is, Harry, nothing pleases that man more than his family—you know that, don't you?"

"Yes, Mother. I know."

"Of course you do." She pushed the lock of hair off his forehead once again. "Remind me to trim your hair tonight, Harry, it is getting entirely too long. You come to me after Miss Williams has given you your bath, all right? I can't trust her with the scissors—the last time she cut Frank's hair put a pudding bowl on his head, then trimmed the front so short he looked perfectly ridiculous. Took months to grow out. Thank goodness your brother didn't notice—he's still too young to care what he looks like. Have you met Harry's little brother and sister?" she asked Charlotte.

"No, Lady Bryden. I've not yet had that pleasure."

"Well maybe the next time you come over to play with Harry you can see them. Harry doesn't play with them, of course, being a good deal older, but he does take extremely good care of them. I trust him more than I trust that Miss Williams. Do you know she once left Margaret and Frank alone in the nursery playing with paints? By the time I went to check on them, Frank had painted his baby sister the most ghastly shade of green— he said he was trying to make her look like a turtle! I wanted to discharge Miss Williams on the spot, but Harry begged me not to. He said Frank and Margaret adored her, and that was worth a good deal more than some ruined clothes and all the soap it took to clean poor Margaret's skin. He was right, of course. Harry has always been unusually mature for his age——"

"Forgive me, your lordship," apologized Telford, rushing breathlessly into the study. "I went to fetch Lady Bryden her tray, and when I returned to the drawing room she was gone." He cast her a wounded look as he finished, "My lady, you promised me that you would stay there until I returned."

She blinked, mystified. "Did I? Well, I'm sorry, Telford, but I had to find my Harry and meet his lovely little friend here. Besides, you had only to ask Lord Bryden, and he would have told you where I had gone. Wasn't he still in the drawing room?"

Telford glanced worriedly at Charlotte, uncertain how much she had gleaned about Lady Bryden's precarious state of mind. "His lordship was not there when I returned," he answered truthfully.

"Well, then, he probably went into the library to have a cigar. Have you met little Charlotte, Telford?"

"Yes, your ladyship."

"Lady Bryden has been telling me the most wonderful stories about her children," Charlotte said, trying to put the butler at ease. It was obvious to her that he was most protective of his charge.

"Did Harry tell you about the time he sneaked into the pantry and ate an entire jar of Mrs. Shepherd's preserved cherries?" enquired Lady Bryden gaily.

Harrison winced. "I don't think Charlotte needs to hear that, Mother——"

"They were soaked in pure Jamaican rum," she continued, ignoring him. "Then he went to his room and promptly threw up red cherry juice all over himself. When the maid went in and found him lying on the

floor, she thought there had been a murder." Her laughter filled the study as she finished, "Poor Harry has not
been able to look at a cherry since!"

"Telford, did you fetch Lady Bryden her tray?"
Harrison asked.

"Yes, my lord. I left it in the drawing room."

"Wouldn't you like to finish your tea, Mother?"

"Not until I speak with your father and let him
know that you are all right, Harry. You know how he
worries."

Harrison prayed for patience. "Telford, would you
ask my father to join my mother for tea in the drawing
room."

"Yes, my lord."

"Don't be ridiculous, Harry," his mother scolded.
Her voice became slightly agitated as she added, "You
know very well your father can't join me for tea."

Harrison regarded her cautiously, wondering if she
had suddenly shifted to one of her rare moments of lucidity. "Why not?"

"Your father doesn't drink tea. Hasn't for years."

"Then Telford will bring him a glass of Scotch. He
still drinks Scotch, doesn't he?"

"Harry!" Lady Bryden sounded shocked. "I don't
approve of you talking about spirits in front of your little friend—whatever will her parents think?"

"That's all right, Lady Bryden," Charlotte hastily assured her. "My father has been known to indulge in a
glass of Scotch himself."

"Well, really, children, this is not an appropriate
subject for either of you," Lady Bryden chastised. "Now,
Telford, I would like you to bring these children some
of those lovely little ginger cakes Mrs. Griffen baked this
morning, all right?"

"Yes, my lady."

"It was delightful to meet you, my dear," Lady Bryden

said, smiling at Charlotte. "Do come again whenever you please." Her gaze grew shadowed. "We don't seem to have many visitors, these days."

"I would be delighted to come for another visit, Lady Bryden," Charlotte told her.

"Very good. Don't forget about Harry's party," she chimed as she went sailing out the door. "It's going to be wonderful. Come along, Telford, we have to start making arrangements." She beckoned for the dutiful butler to follow.

Harrison closed the door, pressed his forehead against it, and slowly counted to three. Then he turned to look at Charlotte.

"Thank you."

"For what?"

"For not making her feel uncomfortable."

Charlotte nodded. "How long has she been like that?"

"A long time." He went to his desk and poured himself another drink.

"Was she like that when you were a child?" Charlotte could well imagine how confusing Lady Bryden's peculiar hold on reality would have been for a little boy.

"No."

Harrison took a swallow of brandy and stared at the painting of his mother and her three children that hung on the wall opposite his desk. His father had commissioned it when Margaret was about a year old, Frank was five, and Harrison was eleven. They were seated in the garden at their country home, beneath the brilliant green foliage of a splendid tree that had been planted some two hundred and fifty years earlier, when the first Lord Bryden had begun the construction of the house. Harrison's father had grown up playing beneath that tree, and he had wanted a portrait of his beloved wife and children beneath it. He had said that every time he looked at the painting, he would see everything that was most important to him.

"Where are your brother and sister now?"

"Margaret is married and living in France, with two children of her own. Frank lives in Chicago, where he is trying to establish himself as something of an entrepreneur."

"Does your mother ever see them?"

"Rarely. Margaret used to visit before she had her children, but now she finds it difficult to travel with them. Also, my mother can be unpredictable. Sometime she is happy and pleasant, but she also has moments where she can be rather volatile. Margaret, understandably, does not like to expose her children to their grandmother's moods. They are quite young and ill-equipped to deal with it."

"What about your brother?"

"Crossing the Atlantic takes over a week. He can't afford the time."

"Does he write to her?"

"He did at first. Unfortunately, she never really understood from whom the letters were coming. For the most part, in her mind Frank is the five-year-old boy in this painting. She can't seem to grasp that her son is grown and living an ocean away, or that her daughter is married with children of her own."

"And what about you? Does she ever recognize you as a man?"

"She used to, but her episodes of being somewhat normal have become more infrequent. It will be difficult to convince her I don't need her to cut my hair," he added ruefully, raking his hands through it.

"I could trim it for you, if you like. Then it wouldn't upset her anymore."

He regarded her in wonder. It had been a long time since anyone other than a servant had offered to do anything for him. "Thank you, but that won't be necessary. But thank you."

He was staring at her intently, making Charlotte feel self-conscious. "I'll be going, then," she said. "Poor Oliver must be wondering what has become of me, as I told him I would only be a few minutes—"

"Charlotte."

"Yes?"

"Let the police help you," he urged quietly. "God knows, I never thought I would be espousing the merits of the police, but they are used to dealing with situations like this. They can find this scum who is threatening you, put him in jail, and that will be it."

She shook her head. "The police cannot help me."

"Why not?"

What could she tell him? she wondered miserably. Because the man who was threatening her was actually her own father? Because he had vowed to beat her mercilessly if she told anyone, and she knew too well that he never made an idle threat? Because if she didn't get him the money, he would do something too horrible to contemplate to her family? Because the police would only listen politely and fill out a report, and then do absolutely nothing? There were thousands of men on the streets of London who fit the description of Boney Buchan. They knew the dark warrens of the tenement buildings and the stinking mazes of alleys and back streets far better than any police constable. The police could never find Boney Buchan. But he could find Charlotte.

And when he did, he would punish her for disobeying him.

"They cannot," she repeated, her voice hollow.

Harrison grit his teeth in frustration. His headache was intensifying now, warning him that he would soon have to resort to laudanum after all. Fighting the pain, he went to his desk and opened the safe hidden in the lower cabinet. He extracted an envelope, then locked the safe and cabinet once more.

"Here is eight hundred pounds," he said, handing her the envelope. "It's all the bank notes I have at the moment. I can arrange for more, but unfortunately it will take a few days. In the meantime, see if that is enough to take care of your situation."

Charlotte stared at it, surprised. Then she reached out and took it. "Thank you."

Harrison nodded. She seemed achingly beautiful to him in that moment, a beguiling combination of strength and vulnerability. He found himself wanting to reach out and touch her, to pull her close and wrap his arms around her, to feel her body pressing against him, all softness and strength and heat. He didn't want her to face whatever dark forces were threatening her alone, and yet he sensed that she would not welcome his assistance. Given his disastrous performance at his last two break-ins, he supposed he did not inspire a great deal of confidence—even in himself. He pressed his fingers against one temple, trying to ward off the advancing pain. His vision was starting to blur, warning him that he had to take refuge in his chamber, soon.

"Forgive me if I don't see you to the door," he murmured, pulling on the velvet rope that would summon Telford. "Telford will escort you back to your carriage."

Charlotte regarded him with concern. "Are you all right?"

"I'm fine." He braced his hands against his desk and pretended to study a document lying upon it. The type on it was wavering and blurry, making him nauseated.

"Sir?" said Telford, appearing at the door.

"Kindly escort Miss Kent out to her carriage." It was an effort for Harrison to keep his voice steady.

"Yes, sir." The butler turned to Charlotte. "Miss Kent?"

"Good night, Lord Bryden," said Charlotte.

Harrison did not look up as Telford followed Charlotte out.

It was only after the door had closed that he took the bottle of laudanum from his drawer and poured a dose into the remainder of his brandy. He swallowed it in a single gulp, then shut his eyes and slumped across the desk in defeat.

There was nothing more he could do for anyone that night.

Chapter Eight

ARCHIE BUCHAN SHIFTED RESTLESSLY ON HIS FEET and vehemently cursed God, Jesus Christ, and the handful of Christ's disciples whose names he could remember.

He hated waiting.

Life in prison had been all about waiting, he reflected bitterly. He had waited for morning so he didn't have to lie against his louse-ridden bed listening to the snores and farts and moans of the others holed up with him. He had waited for his jug of frigid water and harsh soap, because it enabled him to rinse out the foul scum that constantly brewed in his rotting mouth. He had waited for his gluey porridge, greasy soup, and sour milk, because he knew if he didn't eat, he would die. He had waited to start his ten-hour shift of picking oakum or making nets, because if he didn't work he was beaten and sentenced to the crank machine. And then he had waited for night to fall once more, his body aching, fingers blistered and bloody and raw, so exhausted that he scarcely noticed the foul smells and sounds poisoning the air around him.

Patience meant survival.

Some inmates around him had not understood this. They had permitted their bodies to weaken. They had let their minds become brittle. They had failed to keep their rage burning hot within them. But not Archie. He was not about to let himself die or go mad, which were the only two options for escape.

Instead he had focused on the certainty that one day he would be free to eat what he liked, get drunk when he wanted, and bury his cock in as many women as he could afford.

It was this same patient determination that had enabled him to keep watch on Charlotte's house the entire night, waiting. He had seen her go off by carriage the previous evening, and had still been standing there when she returned. He had watched the three young whores who were staying with her return at different times as well. When boredom had set in he had occupied his mind with thoughts of what he might do to each of them if he had the time or the money. When that grew tiresome, he thought about what he would do to Sal when they returned to their shabby room instead. Sal wasn't young or bonny, but she knew a thing or two about pleasing a man, and he didn't have to pay her for the privilege. Once he had his money, though, he'd find someone more to his liking. Someone younger and fresher, who hadn't opened her legs for every prick who ever bought her an ale or told her she wasn't hard to look at. Sal was a bit soft that way. She wanted a man to look after her. Although Archie hadn't done much in that regard, when he quiffed her he made sure he rubbed her muff, which caused her to groan with pleasure.

He had never liked prigging women who just seemed to endure his attention.

"Is he up yet?" demanded Sal, yawning as she emerged from behind the last house in the row.

"No."

"It's still early, Archie," Sal pointed out, scratching herself. "Why don't ye go catch a few winks, an' I'll stay here an' watch for him? There's some crates back there that I piled up, so ye don't have to sit on the ground."

"I ain't tired."

"You look half dead."

"I always look this way."

"I don't know how ye'd know, since ye ain't got no mirror."

"For Christ's sake, Sal, either shut yer gob or go back to sleep. I ain't movin' from here."

"Fine, then," she snapped. "Don't sleep. I don't care."

"Good."

She glowered at him. The man was impossible. All she was trying to do was offer him a little bit of comfort after he had been standing on his feet all night. Most men would have been thankful. They might have chucked her under the chin and told her she was a good girl, then let her lead them back to the nice, dry chair she had made. They might have entrusted her to take over the watch, knowing that she was smart and would be sure to wake them the minute she saw anyone come out of the house. But not Archie. He had to do everything himself. He didn't trust anyone—not even her. It hurt a little, the fact that he didn't believe her ardent promises that she would never betray him. It also made her sensitive to the fact that he made no such assurances to her. In the end, though, it didn't matter if he wouldn't swear himself to her. Lots of men had promised to be true to her, then either fleeced her or lifted the skirts of another woman. She'd known a few girls who'd run around on their men, but that was rare.

Girls knew they'd get a fist in the eye if they looked at another.

"There he is." Archie's mouth curved with satisfaction as young Flynn emerged from the house.

"What's he doin' out so early?" wondered Sal. "If I was him with a nice house and a clean bed, I'd sure sleep later than this."

"Old habits die hard," mused Archie, watching as the slight boy moved quickly down the front steps. "He's used to risin' afore the sun, to get off the street and out o' the doorways afore someone lands a broom on his arse."

"Where's he goin' then, at this hour?"

"Let's find out." Archie lowered his cap, hunched his shoulders forward, then offered one arm to Sal.

"Why, thank ye, Archie," she said, surprised by his unusual show of courtesy.

"We'll take less notice if we look like man an' wife. Straighten yer hair, ye look like ye've been blasted by a gale."

Sal's hands flew self-consciously to her stringy, clumsily arranged hair. "Better?"

"It'll have to do. Come on, I don't want to lose him."

They shadowed Flynn at a distance through the streets. The boy moved quickly, as if he had a purpose in mind. He walked with a kind of jaunty air, his head up, his feet tripping lightly over the sidewalks and cobblestones. His dark blond hair dripped out from underneath a brown cap, and although it was a bit long and ragged, it had obviously been recently washed and combed. His plain coat and trousers were loose-fitting but clean, and his leather boots seemed relatively new. There was a confident, almost swaggering manner to him that one did not find in most eleven-year-old lads from respectable homes, but Archie knew it well. That was what one got when one took a filthy, conniving urchin, cleaned him up a bit, and put him in clean togs.

It was not enough to fool Archie, but at first glance, the lad looked decent enough. That put him at an advantage. Nobs got all addled when they saw a scruffy little urchin about, fearing that the beggar was about to nick something off them. Dressed in his fancy traps with his face scrubbed and his hands washed, young Flynn had a look of near-respectability to him. A few more years in Lottie's tender care, Archie reflected, and he might be just as polished at playing a swell as she was.

But deep down he would still be scum, just like the rest of them.

"Quick little bugger, ain't he?" said Sal, her ample breasts heaving against the constraints of her corset.

"Come on, Sal, keep up—I feel like I'm half-draggin' ye."

"I'm tryin'," she told him crossly. "You'd be havin' a hard time too if you was wearin' these bloody heels. They ain't made for traipsin' all over London."

"I don't know why ye waste good money on boots ye canna even walk in," Archie snapped. "It's nae like ye spend yer time ridin' about in carriages."

"When we're flush in the pocket, I'll be buyin' myself a new pair of boots," she assured him. "I know the ones I want, too; all toffee-colored with leather soft as cream, and tiny little buttons that look like gems."

"Just make sure ye can walk in them," he muttered, dragging her along. "If ye can do that, they'll be worth whatever ye pay for them."

They followed Flynn down several more roads, until finally he came to one of the modest shopping streets near Drury Lane. The shopkeepers were busily opening their stores and setting up tables and stalls in front. These were being filled with everything from handsome leather books to delicate ladies' combs and fans and neatly pressed gentlemen's handkerchiefs. If goods were attractively displayed in the open air, the men and women strolling by might be more likely to make a purchase. For aspiring thieves this left the goods vulnerable, particularly if the shopkeeper had to go into the store for a moment, leaving his display unattended.

Archie watched as Flynn casually sauntered along the street, his hands jammed into his pockets, whistling. The lad knew his business, Archie mused, feeling a flicker of respect. If the boy moved too quickly or looked nervous, he would immediately attract the suspicions of the shopkeepers. But if he took his time and appeared relaxed, then they were apt to think he was a lad with a bit of brass in his pocket, who just might be enticed to part with it.

Flynn meandered down the street, pausing to examine a book here, a pile of fruit over there. Suddenly an explosive sneeze tore from him, causing him to whip out a voluminous red handkerchief and double over. Archie watched with admiration as the boy snatched an apple from a cart just as the banner of red cotton went to his face. Flynn deftly slipped the apple into his pocket while making a spectacular show of blowing his nose, much to the revulsion of anyone who happened to be watching. He then stuffed the wadded up handkerchief into his pocket, cleverly masking the swell of his stolen fruit. He ambled along once more, still stopping to look at whatever happened to catch his eye. After a few minutes he fished the apple from his pocket, polished it vigorously on his sleeve, and bit noisily into it.

Archie was impressed.

"Clever little dip, ain't he?" Sal had also spent enough years picking pockets to recognize raw talent when she saw it.

"Canna imagine Lottie would let the lad go hungry," reflected Archie. "He stole that apple 'cause he knew he could. An' if he's anythin' like me, he'll want more—just to see if he can get away with it."

"Come on then, Archie." Sal grimaced as her shoes bit into her feet. "Let's get it done and over with."

"I want to see what he has in mind, first. Best way to find out what he can do is to watch him."

Sal groaned, but didn't argue. She knew if she made too much trouble Archie would just leave her behind, and she didn't want that.

They strolled along arm in arm, blending in with the other early morning shoppers who were now crowding the narrow street. They paused to look at something when Flynn stopped, then pretended to lose interest and moved on after him. After the lad ignored several opportunities to lift something without the attending shopkeeper's notice, Archie began to suspect that Flynn had a specific destination in mind.

Eventually the boy came to a tidy little shop that sold tobacco and sweets. Beautifully arranged behind the front windows on the left side of the store was a tempting array of succulent candies. The other side of the store specialized in tobacco products. To Archie's surprise, this was the side to which Flynn gravitated. The lad stared through the glass at tall jars filled with dark mounds of fragrant tobacco, and cigarettes and cigars packed in neat little boxes that were decorated with fancy gold lettering and exotic-looking stamps. A handsome collection of smoking accessories complemented the display, including elegant sterling silver cigarette cases, heavy ashtrays made of crystal, marble, and onyx, and an assortment of spectacularly carved pipes.

Flynn stood close to the window, his hands in his pockets. He seemed fascinated with the adult delicacies within, but no one took much notice of him. The round, balding shopkeeper gave him a friendly sort of look, perhaps thinking he might have a copper or two to splurge on a sweet, but in the next moment a gray-haired gentleman entered the store in search of some tobacco, and Flynn was forgotten. The boy edged a little further over, watching as the shopkeeper removed one of the tall jars of tobacco from the front window. The owner then turned to take it to the back of the store, presumably to measure out some for the elderly patron who had just gone inside.

Flynn swiftly withdrew a small knife from his coat pocket, inserted it in the corner of one of the glass panes, then sneezed as he pushed firmly against it. The sound covered the cracking of the glass, which fractured in the approximate shape of a star. He pressed a sticking plaster against the broken pane, pulled the glass out, then thrust his small hand inside and began scooping up the pipes and cigarette cases, stuffing them into his coat pockets. Within twenty seconds he had taken as much as he could carry. He propped the broken fragment of glass back up against its casing, then turned and walked away, whistling.

He had only gone a few feet when the shopkeeper suddenly looked up from his counter and noticed the broken pane of glass.

"Stop, thief!" he roared.

Flynn shot forward like a cannonball, racing amidst the outdoor carts and stalls as he tried to escape. Determined not to lose him, Archie threw off Sal's arm and sped forth as well. He was in reasonable shape for a man of some fifty-odd years, but the bevy of angry shopkeepers and bystanders who raced forth to apprehend the young thief quickly outpaced him.

"Come here, you little bugger!" shouted the enraged shopkeeper, his fury rendering him oblivious to the fact that he had just deserted his store.

"Somebody trip him!" yelled another.

"Look out—he's getting away!"

A veritable mob was now charging after the boy, but its very size made it clumsy. Soon the incensed members at the back were huffing and clutching their chests and dropping off, deciding one troublesome urchin wasn't worth apoplexy. Archie forced himself to keep going, even though a needlelike pain was jabbing his chest and his lungs felt as if they were going to explode. He could just barely see Flynn up ahead. Cursing and praying that he wouldn't drop dead at the same time, he forced himself to run faster.

"Got you, you filthy little bastard!" roared an elated gentleman, grabbing Flynn by his coat.

"Sod you!" The boy twisted around and kicked him hard in the knee.

"Bugger it," the man swore, releasing the lad as his leg buckled painfully beneath him.

Flynn was off again, darting this way and that as he threaded a path through a maze of startled shoppers. A few brave souls thrust out hands and feet in an effort to either grab him or trip him, but Flynn was light and quick enough to slip from their grasp or leap over their legs. When that didn't work, a solid kick to their shins invariably did. But the excitement of his escape was drawing more attention further down the street. A half-dozen youths quickly arranged themselves into a block-ade. Flynn turned and whipped down the nearest lane leading off the street. A few resolute souls from the ini-tial mob ran after him, shouting at the leader of the pack to not let the boy get away.

Archie arrived just in time to hear an outraged streak of high-pitched cursing.

"Let me go, ye friggin' old toff!" raged Flynn, strug-gling mightily to get free of his captor.

"Hold fast, you filthy little tooler, or I'll knock your bloody head off!" returned the man gamely.

"Sod you!" Flynn kicked the man in the shin.

The man responded with a powerful blow to the side of Flynn's head, stunning him.

"Do you want another?" he demanded, shaking the slight boy by the scruff of his neck.

Flynn shook his head, his shoulders slumped in defeat.

"You're nothing but a pissing little scrub," muttered the man, easing his grip slightly.

Flynn smashed his skinny fist into the man's nose.

"Jesus Christ!" The man's hands flew to his bloodied face. "I'll kill you, you little shit!"

Flynn was already dashing away, heading toward the sunlit opening at the opposite end of the alley.

Archie ran a few steps then threw himself forward, stretching his arms and back and legs as far as they would go. "Got ye!" he barked triumphantly, knocking the boy to the ground. He pressed his knee into the boy's back and pinned his arms beneath him.

"What have ye done this time, ye rotten scalawag?" he demanded furiously, swiftly rifling through the boy's pockets before anyone else drew near. He quickly removed two silver cigarette cases, three handsomely carved pipes, and a small box of cigars, which he dropped into his pocket. "Ye'll be the death of me and yer ma, and that's the God's truth of it. Have ye nae shame?" he railed as a small, angry crowd gathered around them. "What'll I tell yer poor ma, who's still grievin' since yer wee brother died just last month—that her only livin' son is off to the coop now, an' she'll just have to make do without him as well?"

Flynn regarded Archie warily. Archie gave him a conspiratorial smile and patted his pocket, indicating that he would help the boy in exchange for a cut of his booty. Flynn nodded curtly, accepting his terms.

"Ye'll be lucky if the peelers dinna haul yer scrawny arse away for good," Archie continued, jerking the boy to his feet. "An' if it weren't for yer poor ma, I'd be of a mind to toss ye in jail myself, ye soddin' little prig!" He cuffed him smartly on the side of the head, knocking off his cap.

"Is this your son?" The shopkeeper was huffing mightily as he pushed his way to the front of the crowd. His face was an alarming shade of purple.

"Aye, I'm afraid so," Archie replied, removing his own cap respectfully. "I'm sorry about all the trouble he's caused ye, sir, an' I'm willin' to let him have whatever punishment ye think is fittin'. Ye can call for a peeler, if ye like, though if he goes to the pound it'll break his mother's heart—maybe ye could throw a poke or two at his chops, if ye think that'll make up for the terrible thing he's done."

Flynn regarded Archie incredulously. "Sod that—"

"I'll be lickin' him proper, whatever ye decide," Archie continued, grabbing Flynn by his ear. "I whips him constant, but it don't make no difference, he's as lazy as Ludlam's dog, he is, an' a scraggy liar besides, but he's my own blood and 'tis my job to see he turns out right, so I'll just hold him for ye while ye give him his due." He dragged Flynn in front of the shopkeeper and held Flynn's arms behind him.

"Here now, leave off, ye great bruiser!" shouted Sal fiercely, pushing her way to the front of the crowd. "Ye should be ashamed of yerself, beatin' on me boy—and just after his own baby brother died, too." Anger glittered in her eyes. "Does yer wife know ye take yer pleasure by bastin' on lads scarce half yer size?"

The crowd murmured in disgusted agreement, despite the fact that a moment earlier it would have welcomed watching the boy get beaten.

"I wasn't going to hit him," the shopkeeper protested, confounded. "But he smashed my shop window and stole from me!"

Sal marched over to Flynn and planted her hands on

her hips. "Well, what have ye to say for yerself? Did ye steal from the gentleman?"

"I did," Flynn admitted, "but only so I could buy ye somethin' pretty—ye've been so sad since the babe died." His expression was angelically tormented. "I did it for ye, Ma."

"Oh, my sweet boy!" Sal threw her arms around Flynn and pulled him hard against her bosom. "Ye're all I've got left now, so promise me ye'll be a good lad and not steal no more—I couldn't bear to lose you, too!" She buried her face in his hair and began to sob loudly.

"I won't, Ma." Flynn's voice was muffled against the cushions of her voluptuous breasts. "I promise."

"There now, he's goin' to be straight from now on, sir, I promise ye." Archie pulled a wrinkled handkerchief from his coat pocket and blew his nose loudly into it.

"But what about what he stole from me?" demanded the shopkeeper.

Sal broke her embrace to regard Flynn sternly. "Right then," she said, holding out her hand. "Let's 'ave it."

Flynn hesitated, then pulled out the remaining pipes and cigarette case from one pocket and gave them to her.

"All of it," Sal said warningly. "Now."

Casting her a disgruntled look, Flynn produced several packages of cigars and cigarettes from the other pocket and added them to her hands.

"There ye are, sir," she said, handing the stolen goods back to the shopkeeper. "Good as new."

He stared at the items in his hands suspiciously. "This isn't all of it," he protested.

Sal turned Flynn. "Are ye holdin' somethin' more?" she demanded.

"No." Flynn shook his head vigorously.

"Turn out yer pockets then," ordered Archie, "so we can see."

Flynn obligingly turned out his pockets. All he produced was his red handkerchief.

"I could have sworn he took more," muttered the shopkeeper.

"Now say yer sorry to the gentleman," ordered Sal.

Flynn regarded him remorsefully. "I'm sorry, sir."

"There's a good lad," said Archie. "Well, sir, I guess we'll just be on our way—"

"Just a minute—what about the damage to my window?" demanded the shopkeeper. "That's going to cost at least half a crown to fix."

"O' course, let me take care of that." Archie pretended to feel around his pockets for some money. "Let's see—I know it's here somewhere—" He shook his head in confusion. "Well, that's the damnedest thing—Mary, have ye got half a crown on ye?"

"Sure enough," she said, rooting around in her reticule. After a moment she shook her head. "Must 'ave left me coin purse at home."

"Well, sir, here's what I'll do," said Archie gamely. "I'll come by yer shop in an hour with the brass, an' I'll fix yer window besides, so ye can keep the money just for the trouble the lad caused ye. Sound fair?"

Archie could see that the shopkeeper would have much preferred to have his money straight away. But what Archie had proposed was so eminently reasonable, there was no possibility he could refuse him.

"Very well," he conceded.

"Right then, lad," Archie continued, frowning at Flynn, "let's get ye home so ye can think on how ye're goin' to change yer ways and be more of a help to yer ma."

"I don't need nothin' fancy from a store," Sal assured Flynn. "All I need is to have me boy with me, an' know he's safe." She snuffled loudly, wiped her nose on a not very clean handkerchief, then wrapped her arm around him.

"I'll see ye soon, sir," Archie called over his shoulder to the shopkeeper as he pushed Flynn through the thinning crowd, "to take care o' that smashed window."

They left the alley and walked down the street together, arm in arm. After they had traveled a few blocks, Flynn broke free from Archie and Sal's hold.

"Right, let's split the swag," he said in a low voice, referring to the cache in Archie's pocket.

Archie scowled at him. "Not here." He gestured at all the people milling about. "We'll take ye somewhere we can look at it safe." He pretended to think for a minute. "Me an' Sal's got a room not far from here. We'll go there."

"I ain't got time for that," Flynn informed him stubbornly. "Just slip me one of them silver cases and I'm off."

"I ain't slippin' ye nothin' here," Archie returned flatly. "I didna risk my neck out there just to be nabbed by a peeler as we're walkin' away. Ye can come with us or shove off—I don't give a damn."

"We got gin," added Sal, trying to entice him. "Good stuff, too, not the piss ye're used to swillin'."

Flynn thought about this a moment. "Fine."

He followed them in sullen silence as they wove their way down a series of narrow streets, crossing garbage-strewn courts and stinking passageways that took them deeper into the criminal rookery known as Devil's Acre. The rotting buildings there had once been reasonably respectable homes in the seventeenth and eighteenth centuries, but years of misery and disrepair had transformed the area into a fetid, vermin-filled slum. Brothels abounded everywhere, coupled with filthy "padding-kens." In these overcrowded lodging houses, those with a few coins to spare could share a filthy bed with several others, in a room stuffed with thirty or more miserable men, women, and children. The entire area was a nest of desperation, populated only with criminals and whores, but Flynn took no notice of it. He followed Sal and Archie gamely through the maze of twisting alleys, confident that he would find his way out of it unassisted.

Finally they entered a dilapidated building. Archie led the way up a creaking staircase to the top, pausing to kick a rat out of his way before he unlocked the door to his room. Flynn followed him and Sal into the hot attic chamber, which stank of gin, urine, and boiled cabbage.

"I ain't splittin' it," Archie said flatly, closing the door behind them.

"What do ye mean?" demanded Flynn, incensed. "I nicked it."

"Aye, and nearly got yerself walloped an' sent to the coop for yer trouble. I'm the one who saved yer scrawny arse, an' I'll be the one keepin' the swag."

"Sod you!" swore Flynn, striding toward the door. He jerked on the handle, only to find it locked.

"There's one more thing I forgot to mention," Archie added, seating himself on one of the two rickety wooden chairs in the room. "Ye'll be stayin' with me an' Sal for a while."

"The hell I will." Flynn cursed as he pulled against the door. "Give me the soddin' key."

"It ain't for long," Archie assured him. "Just until I collects my money from my Lottie."

"Who?"

"Miss Charlotte Kent, I suppose is what you call her. That ain't her real name, though. She's Lottie Buchan, from the town of Inveraray. There was a time when she was almost as good a little prigger as you."

"Ye're a liar," Flynn spat. "Miss Charlotte is a lady—her da's a nob in Scotland!"

"That nob ain't her da," Archie informed him. There was a trace of pride in his voice as he finished, "I am."

Flynn snorted with laughter. "You? Ye ain't fit to scrape the mud off her boots!"

Archie leapt up and heaved him into a small table.

"Stop it, Archie!" shouted Sal.

"I don't tolerate disrespect," Archie informed her, hauling Flynn to his feet. "Not from no one." He raised his fist.

"Think a minute," pleaded Sal, grabbing him by his outstretched arm. "If ye make a great racket, ye'll only have the neighbors comin' up to complain, an' how will ye explain the lad to them?"

Archie hesitated, his great fist suspended in the air.

"Ye dinna want to ruin everythin'," Sal continued emphatically, still pulling on Archie's arm. "Leave the boy be. He ain't goin' to say nothin' more." She cast Flynn a warning look.

Archie glared at Flynn. "Are ye?"

His eyes burning with hate, Flynn shook his head.

Archie responded by heaving him across the room. Flynn smashed into the wall. He stifled a moan and sank to the floor, then curled into a ball.

"Get off of me!" Archie snarled at Sal, wrenching his arm free from her. "An' get me a bloody drink."

Sal obediently went to a small cupboard in the corner of the room and retrieved a bottle and two dirty glasses. She set them on the table, poured a generous shot of gin into each, then handed one to Archie.

"Here's to prime times ahead," said Archie. He raised his glass and drained it, then banged it on the table, motioning for Sal to fill it again. Once that drink was gone, he wiped his mouth on his sleeve and glared at Flynn, who was sitting huddled on the floor against the wall.

"Keep yer mouth shut and do as I say, and ye'll have nae to fear. But try to escape, or do anythin' to make trouble," he added ominously, "an' I swear I'll break every goddamn bone in yer skinny little body."

WHERE'S FLYNN?" WONDERED OLIVER, FROWNING.

"I thought he was with you," said Annie as she took a seat at the dining room table.

Doreen passed a plate of warm biscuits to her. "I've nae seen him all day."

"He was up an' out early this morning," supplied Ruby. "I heard him goin' down the stairs."

"'Tis nae like the lad to be late for his supper," fretted Eunice, serving ladlefuls of fragrant stew into everyone's bowl. "I told him I was fixin' beef-and-barley. That's one of his favorites."

"I'm sure he'll be along soon," Annie assured her.

"He shouldn't be goin' off without tellin' Miss Kent or Oliver, Eunice, or Doreen first," Violet observed. "That's the rule." She slathered a thick layer of butter onto her biscuit, then crammed the entire thing into her mouth.

"Here now, ye're goin' to choke if ye shove it in like that," scolded Doreen.

"A lady tears off just a wee piece, puts a little butter on it, then eats it nice an' dainty," added Oliver, trying to help Violet with her table manners. He pulled a small piece off his own biscuit to demonstrate.

"I'm starvin'," protested Violet, her mouth full.

"I canna see how ye'd be starvin', given that ye ate an entire meat pie, four pieces of toast, three fried eggs, an' four sausages for breakfast," countered Doreen.

"The lass is still growin'," Eunice clucked sympathetically, adding another ladleful of beef-and-barley to Violet's bowl. "Look at the poor thing—she's nae but skin and bone."

"Even so, ye shouldna be chokin' down yer food like a starved dog," argued Doreen. "It ain't proper."

Violet rolled her eyes. She was barely fifteen, and she had already been whoring for three years by the time Miss Kent had taken her in two months earlier. It was her own mother who had first pushed her into the trade, as a way of supplementing their family's meager income. She had been twelve at the time, which was the legal age of consent. Her first time with a man had been terrifying and painful, and she had wept bitterly when it was over. But her mother had called her a good girl when she saw the fistful of coins the man had given her. She had taken them all, sorted through them, then given Violet just one to keep, generously telling her she could spend it or save it, whatever she liked.

After that Violet never gave her mother everything she earned.

There was never any question of whether or not Violet would continue whoring—not if she wanted to go on living with her family. And if she didn't, well, just where would she go? Her "gentlemen friends," as her mother liked to call them, kept food on the family's plates and a roof over their heads, which was somehow made to seem right and noble. After a while, Violet found that both her body and her mind adjusted. She was a working girl, just like the hundreds of other girls who frequented Charing Cross Station and the Strand, looking for customers. Some of them received gifts from their men, like pretty hats with feathers on them, or even silk stockings or soft leather gloves. But when Violet saw the older prostitutes wandering the same areas, their chests heaving with phlegmy coughs, their chalky faces wrinkled and bruised, she wondered if that was all life had in store for her. She had heard about prostitutes who lived fine lives, put up in elegant apartments where they dressed in jewels and furs and drank champagne all day, but she didn't know any like that. Those kind of whores didn't have to actually walk the streets. They were so beautiful and refined, the men came right to them. That was the kind of whore she wanted to be, she decided. Someone elegant, who could pick and choose which man she would let between her legs. That seemed a much better life than walking the streets or slaving in a factory.

She helped herself to another biscuit. Mimicking Oliver, she carefully pulled off a small piece, dabbed a miniscule amount of butter on it, and daintily placed it in her mouth.

"There's a good lass." Oliver smiled with approval. "Now, just remember to chew with yer mouth closed, nice an' quiet."

Violet immediately closed her mouth.

"Good evening, everyone." Charlotte affected an expression of calm as she entered the dining room. She did not want anyone to sense the sick anxiety that had been mounting within her all day. "Where's Flynn?"

"He'll be along shortly," Doreen assured her, taking note of the dark shadows beneath Charlotte's eyes. "Are ye nae feelin' well?"

"I'm fine, Doreen." She managed a smile. "I'm just a little tired, that's all."

"Ye've been doin' too much lately," Eunice scolded, shaking her head. "Goin' off to all them fancy dinners an' balls at all hours—to say nothin' of that night ye dragged the Dark Shadow home with ye. Ye're nae so swack that ye can be doin' those things."

"Ye need to stay in and rest," Annie agreed. "Let the world go about on its own for a bit."

"I'm afraid staying in and resting won't help me to keep things going here," Charlotte responded.

"If ye drop dead from exhaustion, that willna keep things goin' here neither," argued Doreen. "I hope ye're nae plannin' on traipsin' out tonight—ye look as if ye're ready to fall into yer stew."

Charlotte shook her head. "I'm not going anywhere tonight."

In fact, she had no idea whether she was or wasn't. Her father had told her that he would come to her after four days for his money. That meant he could appear any moment. She had waited all day to see if he might send someone with instructions on where she should go to meet him. So far, no one had come. The anxiety of waiting was eroding the fragile calm she was struggling to maintain.

The moment he realized she had obtained only a fraction of the money he had demanded, he would beat her.

She told herself she could stand that. After all, she had endured countless beatings by him as a child, and she had survived. What truly terrified her was the possibility that he would also harm one of her family. She had agonized all day as to whether she should warn them. But if she did, they would insist upon involving the police. And when her father found out, as he ultimately would, that would make him even more furious. Which would cause him to do something brutal. Perhaps not to her, but to one of her brothers or sisters, or maybe even to Genevieve and Haydon.

The fear roiling in the pit of her stomach rose up, nearly choking her.

She desperately wished her brother Jack wasn't away on one of his lengthy voyages. Jack was the oldest of her siblings, and they had always shared a special bond. When they were younger, Jack had been her champion, always trying to protect her from the world. And he might have stayed her champion, if Charlotte had not insisted that he go to sea and visit all the exotic places they had talked about endlessly as children. But even though it might have been comforting to confide in him about her father, it would have been impossible, she realized bleakly. His own violent childhood had given Jack a dangerous, sometimes uncontrollable rage. He was more of a match for Boney Buchan than anyone else in her family, but that didn't mean he would win against him. Genevieve and Haydon had worked for years to civilize Jack, which meant that now he at least understood that there were rules to be observed, and consequences to be suffered.

No one had ever tried to civilize her father.

The only other person she had considered turning to that day was Harrison. She found herself thinking of him constantly, recalling his powerful presence, the intensity of his dark gaze as he asked her to tell him who was threatening her. As if he truly believed that he could help her. And for one brief moment, as she had felt the searing heat of his strong hands upon her, she had almost believed he could. But a gently bred aristocrat like Harrison knew nothing of the sordid world from which she came. He was born to a life of elegance and grace, filled with velvety green lawns and pretty ponies and little iced cakes, with a mother and father who adored him and servants who were employed to see to his every whim. He came from a world that was clean, gentle, and pure. And despite the fact that he had enjoyed some success at being a jewel thief, his last two break-ins had been disastrous; it was obvious his skills were waning. Harrison had been kind enough to give her what by any standard was an enormous sum of money.

For the rest, she would have to count on herself.

"Can I have it?"

Charlotte stared at Violet blankly. "Pardon?"

"Yer supper. Ye ain't eating it. Can I have it?"

"Sweet Saint Columba, I'll get ye more from the kitchen—there's nae need to be grabbin' it off of poor Miss Charlotte's plate when she's scarce had a chance to eat."

"But she ain't eating it," Violet returned, defensive. "She's just starin' at it."

"That's all right, Eunice. I'm not hungry." Charlotte handed Violet her bowl.

"Can I have yer biscuit, too?"

"Now ye're just bein' greedy," observed Annie. "Especially since ye've had three already."

"One of 'em was real small," Violet countered. "And when ye rip 'em into little pieces they don't fill ye up the same as when ye swallow 'em big."

"Here you go, Violet." Charlotte passed her biscuit to the slender young girl as well. Her churning stomach and ragged nerves were making it impossible to eat anything anyway.

"If ye're nae goin' to eat yer supper, then what'll ye have?" asked Eunice, regarding Charlotte with concern.

"I'm really not hungry, Eunice." She rose from the table. "I think I'll just retire to my room and read a bit."

"Would ye like me to fix ye some tea and toast?"

"Maybe later."

"I'll bring ye a tray in an hour. I've made some lovely cod pie—I'll bring ye a plate of that, too."

"I'm afraid I'm not hungry for cod pie," Charlotte told her.

"I am," Violet said enthusiastically, gobbling up Charlotte's stew. She belched.

"Here now, I've told ye afore we'll have none o' that at the table," said Doreen sternly.

"If ye keep eatin' like that, yer belly is goin' to burst," Ruby warned.

"Now leave the poor lamb alone," said Eunice, who always loved to see someone enjoy her cooking. "She's just nae used to havin' so much food about. Ye can have yer cod pie now, Violet, but maybe ye'd like to bide a wee bit, and have it later. I'll set some aside for ye, if ye like."

"I want it now," Violet told her. "I'm starvin'."

"Canna see where she's puttin' it," Oliver marveled. He glanced under the table, checking to see if she was hoarding food in her napkin for later. "Seems to all be goin' into her mouth," he reported, shrugging.

"Eunice told me I ain't got to hide food, because she said I could eat whenever I wanted," Violet told him, shoveling the last spoonful of Charlotte's stew into her mouth.

"Aye, and so ye can," Doreen agreed. "Just make sure ye dinna fill yer belly so full that we have to roll ye from the table," she added, chuckling.

"And please remember to save some dinner for Flynn, Eunice." Charlotte rose from the table and slowly limped toward the stairs. "He's sure to come in any minute."

S HE HUDDLED FURTHER INTO THE CORNER, HER ROUGH, *soiled blanket pulled up over her head, barely breathing. Maybe he wouldn't notice her, she thought frantically, struggling to lie as still as she possibly could on the floor. That happened sometimes, when he came home so stewed that all he could do was stagger across the room, vomit, and collapse on his bed. Then he would sleep like a dead man, except for the disgusting sounds that blared from his nose and mouth. But Charlotte didn't mind those sounds. They told her that he was truly out, which meant* he wouldn't bother with her for hours. Sometimes he even slept well into the next day. She liked that.

A fragile sense of calm would fall over her when her father slept deeply. Then she could move about and do as she liked, as long as she did it quietly. If it were daytime, she would escape their wretched room in the tenement building and wander the streets, looking for something to nick. Things were usually better for her if she could bring home something to give him. It was never enough, of course. If she lifted a wipe, he complained it was only cotton and not silk. If she managed to nip an apple or a bun, he snapped that she should have nicked a rum cake or a meat pie instead. And if she managed to really screw up her courage and lift a pocketbook or a watch, he would snarl that the pocketbook was near-empty, or the watch was only cheap metal and not gold. He would call her a useless little slut, and rage he'd have been better off if she'd never been born. She would listen in distraught silence, her head bent low, silently telling herself that next time she would do better. Then he would crack her hard across the face and arms and back, again and again, until she fell to the ground.

She had never pleased him.

She heard him staggering toward her, and her heart sank. Not so drunk, then. She squeezed her eyes tight and pretended to be sleeping, feebly hoping that he might let her be. Instead he moved closer. Her heart beat faster as the stench of him assaulted her senses, a wretched smell of sweat and drink and filth. She knew she didn't smell much better, but at least she made some effort to clean herself each day with a little cold water and the precious bits of soap she nipped. She clutched her blanket, a ragged shield of thin wool, which could do nothing to protect her from either him or the cold. Please, she thought, not sure whom she was addressing, please don't let him hurt me.

His booted foot stopped by her backside.

"Give over," he commanded thickly. "Now."

She leapt up and scooted away from him, trying to put herself just beyond striking range.

"Here," she said, pulling a thin chain from her sleeve. "And here," she added, extracting a small, worn snuffbox from the pocket of her gown.

He grabbed the two items and turned them over in his grimy hands, his face twisted in drunken confusion as he tried to make out their value in the weak light. Finally, he bit the chain. He grunted in disgust and shoved it into his coat pocket, then turned his attention to the snuffbox. Charlotte knew it was of no great value, for it was only of silver plate and it lacked any stones or other ornamentation that might have increased its worth. But it was pretty enough and in good condition, which meant that her father would be able to sell it for something. She hoped that would be enough to satisfy him.

"Is that all?" he demanded, his eyes dark and heavily glazed.

She nodded.

"Christ, ye're useless," he spat. "All day ye've nae to do but nip a few things so we can eat, an' this is the best ye've got?"

She looked down at her feet, ashamed.

He slapped her hard across the face, causing her to stagger back.

"Ye're just like yer bloody ma," he growled furiously, "good for nothin'. Only way she could earn her share was by quiffin', an' that's the way it'll be for ye, too. But ye're too skinny an' ugly for any man to want a snatch. I should just throw ye out, do ye hear?"

Charlotte bit the inside of her mouth, fighting back the tears threatening to pour from her eyes. If he saw her crying, it would only be worse. Her father hated it when she cried.

"Ye're goin' to fatten up a bit, an' then I'm settin' ye to work," he decided. "Christ knows, ye ain't much to look at, but there's swells out there that likes 'em young an' tight. They'll nae mind how ye look, as long as ye spread easy an' give em' a fair ride."

Blood leaked onto her tongue. She swallowed it, trying to

fight the wave of nausea coursing through her. *Say nothing*, she told herself, fighting the impulse to protest. To say anything would only earn her a beating. Better to say nothing, and pray that he would forget about his ghastly idea when he awoke the next day.

"Tomorrow, we'll nick ye some new togs," her father informed her, lurching unsteadily toward his bed. "An' clean ye up a bit. Swells likes their snatch clean. Then I can charge more for ye. Not too much at first, mind. That'll scare 'em off. I'll let ye learn yer trade, first." He collapsed onto his bed. "Ye'll be a prime piece, once I'm through with ye," he added, mumbling into his pillow. "I promise ye that."

She stood rooted to the floor, afraid to stir for fear that even the slightest movement might rouse him. After a few minutes his snores filled the miserable little room. Once they had become deep and rattling, she permitted herself to move.

She went to the battered old table in the corner and splashed a little water from the chipped jug onto a dirty cloth. Then she held the cloth against her stinging cheek, trying to ease the pain in her jaw. She had gotten off easy that night. Normally he was not satisfied until she was either cowering in a corner, or he had drawn blood. The fact that he had not beaten her more caused a knot of fear to tighten in her gut.

Prime pieces did not attract men when they were covered in cuts and bruises, she realized bleakly.

Even when they were only nine years old.

H ER SKIN WAS BEADED WITH SWEAT AND HER MUSCLES had contracted, as if preparing to fight. She moaned and turned onto her side. *No*, she thought, fighting the hideous memories invading her sleep. *No, no, no.* Pain was crawling up her injured leg, warning her that another spasm was about to strike. She whimpered and pressed her face deeper into her pillow, attempting to summon the strength she needed to endure it.

A rough hand clapped hard against her mouth.

"Hello, Lottie," her father drawled, his breath sour and reeking of gin.

She lay frozen beneath him, overwhelmed with terror.

"If ye make a cheep, I'll kill ye," he informed her matter-of-factly. "If someone comes runnin' in to save ye, I'll kill 'em, too. Understand?"

She nodded mutely.

He glared at her a moment, his calloused hand crushing her mouth. He could have killed her then and there, she realized. He could have wrapped his hands about her neck and squeezed the life from her, or pressed a pillow against her face, or cut her throat with the wickedly sharp dirk he always carried in his boot. But if he did that, he wouldn't get his money. She held fast to this, trying to dredge some fragment of strength from it. She had something he wanted. That gave her a modicum of power, fragile and fleeting though it might be. She stared up at him, trying to hide her fear behind a frozen façade of near calm.

Abruptly, he jerked his hand away.

She swallowed thickly. *Think,* she ordered herself, trying to bring the storm of fear raging through her under some semblance of control. She took a slow, shallow breath, trying to steady herself.

"This is a fine house ye've got for yerself," he said mockingly, gazing about the simple, shadowed bed-chamber. "I'd expect ye to be livin' much grander. I've seen his lordship's house here in London. Makes this place look like a shack." He eyed her contemptuously through the darkness. "Does he nae think much of ye, then?"

"I picked out the house." Charlotte's voice was small.

"Then ye're even more maggot-headed than I

thought," he snapped. "The ward of a bloody marquess doesna live in a cesspit with priggers an' whores. He canna care much for ye, this Redmond, or he'd nae let ye do it. The other wee dips he took on live better 'an this."

Charlotte's heart sank. So he had seen her brothers' and sisters' homes. Of course he would have. Boney Buchan might have been a thief and a drunk and a brute, but that didn't mean he didn't take his work seriously. Especially when five thousand pounds was at stake.

"Still, he's kept ye on all these years, even though ye're well past bein' of age. I dinna suppose even with all that brass he could get one of his nob friends to marry ye. Swells like their women whole and clean, with a bit of backbone to 'em—not a squashed piece of crippled baggage like ye."

She bit the inside of her mouth. *Say nothing,* she told herself desperately. *Don't fight. And don't cry. Just let him feel like he has all the power. That's what he wants.*

"He'll have to keep on payin' for ye then, till the day he kicks the bucket," Archie mused, rifling through the boxes and jars on her dresser. He pawed through the contents of her jewelry box, stuffed most of the items into his pockets, then snorted in disgust. "Ain't ye got nothin' worth more than a few bob?"

"No."

"Why not? Does he nae buy ye nothin' fancy?"

She shook her head.

"I dinna suppose I'd waste the money on ye, either," he muttered, sighing. "All right then, give over." He held out his hand expectantly.

Charlotte reached under her pillow and withdrew the envelope that Harrison had given to her.

"Here." She limped over to him, praying he wouldn't bother to count it.

He snatched the envelope from her hand and went

to the window. For a moment she thought he was going to simply climb out and disappear into the night, leaving her be. Instead he extracted the wad of notes and began to slowly count them in the moonlight, his lips moving as he squinted and frowned at the numbers printed onto the crisp new bills. When he came to the last of them, he scowled.

"Where's the rest of it?"

"That's all I could get. There is no more."

He raised an unconvinced brow. "I told ye I wanted five thousand pounds." He spoke slowly, the way one talked to a recalcitrant child. "An' five thousand is what ye're goin' to give me, Lottie."

"I can't." Her voice was small. She started to back away from him. "I tried everywhere, and that was all I could get. I told you I couldn't go to Lord Redmond. He'd want to know what the money was for, and if he thought for a minute that I was in any sort of trouble, he'd have the police watching over me—and we don't want that." She tried to make it sound as if they were co-conspirators. As if she was on his side.

He stroked the grizzled gray on his chin, thinking. "Ye're right," he agreed finally. "We dinna want that— do we, Lottie?" His voice was heavy with menace. "'Cause the second I see a bobby sniffin' about for me, I'll be right cagged, and ye know how I get when I'm mad." He inched closer to her. "Ye remember what they call me, don't ye, Lottie?"

She nodded.

"Say it," he commanded harshly.

"Boney," she managed, her mouth trembling. "Boney Buchan."

He smiled, either pleased because she had remembered, or because he liked the way it sounded coming from her. "An' why do they call yer old da that?"

She swallowed.

"Why, Lottie?"

"Because you break bones."

"That's right, I do. Lots of bones, Lottie. More than I can remember. But you remember, don't ye?"

She nodded, feeling as if she was going to be sick.

"So ye're goin' to get me the rest of my money, and ye're goin' to get it for me quick. An' if ye tell me ye canna, or willna, I'm goin' to be right cagged, which just might mean that I'll have to break some bones. An' do ye know whose bones I'll break first?"

She nodded furiously. Tears were stabbing at her eyes now. *I mustn't cry,* she told herself, biting down hard on the inside of her cheek. *I mustn't.*

"I dinna think ye do." His mouth split into a hard smile. " 'Cause ye're probably thinkin' it'll be yer bones I'll be crackin', when in fact I've somethin' better in store. Can ye guess what it is?"

Her eyes widened. Oh, God, he was going to go after someone in her family. He understood that was worse than anything he could possibly do to her. She knew he could do it. She would have to warn them, she realized. She'd have to tell all of them that they mustn't go out, or if they did, that they needed to have protection, and then they would want to go to the police—

"I'm goin' to break wee Flynn's bones," he informed her succinctly. "One bloody bone at a time."

She stared at him, stunned. *No,* she thought, feeling on the brink of hysteria. *No, no, no.*

"Have ye nae noticed that he ain't about, Lottie?" He regarded her with something akin to amusement. "He's a clever wee tooler, that's for sure. Caught him just this mornin' fleecin' a shop. Near got away with it, too. But then a mob started after him, an' I had to lend him a hand. He was soddin' mad when he realized I was keepin' him till our business was finished. Refused to believe I was yer da. I had to crack his napper for that one." His expression darkened as he finished, "He kept his gob shut after that."

Charlotte stayed frozen, trying desperately to absorb what her father was telling her.

And then she shrieked in helpless rage and flew at him, striking him as hard as she could in his face.

Archie was too astonished at first to fend off the blow, which sent a surge of ringing pain through his cheek and ear. He recovered quickly enough to grab his daughter by her arms and crack her own cheek with the back of his hand before heaving her to the floor.

"Try that again, ye fuckin' bitch," he swore fiercely, "an' I'll kill ye."

"No, you won't," Charlotte bit back, her entire being roiling with a powerful mixture of hate and fear. "Not if you want your money."

His eyes widened with surprise. "Well, well," he said, "looks to me like my Lottie has grown a bit o' backbone."

"Charlotte?" Oliver's sleepy voice was laced with concern as he called through her chamber door. "Are ye all right, lass?"

"If he steps through that door, I'll kill him," Archie promised softly.

"I'm fine, Oliver," Charlotte managed, trying to make her voice sound bright. "I just stumbled in the dark, that's all."

"Can I come in?" Oliver persisted, unconvinced.

Archie whipped his dirk out from his boot.

"No!" cried Charlotte. Thinking quickly, she hastily added, "I'm not dressed, Oliver. I'll just be a moment." She pulled herself up off the floor and faced her father. "You have to go."

"Ye've one week to get me the rest of my money," he bit out angrily. "After that I'll start sendin' yer precious Flynn back to ye, one piece at a time, startin' with his ears. Got it?"

She nodded frantically, terrified that at any second Oliver would open the door. If he did, she had no doubt that her father would kill him.

"Good." He stuffed the envelope of money in his pocket, sheathed his dirk in his boot, then went to the window. "One week, Lottie," he repeated, wanting to be sure she understood. "No more."

With that he hoisted himself over the windowsill and was swallowed whole into the night.

Chapter Nine

SOMEONE WAS TRYING TO KILL HIM.

It took a moment for this realization to pierce the heavy mantle of sleep that had left him lying helpless on his bed. But once his senses returned, he did not hesitate.

He exploded upward and began to wring the murdering bastard's scrawny neck.

"Please, your lordship," squeaked Telford, his eyes round with shock, "you're choking me!"

Harrison stared at his butler blankly. Telford was trying to kill him? That was ridiculous. He looked to see if his long-suffering butler brandished a weapon, seeking some evidence that he actually meant to harm him.

There was nothing.

"Jesus Christ, Telford," he swore, abruptly releasing him, "what in the name of God is going on?"

"Forgive me, your lordship," Telford croaked. He climbed off the bed and made a halfhearted attempt to regain his dignity by straightening his night robe. "I didn't mean to startle you. I was only trying to waken you. I knocked and knocked before coming into your chamber.

When you didn't answer me, I grew concerned and tried shaking you."

Harrison raked his hand through his hair, trying to leash the adrenaline pounding through his veins. He could have killed Telford. Another moment or two, and he would have either strangled him or snapped his neck. He stumbled over to the table in the corner of his bedchamber and splashed some brandy into a glass. It was reckless to mix alcohol with the laudanum he had taken earlier, but at that moment, he didn't care. He took a hefty swallow, then another. It had been an accident, nothing more. Anyone might have reacted the same way, waking to find some man hovering over him in the middle of the night. And after all, the moment he had realized it was Telford, he had stopped throttling him. That proved he had a complete understanding of what was actually happening around him. Therefore it wasn't paranoia. He downed the rest of his drink, clinging to that feeble piece of logic. He was not turning into his father.

Not yet.

"What time is it, Telford?" His vision was still a bit blurry from his headache, making it difficult to see the numbers on the mantel clock.

"Twenty minutes past three o'clock, sir," Telford replied. "In the morning."

Well, at least that explained his butler's nightgown. Harrison glanced down at himself and saw that he was naked. "And why are you waking me?" he demanded, snatching up his dressing gown from the chair on which he had tossed it. A terrible thought suddenly occurred to him. "Has something happened to my mother?"

"Her ladyship is fine, sir," Telford hurriedly assured him. "She is sleeping. I'm here because Miss Kent is downstairs in the drawing room and she would like to see you."

Harrison frowned. "At this hour?"

"Yes, my lord. I explained to her that you were sleeping and were not in the habit of entertaining guests at this hour, but she assured me that you would receive her." He hesitated slightly before delicately adding, "She seems rather distraught, my lord."

Harrison didn't need to hear any more. He cinched the belt of his robe and raced past Telford, his chest tight with dread.

He found Charlotte standing in the center of the drawing room. Her face was ashen and her auburn hair was falling in tangled disarray about her shoulders. Her simple gray gown was heavily creased, making it almost look as if she had been sleeping in it. But what caught his attention most were her eyes. Their green-and-gold depths were wide and filled with terror. For a moment he could only stand and stare at her, feeling sick and helpless. He knew that stricken look.

He had seen it in his mother's eyes, many years earlier, on the night his father in a fog of madness had tried to kill her.

He fought the sensations reeling through him, trying to distinguish between the past and the present. Then Charlotte turned slightly, and he saw the ugly plum-colored stain upon her cheek.

Rage surged through him, of such intensity he could not speak.

"I'm sorry," Charlotte began, mistaking the fury in his face for anger toward her. "I know I shouldn't be here at this hour—I've no right to be. But I didn't know where else to go." Her voice was strained. "I thought..."

She paused, not certain how she could explain it to him. He was still staring at her, his hands fisted at his sides. She had made a mistake, she realized desperately. She had thought she could turn to him. For some reason she couldn't explain, she had believed that Harrison would want to help her. But she had been wrong. She could see that now.

"Forgive me." She started to limp toward the door.

Harrison moved in front of her. He reached out and gently grasped her chin, tilting her face up so he could better see the bruise seeping across it.

"Tell me who did this," he said, his voice low and soft.

His expression was hard, but his touch was achingly gentle. She stared up at him, uncertain, confused, and yet something in the powerful anger emanating from Harrison made her also feel stronger. It was as if he was enveloping her within the protective shield of his outrage, even though he was only touching the tip of her chin. And in that moment, she needed some of his strength. She needed to feel it coursing through her, giving her the courage to face the hideous situation in which she, and Flynn, and every one of those whom she loved, had suddenly been thrust.

"I need your help." Her voice was barely a whisper.

He said nothing, but escorted her over to a sofa and seated her. When he turned away to pour her a drink, Charlotte gripped the armrest, feeling a need to hold fast to something. She stared blankly at the faded blue-and-marigold-striped fabric, which was worn and threatening to split open near the seam.

"Here," said Harrison, handing her a glass of wine. He adjusted his dressing gown, a flimsy affair of sapphire silk that barely concealed his otherwise naked legs and chest, and seated himself as far away from her as the length of the sofa would permit. He realized it was entirely inappropriate for him to be sitting alone in his drawing room in a state of undress with a young, unmarried woman, but unfortunately, he saw little way around it. She was far too distressed to be kept waiting while he went upstairs to dress, and whatever Charlotte was about to tell him, she would never reveal in the presence of another. Besides, he reflected, nothing about their relationship thus far had fallen within the confines of what might be considered even remotely socially acceptable.

"I want you to tell me everything, Charlotte, starting with who struck you."

She set down her glass and looked away.

Unwilling to let her withdraw from him when she had demonstrated such inconceivable faith by seeking him out in the first place, he moved closer and took one of her hands in his. The hell with propriety, he thought to himself. "Tell me," he urged, his voice gentle. "Let me help you."

She stared down at his enormous hand holding hers. How comforting it was, to have such a warm, strong hand hold fast to her. No man ever held her hand this way. Oliver sometimes patted her hand, his gnarled, aged fingers softly tapping her knuckles as he told her not to fret over something or other. And Jack, Jamie, and Simon always gave her a reassuringly brotherly squeeze when they offered her their arms, to help her in or out of a carriage or to stroll some short distance with her. Their touch was always sweetly caring and protective, a touch that told her not to mind the fact that she was limping in front of the rest of the world. But their touch was nothing like the feel of Harrison's hand upon hers. His palm was like fire against her skin, a searing heat that was spreading through her flesh and making her feel warm and liquid and strange. It struck her as rather pathetic, that an inexperienced crippled spinster like her could be so moved by the mere touch of a man's hand. But she didn't shift away. Instead she tightened her fingers around his, wanting to feel more of his masculine power.

"He has Flynn," she began haltingly.

"Who?"

She bit her lip. What would Harrison think of her, she wondered despondently, when she told him? When she confessed that the man who had spawned her, and then spent ten interminable years terrorizing her and torturing her, forcing her to do all kinds of excruciatingly shameful things, had come back to her? Harrison undoubtedly knew of her past, despite his previous assertion that he didn't listen to gossip. But no one other than Genevieve knew anything more than the broadest strokes of that past. Even Genevieve wasn't aware of all the sordid details. When Charlotte had first gone to live with her, she had not wanted to tell Genevieve everything, out of fear that her new mother might be so repulsed that she would make Charlotte leave. Gradually, over the years, Charlotte had revealed her past in fragments, but Genevieve had never pushed her to tell her more than she was comfortable with sharing. Genevieve had instinctively understood that everyone manages painful experiences in different ways, and that for some children, the very act of calling up dark memories could be destructive rather than healing. For the most part, Charlotte had chosen not to discuss her father. Instead she had worked hard to vanquish his memory.

It was enough that her crippled leg served as a constant, lifelong reminder.

"Who has taken Flynn, Charlotte?" Harrison repeated gently.

"If I tell you, you must promise me that you won't tell anyone else." She held fast to him, her gaze pleading.

"If you want us to get Flynn back, it may not be wise for me to make that promise. We may need some assistance."

She vehemently shook her head. "No one can

know about this, Harrison. I am already taking a great risk by confiding in you. If he finds out that I have told anyone—"

"If who finds out?"

She didn't answer.

"Fine," he relented, realizing he would never find out anything if he didn't agree to Charlotte's terms. "I swear I won't tell anyone. Now, what has happened to Flynn?"

She swallowed thickly. "My father has taken him."

Harrison frowned, bewildered. "Lord Redmond?"

"No, not Lord Redmond." She stared down at the intricately woven Persian carpet, unable to meet his gaze. "My *real* father."

He was unable to contain his surprise. "I thought he was dead."

She nodded. "I think I did, too. Or maybe I've just tried to push that part of my childhood so far away, I just made him cease to exist—at least for me. I never wished him dead," she assured him, although at that moment she was not entirely sure that statement was true, "or hoped that anything bad happened to him. I just didn't want him to be part of my life anymore." She studied the wilted hem of her gown, feeling ashamed. "I realize that makes me a horrible daughter."

"It makes you nothing of the sort," Harrison contradicted firmly. "From what little I know of your background, Charlotte, your father was a common thief who was extremely abusive toward you. I don't think anyone would want someone like that kept at the forefront of either their lives or their minds—especially a little girl who could not possibly defend herself from him."

She kept her gaze downcast. "I think most people who know me today assume that I was an orphan when Lady Redmond rescued me from jail in Inveraray. My real mother died when I was very young. I don't remember her. But until Genevieve found me when I was ten, I lived with my father. He was arrested for stealing at the same time I was, and he was sentenced to several years of hard labor. He didn't serve them in Inveraray, though. Genevieve was told that he was sent to a jail in Perth, and that was the last we ever heard about him. I never tried to find out more." She ran her fingers along the worn fabric of the armrest, feeling guilty as she hesitantly admitted, "I didn't really want to know."

"Didn't you think he might come looking for you one day, after he got out?"

"For a long time I was haunted by that possibility. I used to be afraid that he would escape from prison and come after me. But then Genevieve married Haydon, and my brothers and sisters and I were made their legal wards. Our names were changed, and the whole family moved north to Haydon's estate near Inverness. Haydon and Genevieve were wonderful parents, and they were extremely protective of all of us. After a few years, I started to feel safe. The life I had led before seemed so distant and ugly. I suppose I tried very hard not to think about my real father."

"But he didn't stop thinking about you."

"In prison, you have a lot of time to reflect upon things," she remarked softly, her gaze still fastened upon the floor. "Especially at night."

The thought of Charlotte being thrown into some dank prison cell when she was only a child struck Harrison as appalling. He could scarcely imagine how terrified she must have been, and how overwhelmed she must have felt when Lady Redmond rescued her and took her into her home to live. One might expect that Charlotte would have been so scarred by the experiences of her childhood that she would avoid anything that might remind her of that part of her life. Instead she had devoted herself to helping others who were trapped in the same desperate world she had once known.

Until that moment, he had not really understood the importance of her work. He had thought it noble enough, in the way that any charitable endeavor to help the less fortunate was good and decent. But the slums of London were teeming with violence and despair. With her modest little house and her odd assortment of servants, Charlotte could hardly wage a war on a dark reality that had existed for hundreds of years. Harrison now realized that even if she only succeeded in altering the lives of one or two of the women and children she brought into her refuge house over the years, that in itself was a magnificent accomplishment.

He had only to look at her to understand that.

"When he first spoke to me a few days ago, my father told me he had thought that I was so weak and useless, I probably hadn't survived prison anyway. I don't think he particularly cared whether I had or hadn't."

"Then how did he suddenly find you?"

"He came to London a few months ago, and he said that while he was going about St. Giles, he started to hear about a young woman who was trying to help the less fortunate in London. I suppose I am something of a curiosity to the people who live there—especially given that I have chosen to actually live with those I am trying to help. Once he heard that I was Scottish, my name was Charlotte, and I walked with a limp, his interest was sufficiently aroused that he decided to find me." Her expression was pained as she quietly reflected, "I suppose I don't look all that much different from the way I did then—just a lot cleaner and better dressed."

Harrison regarded her in surprise. It suddenly struck him that the young woman who was seated beside him had no real inkling of her loveliness. He thought of the simplicity of the evening gown she had worn to Lord and Lady Marston's ball, the loosely pinned arrangement of her hair, and the fact that she had not adorned herself with a single piece of jewelry. He had sensed that her sparing approach to fashion was the result of her not wanting to draw too much attention to herself. But the result was an extraordinary softness and naturalness to Charlotte's beauty which was much more appealing to him than the heavily perfumed, overly coiffed, lavishly gowned women who preened about at every function he attended.

"And once he realized that you are now a woman of some means, he decided it was time to reassert himself as your father," Harrison surmised. "Which meant demanding that you give him five thousand pounds."

She nodded. "I tried to explain to him that I didn't have that kind of money, but he didn't believe me. He told me if I didn't get it for him, he would harm a member of my family. When I gave him your eight hundred pounds this evening, I hoped that would satisfy him, but instead he was furious. That was when he told me that he had Flynn. He said if I didn't get the rest of the money to him within one week, he would break every bone in Flynn's body."

Harrison absorbed this in grim silence. "And will he actually do that?"

"Yes." Her voice was ragged. "He will."

He rose from the sofa and began to pace the confines of the drawing room. The pain in his head that had been plaguing him for over twenty-four hours now had abated considerably, thanks to a dose of laudanum and the fact that he had confined himself to his darkened room. But his mind was still clouded and his vision slightly blurred, making it difficult to think.

He did not have four thousand two hundred pounds at his disposal—not immediately, anyway. If he sold some of his investments and rearranged some financing, he might be able to pull the money together within a few days. The question was, would Charlotte's father be satisfied with this, or would he continue to hold Flynn hostage and demand even more?

"I can get you the money, Charlotte, although it will take a bit of time to arrange it," he began. "However, I'm not convinced that giving your father more money is the answer. Paying a kidnapper is always risky. By abducting Flynn, he has demonstrated that he is willing to use violence to get what he wants from you. If he thinks you can scrape together another forty-two hundred pounds in just a few days, what is to stop him from demanding even more? Why wouldn't he just keep Flynn and use him as a constant leverage to extort money from you on a regular basis?"

She regarded him in horror.

"I'm not saying he will do that," he quickly qualified, realizing that he was frightening her even more. He decided not to point out the possibility that her father could just take the money and murder Flynn anyway, to keep the boy quiet. "I'm just saying it is a possibility we have to consider."

"My father is a simple man, Harrison," Charlotte replied. "He drinks, he fights, he steals. Those are the things he enjoys in life. What he doesn't enjoy is having responsibility. He made that amply clear to me every day. Flynn is a means to an end for him, but I don't think he will want to keep him for any longer than is necessary. Once I have given him what he wants, he will release Flynn and leave me alone."

Either that or he'll kill the lad, Harrison reflected silently. "But now he sees his daughter living what to him appears a lavish lifestyle, and he wants a piece of that for himself. If I understand him at all, he probably believes you owe it to him, as some kind of payment for his being your father—regardless of how he treated you as a child. I think he'll continue to blackmail you as long as you give in to his demands. After all, getting money from you is far easier and more profitable than any other schemes he's tried in the past."

"Even if you're right, at this point it doesn't matter," Charlotte argued. "He has Flynn. I have no choice but to give him what he wants."

"And what if he doesn't release Flynn after you give him the money?"

"He will," she insisted stubbornly. "He must."

"Or what?"

"I won't give him the money until I see that Flynn is safe. I will make him release Flynn first."

"Assuming he agrees to that, what happens next month, or the month after that, when your father finds himself short on cash or longing for something he can't afford, and he decides to pay you a visit again? You have enough people in your life whom you care for deeply that make you an easy target for blackmail. You can't possibly protect all of them from your father, and regrettably, even my means are not unlimited."

"I won't ask you again," she assured him fervently. "I promise."

"I don't give a damn about the money. What I care about, Charlotte, is the fact that this vile excuse for a human being thinks he can threaten you and your family and abduct children who have placed themselves in your care. He has to be stopped, don't you see?"

"I can't go to the police, if that is what you are suggesting."

"Why not?"

"Because my father has sworn to me that if he hears that the police are looking for him, he will hurt someone."

"He won't find out until it is too late," Harrison argued. "For God's sake, I know the London police can be inept, but it isn't as if they will place an article in the newspapers announcing that they are looking for him."

"No, they'll just patrol the rookeries of the worst areas in London, asking everyone if they've seen or heard of him, which will be a far quicker way of warning him."

"Just ask them to be with you when your father comes to pick up the money, and they can arrest him. Then at least he'll be off the streets and no longer a danger to you."

"You don't know my father, Harrison," Charlotte objected. "He may be uneducated and unsophisticated, but that doesn't mean he isn't intelligent. He never rushes into anything. He waits. He watches. He listens. And long before the police have any hope of arresting him, he will have figured out that they were there and left." Her mouth was dry as she finished, "And then he will make sure I am severely punished for disobeying him."

"You aren't a helpless little girl anymore, Charlotte," he said, frustrated by the effect her father was having upon her. He seated himself beside her once more and placed his hands on her shoulders, forcing her to look at him. "You're a strong, beautiful woman with a family and friends who care about you, and believe it or not, you are also a respected member of society. So stop talking about being punished as if that piece of filth actually has some right to lay a hand on you. You no longer have to obey him, and he has no right to touch you. Do you understand?"

"I'm sorry," she said, feeling defensive and overwhelmed. "I realize it's hard for you to understand. I know I must seem terribly weak and pathetic to you— limping over here in the middle of the night, looking a mess, begging for your help. I don't know why I came to you, when you have already given me so much money. It's just that when I woke this evening to find him standing in the dark over my bed—when I felt his hand pressed hard against my mouth—for a moment I was eight years old again, and I knew I had to do whatever he said or—" She broke off suddenly, too ashamed to continue.

Harrison stared at her, still holding her fast, helpless. It pained him deeply to see her suffering so. He looked at the wine-colored bruise on her cheek, and felt a terrible, impotent rage fill him. He could see the memories of her childhood flooding through her, filling her with a suffering he could scarcely imagine. He could feel it in the tremors pulsing through her, could see it in the bleached skin of her knuckles as she clutched desperately at the wrinkled folds of her gown, could hear it in her soft, desperate swallows of breath as she fought not to cry. A terrible nightmare had awakened within her, stripping her of the courage and strength that she had demonstrated on the night when she first came into his life. And he couldn't bear it. He couldn't bear to see this magnificent woman, who in her relatively short life had learned more about courage and strength and endurance than most people would ever know, reduced to this shivering, terrified state.

He would have done anything in that moment to ease her suffering, to bring her back from the black precipice of her tortured past. But everything he had said so far had only further agitated her, drawing her deeper into the world she had fought so hard to escape. And so, realizing that his words were all clumsy and wrong and inadequate, he wrapped his arms around her and drew her close, thinking only that he wanted to shield her from her past, and her present, and all the forces that were battering her injured body and soul.

She leaned into him and laid her cheek against his

chest, wearily, trustingly. Her back was rigid and tense, and so he began to stroke her, his hands slowly caressing the narrow expanse along her spine, urging the tightly clenched muscles to relax. She was lean and fine beneath the firm contours of her bodice, but he knew that beneath her delicate form burned a will and a determination to survive forged of pure steel. That was why Charlotte had been able to survive the cruelties and deprivations of her childhood. She had been rescued, yes, but that rescue had come when she was ten years old, and had already known a lifetime of poverty and abuse. It was enough to destroy most people, he reflected, perhaps not in body, but in soul, leaving them destined to live their lives in fear and anger and resentment. But Charlotte had not succumbed to those emotions—or to the equally destructive trap of self-pity. Instead she had learned to accept herself for who she was, which was the result of many forces, including her life with her bastard of a father. Although he had not asked, Harrison was convinced that her father had caused the injury to her leg. But instead of shutting herself away and leading a secluded life of pleasant calm as the ward of a marquess, reading and painting or playing the piano in a mansion filled with beauty and grace, Charlotte had decided to strike back at the harsh world from which she had sprung. She had summoned the strength to limp through its bleak streets and offer help, to try to do something to make a difference.

Her courage was astounding.

He laid his fingers against the elegant curve of her jaw and tilted her head up until she was looking at him. He wanted to tell her not to be afraid. He wanted to assure her that he would help her in any way he could. He owed her that much, at least. After all, she had risked everything she had to save him on the night they met. But he wasn't offering to help her out of some sense of obligation. Nor was he doing it because he pitied her, or thought her weak and pathetic, as she had so wrongly accused him. He wanted to help her because the thought of her suffering even a moment longer at the hands of the man who had tormented her for the first ten years of her life filled him with unspeakable rage. Because he couldn't bear the thought of anyone threatening her, or worse, daring to lay a hand on her. Because in all his life he had never met a woman as brave and selfless and giving as she, nor one who at the same time could be so stubbornly, maddeningly infuriating. Because from the moment he first laid eyes upon her he had felt a desperate need burning within him, which never abated, but only grew hotter and more overwhelming each time he was in her presence. All these things he wanted to tell her, and more. But as he sat there, staring into the liquid depths of her eyes, which in the soft glow of lamplight reminded him of the sun playing upon the soft green leaves of his father's beloved tree, he found himself unable to speak.

And so he bent his head and captured her lips with his, thinking he was almost certainly going mad, and not giving a damn.

Charlotte froze, shocked. She suddenly felt as if the ground had been ripped out from under her. As if everything she had previously understood to be the parameters of her existence, parameters that she had quietly learned to accept over the years, had shifted in an instant. No man had ever kissed her. At the relatively mature age of twenty-five, she had long ago given up any childish fantasy that any man would ever want to. She was well past the girlish bloom of eighteen. Well past the secretly nurtured hope that someday she might meet someone who would see beyond her crippled leg, her awkward gait, her plain, unremarkable features. She had come to accept that she would never know the feel of a man's hands upon her body, the touch of his lips against her mouth, the presumably exquisite sensation of being desired, and feeling desire in return. Therefore the urgent, powerful heat of Harrison's lips upon hers rendered her nearly paralyzed, unable to think or speak.

Harrison's mouth moved like warm velvet against hers, caressing her, coaxing her, igniting a flame deep within her belly. Slowly, he traced the tip of his tongue along her lips. She sat there, her breath trapped within her chest, her senses reeling, clinging to him. Somewhere in the recesses of her mind she was aware that it was wrong for her to permit him to touch her so, but she was unable to summon the slightest inclination to make him stop. It was glorious to be touched with such masculine hunger, his hands moving like a restless flame across the dips and swells of her, awakening her flesh to the sensation of his caresses. Harrison's palms moved down the length of her back, across the flare of her hips, up the expanse of her ribs. She could feel herself melting beneath him, her body shifting and softening as it responded to his touch. His tongue flickered again across her bottom lip, teasing, enticing. Her lips parted of their own accord, stunning her even as she sighed into his mouth. Her mind swirling with the heady sensation of being desired, she tentatively tasted him. Emboldened and aroused, she tasted him more.

Harrison groaned while his hands roamed possessively across the soft curves of her body. It had been well over a year since he had felt anything more than the most distant flicker of desire, and a desperate yearning was flooding through him. The feel and taste and scent of Charlotte was overwhelming, stripping away all sense of time and place, until his entire existence was focused purely upon that moment, and he was aware of only two things.

He wanted her.

And incredibly, she wanted him.

It was this that made him slowly unfasten the small black beads at the front of her gown, revealing the ivory calico of her camisole. He tugged upon the slender length of ribbon holding it closed and slipped his hands inside, peeling the layers of summery fabric off her shoulders to expose the lacey corset she wore beneath. He felt her stiffen slightly, uncertain, and so he pulled his mouth from hers to rain reassuring kisses upon the pink seashell of her ear, down the ivory column of her neck, across the pulsing hollow of her throat. He inhaled deeply of her as he continued his path of kisses, worshipping her with his hands and his lips, his palms cupping the soft round of her breasts as he buried his face between them. She threaded her fingers into his hair, her breaths coming faster now, as he undid several of the fastenings at the front of her corset, nuzzled one breast free from her lace-trimmed chemise and drew its crimson peak into his mouth. She arched suddenly and gripped him tighter, pulling him close. He took in her sweet softness, then moved to her other breast, sucking upon the lush swell until it formed a dark berry against the wet roughness of his tongue.

Charlotte closed her eyes as Harrison eased her back against the sofa, too intoxicated by the sensations eddying through her to summon any sense of propriety. Pleasure was pulsing through her, making her feel wondrously alive and whole and free. She ran her hands down the hard wall of Harrison's back as he leaned over her, marveling at how powerful he felt with nothing but the thin silk of his dressing gown stretched upon his enormous, muscled frame. His lips were on hers again, his tongue plundering the secrets of her mouth, drawing a moan from her as one hand caressed her breast while the other moved down and disappeared beneath the tangled froth of her skirts. There were only two simple petticoats beneath her gown, which posed little hindrance to the ascent of Harrison's hand upon her uninjured leg.

He moved languidly, his fingers trailing upon her ankle, then grazing up her stockinged calf, until he came to the frill of lace where her drawers ended at her knee. He drifted along the length of her thigh, his touch gentle and sure. Then his hand slipped inside her drawers, causing her to gasp. He distracted her with a long kiss while his fingers began to stroke the silky triangle of her womanhood. She felt hot and restless, and a mysterious ache began to blossom between her legs.

She wrapped her arms around him and drew him closer. Harrison continued to stroke her, his hand roaming languidly over the soft mound, then moving away to fondle the creamy skin of her legs. She shifted in his arms, wanting more, but not really understanding what it was she wanted. In the next instant his finger slipped inside her. She sighed with pleasure as Harrison caressed the secret folds of her, altering his rhythm and his touch, lightly, then harder, quickly, then with long, slow strokes, until finally she was shifting restlessly beneath him.

He pressed hungry kisses across her lips and cheeks and neck, over the hills and valleys of her breasts, along the tightly laced contours of her body. And then his kisses were moving down, and before she understood his intent he flicked his tongue into the scorching heat of her. She gasped, with shock and pleasure and desire, all melded into one staggering sensation. It was glorious and it was shameful, it was the most exquisite pleasure she had ever known and also the darkest, and the combination of these forces rendered her unable to move. She should stop him, on some distant, incomprehensible level she understood that, but it would have been like trying to stop her heart from beating wildly within her chest, or her blood from racing desperately through her veins. And so she closed her eyes and held fast to him, acutely aware of the warm summer air against her naked breasts, the soft drape of her skirts cascading over the sofa, the rough feel of Harrison's jaw against her thighs, and the scalding slickness of his mouth upon her. She threaded her fingers into the dark tangle of his hair, opening herself wider, astonished by her wantonness and yet somehow also empowered by it.

A terrible need was unfurling within her now, something deep and hollow and relentless. She writhed beneath him, wanting him to touch her more, to kiss her more, to feel his hands and mouth all over her body until there was no part of her that he did not know and accept. His tongue moved deeper now, and then he eased his finger inside and began to slip it in and out as he swirled his tongue over her, slowly, deliberately. She couldn't bear it, she was certain of it, but again and again he touched her and kissed her and licked her, exploring her and pleasuring her until there was nothing beyond her and Harrison and the most magnificent ecstasy she had ever known. She opened her legs wider, inviting him to know the most intimate secrets of her, too over-whelmed with these sensations to wonder at the trust she was placing in him, which seemed so natural and right. Harrison's tongue swirled faster, his finger thrust-ing deeper, his hand stroking her breasts and her corseted belly, pressing down upon the aching hollow within. *Please, please,* she pleaded feverishly, not know-ing how much more she could bear. *Please, please, please . . .*

Her breaths were coming faster now, shallow little sips of air that could not fill her lungs, and her body had suddenly become still and strained, every muscle and nerve locked in a spasm of desperate need. *Please, please, please,* she begged, not sure if she was whispering the words aloud or not, not certain of anything except that she had to hold on and endure his scalding caresses and intimate penetration while she reached and reached for whatever it was he was trying to give her. She stretched and grasped, until there was no more air to be had, for her lungs were bursting and her blood was pounding and her mind was filled with the excruciating awareness of Harrison's touch, which made her feel more beautiful than she had ever dared imagine. And then suddenly she cried out, in ecstasy and wonder. Ripples of pleasure surged through her as she collapsed against the sofa, fighting to fill her lungs with air as the tension gradually seeped from her body.

Harrison threw off his dressing gown and stretched over her, fighting for some semblance of control as his hardness brushed against her searing wetness. He wanted to plunge himself into her, to slake the unbearable need roiling within him. It had been a lifetime since he had been overwhelmed by such pure desire, a lifetime since a woman had awakened in him the raw hunger of lust. But this was not just lust, although he was far too aroused to understand just what, precisely, it was. He pressed himself a little further into Charlotte, feeling as if he had been awakened from a lonely sleep, to find this magnificent woman waiting for him, with her enormous eyes and her gentle, healing touch. She was an enchantress and an enigma, one minute shy and retiring, an instant later brandishing the most stunning courage and passion he had ever known. She moved him, confronted him, inspired him, making him feel stronger than he really was. His desire for her was staggering, rendering him unable think of anything beyond that moment. And so he eased himself into her, wondering if it was actually possible to die from such excruciating pleasure.

Charlotte looked up at him, her eyes wide. He

searched her gaze for some sign of reluctance, vowing
that if he saw it he would stop, although he had no idea
how he would manage such an extraordinary feat. But
all he saw was trust, simple and absolute. He bent his
head and brushed his lips over hers, tenderly, wanting to
make her understand with his touch what he barely understood himself. And then, feeling the last taut threads
of his control begin to break, he whispered her name,
and buried himself inside her.

She stiffened suddenly. He summoned every fragment of his self-control to hold perfectly still, hating
himself for having caused her pain. He would have done
anything to ease her suffering, but he had no experience
with virgins, and didn't know whether even the movement of withdrawing might only cause her further distress. And so he kissed her lips, her eyes, her cheeks,
raining tenderness upon her, whispering soothing words
as he waited for the clench of her body to ease. She exhaled a shivering breath, and with it her body started to
soften.

He began to move within her, slowly, leashing the
unbearable desire surging through him as he forced
himself to take care. He tasted her deeply now, and he
could feel her desire once again as she began to sigh and
shift against him. Her hands moved over his naked back,
his shoulders, his buttocks, learning the hard contours of
him, shyly at first, and then with a fierce possessiveness.
Never before had he been so moved by a woman's
touch. He was losing something to her, he understood
that now, could feel it with every aching thrust, every
beat of his heart, every desperate breath. She was exactly
what he had never thought to find, someone strong and
independent and caring, a woman who had seen him
near his very worst and hadn't turned away in horror.
But there was much about him that she didn't know, and
the realization was agonizing. He had no right to her, he

understood that, for he could only offer her a lifetime of uncertainty, and ultimately, a burden that was far too great for even someone as strong as she.

He groaned and moved faster within her, holding her tight, wanting to make her part of him, so that when she left him she would still carry some part of him with her. It was foolishness to indulge in such fantasy, but still he clung to it, pushing aside the world that existed beyond them.

Stay with me, he pleaded silently, knowing he could never ask her to make such a sacrifice, not when he knew firsthand what kind of misery that life would entail. Again and again he pulsed within her, feeling as if he were dying as she opened herself to him and wrapped her arms around him and kissed him with fervent ardor. She was writhing against him now, her breaths puffing in hot little gusts, her fingers clawing at his shoulders as she lifted her hips to sheathe him deeper in her. He tried to slow himself, to gain some semblance of control, but she was rising up and gasping for air as she clenched her body around his, until he could endure no more. He buried himself deep inside her, feeling shattered and lost as he poured himself into her.

Charlotte lay completely still, holding Harrison tight, feeling the powerful drumming of his heart against hers. Nothing had prepared her for what had passed between them. She had understood the rudiments of the sex act from the time she was seven, for the whores who had peopled the landscape of her childhood had thought nothing of making lewd comments to a young girl who was indubitably headed for the same career. She also had her father to thank for crudely educating her on what a man expected of a woman. But then he had broken her leg, putting a quick end to his hopes for making her a prostitute. Most men would tolerate almost anything from a whore, including filth and ugliness and disease.

But mercifully, that didn't include raping a child who was also a helpless cripple.

In that perverse way, her leg had actually protected her.

None of that, however, was remotely related to what had just occurred between her and Harrison. She held fast to him, memorizing the weight of his body upon hers, the sheen of his skin beneath her palms, the feel of his breath upon her neck. Her body was liquid, as if she had been soaking in the hottest of mineral springs, and the pain which she lived with constantly had seeped away. She supposed on some level she felt ashamed. After all, unmarried women did not share their bodies with men, at least not in the world Genevieve had made her a part of. But that tenet of polite society seemed inconsequential against what had just raged between her and Harrison. Charlotte had never expected to experience such passion—had never known such a thing was even possible. She had long ago accepted that no man would find her desirable. Yet Harrison had. And more, his feverish longing had roused the flames of her own need, until she wanted him just as much as he wanted her.

A melancholy yearning began to unfurl within her, deep and relentless and frightening. She closed her eyes and turned her head to the side, her arms wrapped around him as she fought the tears pooling in her eyes. She did not want him to sense her longing. It would only make her seem pitiful and foolish, and she could not bear to have him think of her so.

Not after the way he had looked at her as he gave himself to her.

"I must go," she murmured, seeking to break the spell that had woven around both of them. She unwrapped her arms from his back, trying to put some distance between them. "Oliver is outside waiting for me."

Harrison hesitated. He did not want her to go. Did

not want her to move from underneath him and adjust her clothes and hurry out the door into the cruel world beyond. He wanted her to stay with him. Wanted her to go with him upstairs and climb into his bed and let him hold her in his arms while he watched her fall into a deep and restful sleep. He wanted to see the soft play of sunlight spilling across her face as morning broke, wanted to see her gradually waken, all sleepy and disheveled and warm. He wanted to keep her with him, not just for that day, but always, to know that whatever fate awaited him, she would be there, ready and willing to share it. All this he wanted, and so much more. But it was impossible. He understood that. And so he cradled her face between his hands, forcing her to look at him, agonized by the sparkle of tears upon her lashes.

"I'm sorry," he said, despising himself for the distress he had obviously caused her, and the fact that he could never make it right.

Charlotte regarded him in surprise. How could he be sorry about something that had been so exquisite? She could hardly consider herself ruined for any other man.

There never had been any other man, and she was utterly certain there never would be.

"I'm not," she whispered solemnly.

He arched a brow in surprise, once again confounded by her. He found her assertion comforting. Even so, he knew he owed her more.

"I will do everything within my power to help you, Charlotte," he vowed. "I will find you the money you need to give to your father for Flynn. But I want to be there with you when you make the exchange, to make sure that both you and Flynn are safe. I also want to explain to your father that there will be no more blackmailing." He traced his finger gently around the stained contours of her bruised cheek, struggling to control the anger burning within him as he finished quietly, "And tell him that if he ever so much as lays a finger upon you again, I will tear him apart."

She stared at him, mesmerized by the low cadence of his voice, the protective fury in his gaze, the unberable gentleness of his touch. She could never allow him and Archie to meet. It would have been wrong to expose something as strong and beautiful and giving as Harrison to the foul brutality of a man like Boney Buchan. But she did not tell him that. Instead she laid her hand against his cheek, memorizing the heat of his skin against her palm, the chiseled contour of his jaw, the dark sureness of his gaze.

"Thank you."

He nodded. And then, realizing he had no choice but to release her, he rolled off her and turned away, giving her a modicum of privacy as he donned his dressing gown.

Charlotte rearranged herself as best she could, hoping that Oliver wouldn't notice anything amiss as she clumsily buttoned her gown and tidied her hair.

"You may turn around now," she said at last.

Harrison turned to look at her and felt his heart wrench. "I will have the money for you in a few days. I will send word to you when it is ready. Then we can arrange to meet your father. Do not worry about Flynn," he added, fighting the desire to pull her back into his arms. "He's a strong, clever boy who knows how to handle himself. He'll be fine."

Charlotte wasn't so sure about that, but she didn't argue. There was no point in imagining the worst. Permitting herself to break down in hysteria was a luxury she didn't have. She had to stay strong, for the sake of Flynn, and Annie, Ruby, and Violet, and all those she loved. On some level she didn't completely understand, she even had to stay strong for Harrison.

"Telford will show you out," Harrison continued, pulling upon a velvet rope to summon his butler. "Somehow I don't think Oliver would appreciate seeing me escort you to the door in my current state of undress." He opened the door to the corridor, afraid that if they shared even one more moment alone, he would lose his resolve and drag her back against him.

Charlotte stood before him, staring at the deep lines etched into his face, and the haunted depths of his eyes, which were torn between the most powerful longing and the most excruciating regret.

"Harrison," she began softly.

"You rang, my lord?" asked Telford, fumbling sleepily with the tie of his flapping dressing gown as he rushed down the hallway.

"Miss Kent is leaving now," Harrison informed him. "Kindly escort her out to her carriage."

"Certainly, my lord." Summoning an extraordinary dignity despite his rumpled state, Telford turned and gave Charlotte a courtly bow. "After you, Miss Kent."

Charlotte turned and limped silently down the hall, her gaze down so that neither Harrison nor Telford could see the tear that had somehow managed to defy her fierce determination not to cry.

LEWIS SANK BACK INTO THE SHADOWS, WATCHING IN silence as Charlotte's carriage clattered into the fog-laden gray of London's early morning light.

He had been keeping an eye on Lord Bryden's home all night. It had been a relentlessly dull assignment, but it was one he had given to himself, so he could hardly complain. If Chief Inspector Holloway knew that one of his senior detectives was spending his nights watching the home of one of London's most respected citizens, an earl who was renowned as a successful investor, a dutiful son, and by all accounts a law-abiding member of society, he would have hauled Lewis in for a lecture on not wasting his goddamn time when there were bloody murderers running about. Chief Inspector Holloway disliked Lewis immensely, and never failed to make his antipathy known. He suspected Lewis thought himself smarter than he.

On that point, the chief was uncharacteristically astute.

When he was first transferred to the Detective Branch, Lewis had made the grave error of admitting to Chief Inspector Holloway that he had a university education. He was swiftly informed that only fribbles and fools wasted their time at university. Everything Chief Inspector Holloway knew had been learned through what he termed the "school of life," as if the boundaries of his own narrow little existence set the limits to which all men should aspire. He told Lewis that was where all his police officers and detectives should be schooled, not prancing about some bloody university memorizing useless scribblings from ancient Greece. Lewis had pointed out that there was actually a great deal to be learned from books, and that modern law enforcement was inextricably tied to the fields of science, forensic medicine, psychology, and the law, all of which needed to be studied in far greater depth than what might be gleaned from merely walking the streets of London.

That comment had earned him a six-month assignment investigating a series of larcenies of wet linen stolen from their drying lines in north London.

His rise through the ranks had been frustratingly slow. But his intelligence and determination had proven irrefutable, and ultimately, the chief had little choice but to promote him. At his current level of First Class Inspector, however, he had hit the ceiling, unless there was an opening for a Chief Inspector somewhere. Old

Holloway wasn't going anywhere, unless the arrogant fool suddenly dropped dead.

One could always hope.

Lewis withdrew his pocket watch and studied the time. Twenty-two minutes past four o'clock in the morning. He took out his notebook and recorded it, then calculated the length of time of Miss Kent's visit. One hour and twelve minutes. He had not been close enough to make any reliable observations about her apparent frame of mind at the time of her departure, but he had noted earlier that she had seemed rather agitated when she arrived at exactly ten minutes past three o'-clock. Lord Bryden's butler, who was dressed in his nightclothes, had answered the door, and he had also escorted her back to her carriage as she left. Her elderly driver, Oliver, had waited for her, stepping down from his seat only to help her in and out of the carriage. Lewis thought for a moment, trying to decide if there was anything else that needed immediate notation. He would compose a more detailed report later, when he was seated at his desk with a pen and good lighting, as was his habit. Lewis was a great believer in notes. He prided himself on having an excellent memory, but that didn't mean he didn't realize that even the most important details could be subject to the shifting variations of time and imagination. If it was recorded in the notes, then it was fact.

Everything else was merely speculation.

He placed his notebook back in his pocket, then withdrew the pristine linen handkerchief that Constable Wilkins had found on the ground the night that Lord Pembroke's home was broken into and his butler murdered. It was this monogram that had led him to Lord Bryden, as well as a half dozen other men who had attended several balls at which Lady Pembroke had recently worn her esteemed ruby necklace. Four of the men had proven far too ancient to be able to perform the kind of physical feats for which the Dark Shadow was renowned. The fifth, Lord Berry, had turned out to be as short and round as a turnip, causing Lewis to dismiss him as well.

Only Lord Bryden was even remotely of an age and physique that might have made him capable of such feats, although at forty years, Lewis was skeptical that he could scale walls and trees. However, since he was the only remaining possibility, Lewis had decided to do a little investigating into Lord Bryden's circumstances, to see if there was anything that might suggest even a tenuous link between his lordship and the elusive thief known as the Dark Shadow.

Upon initial examination, there was nothing. Lord Bryden apparently enjoyed a solid financial situation, based upon a number of excellent investments that had proven extremely profitable over the years. He didn't drink to excess. He gambled, but only for entertainment, and with a reasonable amount of success. He had once been considered something of a rake, but again, no more so than most eligible lords who had been blessed with a relatively pleasing appearance and the allure of their title and their money. But Bryden's romantic dalliances had dwindled in the past year or two, perhaps in part because of the declining health of his mother. Lady Bryden was reputed to be completely mad, although Lewis could not ascertain whether or not this was true, since she had not been seen in public for several years. It was entirely possible that she was merely suffering from the unkind ravages of age, and preferred not to venture from her home anymore. Lord Bryden himself seemed to enjoy attending social functions with relative regularity, and was considered something of a coup when he attended a dinner party, as the hostess could then try to match him up with one of her vapid unmarried lady guests.

Lewis suddenly found himself thinking of Annie, the beautiful young girl who had stood before him in the rain the night he had gone to question Miss Kent. He had thought of Annie often since that night, at odd moments, when his mind should have been firmly focused on his case, or on the mundane preparation of his dinner, or when he was tossing restlessly upon his bed, fighting to fall asleep. She was a far cry from the milky-skinned, sharp-featured, tightly laced young women of polite society, who Lewis suspected regarded him with either pity or contempt. Not that he inspired much idolization. With his rumpled clothes and his worn shoes and his cramped, gray little flat, which he hardly ever saw because he was always working, he was scarcely an enticing catch. But Annie had not looked at him the way most women did, their narrow eyes swiftly assessing and finding him wanting, or worse, not even worthy of an assessment.

Annie's brandy-colored eyes had flashed furiously at him through the rain, her gaze afire with challenge. She had tossed back the damp chocolate silk of her hair and waited, acting as though she actually believed Lewis could do something to right the wrongs that had been inflicted upon her. Of course this was due to the fact that Lewis was a member of the police force, and therefore obliged to protect the innocent and uphold the law. But somehow he had sensed there was more to their exchange than that. Surely that explained the extraordinary sensations Annie had aroused in him when she realized he would do nothing. Her icy contempt had left him feeling angry and frustrated, not just with the fact that he didn't have the time to go tramping about St. Giles searching for the bastard who had beaten her, but also because she had been with someone who had dared raise his hand to her. A keen intelligence burned in Annie's eyes, coupled with a tantalizing femininity that filled her lush body as she turned away, dismissing him with the condescension of a queen. She was a whore, he reminded himself endlessly, yet he could not bring himself to think of her so. Annie was too full of beauty and rage and light for him to dismiss her as such. Besides, by seeking Miss Kent's assistance, it was clear she was trying to extricate herself from her former life. She was a young woman of experience, who had seen the rougher side of life, but was too much a fighter to have been broken by it.

He was drawn to her, he realized, appalled.

And not just because of the promise she flaunted in the cherry swell of her lips and the soft curves of her charming body. No, there was more to Annie than that, he was certain of it. He prided himself on his highly tuned intuition, which when combined with his relentlessly logical mind, was almost always correct. What then was he to make of his schoolboy attraction to a whore who actually fancied herself better than he?

He pushed his hand through his hair, disoriented. Clearly he needed some sleep. That explained why he was wasting so much time thinking about nonsense when he needed to focus every grain of his attention on the most important case of his career. He stared at the now-crumpled ball of linen in his hand, marshaling his attention back to the question of Lord Bryden and the dropped handkerchief.

On the surface, Lord Bryden's life looked to be neatly in order. But Lewis knew better than to be satisfied by appearances. Everyone had ghosts in their past, and as he had correctly surmised, Lord Bryden was no exception. It had only taken a little digging to uncover the unfortunate circumstances surrounding his father's untimely deterioration and death.

When he was barely in his fifties, the former earl had begun to exhibit some rather bizarre behavior.

Ultimately, it was widely rumored that he was suffering from some form of premature dementia, perhaps brought on by syphilis. Unfortunately, at the time Lord Bryden was still sufficiently in command of his faculties to appear capable of administering his estates. This resulted in his investing his entire fortune in a rather risky venture, which subsequently collapsed, virtually wiping him out. His lordship was then forced to liquidate many of his assets, including properties in Somerset and Norfolk, and a formidable art and jewel collection. Unfortunately, this did little to stabilize the family's ruined financial situation. Despondent and of an increasingly feeble mental state, his lordship finally shot himself, just three days shy of his fifty-sixth birthday. His eldest son was thrust into the position of earl at the relatively tender age of twenty-four.

It was tragic, mused Lewis, but not highly unusual. History was full of drunken or dotty fathers who managed to obliterate their family's wealth before they died. What was atypical in this case was the remarkable ability of young Lord Bryden, who until the moment of his father's death had been something of a wastrel, to consolidate what little remained of his assets and rebuild his family's fortune. In the span of a few short years, the new earl had somehow been able to raise enough equity to make investments that began to show extremely profitable returns. His father's debts were cleared. The family's remaining homes were well kept and even expanded upon. His lordship even sought out some of the artwork that had previously been sold to satisfy his father's debtors and bought it back, at many times what the buyers had paid his father. Given how dire his financial situation was reputed to have been, Lord Bryden's rise to riches again was nothing short of extraordinary. Over the course of a year or more, young Lord Bryden had either begged, borrowed, or stolen sufficient funds to make the investments that would put his family firmly back upon the privileged list of English society.

It was the year that captured Lewis's attention.

The Dark Shadow had been stealing jewels all over London for several months now. At first, it was assumed that the initial thefts were unrelated. But as more thefts occurred and it became evident that they were linked, London society dubbed the thief the Dark Shadow, after a daring thief who had terrorized London's bejeweled society for approximately a year, beginning in the summer of 1859. What was unique about those robberies was the fact that no jewelry chest or safe was ever emptied; as was the case presently, only select items of considerable value or beauty were stolen. None of the pieces were ever recovered. And then, abruptly, the break-ins stopped. It was assumed that the Dark Shadow had been captured and jailed for some lesser offense, or perhaps he had died or been killed. The most popular theory was that he had gone into luxurious retirement in some villa on the Mediterranean.

Or maybe, mused Lewis, staring at the ring of amber still glowing faintly around the drapes of Lord Bryden's study on the main floor, he had just become so successful he had no longer needed an alternate source of income.

The handkerchief remained problematic. It struck Lewis as almost inconceivable that the man who had been cleverly slipping in and out of the homes of London's aristocracy and disappearing into the night would suddenly become so careless that he would drop a monogrammed handkerchief at a crime scene. The Dark Shadow was no fool. Neither, apparently, was Lord Bryden. Why would he even take such an item with him when he was about to commit one of his crimes? Was he baiting the police, perhaps daring them to catch him? Did he on some level even want to be

caught? Lewis was well aware that many criminals enjoyed the sport of outwitting the police even more than
they enjoyed performing their actual crimes. It was entirely possible that the Dark Shadow had grown weary
of staying so far ahead of the police, and had decided to
toss a clue in front of them as a way of making the game
more interesting—or even to bring it to an end. Or was
the explanation something far more mundane? Had
Lord Bryden's valet placed the handkerchief in the coat
he had chosen to wear that night, without his lordship's
knowledge? Or had Lord Bryden merely been in the
vicinity of Lord Pembroke's home that night, and
dropped the handkerchief quite innocently? Was the fact
that the Dark Shadow had last been active in the same
year that young Lord Bryden had been frenetically trying to raise funds to hold his estates together and support
his understandably distraught mother, younger brother,
and sister, merely a coincidence?

Lewis carefully placed the wrinkled square of fabric
back in his pocket. It was possible.

The appearance of Miss Kent at Lord Bryden's
house in the middle of the night, however, made the
possibility of mere coincidence highly improbable.

Chapter Ten

"GOOD MORNING, HARRY," SAID LADY BRYDEN, sailing into the dining room. "I'm glad I found you before you went off—we have much to discuss—good gracious, is that coffee you're drinking?"

Harrison looked up from his newspaper and eyed his mother carefully, trying to ascertain her state of mind. "Good morning, Mother. How are you feeling today?"

"Really, Harry, what on earth has gotten into you? If your father finds out you are in here reading his paper and drinking his coffee, he will be quite annoyed, I can assure you."

"Father isn't here, Mother," Harrison told her.

"That is no excuse, and you know it," Lady Bryden returned firmly. "Telford," she said, fixing her gaze upon him, "would you be kind enough to bring my son a cup of tea, with plenty of milk and sugar in it? And perhaps one of Mrs. Shepherd's lovely cinnamon buns—the ones with the sticky syrup on them. Harry just loves them."

Telford regarded Harrison helplessly.

"That won't be necessary, Telford," Harrison assured him. "I've finished breakfast, Mother. I'm just about to go out."

"Really?" Lady Bryden regarded him uncertainly, confused that she did not know her son's itinerary for the day. "Where?"

Harrison hesitated. In fact he had an appointment that morning to meet with his barrister and solicitor, to finalize the details of liquidating some of the shares he held in three different companies. When he went to him the previous day, his solicitor had advised him not to sell, as the companies were still relatively young and had not nearly reached their full potential. Unfortunately, time was a luxury Harrison could ill afford. If all went well, he should have the money in hand within a few days.

Then he would meet Charlotte and determine how they were going to give the money to her father in exchange for young Flynn.

Guilt clawed at his belly. He had been tormenting himself endlessly over what had happened between him and Charlotte two nights earlier. Harrison understood that his mind had been clouded from the effects of both his headache and the laudanum he had dosed himself with prior to Charlotte's arrival. Even so, what he had done was appalling. Charlotte had come to him frightened, alone, seeking his help and guidance and support, because on some level he barely understood, she trusted him. And he had taken advantage of her. There was no way to paint it any plainer than that. He had used his considerable experience to seduce her when she was most vulnerable. He had eased her back and buried himself deep inside her, taking her in a frenzy of passion as if she were some common harlot who had dropped by to service him.

Self-loathing poured through him, intensified by the sudden hardening between his legs. What the hell was the matter with him?

"Harry? Are you all right? You suddenly look ill."

"I'm fine," Harrison assured his mother, forcing himself back to the present. "I'm meeting a friend for lunch," he added, in answer to her previous question.

"Who?"

"His name is Lawrence." Harrison was never certain how much information to give his mother during these exchanges. Sometimes she easily accepted whatever he told her with nothing more than a perfunctory nod, while other times she became fixated upon some seemingly inconsequential detail and worked herself into a near frenzy over it.

"Is that Lord Shelton's son?" she enquired, drawing her finely shaped brows together. "The one who is afraid of horses?"

Harrison debated whether or not to correct her. Ultimately he decided it was easier for his mother to have an image in her mind of whom he was going to see than not. "The very same," he lied.

"Then you must be sure to invite him to your party, Harry," she declared enthusiastically. "I promise you it is going to be great fun. We're going to have all kinds of lovely games on the lawn, and ice cream and cakes, and ponies…" She stopped suddenly, frowning. "You don't think poor Lawrence will be sick when he sees them, do you? That's what happens to him, you know. He simply throws up everywhere the minute he gets near a horse. His parents have tried everything to make him stop. They've even taken him to a doctor who suggested it might be the smell of the animals that was offending him so. So his nursemaid tied a scented scarf around his face to try to mask the smell, but that only caused him to vomit all over the scarf, poor thing, which I'm sure he found most upsetting."

"I believe he has gotten over his fear of horses, Mother," Harrison assured her.

"Well, that's a relief to his parents, I'm sure. A gentleman can't have much of a life if he cannot bring himself to mount a horse without getting sick all over the place. People tend to notice that sort of thing."

"To say nothing of the poor horse," quipped Tony, striding into the dining room.

"Mr. Poole," said Telford, startled by Tony's sudden appearance, "how did you get in?"

"The front door was left slightly ajar. I called hello, but nobody answered, and I could hear all of you chatting away in here, so I thought I'd just save you the trouble of answering the door and come on in. Good morning, Lady Bryden," he said, taking her hand and kissing it. "I must say, you look particularly lovely this morning. You seem to get younger and more radiant every time I see you."

"Mother, you remember my friend Tony Poole," said Harrison, seeing confusion cloud his mother's eyes as she stared at her young admirer. "He has been a visitor here many times."

"Yes, of course." Lady Bryden smiled politely. "How are you, Mr. Poole?"

"Just wonderful, thank you, Lady Bryden," said Tony, seating himself at the table. "Now Harry, you really let me down last night, I'm afraid. There I was at the Fenwicks' ball, telling everyone that you had sworn to me that you were going to attend, and then you never showed up, you coward. Lady Elizabeth was shadowing me all night, and every time she appeared she had a different fool dangling on her arm. I think she wanted to be sure that when you finally arrived you would see that she was having a marvelous time without you. While she seemed gay enough early on, as the hour grew later and the fellows traipsing around after her got progressively younger and more pitiful, you could almost feel the irritation seething from her across the room. By the end of the evening she was desperate enough to accept a dance from Lord Beckett's bran-faced son, and he barely comes up to her shoulder—she spent the entire time trying to keep him from bumping his nose into her chest!" He laughed.

"Why, Harry, did one of your friends give a party yesterday?" asked Lady Bryden.

"There was a gathering at Lord and Lady Fenwick's," Harrison replied.

"Why didn't you go?"

"I didn't feel like going out."

"Really, Harry, this shyness of yours just won't do," Lady Bryden chided. "You have to make yourself go out, and once you are there I'm certain you will find that you will have a wonderful time."

"I'm sure you would have, Harry," Tony agreed, rising from the table to inspect the feast of breakfast foods laid out on the marble-topped sideboard. "Lady Whitaker was there, and everyone was fawning all over her because her husband had just purchased a magnificent diamond necklace for her from some jewel dealer he met from Belgium," he recounted, heaping a selection of meats and rolls onto his plate. "The stone at the center of the necklace is apparently quite well known— it is called the Star of Persia, or some such thing. People were saying it once belonged to an empress, and that it is unspeakably valuable because of its clarity and its unusual shade of pink. It aroused such fascination that it was even mentioned in the *Morning Post* this morning, if you can believe that," he finished, chuckling. "That just shows you just what a dull night it was."

Lady Bryden dropped her teacup, spilling its contents all over the table.

"Let me help you, my lady," offered Telford, rushing forth with a napkin.

"Leave it!" Lady Bryden's entire body was rigid as she fixed her gaze on Tony. "I believe, Mr. Poole, that you must be mistaken." Her hands gripped the table as she spoke, as if she were struggling for support. "The Star of Persia belongs to me. It was a gift from my husband on the night that my darling Harry was born. Although I seldom have an opportunity to wear it, it is a gift I nonetheless cherish deeply. I would never sell it, ever. It is a precious heirloom, and an irreplaceable memento of the birth of my first child. I plan to give it to Harry when he grows up, so that he may present it to his wife when she bears their first child. So you see, Lady Whitaker could not possibly have been wearing it last night. Whatever Lord Whitaker purchased may have been very exceptional, but it was most assuredly not the Star of Persia."

Tony glanced uneasily at Harrison.

"Of course you are right, Mother," Harrison agreed, his voice low and comforting. "Lord Whitaker probably bought something that merely resembled the Star of Persia, and people got confused about its history. Either that or the dealer lied to him about the stone. Either way, you have nothing to worry about. Your necklace is perfectly safe."

She nodded, but her gaze was panicked, as if she didn't know whether or not to believe him.

"Would you like to see the necklace?" she asked Tony. "I can get it for you if you like. It will only take a moment."

Again, Tony stole a glance at Harrison, whose eyes told him in no uncertain terms that he was not to accept her offer.

"Perhaps another time," Tony said amiably. "These sweet rolls look absolutely delectable, Telford," he remarked, changing the subject. "You must tell Mrs. Griffen I simply adore her baking." He piled two of them onto his plate and returned to the table, where he tucked into his meal with great enthusiasm.

"Mother, would you like some more tea?" Harrison could see that she was still upset by the mention of her necklace.

"No, thank you, Harry." She released her grip upon the table and stood. "I really must get back to organizing your party." She managed a forced smile. "Has Harry told you about it yet, Mr. Poole?"

Again Tony looked to Harrison for guidance. Harrison gave him a slight nod.

"Yes, Lady Bryden, he did," Tony assured her. "It sounds like it's going to be wonderful."

"And can you come?"

"Nothing could keep me from it."

"Splendid. Well, then, I must get to work writing the invitations. You boys eat—but no coffee, Harrison, is that clear? It isn't good for you."

"Yes, Mother. Where did you want to write your invitations?"

"Why, I thought I would work on them at my desk in my room. Why?"

"Telford will see you upstairs, then."

"Really, Harry, that isn't at all necessary. Telford has better things to do than escort me around the house. I'm not an invalid, you know, and I'm quite aware of where my own chamber is."

"Actually, your ladyship, I was just about to go upstairs anyway," Telford assured her.

Lady Bryden regarded him suspiciously. "Why?"

"I need to fetch something from Lord Bryden's wardrobe," he quickly improvised.

Because of his mother's condition, Harrison preferred to keep his staff to a minimum, and therefore he
did not employ a valet. Fewer servants meant he could
afford to pay the ones he did have better wages, which
made them less apt to seek employment elsewhere. Loy-
alty and discretion were important to him. He did not
want servants who came and went and then gossiped to
others about his mother's fragile state of mind. Also, he
had learned over the years that his mother did not tolerate change very well. She needed routine and familiar
surroundings and people in order to function well.

In that respect, her illness resembled the senility that
had gradually broken the mind of her husband.

"Very well, Telford, if you are planning to go upstairs anyway, then you may accompany me—although I
really don't feel it is necessary." She smiled at Tony once
more. "Very nice to see you again, Mr. Poole. I shall
look forward to seeing you at Harry's party."

"And I look forward to attending," Tony assured
her, politely rising from his seat. "I'm sure it's going to
be grand."

Harrison also rose from his chair as his mother left
the room. When she and Telford were gone, he sank
back down and took a final swallow of his coffee.

"Did Lady Bryden really own the Star of Persia?"
asked Tony curiously.

Harrison nodded. "Unfortunately, it was one of the
many things my father was forced to sell after his investments began to fail."

"But he didn't tell her?"

"I suspect he wasn't thinking clearly at the time,"
Harrison replied carefully. "He was completely overwhelmed by the debts that surrounded him. But he also
wanted to protect my mother from the knowledge of
just how badly he had handled their wealth. I suppose at

first he thought that he would sell a few things and re-
lieve some of the financial pressure on him, and hope
that eventually some of his investments would bear
fruit." His expression was grim. "Unfortunately, that
was not the case."

"So did your mother ever learn about what happened to her jewels?"

"Yes," Harrison replied shortly. Even though Tony
had been a friend of his for nearly two years, he did not
like discussing his family's past with him. Some things
were better left buried. "Her memory, however, became rather selective after my father died."

"Maybe you should go to Lord Whitaker and offer
to buy the necklace from him," Tony suggested. "It
would undoubtedly please your mother to have it back
in her possession."

Harrison's expression was noncommittal. "My
mother's reactions to things can be a bit unpredictable.
Also, it is doubtful that Lady Whitaker would be willing
to part with a piece that has already generated her so
much admiration and publicity."

"You're right about that. She was positively glowing
as everyone crowded about her, gawking at her great
prow of a chest. I don't imagine she's had that many
people toss her a second glance since the day she was
married, and that was before I was born!" Tony
laughed. "But if you are interested, you'd best make an
offer quickly, before the Dark Shadow swoops down
and steals the thing away. Everyone last night was natter-
ing on about how once he gets wind of the fact that this
famous necklace is in London, he'll be positively desperate to add it to his collection. It must be worth at least
ten times whatever your father paid for it over forty
years ago."

Tony was probably right, Harrison realized. The

thief currently playing the Dark Shadow had demonstrated his eye for the very best, and showed remarkable restraint each time he slipped into a house. Just as Harrison had, some sixteen years earlier. Harrison's rationale for doing so had been simple. He had only taken what he knew for certain had belonged to his estate. Those magnificent jewels his father had sold at a fraction of their value, in a heartbreaking moment of madness and desperation. Everything else Harrison had left untouched. That had the advantage of delaying the moment in which the owners of the purloined jewelry realized that something had been taken. By the time the police had been called in to investigate, they were rooting around a house that had been robbed days, or sometimes even weeks earlier. There were, quite simply, almost no clues to be had. All that was certain was that someone had slipped in and out unnoticed, destroying nothing, and harming no one.

That was the critical difference between himself and the man who had stolen his guise.

Harrison had been determined to reclaim what he believed was rightfully his, without causing injury or bloodshed. The current Dark Shadow was apparently only interested in stealing the most valuable jewels he could find. He didn't give a damn who got hurt or killed in the process. The longer he continued at his game, the greater the risk of more people being injured. For that reason alone he had to be stopped. But Harrison also had a more personal need to bring the daring thief's career to an end. By adopting the persona Harrison had created, this new burglar had aroused much interest in the past exploits of the Dark Shadow. While the detectives who had worked on the case sixteen years earlier had never been able to uncover Harrison's involvement, it was possible this time he would not be so fortunate.

Some earnest young detective might take a renewed interest in examining the Dark Shadow's past exploits, to see how they compared to those of the present. That was dangerous. Whether the man playing at the Dark Shadow realized it or not, by emulating the thief Harrison had created, he had the power to bring Harrison's carefully constructed life crashing down around him.

Harrison could not permit that to happen.

"That was absolutely delicious," said Tony, finishing off the last of his sweet roll. "That Mrs. Griffin of yours really is a gem. You mustn't let her slip through your fingers, Harry, or I'll be forced to find someplace else to drop in for breakfast. I have an idea," he said brightly, setting his napkin aside. "Let's go down to the Marbury Club and see if anyone is taking bets on whether the Dark Shadow will try to nick Lady Whitaker's necklace tonight, before she and Lord Whitaker leave for Paris tomorrow. I'm bound to make a few pounds out of old Lord Sullivan on that."

"How do you know which way Lord Sullivan will wager?"

"I don't," he replied, shrugging. "I just tell him how I plan to bet, and he bets against me. He doesn't really care whether he wins or loses, he just enjoys the sport of telling everyone how completely idiotic my predictions are. If I bet that the Dark Shadow will try to steal the necklace tonight, Lord Sullivan will pronounce me a fool, and wager that the Dark Shadow will wait until Lady Whitaker returns from her trip abroad. There will be a lot of gruff arguing as Lords Shelton and Reynolds jump into the fray, a few names will be called, and then we can all have lunch. I think they're serving boiled leg of lamb with white sauce today—that's one of my favorites."

Harrison's mind began to race. Tony was probably right, he realized. If the Dark Shadow knew about the

Star of Persia—and given the attention the stone had aroused the previous evening, Harrison could not imagine that he didn't—then he would most likely attempt to steal it that night, before Lady Whitaker had a chance to take it abroad. If Harrison had wanted to steal the necklace, he certainly wouldn't have waited around for a month or more to see if it would return.

No point in permitting such a magnificent piece to go to France, where some other eager jewel thief could find it too tempting to ignore.

"What do you say, then, Harry? Are you up for a visit to your club?"

"Not today, Tony, I'm afraid," Harrison replied. "I have a meeting scheduled for this morning, and then there are a number of matters I must attend to this afternoon. Sorry about that." Tony was not a member of the Marbury Club, and therefore he relied upon Harrison to take him there as a guest. "Since Telford has gone upstairs with my mother, I'll see you to the door." He rose from the table.

"That's a pity." Tony looked genuinely disappointed as Harrison escorted him into the foyer. "What about tomorrow, then?"

"Tomorrow might be a possibility. We shall have to see."

"Very well. Are you planning to attend Lord and Lady Beckett's party tonight? It promises to be quite grand. If you go, I shall do my utmost to protect you from Lady Elizabeth," he joked. "Given her profound irritation with you last night, I fear you will need my protection."

"I don't know whether I'll be going or not," Harrison replied evasively. If he were going to break into Lord Whitaker's home that night, preparations had to be made. He did not want to waste time at some bloody party.

"Fine then, abandon me," his friend teased. "I shall tell all the men that you're off having a torrid night of pleasure with a beautiful young French dancer, and inform all the women that you are preoccupied with going over your plans for a massively expensive addition to your country estate. That will give them all something to talk about."

"I don't particularly want them talking about me," Harrison said, opening the front door.

"That's impossible," Tony pointed out. "You're titled, wealthy, relatively young, unattached, and from what I hear, women don't find your appearance altogether hideous. If you show up, they will gossip about how much you are currently worth, whom you are going to dance with, and who has a chance of ultimately becoming your bride. If you don't show up, they will gossip about how much you are currently worth, whom you danced with the last time they saw you, and what on earth you could be doing that could take precedence over attending such an important party. That is where I, as your friend, simply have to intervene. I don't want them to think you're at home padding about in your slippers, reading dusty books and sipping cocoa. It isn't good for your image, Harry," he finished, going out the door. "Trust me."

Harrison watched as Tony climbed into his waiting carriage. He didn't really give a damn about his image, he thought, closing the door. People could think whatever the hell they wanted about him—as long as they left his mother and the memory of his father alone.

And never found out the truth about the exploits of his past.

The Dark Shadow's reign of thievery was coming to an end, Harrison decided, filled with a sudden sense of urgency. If the thief were anything like him, he would not waste a moment trying to steal the exquisite Star of

Persia. Harrison would break into Lord Whitaker's home that night, wait for the Shadow to appear, and confront him a final time. And this time, he would make sure no one else got hurt.

Even if that meant Harrison had to kill the murdering bastard himself.

Chapter Eleven

HE LAY PERFECTLY STILL, HIS BREATH TRAPPED TIGHT within his chest, slowly counting.

He had already started to hold his breath three times before, and had been unable to contain it for his usual time. His weakness infuriated him. It was possible that the dusty, dank air trapped underneath the bed where he hid was too wretched for his lungs to tolerate. It didn't matter. Excuses were for cowards and weaklings. Each time he had failed he forced himself to start over, sucking in a great long draught of air as he forced his chest, lungs, and abdomen to relax. But his body was treacherous. It protested. It twisted and strained and grew taut. His chest swelled until his ribs ached, his face contorted and became hot and bloated. *A few seconds longer,* he commanded, fighting for dominance of his physical needs. *A few seconds more...*

His mouth betrayed him, exploding open like a sudden yawning tear. He inhaled a stale breath of air, furious and frustrated. What the hell was the matter with him? He was about to perform the perfect crime. Each of his preceding robberies had been but an insignificant rehearsal for what he was about to do. Yet here he was gasping like a newborn, unable to summon either the discipline or the focus to achieve one of his most basic skills. Was this a warning that he was somehow off tonight? Should he reconsider going through with his carefully cultivated plan? Was the uncertainty that had started to nag him after he wrestled with Bryden several nights earlier an indication that he was losing his edge?

He gave himself a mental shake. He was not losing a goddamn thing. As for his edge, it had been too keenly honed after far too many years of bitterness and anger to be even remotely blunted by some cursory physical discomfort. Suffering was a catalyst for strength and determination. It had enabled him to shed his pathetic little existence and transform himself into someone of accomplishment and renown. In that unexpected way, what had happened to his family had actually been good for him.

It was far easier to sever one's roots when the ground in which they lay was putrid.

He heard a noise. He strained to listen, his ears attuned to the farthest corners of the house he could manage from the confines of the guest bedroom he had chosen. Whatever the noise was, it did not repeat itself. He permitted himself to relax a little, settling back against the hardness of the floor.

His evening had been passed listening to the sounds of the household, from Lord and Lady Whitaker's animated arguments over what they needed to pack for their sojourn to Paris, to the irritated mutterings and frantic footfalls of their harried servants as they bustled to and fro. Eventually, a chilly calm descended upon the house. A series of polite "good nights" were exchanged. Doors were closed, water splashed in basins, beds squeaked. The soft orange light beneath the door was extinguished. And still he waited. For what he estimated was at least two hours more, until he could be sure that the warm waters of sleep had enveloped everyone within, save himself.

And, if God was generous, Bryden.

He flexed his fingers, slowly opening and closing his fists as he considered the two ways the night might unravel. The first was that he would simply break open the safe in Lord Whitaker's study, steal the Star of Persia, and make his way from the house with one of the most valuable diamonds in Europe tucked safely in his pocket. If that was all the evening held for him, he could hardly complain. His personal wealth would have increased severalfold in just one night. And the Dark Shadow could still go on to steal more whenever he felt it was necessary or even just amusing to do so.

He sighed. The idea of squeezing into more tight, dank spaces and waiting for hours on end to sneak out and nick some glittery bauble struck him as vaguely unappealing—even a bit torturous. Perhaps it was just his mood, or the fact that it was so bloody hot and close under the bed. More likely it was the recognition that each robbery had become progressively less exhilarating for him, despite the inherent danger and the exorbitant value of whatever he had stolen. If it were completely up to him, he would actually have preferred that this particular night be his last as the Dark Shadow.

Unfortunately, that was something that was beyond his control.

Suddenly restless, he shimmied out from under the bed, eager to get on with it. He stretched briefly, then reached under the bed and withdrew his carefully wrapped bundle of cracksman's tools. He didn't particularly like cracking safes, but it was a skill that could be learned like any other, and he figured he was about as good or even a bit better than any of the other cracksmen out there. At least he had the advantage of being able to afford the very best tools. He was also able to ascertain the degree of difficulty in opening a safe relatively quickly. If it didn't look as if he could do it within fifteen minutes, he didn't bother with it. There was always a jewel box somewhere holding a few pretty pieces that her ladyship hadn't bothered to give to her husband to lock up. He was quite certain, however, that Lord Whitaker would not have permitted such casual treatment of something as valuable as the Star of Persia. No, that stone could only be in Lord Whitaker's safe.

He had some work ahead of him.

He opened the door to the guestroom a crack, peered into the hallway, and listened. Silence. Satisfied that everyone was asleep, he slipped into the corridor, the black of his attire causing him to melt into the darkness. He made his way quickly down to the main floor. Then he crept along the walls, stealthy as a cat, searching for the door to Lord Whitaker's study. Once he had reached it he held still a moment, listening.

If Bryden had come, he was most likely in the study, lying in wait, just as he had been that night at Lord Pembroke's house. He set down his bag of tools and carefully withdrew his pistol from the waistband of his trousers. Then, moving with the silent grace for which the Dark Shadow was renowned, he eased the door open and pointed his gun at the darkness within, ready to fire at the slightest movement.

There was no one there.

A preliminary disappointment flushed through him. Not altogether convinced that he was alone, he entered the room, cautiously, his pistol ready. There was no great wardrobe in Lord Whitaker's study in which Bryden could hide. There was a modestly sized sofa at one end, but it sat upon feet that lifted it barely three inches off the floor. No space there for him to lie. His gaze darted to the drapes, which were closed and long enough to brush against the floor. Moving silently, he inched closer, studying the fall of the curtains. There were no bulges to suggest a man concealing himself behind them. A quick inspection of the floor revealed no feet peering out from beneath the fabric's hem. Turning, he advanced toward the desk, which was the final place a man might hide. His chest pounding, he leapt around it, his pistol pointed squarely into the black cavern beneath.

Empty.

He raked his gaze across the study once more, wary. He had been all but positive that Bryden would try to catch him. After all, Bryden had to have suspected that the Dark Shadow would want to steal the Star of Persia that night.

Or had his lordship thought that he would wait until Lord Whitaker returned from Paris?

He stood frozen, his pistol ready. Perhaps Bryden was still going to spring from somewhere. But after a span of relentless quiet, except for the ticking of a mantel clock somewhere in the dining room, he began to accept that Bryden was not there. He lowered his pistol and permitted himself to relax slightly, genuinely disappointed.

It was just another robbery, then.

He retrieved his tool kit from the hallway, closed the study door, then moved behind Lord Whitaker's desk. He set his pistol down upon its polished surface and opened his bag. He removed a small dark lantern, struck a match and lit the stubby candle within. A feeble yellow glow spat forth, barely enough to light a foot in front of the lantern, but ample for his purposes. He scanned the walls behind the desk, which were elegantly paneled in dark English oak. Sliding his fingers along the lower wainscoting, he felt for a slight variance in the spacing between the panels. After a moment he found it.

He gripped the wood trim at the top and pulled, causing the panel to swing open and expose the black iron safe behind. He moved his lantern closer, inspecting the formidable door's make, markings, and lock. It was a Chubb brand, well regarded for its strength and reliability. A quick study told him that it was an old model, however, manufactured before the improved locks that the company had introduced in 1860.

Thankfully, Lord Whitaker was not a slave to new-fangled technology.

He knocked lightly upon the safe door, trying to ascertain its depth and strength. The more recent safes were made heavier and more durable, with casings that were resistant to almost any drill. With the right tools and sufficient skill, however, the older models could be penetrated. He debated the best way to crack it. He considered using a peter-cutter, which fixed a center bit into the keyhole of the lock, after which a drill was attached. With sufficient strength and determination, the lock could be broken and the door forced. It could be a time-consuming job, however, and the results were not certain. Blowing the lock apart with gunpowder was another option, but that would be too noisy.

Ultimately, he removed his drill, center bit, a lock to hold the drill fast, a metal saw, and a heavy, stout crowbar called a jemmy. He would drill and cut an opening above the keyhole, making it just big enough for him to slip his hand through. Then he would reach inside, pull back the bolt of the lock and open the safe door.

A bit time-consuming, but beautifully simple and sure.

He carefully laid his tools out on the carpet before him, in the precise order in which he intended to use them. He rubbed his sleeve over the metal door, polishing the spot where he planned to drill. Then he fixed his bit onto his drill, pressed it hard against the black metal and began to turn the crank, driving its sharp point into the safe's cool surface.

It took him a little longer than he had anticipated to carve and chisel an opening sufficiently big for him to put his hand through. When he finally had succeeded, his mask and clothes were wet with perspiration, and his arms aching from exertion. None of that mattered, however. Filled with anticipation, he eased his hand into the hole he had cut and felt around for the mechanism of the lock. Then he closed his eyes and ran his fingers over it, learning its structure. Once he was sufficiently acquainted with the complex nooks and rounds, he found the bolt and gently pushed it back.

The door slipped open.

His heart pounded with triumph and relief. The hardest part was over. He reached deep into the safe's grotto, searching for the box or bag in which the magnificent Star of Persia would be resting.

"It isn't there," drawled a voice.

He froze.

Summoning calm, he gradually extracted his arm from the empty safe. He was in a squatting position, which was advantageous, he realized, squinting through the gloom at the sober-faced man who had managed to creep into the study without his knowledge as he labored on the safe. His fingers lightly grazed the carpet, grasping the jemmy. He stood slowly, concealing the iron bar behind his sleeve.

"I'm placing you under arrest," Lewis informed him, leveling his pistol upon him. "If you have any weapons, I advise you to drop them. You won't be harmed as long as you cooperate."

His captor could only be a police officer, he realized, to spew such utter nonsense with such grave sincerity. His lack of uniform suggested that he was an inspector. That made him feel a little better, at least.

He would have hated to think that he had been lured into a trap by some lowly, underpaid constable.

"My pistol is on the desk," he said quietly, making it sound as if he were resigned to his fate. And then, because he sensed his captor was quite sensibly wary of him, he added in a reassuring voice, "I won't fight you. I know when I've been bested."

Lewis stared at him guardedly. Lord Bryden was a gentleman, who probably considered his word to be infallible. Unfortunately, he was also a cold-blooded murderer, who had cut down two men without mercy during his illustrious career as a jewel thief.

Lewis did not intend to become his third victim.

"Step away from the desk, slowly," Lewis commanded, seeking to put some distance between the thief and his weapon. His voice was unnaturally high, betraying his nervousness. He cleared his throat. "Very good. Now don't move."

He had no experience in arresting a criminal as dangerous as the Dark Shadow. All he had to do was get the manacles on him, and then he could be sure the thief was under control. He was tempted to call for Constable Wilkins, who was positioned on the uppermost floor. Lewis had ordered him to watch all the servants' doors, in case the Dark Shadow decided to enter by way of the roof. Lewis knew that on occasion he had done so in the past. But not that night. Lewis wasn't sure how the thief had entered Lord Whitaker's home. At that particular point, it scarcely mattered. He had finally caught him. As long as the Dark Shadow didn't try to evade arrest, his deadly career was finally over.

Lewis's own career, on the other hand, was just about to begin.

"That was most clever of you, Inspector, the way you set this entire evening up," the Dark Shadow remarked, his voice laced with admiration. "I suspect you knew that the Star of Persia once belonged to my family. You must have realized I would want to get it back."

"I hoped it would capture your attention," Lewis admitted. "Once I suspected it was you who was responsible for the robberies, Lord Bryden, I began to look for a pattern—not in how you robbed, which was self-evident, but in what you robbed. I started to look more closely at your thefts of the past, and the history of those particular jewels. That was when I discovered they all had a unique link to one another. Each piece had been part of your estate before your father died—some of them for several generations. That is when I came up with the idea of getting Lord and Lady Whitaker to pretend they had the Star of Persia in their possession. I felt certain you would be eager to reclaim that particular piece."

"Very astute of you." His captive tilted his masked head in tribute.

Lewis nodded. He had not expected Lord Bryden to be quite so civilized in his arrest. That was the way of things amongst the aristocracy, he supposed. They might succumb to the baser acts of stealing and murder like any other common criminal. But when they realized they had been caught, they remembered who they were and conducted themselves accordingly.

Which was going to make Lewis's job considerably easier.

"If you'll just hold out your hands for me, I'm afraid I'm going to have to put these manacles on. It's just a formality, you understand," he added. "I'm required to do it."

"I understand," the Dark Shadow assured him. He obligingly raised one hand, patiently watching as his earnest inspector bent his head to fix the manacle onto his wrist.

Then he smashed him across the back of his skull

with his jemmy, causing Lewis to crumple heavily onto the floor.

He stood above him a moment, his weapon poised to bash him again if he so much as twitched. He didn't want to kill him, he reminded himself, fighting for control. After all, this inspector was now an essential component of finishing the game.

"Drop it," commanded a low voice suddenly, "before I blow your goddamn head off."

He looked up, startled. The room was still cloaked in shadows, relieved only marginally by the thin spit of light from his small lantern. It didn't matter. He knew the masked figure standing before him.

"Good evening, Bryden," he said, trying to contain the sheer exaltation pulsing through his veins. He was not to be denied after all. "I was worried you weren't going to show up."

"Drop your jemmy and move away from him," Harrison repeated, holding his pistol steady.

Once Harrison had seen Inspector Lewis slip into Lord Whitaker's study, he had thought that it was over. He had half-toyed with the idea of just stealing out of the house then and there, leaving the Metropolitan Police Force to enjoy the splendid victory of the Dark Shadow's arrest. But the moment he realized that there were no eager police constables lined up in the corridor to rush in and assist the intrepid detective, Harrison had hesitated. His own previous altercation with the jewel thief made him absolutely certain that his nemesis would not surrender easily. And so he had waited, wondering if Inspector Turner had any idea just how dangerous the man he had conspired to trap was.

The moment he heard the sound of a body crashing to the floor, he knew the inspector had lost.

"I must say, I'm glad you decided to come," the Dark Shadow remarked blithely, ignoring his order.

"What with the police and Lord and Lady Whitaker going to such trouble to lure me here, it would have been a shame if you missed it." He tapped his jemmy lightly against his palm.

Harrison inched closer, shrinking the distance between them. "You might as well drop your jemmy. I don't plan to get close enough to you to let you use it on me, and if you try to use it on the poor inspector, I promise I'll shoot you before you land a single blow."

"You're right," the Dark Shadow conceded, sighing. "It seems the game really has come to an end." He shrugged his shoulders, then leaned toward the desk, ostensibly to toss his jemmy on it.

Instead he grabbed his pistol and pointed it at Bryden.

"Now, this is a fascinating development, don't you think, Bryden?" His voice was taunting. "Once again we are equally matched—more or less. The only difference is that I have the ballocks to actually shoot you, whereas you, I'm afraid, are rather unsure as to whether or not you are desperate enough to shoot me."

Harrison raised his pistol higher, aiming at the bastard's head. "Don't put me to the test," he warned softly.

The Dark Shadow stared at him a moment, his gaze unfathomable. Then he suddenly shifted his aim from Harrison to the pathetically vulnerable inspector's head. "Drop your weapon now, Bryden," he snarled, "or I'll blast the handsome inspector's brains all over Lord Whitaker's impeccably woven Turkish carpet."

Harrison hesitated. He could not be sure that the Dark Shadow would actually carry through with his threat. But the memory of poor Lord Pembroke's butler filled his mind, a silver shaft protruding from his chest. There had been blood everywhere that night, leaking all over the rumpled white of the butler's nightshirt. No one could save him. Just as no one could save Inspector

Turner if the bastard standing over him blasted a gaping hole in his skull.

His body rigid with fury, Harrison reluctantly dropped his pistol.

"Excellent choice." The Dark Shadow nodded with approval. "And now if you'll forgive me, I really must be off." He edged his way to the windows, his weapon still leveled at the prone figure of Inspector Turner. "I'm sure you and the inspector here will have much to talk about after I leave." He parted the curtains and raised the sash.

"You can't get away," Harrison said. "There are constables posted outside watching the house. They'll shoot you long before you make it to the ground."

"Actually, I don't believe the inspector has much help in this," the Dark Shadow remarked, peering outside. "I had a good look around before I came in, and I didn't see anyone unusual hanging about. However, you're absolutely right, there's probably a constable or two lurking somewhere. Let's give them something interesting to find, shall we?"

He aimed his pistol at Inspector Turner's head.

Harrison roared with rage and lunged toward him, grabbing his arm just as the weapon discharged. The Dark Shadow heaved Harrison aside, then vaulted himself over the windowsill. By the time Harrison reached the window the thief was already nimbly making his way through the darkness of the garden behind the house.

Harrison swore and hoisted one leg over the sash. He would find him and kill him if it was the last thing he did, he vowed, dragging his other leg over. He would tear him apart with his bare hands—

"Stop or I'll shoot!"

A terrified young constable raced into the study

brandishing a quivering pistol. When he saw Inspector Turner's body, his face contorted with horror.

"It wasn't me!" Harrison realized it looked as if he was the one who had shot the inspector. "The Dark Shadow is getting away—"

"Shut your gob!" Constable Wilkins snapped, his pistol trembling. "You're under arrest, do you hear? And if you so much as sneeze, I'll kill you, do you understand?"

Harrison closed his eyes, fighting the mounting pressure that was starting to spread against the front of his skull. It was over, he realized. No one would believe that there had actually been another thief there with him, who had broken into Lord Whitaker's safe and then shot the inspector as he tried to arrest him. Besides, the police had already decided that Harrison was the Dark Shadow. That was why they had created the fantasy lure of the Star of Persia.

Someone had finally deciphered the evidence of his past.

He slowly climbed back into the study, feeling old and defeated.

And agonizingly aware that he had failed, leaving both Charlotte and Flynn hopelessly vulnerable.

Chapter Twelve

"THEY'VE CAUGHT HIM!"

Oliver swiftly took in Annie's panicked face and the wild tangle of hair falling down her shoulders. "Caught who, lass?"

"Is it Flynn?" asked Eunice fearfully.

"No—it's the Dark Shadow." Annie's expression was grave as she looked at Charlotte. "He's been arrested, Miss Charlotte. They've locked him up at Newgate. They're goin' to see him tried at the Old Bailey for thievin' an' murder."

Charlotte gripped the spoon she had been using to stir the batter for Eunice's pound cake. A sickening roar was pounding through her ears. "Are you sure?"

"There's talk of it all through London. They say he was caught last night tryin' to nick some rare diamond from a Lord Whitaker—only there weren't no diamond to be nicked. It was a trap laid by the peelers. The Shadow shot one of 'em, too—that same detective who came to the house the night ye brought him here. Shot him as he lay on the floor, helpless as a babe, the filthy wretch!"

The roaring in Charlotte's ears became overwhelming, making her nauseated. "Is he dead?"

"They say he ain't." Annie's eyes were smoldering with emotion. "I'm hopin' he ain't—even if he is a peeler."

"Why?" wondered Violet. "Did ye fancy him?"

"Course not!" Annie returned heatedly. "It just seems an awful shame to have a man like that snuff it while he's just tryin' to uphold the law."

Violet glanced at Ruby, clearly astonished.

"So who is the Shadow, then?" demanded Doreen. "Is he a swell?"

"Not just a swell," Annie replied, "he's an earl. Lord Bloody Bryden, they're callin' him now. Lives in a fancy home over on St. James Square, an' has a great country estate, too."

"I knew it!" Ruby exclaimed. "I can always tell by a man's hands. His was lovely clean—remember, Miss Charlotte? An' he talked so fine—"

"What would an earl who's got two fine houses be doin' runnin' about London at night tryin' to nip jewels?" Eunice frowned, confounded.

"Maybe he did it for a lark," suggested Violet. "Wanted to see what it was like to prig."

"An' after he did it once, he got a taste for it," added Ruby. "That happens sometimes—just like drink. Ye like it so much ye have to do it again, just to feel the same thrill."

"A shame," lamented Doreen, shaking her head. "If he'd but changed his ways after Miss Charlotte brought him here, he'd have been able to live out his days in peace an' quiet. Now it's the hangman's noose for him, an' for what? A bit o' brass, which he scarce needed."

"Maybe the lad had debts," Eunice suggested. "Maybe his real taste was nae for stealin', but for wagerin', which he could ill afford."

"Even so, he played an awful risky game. Especially when he had so much to lose. He must have known he couldna stay ahead o' the bobbies forever."

"Now, lass, ye mustn't blame yerself," soothed Doreen, suddenly noticing the pallor of Charlotte's cheeks and the taut skin of her knuckles. "After all, ye scarce had any time with him. I'm sure if ye'd had but a few days more—an' if he hadna been sufferin' that fierce headache, an' been well dosed with laudanum—ye'd have done yer best to change his ways. As for the inspector, well, ye had nae way of knowin' the Dark Shadow could actually murder. Ye said yerself he had nae but a hairbrush on him the night ye crossed paths."

"Seems the lad fell a long way in a short time," reflected Oliver grimly. "A dirk in the chest o' poor Lord Pembroke's butler, then a bullet in the inspector. I'd have nae thought he could be so cold." He paused a moment, hesitant. "Did ye know about Lord Bryden, lass?"

Charlotte regarded him helplessly, feeling as if her world were spinning completely beyond her control. The women in the kitchen regarded her with interest, perhaps thinking that Charlotte might have casually met Lord Bryden at one of the dinners or parties she had recently attended. They did not know of Charlotte's visit to Harrison's home several nights earlier. Charlotte had begged Oliver not to say anything to anyone about it, and of course he had honored his word.

"Did ye know who the Shadow really was?" Annie's voice was taut. It was apparent the shooting of Inspector Turner had upset her.

"Yes," Charlotte admitted. The air in the kitchen suddenly was thin and hot, and she couldn't seem to fill her lungs. "And everything that's happened—to Lord Pembroke's butler, and to Inspector Turner—is because of me."

"Dinna be daft," scolded Doreen impatiently. "Ye

saved the man's life by bringin' him here when ye did, or else he might have bled to death or been hanged. As for turnin' him over to the peelers, well, till then, he'd nae killed anyone—he'd only snatched a few bonny jewels."

"None of us thought he'd go on to murder." Eunice clucked her tongue. "Somehow he didna seem the type."

Shame was surging through Charlotte now, coupled with a suffocating despair. "I made him commit those robberies," she confessed miserably. "He was doing them for me."

Oliver regarded her incredulously. "What in the name o' Saint Andrew are ye blatherin' about?"

She had to tell them, she realized. There was no way around it. "When I realized that Lord Bryden was the Dark Shadow, I tried to blackmail him," she explained. "It was totally wrong, of course, but at the time I couldn't see that. I needed a great deal of money quickly, and all I could think was that Lord Bryden had the means to give it to me. I didn't know he would have to steal it, but I didn't really care. All I knew was that Flynn was in danger. I needed five thousand pounds to get him back, and Lord Bryden was the only one I knew who could get it for me without asking too many questions."

"Here now, what's this about Flynn?" Oliver's expression was incredulous. "I thought ye said he'd sent word that he'd moved on, an' we were nae to worry about him."

"I lied to you. I'm dreadfully sorry, Oliver, but I didn't know what else to do." Her words were coming faster now, her voice edged with hysteria. "I couldn't tell you the truth, because he said if I told anyone he would hurt Flynn, or one of you, or even Grace or Annabelle or Simon—"

"All right now, lass, take a breath," commanded Eunice, wrapping a strong arm around her. "Who said they would hurt Flynn?"

"If someone's been threatenin' ye or has hurt the lad, I'll beat their arse from here to Sunday!" raged Doreen, clutching her thin hands into fists.

"It weren't Jimmy, was it?" Annie's eyes were flashing with anger now. "Is that bruise ye got on yer cheek the other night from him?"

"Ye swore to me up and down that ye'd stumbled and fallen," interjected Eunice. "Is that nae the truth?"

Charlotte held fast to the worn wooden boards of the table. The past she had tried so hard to extract herself from, however imperfectly, was about to envelop her once more. In her life with Genevieve and Haydon, Boney Buchan had become a distant phantom, one who had left her physically and emotionally scarred, but who no longer had the power to hurt her. That had changed. Her attempt to keep him a secret and deal with him on her own, according to his rules, had been a mistake. And now both Flynn and Harrison were going to pay for it.

"Flynn has been taken by my father—my real father." Her voice was hollow and ashamed. "He goes by the name Boney Buchan. I haven't seen him for years, not since I was ten years old, and we were arrested for stealing. He went to prison in Scotland. Now he's here in London."

"And once he found ye he decided to squeeze ye for a few quid." Oliver's wrinkled face was contorted with fury.

Charlotte nodded. "He wants five thousand pounds. I told him I didn't have it, but he didn't believe me. He said he'd do something dreadful to my family if I didn't get it for him. So I went to Lord Bryden and I asked him for the money, in exchange for my silence. By then I had realized he was the Dark Shadow. He gave me eight hundred pounds, which was all he had in his possession at the time. But when I gave it to my father, he said wasn't enough, and then he told me that he'd taken Flynn. So I went back to Lord Bryden, and he promised to get the money for me. That's what he was doing at Lord Whitaker's. He was trying to steal enough for me to pay my father and get Flynn back."

"Ye should have told us lass," Oliver admonished sternly. "Ye know we would have done everythin' we could to help."

"I wanted to tell you, Oliver, but I was afraid," Charlotte explained. "My father can be very violent. He swore to me that if I told anyone about him, he'd do something dreadful—not just to me, but to Flynn or one of you."

"Right, then," said Annie, braced with the need to take action. "Tell us what this Boney Buchan looks like, an' me, Ruby, an' Violet will put out the word that we're lookin' for him. There's sure to be someone about who won't mind squeakin' on him in exchange for an ale or a couple o' meat pies."

"Once we find him, we'll get Flynn, an' then he won't hold nothin' over you," Ruby continued. "I've a few friends I can ask for help, too, to make him understand he ain't to bother you again."

"I don't think anyone can make him understand that." Charlotte's voice was strained. "He's very violent."

"So are half the men in St. Giles—and half the women, too!" scoffed Annie, unimpressed. "Yer da must be near fifty by now, ain't he?"

"I don't really know," Charlotte admitted. "I suppose so."

"Then he ain't near so strong as he was when ye was just a girl," Annie decided.

"Annie's right," Ruby agreed. "Just look at who he's threatenin'—a scrawny, half-starved lad an' a lady with a crippled leg." She snorted in disgust. "It's disgraceful, is what it is. Some of the lads I know would be happy to give him a proper fanning just for that."

"To say nae of what yer brothers will think once they find out," added Eunice. "I canna imagine Jack would leave much of him standin' if he ever got his hands on him."

"Jack mustn't ever know," Charlotte objected. "Please, Eunice—we can tell Simon and Jamie, but not Jack. He would be furious if he learned that my father has been threatening me. He might do something terrible—something that might land him in jail."

"The lass is right," Oliver agreed. "Simon and Jamie will keep a cool head, but Jack won't. 'Tis in the lad's blood to swing his fists first an' talk later."

"It scarce matters, since he's still away on one of his voyages," Doreen observed. "I dinna think he expected to be back till next month, at the earliest."

"Fine, then, I'll ride over to Mayfair and tell Simon, Jamie, Annabelle, and Grace what's happened." Oliver rose from the table. "An' we'll send a note to Miss Genevieve and his lordship, who are visitin' in the country, and ask them to take the next train to London straight away."

"If they get the note this evening, they could be here by tomorrow afternoon," Eunice reflected. "Then we can all decide how we're goin' to handle Boney Buchan."

The fierce determination and energy filling the warm kitchen flooded through Charlotte, making her feel stronger. Now that the news about her father was in the open, the crushing burden she had been carrying since he had first accosted her had suddenly eased a little. She had been wrong to try to deal with him on her own, she realized. She had thought that by keeping his vile threats a secret, she was protecting the people she cared for. Instead she had left them all exposed, increasing her father's ability to hurt them. She would not make the same mistake again.

"I'll go with you to Mayfair, Oliver, so I can explain everything to my brothers and sisters myself," Charlotte decided, rising from her chair. "But first we have to make a stop at Newgate."

Oliver regarded her uncertainly. "Are ye sure that's wise, lass? If the police suspect ye've known the Shadow was Lord Bryden—"

"Wise or not, I am going to see Lord Bryden." She swallowed thickly, trying to control the emotions churning through her. "I want to know how he is faring. I want to apologize for putting him into such a terrible position. And I want to see if there is anything I can do to help him. I'm sorry, Annie," she apologized, sensing the girl's outrage, "but the Lord Bryden I know is very different from the man who was arrested last night. I cannot explain why he shot Inspector Turner when he was helpless—if that is indeed true. But whatever he did—whyever he did it—there's something I have to tell him . . ." She stopped suddenly.

"That's all right lass." Troubled by her obvious distress, Oliver glanced uncertainly at Eunice and Doreen, who both nodded.

"All right then," he conceded, reluctant. "I'll fetch the carriage and take ye to Newgate, if that's where ye're fixin' to go."

NEWGATE PRISON WAS A GRIM-LOOKING FORTRESS OF austere granite, the mere sight of which could ignite a flame of fear deep within the bosoms of even the most law-abiding of London's citizenry. There had been a prison standing on its misery-soaked site from the early twelfth century, although it had been rebuilt in 1770 and again some ten years later. For nearly a hundred years since it had enjoyed the dubious distinction of being London's chief prison, and until 1868 had been a favorite place for finding the foulest entertainment. To that year all executions at Newgate were carried out in view of the public, and they proved wildly popular.

Every Monday morning at eight o'clock a veritable tidal wave of shoving, shouting men, women, and children would swarm the road outside the Debtor's Door, to watch the parade of despondent souls condemned to be executed that day. Murderers were hanged on Monday, and they proved a far greater attraction than watching those being hanged for burglary, forgery, or sodomy writhe and kick at the end of a rope. When the lever of the gallows was pulled the condemned dropped only about one or two feet, which made it almost certain their deaths would take several minutes. For those flush in the pocket, a seat could be found overlooking the gallows for as much as ten pounds—a fortune, but generally agreed upon as well worth it. Booths selling food and drink were set up around the scaffold, and vast quantities of warm ale, watery brandy, and greasy pies made of questionable meats were consumed, the dank air heavy with merry camaraderie.

Unfortunately for those who loved nothing better than a good hanging, a change in the laws during the 1830s limited the crimes punishable by death. In 1868 public hangings were abolished altogether, putting an end to what the socially conscious of British society argued was a grotesque form of amusement. After that, murderers were hanged in private, their bodies discreetly buried in unmarked graves within Newgate's virtually impenetrable walls.

For that small boon, Harrison was supremely grateful.

He leaned against the cold stone wall of his cell, his arms folded across his chest, staring up at the pale wash of sunlight filtering through the heavy black bars of his tiny window. The furnishings surrounding him were spare: a rickety stool that threatened to collapse beneath his weight, a table bearing a badly cracked jug and basin, a roll of gray bedding, a shelf bearing a Bible, prayer book, plate, and mug, and finally, in a corner, a chipped and stained chamber pot. There was an iron candlestick embedded in the wall, bearing the half-melted remains of a cheap yellow candle. Spartan furnishings by any measure, and certainly a significant departure from the luxuries to which he was accustomed.

Strangely, he found himself not terribly bothered by the rough simplicity of his cell. There was nothing there of beauty or color save the lemony-gold beam of sunlight, which trickled through the window with cheerful abandon, utterly oblivious to the fact that the architects who had designed and redesigned Newgate over the centuries had clearly intended for each cell to be relentlessly somber. The sunshine cast its golden veil across the bleakness before splashing against the worn stone floor, the stripes of the bars breaking it into smaller segments that could be counted and contemplated as they shifted in size and brightness over the course of the morning. Staring at that playful puddle of light had given Harrison the means to calm himself and focus his mind, to set aside the rage and frustration that had consumed him from the time of his arrest to his arrival at Newgate.

When he had first trudged through the prison's endless narrow corridors, through countless locked gates and iron-fortified doors, his hands shackled helplessly behind his back, he had been overwhelmed with a fury and despair unlike anything he had ever known. A dull ache had started to seep through the front of his skull, and his vision began to blur. He knew then that if he succumbed to one of his incapacitating headaches, for which no laudanum would be provided, he would truly be lost. He forced himself to breathe deeply, even though the air was fetid, and worked to calm the rapid pounding of his heart, which seemed to be in tandem with the throbbing in his brain.

To his amazement, he was able to hold the headache at bay.

He was able to enter his cell, which his decrepit little warder proudly assured him was one of the better ones, assigned only to those prisoners of the more respectable classes like himself who had the ill fortune to spend time at Newgate, and look as if he gave it his discriminating approval. He was able to remain standing while the warder removed his manacles and chatted away about how all the prisoners used to be kept in common wards until Newgate was redesigned into a single-cell system, and how he was lucky enough to have his ward all to himself, Newgate being decidedly short of respectable prisoners on that day. Harrison was able to stagger to his bedding and lower himself onto it, to keep his breathing steady while squeezing his eyes shut, telling himself that he would not, *would not,* permit his goddamn treacherous body to succumb to its infernal weakness.

Incredibly, his headache had been suppressed.

It had tormented him, certainly, for several hours, but not to the extent that had long been its norm. It had never progressed to anything more than a pounding pain that was unpleasant, even nauseating, but scarcely debilitating, comparatively speaking.

On a day when his very life was crashing down around him, he found that small, unexpected victory enormously gratifying.

Once his pain had abated, he had been able to think more clearly. He realized then that he would have to shackle his emotions, tightly leashing both his anger and his fear, so he could assess his situation and determine what, if anything, could be done to improve it. It was difficult, but not impossible.

The beam of sunlight had helped immeasurably.

His greatest concern at that moment was for his mother, Charlotte, and Flynn. He had faith enough in Telford to know that his butler would never reveal to his mother what he had undoubtedly learned by now: that Harrison had been arrested for burglary and murder. His arrest had occurred too late to make the early edition of the newspapers, but London would be rampant with talk of it, which meant that every gossiping servant, delivery person, and newspaper reporter would be hammering on his door, demanding to know if it were true, pleading for some titillating details. Telford would protect his mother for as long as was possible, making some excuse or other for Harrison's absence, which she would most likely accept, at least for a short while.

Harrison planned to send letters to Margaret and Frank, telling them what had happened and asking them to come as quickly as possible. Although Harrison hated the thought of disrupting their lives, there was no help for it. Frank would have to leave America and focus on learning the details of running the properties and managing the investments. If Harrison's trial went badly, his younger brother might well end up being the next Earl of Bryden. He tried not to think about that. And Margaret would have to leave her children for a period to help tend to her mother, who would be devastated when she finally learned that Harrison had been arrested for murder.

For the first time he could remember, he found himself hoping that his mother's delusional state continued to separate her from reality. Somehow that seemed a kinder fate than facing the truth.

His other great concern was for Charlotte and Flynn. Harrison's barrister was to have arranged for the money he had requested and brought it to his home that morning. After his arrest, Harrison had sent word to Mr. Brown to meet him at Newgate instead. When he arrived, Harrison would direct him to discreetly take the money to Charlotte, along with a note he had yet to write.

There was much he wanted to tell her.

He wanted her to know that he wasn't the thief and murderer she believed him to be—at least, not entirely. He also wanted to warn her that under no condition was she to face her father alone. Finally, he wanted to make her understand how much she had come to mean to him, despite the fact that they had known each other such a brief time. That she was stronger and more inspiring to him than any woman he had ever known. That her courage, her determination, and her selflessness had shone a brilliant light into his life, at a time when he had felt surrounded by bitter gloom. All this he wanted to tell her, and more. But to do so would only implicate her, should the letter fall into the wrong hands. And so he would merely pen a brief note, saying it had been a pleasure to meet her, and wishing her all the best with her refuge house.

Not even the cleverest of prosecutors could extract much incriminating evidence out of that.

A key scraped in the lock, and the heavy wooden door swung open. Reluctantly, Harrison tore his gaze away from the shaft of sunlight. The emaciated form of his warder, Mr. Digby, with his stringy yellow hair and his pitifully stooped frame, clad in an ill-fitting frock coat and striped trousers that seemed far too fine for wearing while skulking around a prison, entered his cell.

Behind him limped a remarkably alive Inspector Lewis Turner.

"Inspector Turner here to see ye, yer lordship," announced Digby solemnly, holding himself as straight as his stooped back would permit.

The warder's generously furrowed face was sober, and Harrison thought he detected just a hint of pride in his flaccid-lidded eyes, as he waited for Harrison to acknowledge his announcement. It was clear that Mr. Digby may have once aspired to something better than being a prison warder, and was consequently impressed by both the social stature and notoriety of his latest prisoner.

"Thank you, Digby," said Harrison politely, his tone betraying none of the relief he felt at seeing that the inspector had survived the Dark Shadow's assault. He was about to add "That will be all," more because he thought the man might appreciate it than because he thought Digby might actually hover around waiting to see if he could provide something further to his charge, but Inspector Lewis quashed the opportunity with a curt dismissal.

"Leave us," Lewis commanded abruptly, banging the walking stick upon which he leaned.

Digby cast a questioning glance at Harrison.

"That will be all, Digby," Harrison said to him. "Thank you."

"Yes, yer lordship," the warder replied, bowing his head slightly. "If ye need me, all ye need do is call."

With that he backed his way out of the cell and turned the key once more, leaving Harrison and Lewis alone.

"Inspector Turner, I am delighted to see you looking so well," Harrison remarked cordially. "Won't you sit down?" He gestured at the decrepit wooden stool.

Lewis glared at him and stayed where he was. In fact he would have liked very much to sit down, but he wasn't about to accept hospitality from the bastard who bashed him on the head and then shot him while he lay helpless and unconscious. Fortunately, Bryden was an extremely poor shot—either that, or the darkness of the room had hindered his ability. Whatever the reason, the bullet had only entered the upper part of Lewis's thigh. After an interminable amount of poking, prodding, and stitching at the hands of a surgeon who would have been better suited to a career in butchery, Lewis had been told he was extremely lucky and that he should take to his bed for a week, to rest and give the wound a chance to heal.

Instead Lewis had demanded a walking stick.

"I see you've got your warder placed firmly under your heel," he observed acidly, detesting the way the old man had acted as if Lord Bryden were some kind of hero. "I suppose compared to most of the scum he's had to guard over the years, you're almost royalty."

"Maybe I'm just one of the few prisoners who have ever treated him with a modicum of respect," Harrison countered. "You might want to try it one day your-self—you'd be amazed at the results."

Lewis regarded him evenly. "Don't you dare lecture me, Bryden. You're the one who has spent the better part of his life breaking into people's homes like a com-mon thief, pilfering jewels and murdering people. If you're under the illusion that you are somehow better than me because you were born with a title, then you are sadly mistaken."

"Forgive me. I would never profess to believe that I was better than you, Inspector Turner. You are a man of education and intellect, and you have a singular deter-mination which I happen to admire. I have little doubt that if you work hard, your career will be nothing short of brilliant. I know of very few men born to titles who can make the same claim."

Lewis stared at him guardedly. Was Lord Bryden ac-tually complimenting him?

"Why did you do it, Bryden?" he demanded, curious. "I understand that when you started, years ago, it was because your father had squandered your fortune. You were determined to get some of it back, even if that meant stealing it. I'm sure you believed you were only reclaiming what by right was already yours. What made you start again? I've investigated your finances, and unless there is something buried in there that not even your bankers are aware of, your financial situation is sound. Why start running about in the middle of the night stealing jewels, most of which you could have afforded to buy if you wanted to?"

Harrison stared impassively at the rectangles of light upon the floor. His situation was impossible. If he admitted to the thefts he had committed sixteen years earlier, then he would be inextricably tied to the more recent rash of thefts, two murders, and one attempted murder, which could only be punishable by hanging, his status as an earl notwithstanding. Somehow he did not think Inspector Lewis would accept his explanation that yes, he had committed those earlier thefts, and yes, he had been present at several of the recent thefts, including the one the previous night where the inspector had unfortunately been shot, but only because he was actually trying to capture the man who was running about pretending to be him—or, more accurately, pretending to be the man he had once been. It sounded preposterous even to him, for God's sake. Therefore his only choices were to deny everything, which was ridiculous, given that he was caught trying to climb out Lord Whitaker's window the previous night, or say nothing, which would be interpreted as a sullen admission of guilt.

Either way, the outcome was the same.

"Tell me something, Inspector Turner," Harrison began, still staring at the play of sunlight against the floor. "Was there ever a moment during your investigation in which you thought the evidence didn't quite make sense? Where you were faced with a number of apparent facts that didn't fit together?"

Lewis was careful to keep his expression composed. In truth, there were several elements of evidence that did not make sense to him. He thought back to Lady Pembroke's bedchamber, with its overturned furniture, the black woolen cap and mask left lying under the bed, and the fact that the bedcovers had been neatly rearranged despite the fact that the thief had not yet returned the jewelry chest key to its hiding place. All those things had bothered him. Despite the fact that he had finally solved his case, they still struck him as perplexing.

"Many investigations present evidence which at times can seem odd or conflicting," he allowed. "It is the investigator's challenge to sift through it all and make sense of it."

"And do you believe you have done that, Inspector Turner?" Harrison continued to study the floor as if it were a magnificent work of art. "Do you think that you have made sense of every scrap of evidence?"

"Not entirely," Lewis admitted. "I still have some questions."

"And that must trouble you a little," Harrison mused. "Because you know I have the funds to hire the most brilliant defense lawyers in London, and if there are any holes or inconsistencies in your investigation, however small or insignificant they may seem, my lawyers will focus a great deal of attention on them. Which could be problematic for your case, and even a little embarrassing for the police."

"You were found in black clothes and a mask in Lord Whitaker's study last night, trying to escape out the window. That is a fact."

"One I don't deny."

"And you broke into Lord Whitaker's safe with

your safecracking equipment searching for the Star of Persia, all of which we have as evidence."

"Now, that, I'm afraid, I do have to deny," Harrison said. "I can quite honestly say that I have never broken into a safe in my life, although there have been times when the lock on my own safe has been a bit recalcitrant and I banged upon the door a few times."

"Then you did a marvelous job of just pretending to break into the safe, given that you drilled a hole right through it and got the door open. You also struck me over the head with a jemmy and then shot me."

"Did you actually see me shoot you?"

"Of course not! You knocked me unconscious first."

"Forgive me for asking, Inspector, but if I knocked you unconscious, why on earth would I need to shoot you?"

"I don't know," snapped Lewis, suddenly irritated. His leg was throbbing like the devil, he hadn't slept more than a few hours in the last few days, and he had no bloody patience for whatever game Bryden was playing. "I suppose because you were afraid I might identify you."

"Could you have identified me?"

Lewis was about to assure him that he could, but stopped. Bryden had been wearing his cap and mask when Lewis came upon him in Lord Whitaker's study, he reminded himself. "No," he reluctantly admitted.

"Why not?"

"You know very well why not. You still had your mask and cap on."

"So if you didn't see my face and you were knocked unconscious, what could possibly possess me to shoot you?"

"Maybe because you are a bloodthirsty son of a bitch who enjoys killing people."

"Maybe," Harrison allowed. "That is certainly a possibility. But if I was so intent on killing you just for my own vile pleasure, and you were lying unconscious on the floor, how is it that I missed so completely and only managed to strike you in what I presume, given your limp and your reliance on a walking stick, was your leg?"

"I guess you are a very bad shot," Lewis returned acridly. "Which is rather fortunate for me."

Harrison lifted his gaze and regarded him seriously. "It was very fortunate for you, Inspector Turner, that whoever shot you did not strike you in the head, as might well have been the case, or in a far more vital area than your leg. What is curious, however, is that if this was the same man who shot poor Lord Haywood on the steps of Lord Chadwick's home from a distance of some twenty paces, it would appear that in actual fact he is a very good shot. Which begs the question: Why did he miss killing you? What interfered with his aim?"

"Constable Wilkins entered the room as you shot me. I suppose he distracted you."

"Did Constable Wilkins tell you that?"

"He told me he came in and found you trying to climb out the window."

"Then it wasn't him who distracted whoever shot you, was it? By his own admission, Constable Wilkins came in after the pistol was fired."

"What the hell are you trying to say, Bryden?" demanded Lewis. "Are you asking me to believe that you are merely a concerned citizen who just happened to be in Lord Whitaker's study last night? Am I supposed to think that you're some kind of bored aristocrat who goes about at night in a mask trying to track down criminals, and that you were really there because you were trying to capture the Dark Shadow?"

"I'm only asking you to continue to look at the evidence," Harrison replied seriously. "You're an educated man, Inspector. You have been trained to examine, to analyze, and above all, to ask questions—especially about things that don't make sense. And I know there are a number of things in this investigation that trouble you. Yes, I was in Lord Whitaker's home last night. Yes, I was wearing a mask. But I was there for the same reason you were. To find the Dark Shadow, and see that he was finally caught and brought to justice before he had a chance to steal or kill again."

"How terribly noble. Forgive me for being somewhat incredulous, but why would you do such a thing?"

"The Dark Shadow is a menace to society. He needs to be caught."

"Why not just let the police do it? That's my job, not yours."

"I did let you do it, Inspector, for three months. But unfortunately, you failed. And as the Dark Shadow grew bolder, I realized you needed some help."

"That was very generous of you, Bryden." Lewis's tone was laced with sarcasm. "But that still doesn't explain why you were suddenly so interested in this particular case. London is full of thieves and murderers. Why not try to capture one of the thousands of other culprits threatening our citizens' welfare? Why was your interest exclusively in the Dark Shadow?"

"My reasons are not your concern."

"I disagree. If you're asking me to believe that you're innocent in all this, that you are nothing more than an honest, law-abiding earl who was willing to go to the trouble of breaking into people's homes so he could help capture one of London's most notorious criminals, you need to tell me why. No one does anything without motivation, Bryden. Greed, lust, passion, fury, vengeance—take your pick. There's always a reason. Why would you go to so much trouble—not to mention risking your life—in order to capture a criminal who had nothing to do with you?"

"Sometimes we have to do things whether we want to or not. This was one of those times."

"And just what the hell is that supposed to mean?"

"It means I'm relieved you didn't have your brains splattered all over Lord Whitaker's carpet, Inspector, as might have been the case." He turned away, fixing his gaze upon the shifting yellow bars of sunlight once again.

Lewis stared at him, angry and frustrated. What kind of game was Bryden playing with him? Did he honestly expect Lewis to believe that he was innocent? It was ridiculous. And yet some of the questions he raised were troubling. More, he didn't get the sense that Lord Bryden was lying.

While that was hardly evidence of his innocence, it was definitely unsettling.

He began to limp toward the door, then stopped. "By the way, this is yours, is it not?" He casually fished a linen square from one of his pockets.

Harrison barely glanced at the handkerchief in Lewis's hand. "Regretfully, no."

"Why do you say 'regretfully'?" wondered Lewis, watching him closely.

"Because I don't have a handkerchief here, and I could use one." His tone was irreverent as he continued, "Despite Digby's heroic efforts to keep this place clean, I do believe some of these surfaces could benefit from a good dusting."

"Then I'm sorry I can't give you this one. Unfortunately, it was found on the ground outside Lord Pembroke's house on the night his butler was killed, and therefore is evidence. I only thought it might be yours because it has the letter *B* stitched into one corner.

Would you like to take a closer look at it? Perhaps you dropped it while you were—"

"It isn't mine, Inspector."

"Of course." Lewis stuffed the handkerchief back in his pocket. "You have another visitor. Miss Charlotte Kent. She's waiting in one of the offices downstairs."

Harrison was careful to keep his expression neutral. He could not permit Inspector Turner to think that he had any relationship with Charlotte, or her association with him might incriminate her.

"I barely know Miss Kent, Inspector. And while I appreciate her desire to visit, given her preoccupation with reforming criminals, I do not believe that Newgate is an appropriate place for a lady. Also, I do not find myself currently in the mood for a righteous sermon on morality and punishment. Kindly give her my regards and send her away."

Lewis was impressed. But for the faint tightening of the muscle in Lord Bryden's jaw, he might almost have believed his performance. "I already told her she shouldn't see you. I warned her that people might misconstrue her desire to visit, which could be damaging for her reputation. Would you like to know what she said?"

Harrison sighed, as if he found the subject tedious. "She's obviously here because she thinks I'm the Dark Shadow, and she'd like to have a hand in reforming my black soul before it's too late. Tell her I'm not interested—"

"She said her reputation had already been in tatters for years, and that she'd been in jail before and didn't think there was anything in Newgate that she hadn't already seen," Lewis interjected. "She was quite adamant that she wasn't leaving without seeing you, and she warned me that you would likely refuse her. She said to tell you that she didn't care if she had to wait here all night—she was more than prepared to do so."

Harrison rolled his eyes, affecting an air that said he found well-meaning spinsters with the reformation of souls on their minds incalculably tiresome.

"Very well, Inspector," he relented, masking the vortex of emotions surging through him beneath a cloak of patent indifference. "Send Miss Kent in if you must."

Chapter Thirteen

DESPAIR GRIPPED CHARLOTTE LONG BEFORE THE ANcient little warder named Digby finally appeared.

She had sat for nearly two hours in a bleak office on the ground floor of Newgate, waiting for Inspector Turner to make whatever arrangements he deemed necessary for her to be taken to Harrison's cell. The chamber was a waiting room for visitors, in which they were required to sign a book detailing the date and time of their visit, and the unfortunate prisoner they wished to see. After that they could choose between one of two hard chairs, and contemplate their surroundings. There was little to contemplate, other than a battered desk littered with papers and a shelf exhibiting somber facial casts of two of Newgate's most notorious murderers.

As the minutes dragged into hours, a terrible helplessness seized her. Her mind retreated to the prison governor's office in Inveraray, Scotland, where she had sat as a filthy, tattered child of ten and waited in terror to find out what was to become of her. Whatever it was, she had been certain it was going to be dreadful. She had heard stories of children being hanged for theft, or strapped to a whipping table and flogged until the pale flesh on their backside was broken and weeping blood. Someone had said they only did that to boys, but Charlotte wasn't sure if they meant whipping or hanging, or both. The judge she had appeared before a few days earlier had called her a disgrace, and had sentenced her to thirty days in prison, to be followed by three years in a reformatory school in Glasgow. Charlotte didn't know where Glasgow was, or what a reformatory school was, or if she was to be whipped once she got there. The woman who shared her cell had said it was just like prison except they forced the children to work night and day until they died from exhaustion—a blessing, the woman assured her, since living there was so unbearable. And as Charlotte had sat shivering, her injured leg stiff and pulsing with pain, her shoulders hunched against the damp cold that pervaded every inch of Inveraray jail, she had felt the same kind of overwhelming desolation that she felt now, some fifteen years later.

Except on that day, years earlier, the door had opened and Genevieve had walked in. She had taken Charlotte's grubby hands in her own clean ones, had brushed the matted tangle of her hair off her face, and had leaned down low, so that her gentle eyes met Charlotte's.

And Charlotte had felt the faintest flicker of hope, that maybe, just maybe, God was watching her after all.

"This is it, my lady," said Digby solemnly after leading her through a miserable warren of grim corridors. Once again he sorted through an enormous ring of keys.

Charlotte bit her lip and waited as the warder held a heavy iron key up to the faint cast of leaden light filtering through the stone passage. He squinted at it, ran his gnarled fingers over its black contours, squinted at it some more, then rejected it in favor of another. He stared intensely at this one also, examining it with dark little eyes that nearly disappeared beneath the crumpled folds of his lids. Finally satisfied, he inserted it into the lock and opened the door.

"Miss Kent is here to see you, my lord," Digby announced with a ceremonious bow.

Harrison turned from the disintegrating light from the window to see Charlotte appear at the entrance of his cell. For one long, frozen moment, everything stopped. All he wanted was to pull her into his arms, to feel her small, soft form pressing against him as he buried his face into the fragrant silk of her hair, losing himself to her gentleness and strength and hope, which was so at odds with the stark wretchedness of his surroundings.

Instead he remained where he was, affecting as indifferent an expression as he could muster.

"Good afternoon, Miss Kent," he said politely, his tone cool and markedly formal. "I must confess, I had not expected the pleasure of your company in this desolate place."

That remark was for Digby's benefit. Although he sensed the old warder actually liked him, he did not want to give anyone the slightest indication that his relationship with Charlotte went beyond anything than a superficial acquaintance.

"I must apologize for the austerity of my surroundings," he continued mockingly. "Please do come in— would you care for some refreshment?"

Charlotte shook her head, bewildered by his indifferent gaze, his dry tone, his apparent utter lack of pleasure at seeing her.

"Oh, come now, you must have something," Harrison insisted. "Mr. Digby, is there not something you could bring Miss Kent, to refresh her after what I am certain must have been a most tiring journey and wait? A little tea, perhaps, and maybe a sweet biscuit or two? I shall be able to compensate you handsomely for any trouble you go to when my barrister arrives later today."

The mention of compensation made Digby's eyes swell from their voluminous folds. "I can boil tea," he assured Harrison earnestly. "With milk, too, if ye want. I've biscuits as well—me own biscuits, that me wife makes for me tea."

"Thank you, but no." Charlotte's stomach was churning now. She thought she was going to be sick.

"The biscuits is fresh," Digby added, trying to convince her. "With ginger an' currants. An' I'll be sure to find ye a nice clean china cup for yer tea, so ye needn't worry about that, miss." He regarded her imploringly. It was clear he wanted to perform this task—whether for the money or because he enjoyed the sensation of appearing more a valued gentleman's butler than a detested prison warder, Harrison could not be sure.

"That sounds splendid," Harrison said enthusiastically, as if the warder had offered to fix a spectacular feast for them. "Do bring it, Digby. I'm certain once Miss Kent sees your wife's biscuits she won't be able to refrain from trying one of them."

"Yes, yer lordship." Digby's mouth split into a grateful smile, revealing a pitiful jumble of yellow teeth. "I've got to go down to the kitchen, but I won't be but a few minutes." He scurried out into the corridor, his weighty ring of keys jangling as he locked the cell door behind him.

Harrison waited until the sound of those keys had retreated down the stone corridor, past the opening and closing of the heavy oak door that sealed his ward off from the rest of the prison. Only then, when he was utterly certain that he and Charlotte were alone, did he permit the mask of his insouciance to fall.

"You shouldn't be here, Charlotte," he began, his voice low and urgent. "I have told Inspector Turner that

I barely know you, and suggested that you are only here in the interests of reforming yet another lost criminal soul. If you happen to come upon him, do everything you can to reinforce that impression."

He began to pace, ignoring his overwhelming desire to touch her, speaking quickly as he ran through the list of things she needed to know.

"I have arranged for the money for your father. My barrister will have it delivered to you after he meets me here later today. I had originally planned that he would take it to you directly, but since you have come here, that is no longer wise. I can't be sure that Inspector Turner won't have him followed, and I don't want you to be associated with me any more than you already are. I will instruct my barrister to return to his office for the remainder of the day, and arrange to have a series of items delivered tomorrow to various addresses by a half dozen couriers instead. If Turner assigns just one man to watch him, which is most likely, by the time he sees the couriers departing it will be too late for him to summon assistance to have them followed as well. What is absolutely vital is that you do not under any circumstances try to give the money to your father on your own." He raked his hand through his hair, feeling rushed and agitated.

"Since I cannot be with you, I want you to swear to me that you will enlist the help of your family. If you won't ask Lord Redmond to go with you, then take both your brothers, Jamie and Simon—and take old Oliver, too, just to be sure Buchan understands he is outnumbered. If your brothers are good with their fists, fine, but if they are not, then at least one of them should carry a pistol, even if they don't intend to use it except for show. Your father is a violent man, and he needs to be dealt with in a way he understands. Tell Oliver to bring that dirk of his as well. Finally, do not under any circumstances put yourself within reach of Buchan's grasp. Let one of your brothers give him the money. But don't let them give Buchan any money until after Flynn is safely restored to you. We don't want Buchan deciding to hang on to Flynn a little longer, thinking that maybe he could squeeze a few more pounds from you." He stopped suddenly, hoping he had covered everything. "When Digby returns with the tea, tell him you have to leave immediately. You can't be in my company a second longer than necessary—it will only give people reason to talk. Do you understand?"

Charlotte stared at him in stricken silence, fighting the tears threatening to leak onto her cheeks.

Harrison regarded her helplessly, taking in the fragility of her stance, the paleness of her skin, the acute pain shimmering in her eyes. The sight of her suffering sliced into him like a blade, severing the cool rationality he had fought so hard to maintain from the moment she had stepped into his cell. His mouth was dry and his body was aching with the need to hold her, to feel the soft beat of her heart against his chest, and the coral silk of her lips against his mouth. Unable to bear the hopelessness that stretched between them, he closed the distance in two strides, wrapped his arms around her and crushed his mouth to hers, enveloping her in his strength as she clung desperately to him.

He tasted her deeply, exploring every sweet secret of her mouth as he plunged his hands into her copper-colored hair, drinking in her passion and her tenderness as he returned it with his own, trying to make her understand with his touch what he had completely failed to tell her with words.

I love you, he said silently, running his fingers across her cheeks, down the smooth column of her throat, over the soft curves of her body. *And if I could, I would spend the rest of my life showing you,* he pledged, raining kisses upon her neck as he pulled her protectively against him, until they were molded together. *And I would never let a moment go by where you didn't feel it,* he vowed desperately, burying his face into the swell of her breasts, where he could feel the frantic pounding of her heart against his cheek. He raised his head to kiss her again, overwhelmed with desire coupled with excruciating sadness. He wanted to take her, to lay her down upon the hard gray bedding and lose himself to her beauty and courage, to let her rescue him from the misery of his surroundings and the wretchedness of his life. And in return, maybe he could make her understand the depths of his love for her, which had started the moment she pushed a silver hairbrush at him, looking at him as if she believed he were capable of taking on the world.

He had wounded her; he understood that. He could not be sure that he wasn't hurting her more by showing the depths of his feelings for her. He hoped not. But time was their enemy. And so he slowed his kisses, fighting to calm the desire within him, and that which he had roused within her. Easing his hold upon her, he gently moved his lips across her cheeks, her mouth, her eyes, until finally he could hold her without devouring her.

"I'm sorry, Charlotte," he apologized, his voice rough. "If I could change all of it right now, I would. Except for one thing."

Charlotte raised her eyes to his, feeling his rage and desperation and need fill the cell until there was no room for anything else. Her voice was barely a whisper as she asked, "What?"

"Meeting you." His gaze was filled with tenderness. "That I wouldn't change—ever."

"I don't see why you wouldn't," she countered painfully. "If not for my asking you for money, you would not have been forced to do the terrible things that have brought you here." Her voice began to break. "You would not have been compelled to kill—"

"No, Charlotte." God almighty, did she honestly believe that she had turned him into a murderer? "You're wrong," he told her flatly. "Everything I have done— there have been other reasons for it—things that had nothing to do with you. And despite what others may say, I didn't kill Lord Pembroke's butler that night his home was robbed—just as I didn't shoot Inspector Turner last night. You must believe me when I tell you that. I don't really give a damn what others think, but you—" He stopped suddenly and turned away, unable to face her. "I need you to believe that I am not a murderer." His voice was laden with bitter regret as he finished, "The rest of the world can go to bloody hell."

Charlotte stared at his rigid, towering form, which seemed so straight and powerful and beautiful against the barren gloom of the cell. And suddenly she was filled with an emotion she could not immediately identify. It surged through her, tightening her muscles until she felt like a coiled spring about to erupt. Heedless of her limp, she marched across the worn stone floor of the cell, grabbed Harrison by his shoulders, and turned him to face her. His surprised gaze met hers.

There was no doubt in her mind that Harrison was telling her the truth. She had always known he abhorred violence—she had sensed it from the very moment she had come upon him in Lady Chadwick's bedchamber. She had felt it in the gentleness of his touch when he had grabbed her as she stumbled, had seen it in his reluctance to take her hostage, even though she practically begged him to do so. When she had learned that Lord Pembroke's butler had been stabbed in the chest, her reaction had been horrified disbelief, because she had known that Harrison would never have performed such a terrible deed willingly. But now he was saying he hadn't done it.

Which meant he was in Newgate waiting to be tried and hanged for a murder he didn't commit.

"If you didn't kill Lord Pembroke's butler, and you didn't shoot Inspector Turner last night, then who did?" Her voice was remarkably even, given the fact that she was almost ready to strangle him herself.

"I don't know." Harrison was startled by her obvious fury. Whatever reaction he might have predicted from her, it was not the barely leashed anger he was currently seeing. "There was another man there. He is the jewel thief who has been breaking into wealthy homes in London these past few months, not me."

Charlotte regarded him incredulously. "Are you saying you're not the Dark Shadow?"

"The answer to that is a bit complicated." He sighed. "The night you found me in Lady Chadwick's bedchamber, I was there trying to catch him, not to steal her jewelry. I knew she had recently acquired an exquisite emerald necklace that had once belonged to a celebrated French noblewoman who was executed in the French Revolution. I broke into Lord Chadwick's home because I thought the Dark Shadow would try to steal that necklace that night. When you found me, I was looking through her jewelry case just to make sure that it was still there, not to take it."

Charlotte frowned, trying to make sense of what he was saying. "How could you possibly have known that the Dark Shadow would try to steal it from Lady Chadwick on that particular night?"

"I didn't know for certain," Harrison allowed. "I had been following his thefts for months, making note of every available detail, trying to link them into some kind of pattern, or perhaps a series of patterns. And I realized that as he grew bolder the Dark Shadow developed a penchant for pieces that were either greatly admired or famous. Lady Chadwick had worn her new necklace to a party the night before, where everyone had made a great fuss over it. That evening she and her husband were hosting a dinner in their home, and I didn't believe she would wear it two nights in a row—especially given that their party was an intimate affair, and the necklace would have seemed too ostentatious. Therefore three elements were in place: the first being the jewelry's recent notoriety; the second, the fact that it would likely not be worn that night; and the third, its availability, as the entire household would be occupied downstairs for most of the evening. It was a perfect set of circumstances for a jewel thief."

"If you were so certain the Dark Shadow would try to break into Lord Chadwick's home that night, then why didn't you simply warn them so they could contact the police?"

"The police had been trying to catch him for months, without success. I had little faith in their ability to do much other than scare him off. I wanted him caught, not chased away."

"Why did his capture mean so much to you, Harrison?" Charlotte thought of Lady Bryden, and the magnificent jewelry she had been wearing on the day Charlotte had met her. "Had he ever stolen anything from you?"

Her eyes were wide and filled with concern. It was as if she believed that if Harrison just told everyone the truth, that somehow his life might be restored to him. Unfortunately, he knew otherwise. The public was anxious for the case of the Dark Shadow to be solved, and Inspector Turner believed, not unreasonably, that he had done just that. Harrison was certain he would not be impressed by any partial confession. Besides, even if Harrison were tried only for the crimes he had committed sixteen years earlier, that would still be more than enough to keep him rotting in prison for years, during which his mind would almost certainly disintegrate beneath the same illness that had afflicted his father.

Either way, his life was finished.

The only person whose understanding he cared about at that moment was Charlotte. She had met him at his very worst; yet, instead of condemning him, she had risked herself to help him, even when he tried to refuse that help. It was cruel and unfair, he thought as he stared down at her, that this lovely, unassuming, determined young woman, who would finally delve beneath the lies and artifice and open up his heart, had only come into his life at the very instant when it was spinning beyond his control. In many ways, he and Charlotte were of the same spirit. Charlotte was a survivor, as was he. And because she had been forced to do things in order to survive, she did not judge others with the same pious superiority that virtually every other woman he had ever known did. That was why she had tried so desperately to help him on the night they met. It was why she had trusted him enough to turn to him for help when she needed it. And it was why she had opened herself to him, giving of her heart and body and soul, and then refused to pretend to be horrified or ashamed by the glorious passion that had burned between them. In her own quiet, courageous way, Charlotte was far stronger and more honest than he. He was humbled and awed by her.

And in that moment, all he wanted was to hold her close, and tell her the truth.

"When I was twenty-four, my father killed himself," he began, his voice taut and void of emotion. "He shot himself in the head, either in a moment of utter madness or with complete lucidity—I can't be sure which. His mind had been eroding for years. What began as a few amusing incidents of forgetfulness and confusion had gradually turned into something far more hideous."

"What happened to him?"

"He began to have excruciating, nauseating headaches, for which nothing could provide any relief except to shut himself in his room in absolute silence with the curtains drawn for a day or more, during which he refused any food, drink, or company. My mother summoned a succession of doctors from all over England and across the Continent, whose diagnoses varied from saying he merely suffered from a too rich diet, to having an insufficient supply of blood to his brain. One insisted a tumor was causing his pain, and was quite anxious to crack open his skull and take it out. He told my mother he didn't expect my father to survive the operation, but said the advance of science would be nobly served by his attempt. Needless to say, she ordered him from the house.

"Another suggested he was suffering from a form of headache called migraines, and he began dosing my father with a myriad of foul concoctions made from valerian root, Peruvian bark, hemlock, camphor, myrrh, and opium, among others. When they all failed to provide relief, the doctor burned blisters behind his ears and pulled out three of his teeth, which merely added to his suffering. He even bled him, for God's sake. And my father only got worse. His headaches persisted and his mind continued to deteriorate.

"The problem was, none of us realized just how severe that deterioration was. Whenever he forgot something or grew enraged for no apparent reason, we attributed his absent-mindedness and fits of violence to the medications he was taking. My mother insisted his outbursts were completely understandable, given how much he was suffering—even when he tried to strangle her one night. She had always been extremely protective of him, and nothing could dissuade her from the idea that once she found a cure for his headaches he would return to his former self. In the meantime, his children and his servants were to treat him with respect, tolerate his wildly vacillating moods, and make discreet excuses for him if anyone beyond our household noticed his increasingly bizarre behavior. And while we were all going about pretending he was fine and respecting his dignity and his privacy, my father managed, through no fault of his own, to virtually bankrupt us. And then he went into his study and shot himself."

Charlotte watched as Harrison struggled to keep his expression even. She could see that this was enormously painful for him, despite his attempt to make it sound as if he was talking about something that had long since lost its power to hurt him. Yet she also sensed his desperate need to talk about it, to share this terrible part of his past that had altered the course of his life.

"Go on," she said quietly.

"I was twenty-four. And perhaps no more of a fool than the other young, callow nobles with whom I associated, but unfortunately, my lack of responsibility had disastrous consequences. I had fancied myself in love with a dancer from a music hall, and that affair managed to take up most of my waking hours. I had not made any effort to learn anything about our family's finances or investments, or just what it was, precisely, that paid our bills. I suppose I thought there were heaps of money sitting in the bank, and that when I finally became earl in ten or twenty years, I would simply inherit that money and use it to keep everything going. As I quickly learned after my father's funeral, that was not the case.

"In the two years preceding his death, my father had made a dreadful series of investments in business ventures that initially appeared promising but then failed, dragging him deeper into debt. He began to use anything as collateral, including properties, artwork, and our family's jewel collection, which was significant. The men with whom he did business were most accommodating about accepting collateral as payment. They even helped him by providing discreet buyers. The documentation for all of this was confusing and incomplete, but I soon began to suspect that my father had actually been defrauded. I went to the authorities, who told me there wasn't enough evidence to proceed with an investigation, which would be long, costly, and almost certainly unsuccessful. And so I was left with a staggering pile of debt, several overmortgaged properties, and a mother, brother, and sister who were crushed by my father's death and couldn't comprehend how our finances could possibly be so dire."

"And so you decided to steal some of it back—starting with the jewels."

He nodded. "The banks were unwilling to extend me any more credit. And I was furious that I had let this happen—that I had somehow been naive enough to believe my mother when she insisted that my father was perfectly capable of conducting his business affairs. Once I realized the truth, I had to do something quickly. Since I believed everything we had lost had effectively been stolen from us, I decided to just bloody well steal it back. Of course stealing the artwork was impractical—too cumbersome, and nearly impossible to sell anyway. But the jewels were another matter. They were small and easy to sell, because they could be removed from their settings and sold as loose stones.

"So over a period of a year, I broke into houses and took only those jewels I believed were rightfully mine. The newspapers dubbed me the Dark Shadow, and in my anger and my arrogance, I was quite happy to have them romanticize me in their writing. They took great pleasure in describing my latest thefts, and much of London enjoyed the fact that someone was running about stealing jewels from the rich, yet not actually hurting anyone. I sold the jewels and reduced my debts, while also making some careful investments. Fortunately, my instinct for business was sound, and gradually I began to rebuild my family's wealth."

"How long were you breaking into houses?"

"Almost a year. I might have continued for longer, but I had a bad fall one night as I was climbing out of a window and I injured my back. For a moment I didn't think I could get up. That was when I knew I'd had enough. It was foolish to think I could keep on and not get caught, and my mother, Margaret, and Frank needed me. So the thefts stopped abruptly. People speculated that the Dark Shadow had been killed, arrested for a lesser crime, or retired to a villa in the Mediterranean.

Then suddenly, a few months ago, someone adopted my guise and started stealing again. He actually left notes identifying himself as the Dark Shadow. At first I just ignored it. I thought he would quickly be captured and that would be the end of it. But as he grew bolder and the police failed to capture him, I grew concerned that some earnest investigator might open the old files on the Dark Shadow and see if they could solve the mystery of his identity by looking at the past instead of the present. Whether this new thief realized it or not, his thefts were posing a threat to me and my family."

"So you decided to try to capture him yourself."

"Yes. And I came damn close. That night at Lord Pembroke's house, I actually confronted him. We fought, but unfortunately he got away after tearing off my mask."

"Did he see your face clearly?"

"Yes. He recognized me—he said my name. Then he hurled a blade at Lord Pembroke's butler before I could stop him. I got away, but I knew time was running out. Whoever this Dark Shadow was, he had the advantage, because he knew I was after him. If he hadn't already made the connection to my past, he did that night. Which meant he could start leaving evidence that would point to me." He shook his head, infuriated by his own stupidity. "I still believed I could outwit him, because I thought I could anticipate his next move. When I heard that Lady Whitaker was flaunting the Star of Persia, I was certain the Dark Shadow would want it. I didn't realize that Inspector Turner had already linked me to the thefts. He had found a monogrammed handkerchief of mine outside Lord Pembroke's home on the night his butler was killed, which quickly led him to me."

"Did you drop it?"

He shook his head in frustration. "I don't remember." He did not tell her that there were many things he had been unable to remember of late. "I'm usually extremely careful about what I carry on me when I'm the Dark Shadow. But I suppose it's possible that it was in one of my pockets and I just didn't realize it."

"Or that once the other Dark Shadow realized who you were, he stole a handkerchief from you and purposely dropped it to point the police in your direction," Charlotte theorized.

Harrison frowned. "How would he have gotten his hands on one of my handkerchiefs?"

"He could easily have picked one of your pockets without your noticing. Even I could do that, and I'm sadly out of practice. Or he could have hired some young pickpocket eager for a quick coin to do it. Or he could have broken into your home and taken one."

Harrison preferred to think that someone had taken a handkerchief from his person, rather than breaking into his house. He realized that was ironic, given all the break-ins he had committed during his life.

"Did you explain all of this to Inspector Turner?" Charlotte asked.

"Inspector Turner is overjoyed that he has captured the Dark Shadow—especially given that he believes I tried to kill him last night. In fact I kept him from getting his head blown apart, but he doesn't know that. If I tell him I was the Dark Shadow, but am not anymore, he will simply dredge up my old crimes and point out how closely they match the new ones. That will only further implicate me. I'm afraid there is nothing to be gained by telling him the truth, Charlotte. I've told him I was trying to catch the Dark Shadow, but that made little impression upon him. Unless this new Dark Shadow is caught before I go to trial, there is no reason for Turner to question the solidity of his case. Unfortunately, I don't believe this thief is going to steal again."

"Why not?"

"Because my capture brings his career to a perfect end," Harrison explained. "To have another man hang for his crimes, bringing the case of the Dark Shadow to a close."

"Or to have you in particular hang for his crimes, Harrison. Has it not occurred to you that this man could be driven by his desire to see you take the blame for his actions? Why else did he just happen to have one of your handkerchiefs available to drop as evidence on the very same night you confronted him?"

"We don't know for certain that he did that," Harrison pointed out.

"Even if he didn't, I don't believe it is a coincidence that this man just happened to decide upon the guise of the Dark Shadow," Charlotte argued. "His thefts were meticulously planned and executed, which demonstrates he is intelligent. Yet he started leaving notes identifying himself as the Dark Shadow. Why would he select a guise that had been made famous nearly two decades ago?"

"At the risk of sounding conceited, because he admired my reputation."

Charlotte shook her head. "He may have admired it enough to adopt your methods, but that doesn't explain why he elected to go by the same name. Why not let the public give him his own name, based on his own feats? Or create a name for himself? Criminals love notoriety, and they like to be known for their deeds, however ugly they may be. Their legacy may be brief, but in my experience, they like it to be their own."

"Are you suggesting that whoever is doing this has actually been trying to get me arrested for these crimes?"

"I'm not sure," Charlotte said. "But if that is the case, then he has accomplished what he wanted. Your arrest. The only thing that might make him steal once more is if he thought you had been released."

"Inspector Turner is convinced he has captured a dangerous murderer. Unless we produce the real Dark Shadow, he has no reason to let me go."

"Is there anyone you can think of who might have a desire to see you punished?"

"Several come to mind," Harrison reflected ruefully, thinking back to the indiscretions of his youth. "But I find it hard to believe that any of them could have coddled their anger this long, to a point where they would go to such drastic measures."

"It is possible one of them is angrier than you think, and has just managed to hide it until now." Charlotte thought for a moment. "We have to get Inspector Turner to say he will release you. That's the only way we might be able to rouse this Dark Shadow to action again. We have to make him think his plan has failed, and that you are still a threat to him."

"Turner will refuse. All you will succeed in doing is further incriminating yourself. I won't let you do that, Charlotte. I don't give a damn about what happens to me, but you—"

"I'm not going to ask him to actually release you," Charlotte interjected, "only to *say* that he has released you. We need to set a trap, and to do that we need the Dark Shadow to believe that you have been cleared of all suspicion. If my instincts are right, whoever is trying to implicate you will not be able to tolerate your going free. Secondly, I don't intend to speak to Inspector Turner myself. I know someone who will be far more effective at getting him to agree to our plan than I."

Harrison regarded her curiously. "Who?"

"Annie. She was most upset to learn that he had been shot. If I recall his expression correctly on the night he met her, Inspector Turner will be quite willing to see her."

"He may be willing to see her, but that doesn't mean he'll agree to go along with your plan."

"If he won't, then we'll have to come up with another one. What I won't do, Harrison, is stand by and watch you be tried and sentenced for crimes you did not commit. If it comes down to having to admit to the crimes of your youth so you can avoid being tried for murder, then that is what you must do."

"My past will only further condemn me."

"Or it may absolve you."

"To the extent that I'll be sentenced to years of incarceration as opposed to being hanged. I'd rather hang and get it the hell over with."

"I wouldn't."

He regarded her with aching regret. "I'm sorry, Charlotte. I never meant to drag you into all of this. And I never meant to hurt you."

"The only thing that is hurting me now is watching

you resign yourself to this fate. We can change our fates, Harrison. I did it. So can you."

"That was different."

"You're right. I didn't have the advantages you have."

"What advantages?"

"You're strong, educated, wealthy, and respected. You come from a privileged background, and you know you can withstand the storm of scandal that will surround you once this is over. Most important of all, you are loved." Her voice was softer now, almost ragged. "That was the only thing I had when Genevieve took me out of prison. She gave me love, and a family who loved me and made me feel safe." She reached out and hesitantly laid her hand against his chest, so that her palm could feel the beating of his heart. "And that is what I will give you, Harrison. If you'll let me."

Even as she spoke the words, she was astonished. But there was no time for shyness and propriety, or for words to be left unspoken. And somehow Harrison brought out a completely different woman in her than the quiet, retiring, selfless Charlotte Kent she had always been to the rest of the world. Harrison made her feel passionate and angry. He made her want to fight, not just for the injustices of others, but for herself as well. All her life she had believed that she would never meet a man who would love her with the passion that she longed for. But Harrison did. She could feel it in the fervor of his touch, the hunger of his kiss, the desperate longing of his body. He made her want more from life than what she had previously accepted.

He made her want him.

And if she lost him, she did not think she could bear it.

Harrison closed his arms around her. "From the moment you shoved that bloody hairbrush at me, I knew you were trouble," he murmured, pressing his lips to hers. He kissed her deeply as his hands roamed across her, trying to memorize the feel and taste and scent of her, his senses ablaze with desire and regret. "Charlotte, I—"

"Here we are," called out Digby cheerfully, his key grinding in the lock.

Charlotte turned away, frantically smoothing her hands over her hair and gown as an oblivious Digby picked up the heavy tray he had set down upon the corridor floor.

"Digby, you've really outdone yourself," marveled Harrison enthusiastically, momentarily blocking the old warder's view of Charlotte as he strode forward to examine the tea Digby had prepared. "Just look at those biscuits—they look glorious."

"They're a bit broken," Digby apologized, glancing ruefully at the plate of fragmented cookies. "But they taste good."

"I'm sure they are absolutely splendid," Harrison agreed. "Come, Miss Kent, may I offer you a cup of tea?"

"I'm afraid I cannot stay any longer, Lord Bryden," Charlotte replied, trying extremely hard to not look like a woman who had just been in the throes of a passionate kiss. She pressed her lips together, fearing they might appear swollen. "I have a number of things to attend to."

Digby looked crestfallen. "Are ye sure, Miss Kent? I found a nice clean cup just for ye—I washed it meself."

"That was extremely kind of you, Mr. Digby, and I am most grateful," Charlotte assured him. "Unfortunately, I do have to be off. Thank you for agreeing to see me, Lord Bryden," she continued, turning her attention to Harrison. "I hope you will reflect seriously upon all the things I have said."

"I shall indeed," Harrison promised gallantly. "Well,

Digby, since we cannot convince Miss Kent to stay, I hope you won't mind escorting her out." He gave the old warder a meaningful glance, as if he couldn't wait for him to hustle his pious guest out of there.

"As ye wish, milord," said Digby, nodding with understanding. "After you, Miss Kent."

Charlotte kept her spine stiff and her expression frozen as she limped out of Harrison's cell. Panic ignited within her as Digby locked the heavy door behind her. She imagined herself banging the unsuspecting warder on the head, stealing his keys, opening the door and freeing Harrison. Which would, of course, accomplish nothing. As if sensing her despair, Harrison began to whistle cheerfully as he poured himself a cup of tea. His apparent calm, real or forced, enabled her to take hold of herself. She waited in silence for Digby to finish locking the door before leading her down the dark end of the corridor.

It was only after the door to the ward had banged shut that Harrison stopped his idiotic whistling. He stared blankly at the cracked china teacup that Digby had brought especially for Charlotte.

And then he picked it up and heaved it against the window, causing the delicate shell to shatter against the iron bars.

Chapter Fourteen

"A LADY HERE TO SEE YOU, INSPECTOR, SIR. SHE SAYS it's most important."

Lewis scowled at the obsequious young police constable standing nervously before him.

Everyone at Metropolitan Police Headquarters, otherwise known as Scotland Yard, was in the throes of anointing Lewis as the brilliant young detective responsible for finally catching the infamous Dark Shadow. He had gone from being a laughingstock to being a hero—at least amongst the police and the victims of the elusive jewel thief. Journalists had been crowded outside the building for two days, waiting impatiently for further details surrounding Lord Bryden's capture. Unfortunately, they also wanted to know more about Lewis, including personal details about his upbringing, his marital status, and, appallingly, the precise nature of his injury. It was this sudden, wholly unexpected invasion of his privacy that had caused Lewis to retreat to his desk after his initial announcement to the press. Let Chief Inspector Holloway make the statements, he thought acidly. The chief apparently enjoyed standing about pontificating about how he had seen to it that London was a safer place to live, as if he were personally responsible for Lord Bryden's capture.

"Who is she?" demanded Lewis.

"A Miss Annie Clarke, sir," replied the young officer. "She claims to know you. She says she met you one night at the home of Miss Charlotte Kent."

Lewis instantly forgot about the clutter of papers and assorted pieces of evidence on his desk. "Where is she?" he managed, fumbling with the buttons of his rumpled brown coat.

"Waiting out front, on the bench in front of Sergeant Jeffrey's desk. If you like I can escort her to you—"

"That won't be necessary." Lewis grabbed his walking stick and began to hobble toward the front desk, grimacing as he fought the pulse of pain that snaked down his thigh every time he put pressure on it. His face felt a little flushed, which he hoped wasn't noticeable. He would have to make some comment about the heat of the day, when he saw her, just in case. He didn't want her to see him limping toward her and think he was about to faint.

"Good afternoon, Miss Clarke," he said, affecting a bland formality that he hoped masked his powerful attraction to her the instant he saw her.

She was far lovelier than he remembered. The bruising around her eye had faded, and she regarded him with wide, intelligent eyes that seemed to delve deep into him, searching and assessing. There was no fear there, yet he sensed that there was no judgment, either, or if there was, it was not the scornfully dismissive type she had hurled at him the night he had refused to go after the man who had beaten her. He had long regretted his decision to not at least take some steps to find that bastard. What on earth could she have thought of him that night, except that he was an uncaring prick who didn't give a damn when a man smashed his fists into a helpless girl? He met her gaze with feigned calm, trying not to let her see the effect she was having upon him.

"Good afternoon, Inspector," she replied politely.

Annie rose from the hard little bench on which she had been seated, trying her best to remember all the proper manners that Charlotte had attempted to teach her. She felt completely ill at ease in the legal confines of Scotland Yard, with all those bacon-faced peelers staring down their noses at her. She was dressed in one of Charlotte's day gowns, with a prim bodice that buttoned all the way up to her neck, long, slightly puffed sleeves, and a generously full skirt that swished importantly about her as she walked. She was also wearing one of Charlotte's hats. At first she had thought it was a bit plain, but once Charlotte and Doreen had pinned her hair up and then set the hat into place, Annie had to agree that it was actually rather elegant on her. She had been surprised by how nice and ladylike she looked. Charlotte's clothes made her feel a bit different—almost as if she were a woman of quality, instead of just a fashionably dressed whore. Former whore, she reminded herself adamantly. She sensed that people were looking at her differently as well. Certainly Inspector Lewis seemed to be staring at her a bloody sight different than the night he'd found her standing all drenched and bruised and ranting in the rain.

"I'm sorry about your leg." She bit her lower lip, suddenly uncertain as to how she was supposed to act. Inspector Turner was far more pleasing to look at than she had remembered, a fact that was making her feel decidedly wobbly inside. "It ain't too bad, is it?"

"No," he assured her. "It isn't too bad."

"Well, that's a relief." Annie glanced about, feeling

as if everyone in the entire police headquarters was staring at them.

"Would you like to take a short walk?" Lewis had briefly considered escorting her back to his desk, but he did not have his own office, and Annie had already attracted enough attention there. Taking her for a walk was the only way they could speak privately without compromising her reputation.

He tried not to contemplate exactly what that reputation was.

"A walk would be nice," she replied.

"If you don't mind, we'll leave by one of the doors at the back of the building," Lewis suggested, recalling that there was probably still a flock of journalists waiting out front.

She pressed her lips into a tight line. Obviously he was embarrassed by the prospect of being seen in public with her. "If ye like."

Lewis thought he saw a flicker of anger burning in her gaze. Did she not understand he was trying to protect her privacy as well? Bemused by her reaction, he escorted her to the back of the building, trying hard to ignore the curious stares that followed them. He told himself the police officers and detectives were only fascinated by Annie because she was so strikingly pretty. Also, he had just solved the case of the Dark Shadow; therefore, everything he did was suddenly of interest to them. Even as he ran these rationalizations through his mind, logic dictated that he at least acknowledge the more obvious reason for their stares.

Annie radiated pure sexuality.

It permeated the lush curves of her body, the soft scallops of her mouth, the easy, compelling sway of her hips. She was not dressed provocatively, for which Lewis was enormously grateful, nor had she dabbed any artificial color on her cheeks or lips. Nevertheless, there was something about her that was overwhelmingly, intoxicatingly alluring.

Or did he just think that because he was so drawn to her?

"That's better," he said, escorting her out the door and into a brilliant wash of sunlight. "Now we won't have any prying journalists to contend with as we make our way down the street."

Annie looked at him in surprise. "Was that why ye wanted us to slip out back, then? On account of them?"

"They've been making my life a misery since they heard the news about my encounter with Lord Bryden the night before last," Lewis explained. "They want to know where I was born, who my parents were, what does my father think about me being a detective. One of them even had the nerve to ask my how much money I make a year, as if that were any of their damn business. I bloody well wanted to throttle him."

He stopped suddenly, wondering if he should have used profanity in her presence. She appeared not to have noticed, or if she had, she was electing not to make an issue of it. He liked that. Even so, he would have to be more careful. He did not want her to think that he was speaking crudely in front of her because he didn't respect her enough to behave like a gentleman.

"Next time tell 'em to mind their own bloody business," Annie advised, "or ye'll put a fist in their bone box."

"Somehow I don't think my chief inspector would approve of such candor," Lewis reflected, amused by her straightforwardness. "The police force has borne a lot of mockery and criticism in the past few months. Now that the Dark Shadow has been caught, the chief wants to enjoy the moment to the utmost."

Annie fixed her gaze onto the street and said nothing.

Lewis regarded her uncertainly. He wondered if she

would accept his arm if he offered it, or refuse it because she lumped him in with all the other peelers who clearly made her feel ill at ease. Deciding to take a chance, he offered her his arm.

Annie looked up at him in surprise. She supposed he was only doing the gentlemanly thing. Even so, she found herself extremely pleased that despite the fact that he was a peeler, he respected her enough to pretend she was a lady, at least in front of others. She laid her gloved hand against his sleeve, lightly, the way Charlotte had instructed her to if ever a gentleman might offer his arm to her. The hard muscle of his arm flinched as her fingers grazed it. She wasn't sure what to make of that. Mindful of the fact that he was limping, she began to walk slowly with him down the street.

"When I heard ye'd been shot, I imagined the worst," she confessed. "I thought ye'd snuffed it, for sure. I was glad to hear ye hadn't."

"I was lucky." It pleased Lewis to think that she had actually been worried about him. "The bullet only hit me in the leg."

"Will it heal all right?"

"Yes." He didn't want her to think that he would be limping about with a cane forever.

"Well, that's a mercy." She looked away, feigning a sudden fascination with a carriage that was clattering down the street. "Yer wife must have been awful scared."

"I'm not married."

She glanced back at him. "Ye ain't?"

"No." He thought he detected a trace of relief in her eyes. Or was he just imagining that because he wanted to believe she might actually be interested in him?

"Why did you come to see me today, Miss Clarke?" He studied her a moment, watching the reluctant tightening of her pretty little mouth. "Did Miss Kent send you?"

"In a manner of speakin', yes," Annie admitted. "She wanted me to ask ye somethin'. But I also wanted to come and see ye as well," she swiftly added, "just to see for myself that ye wasn't hurt too bad."

"I'm moved by your concern." His tone was slightly arid. He knew it was absurd to think that Annie had come just to see him. She had not been thinking feverishly about him night and day. She probably had a long line of men waiting to sample her various charms, her stay at Miss Kent's house of refuge not withstanding. "What did Miss Kent want you to ask me?"

"It's a bit of a favor, really." Annie could feel his sudden coolness. She wished she hadn't been there to ask anything of him. She wished she had only been there to go for a walk with him, to stroll along in the summer sunshine, her big skirts swishing along the sidewalk, venturing a polite smile now and again at the other gentlemen and ladies passing them, as if she were a proper lady.

"Go on."

"It's just that Miss Kent is sure Lord Bryden ain't the man ye're lookin' for," she blurted out suddenly. "She swears he ain't the Dark Shadow. Only now that ye've got his lordship in the coop, she's sure the real Dark Shadow will never be caught. She thinks he knew Lord Bryden was tryin' to nab him, an' now that ye've got Lord Bryden instead, the real Dark Shadow will just go about his regular life, laughin' all the way to his grave while his lordship gets stretched for his crimes."

So that was it, Lewis mused. Miss Kent's relationship with Lord Bryden must have been just as intimate as the facts had suggested on the night Lewis watched her visit his home in the middle of the night. He wasn't surprised by that, given her insistence upon seeing Lord Bryden in prison the previous day. While Lewis could find no evidence that the two had ever met prior to Bryden taking her hostage at Lord Chadwick's house—assuming that the masked man was Bryden—Lewis was now convinced that Miss Kent had played a vital role in helping Bryden escape that night. What he found most intriguing was that two people of such opposite character and background could be so attracted to one another. Lord Bryden was confident, bold, outspoken, and had once enjoyed a reputation for seducing some of London's greatest beauties. Miss Kent was hardly the kind of woman with whom he typically dallied. She was a shy, fading, crippled spinster from crude beginnings, who would never be accepted amongst the aristocratic society she had been brought into. He found himself wondering if Bryden actually cared for her, or if he had merely used her to help him escape and advance his own ends.

"And just how is it that Miss Kent can be so entirely certain of Lord Bryden's innocence?" he asked.

"I ain't sure," Annie admitted. "She wouldn't tell me that. And I don't know enough about Lord Bryden to say whether it's true or not. I mean, ye did see him shoot ye while ye was lyin' helpless. Why would he do such a filthy thing if he ain't the Dark Shadow?"

Lewis didn't answer. He couldn't, because he hadn't actually been conscious when he was shot, as Lord Bryden had so aptly pointed out.

"All I know for certain is that Miss Kent is as fine a lady as ye're ever like to meet," Annie continued fiercely. "She's different from everyone I've known—an' I've known plenty." She cast him a challenging look, making it clear that she made no apology for her life. "She's lived with the lowest, blackest scum ye could imagine, an' the highest, fanciest swells. She's even been locked in prison herself, though ye'd never know it to look at her. And she knows ye have to look down deep to really see what a person's about. An' if she's looked down deep inside Lord Bryden and says it ain't in him to murder, then I believe her. I ain't sayin' ye should just toss his lordship out the door and that's that, or nothin' like that," she swiftly clarified. "He must have been up to somethin', bein' at Lord Whitaker's house in the middle of the night, and then shootin' ye when ye was helpless. But Miss Charlotte says ye'll never catch the real Dark Shadow if Lord Bryden hangs. If ye're a man of justice, ye should at least make sure ye hang the right man, or else his soul will haunt ye to yer grave."

Lewis was silent a moment, giving no indication that the possibility of Lord Bryden's innocence had ever crossed his mind.

In fact it had been nagging at him constantly in the long hours since he had faced Bryden at Newgate.

He considered himself a good detective. He noticed details, whether when examining the scene of a crime, analyzing a course of events, or questioning a witness. His penchant for accurate record-keeping helped him to keep facts straight, instead of distorting or embellishing them, as many other detectives and police constables were prone to do. He was also extremely logical, at least when it came to criminal matters. And despite the fact that most of the evidence pointed to Lord Bryden, Lewis could not deny that many pieces simply did not fit together. Moreover, he could not dispute Bryden's argument that there really had not been any need to shoot Lewis, given that he was unconscious and he couldn't possibly have identified whoever was behind the Dark Shadow's mask anyway. But what bothered him most was the fact that he considered himself a reasonably astute judge of character.

And something kept telling him that Lord Bryden

was not the kind of man who would take the life of another over a few pieces of jewelry.

"If Miss Kent doesn't expect me to release Lord Bryden, then just what, exactly, are you asking me to do?"

Annie looked up at him in surprise. His expression had been so dark as they walked along, she had thought she had succeeded only in making him angry. Now she understood he had looked that way because he had been thinking. She liked the fact that he was a man who took the time to think before he spoke. Almost every other man she had ever known had exploded with either lust or fury long before he ever took a minute to actually use his brain. It made her feel a little awkward that she wasn't as smart or as schooled as him, but when she was with him he didn't do anything to make her feel the lesser for it. She knew a peeler like him would never consider having an honest interest in a whore like her—even a whore who was set on changing her ways. She'd known plenty of girls who quiffed their share of peelers, but it was always so the bastards would leave them alone to earn their trade. Inspector Turner hadn't made any unseemly advances toward her, though. If anything, he was treating her as if she were a proper lady, offering her his arm and walking along the street with her for all of London to see. Of course he had only agreed to see her because of her association with Miss Charlotte, and the fact that he suspected Miss Charlotte knew more about Lord Bryden and the Dark Shadow than she was letting on. Even so, it was awfully prime to be out strolling in his company, with her hand resting comfortably on his strong arm and him talking to her as if he actually gave a damn what she was thinking.

"We need to set a trap," Annie told him. "An' we need to do it fast. If the real Dark Shadow thinks Lord Bryden is about to swing for his crimes, he may just decide to pack up and leave London till it's all over and done. He may even leave for good."

"Assuming there is another thief, he may just decide to sit back and do nothing, and wait for Bryden to hang."

"Either way, he goes free while his lordship dangles," Annie complained fiercely, shaking her head. "It ain't right. We need to make him think that Lord Bryden has got off. If Miss Kent is right an' the Dark Shadow was tryin' to pin his crimes on his lordship, then if he thinks Lord Bryden's been let go, he'll probably want to do somethin' more to get him arrested again. Miss Kent's got an idea, which she thinks will bring the Dark Shadow runnin' to his lordship like a cat to a kipper. Ye need to make sure ye've got lots of peelers about to catch him when he does."

Lewis nodded and leaned a little closer into her, ostensibly so that no one would overhear their conversation. The delicate scent of orange water filled his nostrils. He would not have thought an experienced girl like Annie would have opted for such a sweetly modest fragrance. Perhaps Miss Kent would actually succeed in her attempted reformation of Annie's battered life.

He sincerely hoped so.

"Tell me more," he murmured, hoping he wasn't about to make the biggest mistake of his career.

Chapter Fifteen

DAILY TELEGRAPH
JULY 28, 1875

Lord Bryden Released

The Earl of Bryden was released early this morning from Newgate Prison. His lordship had been detained there on suspicion of being involved with the recent jewel thefts and murders that have been attributed to the persona "The Dark Shadow." Inspector Turner of Scotland Yard explained that while Lord Bryden had been apprehended at the home of Lord Whitaker under irregular circumstances, the police are now satisfied that Lord Bryden is not, in fact, the elusive murderer and thief who has been plaguing London these past months. Lord Bryden is said to have cooperated fully with the police upon his arrest, providing them with vital information regarding the Dark Shadow's identity, based upon his two encounters with the notorious thief. The police expect to make an arrest imminently.

Lord Bryden plans to leave London immediately for an undisclosed destination.

• • •

Aᴌᴌ ɢᴏᴏᴅ ᴛʜɪɴɢs ᴍᴜsᴛ ᴄᴏᴍᴇ ᴛᴏ ᴀɴ ᴇɴᴅ.

This was how he consoled himself as he inched his way through the velvety night air. He crept up the expansive marble staircase that led to the magnificent drawing room on the second level, which Lady Bryden used when she imagined herself gaily entertaining phantom guests from a party that had happened twenty years earlier. Past a cluster of wilting potted ferns. Around a couple of filmily draped ancient statues, pillaged decades earlier by some arrogant British collector who believed such treasures were better suited to the stuffy, velvet choked interiors of England than the brilliant sun-drenched temples of Greece.

He would go to Greece, once this was all over. Greece, Italy, Spain—he'd go anywhere that was hot. There he would sit and drink vast quantities of fine wine and eat wondrous dishes that had been prepared with exotic spices while he contemplated his life. He could afford to take some time off now. He could afford to do whatever the hell he damn well pleased.

That had been an unexpected benefit.

He would find himself a woman. Perhaps he would indulge in a Spanish mistress, with long black hair and heavy, bronze-nippled breasts, who knew how to ride a man long and hard and needed only gifts and money and copious amounts of flattery in return. It had been a long time since he had thrust himself into a woman. Caution had prohibited such intimacy except with whores, but they could leave you pissing pins and needles, and besides, he had grown to dislike the sweaty unwashed smell of them, even though there was a time when he had simply equated that odor with sex. No more. He understood the difference between clean and dirty now. He understood the great divide between the world of those who wore precious jewels and lived in mansions with rococo plasterwork and marble fireplaces and brilliant oil paintings, and those who struggled to see that there was enough stringy beef and wilted cabbage left over to be fried up into a greasy pan of bubble and squeak.

After a year or so of indulging in travel and pleasure, perhaps he would consider finding a wife. Someone young and sweet and impressionable, who would listen to his fanciful stories and admire his elegant manners and be suitably awed by his charms and his wealth. Not the daughter of an aristocrat, though. The daughter of a British peer would be far too concerned about his pedigree. He could not afford to have some meddlesome lord snooping around making enquiries about his background. He would have to be satisfied with a girl of a lesser class—perhaps the daughter of a wealthy banker or businessman. As long as she was pretty and well mannered, and not exceptionally clever. A clever woman would ask lots of questions, and he scarcely needed that.

He wanted to put his past behind him, not constantly be made to account for it.

A procession of valises lined the corridor leading to the bedrooms on the next floor. So it was true, he mused. Bryden was leaving the country—apparently for a considerable length of time. He supposed he could have found out easily enough where Bryden was going, but the idea of chasing him all around the Continent and bringing the game to an end in some hotel room far from London wasn't nearly as satisfying as confronting the bastard in his own home. Besides, although loath to admit it, he was getting a bit weary. At thirty-one years he was scarcely old, but he was definitely starting to feel his age. Clambering up and down the sides of buildings and heaving himself in and out of windows had taken its toll. Time to end it and move on to the next stage of his life.

He stood before Harrison's bedchamber door. His chest tight with anticipation, he silently turned the handle.

The room was dark but for a faint spill of ghostly light filtering through a narrow opening in the drapes. Harrison lay on the bed fully clothed, snoring peacefully. Too much drink or too much laudanum, probably both, had caused him to fall asleep with his clothes on. Three imposing steamer trunks sat at the foot of the bed waiting to be moved downstairs, and more valises sat expectantly upon the floor, with piles of immaculately pressed shirts, trousers, vests, coats, boots, shoes, and other personal effects arranged neatly within them. Wherever his lordship thought he was going, it was obvious he anticipated being away for a considerable length of time.

He locked the bedroom door behind him, a precaution against the sudden entrance of any servants. Then he went to the window and opened it, swiftly assessing the route for his escape. Reaching into his coat pockets, he withdrew a half dozen pieces of stolen jewelry. It was a shame to lose them, but there was no help for it. Greed had kept him from planting this evidence earlier. That had been an error. Somehow he did not think the police would have been quite so quick to release Bryden if they had found evidence of the Dark Shadow's recent thefts in his home. This time, when the intrepid Inspector Turner arrived to investigate, he would discover a few key stolen jewels hidden amongst Bryden's personal effects. That would seal his guilt.

The case of the Dark Shadow would finally be closed.

He stood still a moment, expecting to feel a rush of pleasure at the prospect of Bryden's destruction. Instead he felt curiously hollow. He attributed it to the fact that it was disappointing that he would not receive any acclaim for solving the case. After all, it was because of his determination and superior intellect that Bryden was finally being brought to justice. If there were any justice in the world, he would have been hailed for his tenacity and brilliance. He would have to find satisfaction in the knowledge that he had managed to succeed where so many others had failed.

The considerable wealth he had accumulated in the process would ease the frustration of not being able to share his victory with anyone else.

He bent down and set to work concealing the jewels deep within the contents of several valises, taking the time to wrap each piece in a handkerchief or some small article of clothing first. It had to look like Bryden had made an effort to try to hide them, rather than carelessly stuffing them in amongst his clothes. When he was finished, he pulled his loaded pistol from his belt and rose, ready to confront Bryden for the last time.

The bed was empty.

"Good evening."

Startled, he turned around, only to find a very awake and very lucid Harrison standing several feet behind him.

"Well, now, this is a fascinating turn of events," he murmured, leveling his pistol at Harrison. "I'm actually rather amazed to see you up this late, given that you are usually passed out on brandy and laudanum by now. Head not bothering you tonight, Harry?"

Harrison regarded him coolly, giving no indication of how deeply those words, said in that agonizingly familiar voice, wounded him.

"I'm actually feeling quite well tonight, Tony," he assured him. "Thank you for your concern."

Tony peeled off his mask and cap and tossed them

onto the floor. He had planned to take them off any-way—just before he killed him. He wanted Harrison to know that after so many years of guarding his secret and evading justice, the man he had counted as perhaps his closest friend had ultimately outwitted and exposed him.

"I imagine you're rather surprised to see me dressed as you, or rather, a younger, fitter version of you," Tony reflected. "Must be bloody infuriating to realize that all this time you've been running about trying to find the Dark Shadow, I've been right under your nose."

"I'll admit, I'm a bit surprised to find out what you've been up to lately," Harrison conceded. "If you were having financial difficulties, you could have come to me, you know. You didn't have to resort to stealing."

A bitter laugh escaped Tony's throat. "Is that what you really think, Harry? That this is about the money?"

Harrison's expression was impassive. "Isn't it?"

Tony shook his head. "Poor Harry. You've spent so many years trying to put your past behind you. So many years creating a fine upstanding image for yourself that had nothing to do with your past escapades. But I've had my suspicions about you from the very beginning. That's what made me seek you out in the first place, that day I made sure we were introduced at Lord Beckett's party. And even though I believe I played the role of adoring friend beautifully, you never let me get too close. I had to start showing up on your doorstep and insisting we go places together, because you would never have initiated such a thing on your own. At first I thought you sensed there was something suspicious about me. I realize now that you don't let anyone get close to you. It's no wonder you haven't any real friends."

"Given the way this friendship has turned out, I be-lieve my penchant for solitude is understandable," Har-rison reflected drily.

"Well, fortunately for you, Harry, you won't have to keep your little secret any longer," Tony returned, still keeping his pistol trained upon him. "The jewels were nothing compared to finally confronting you. I've been dreaming of this moment for nearly sixteen years."

Harrison raised a skeptical brow. "You were barely more than a lad sixteen years ago."

"I was fifteen," Tony informed him tautly. "And I wasn't the son of a viscount, although I do believe I have played that particular role extremely well. I was the son of a policeman—an inspector, actually. Police Inspector Rupert Winters. Does that name mean anything to you?"

Surprise drifted across Harrison's face.

"Ah, I see you do remember him. It's good to know that he at least made some impression on you. Although at the time, you must have thought he was little more than the bumbling fool that the rest of London painted him, given his inability to catch you."

"I never thought your father was a fool, Tony."

"Of course you did," he countered. "How could you not? You were the clever Dark Shadow, who spent a year slithering in and out of London's mansions and taunting the men who tried to catch you. And my father was just a hardworking, underpaid police inspector, who had been assigned the biggest case of his career. The pressure upon him to catch you was overwhelming—and only became worse each time you stole again. Then the newspapers began to ridicule the police and detectives working on the case, and my father bore the brunt of their scorn. He vowed to catch you, or die in the attempt. Do you know what happened to him?"

"Inspector Winters was killed long after the Dark Shadow's thefts stopped," Harrison replied, struggling to remember the details. "It was in the newspapers. He was working on another case, and some criminal attacked him in an alley and killed him. It had nothing to do with me."

"It had *everything* to do with you, you son of a bitch," Tony bit out coldly. "My father became obsessed with catching you, to the point where he could barely eat, or drink, or sleep, or even acknowledge that he had a wife and children as he locked himself in his study to pore over his papers, or scoured London searching for clues. Catching you became his life. And when you suddenly stopped stealing, he refused to believe it. He waited and waited for you to steal again, so he could finally lock you up and be celebrated for his efforts. But you didn't steal again. Yet instead of being grateful that your criminal spree was finally over, the public turned on him. The newspapers joked that the Dark Shadow got too old and fat waiting for Winters to catch him. My father was painted as a fool. He started drinking, and he took out his anger on his family. His career was destroyed. He was assigned to minor cases in the worst areas of London, and it was while investigating one of those that he had his head bashed in by some thug, leaving my mother, sister, and me destitute. So don't you bloody well stand there and tell me it had nothing to do with you, you goddamn bastard. It had *everything* to do with you. Your little penchant for jewels destroyed my father and got him killed, which, as I'm sure you can understand, had a rather devastating effect on the wife and children he left behind."

Harrison stared at him, unable to respond. It had never occurred to him that his thefts had hurt anyone other than the people from whom he had stolen. In his mind, they had been accomplices in the ruin of his father, and they deserved to be hurt. He did not believe he could be held accountable for Inspector Winters's death. But he could not deny that his actions had played a significant part in the destruction of the man's career and his life.

"For years I hated you," Tony continued bitterly. "As I got older, hating you wasn't enough—especially since I didn't know what had become of you. And so I began to go through my father's notes on the Dark Shadow's crimes, devouring every little detail, desperately hoping I could solve the mystery of your identity. My father had written scores of pages theorizing the kind of man the Dark Shadow might be, listing the various possibilities of class, education, and intellect. The possibility he favored was that the culprit was either an aristocrat or a servant to an aristocrat—someone who knew his way around the homes and parties of the rich. It had to be a man of relative youth, who was physically capable of climbing up and down trees and scampering across rooftops. And it had to be someone who had a motive. That was where the possibilities became overwhelming. Virtually all servants believe that they are entitled to a better lot in life than the pompous pricks they serve. And there are countless aristocrats suffering financially, or second and third sons of peers who bristle at the unfairness of their allowances. All of these men might have thought stealing a few jewels was a perfectly reasonable way to augment their incomes."

"So you decided you would have to draw the Dark Shadow out," Harrison surmised.

"Exactly. I knew that if the Dark Shadow was still alive, there was a chance he might still be in reasonably good shape, given the feats he was physically capable of some sixteen years earlier. That was how the idea of trapping you in a new series of thefts was born. I learned everything I could about your methods, then set out to copy them. I created a new identity for myself: the Honorable Tony Poole, the pleasantly amusing son of some minor viscount, so I could infiltrate London society and study the men who comprised my list of possibilities. It was rather amazing, really, how quickly I was accepted. It demonstrates how vital the right accent, wardrobe, and story can be. You clean yourself up, affect an air, and casually mention to a few people that you're a viscount's son, then they introduce you to a few others, and by the third time you're introduced, it's accepted as fact."

"You've played your role very well, Tony."

Tony snorted with contempt. He was not about to accept compliments from Harrison. "I didn't consider you too strong a possibility at first, despite the fact that you were within the approximate age range and seemed fit enough. There were so many others who had wives dripping in jewelry, or who had a proclivity for wearing jewelry themselves, or who were still scrambling about financially. But I became intrigued when I learned about your father's suicide, and the nasty business about all the debts he left behind. That was when I decided to establish a friendship with you, to see if I could find out anything more. Unfortunately, you never wanted to talk about your father, and you were reluctant to let me spend time in the company of your mother. I had to rely on gossip to put the pieces together. My suspicions grew, but I didn't know for certain until you showed up at Lord Pembroke's house and I managed to tear your mask off."

"And that's when you dropped one of my handkerchiefs. You were hoping that would lead the police to arrest me."

"I didn't do that until I was absolutely sure you were the Dark Shadow," Tony pointed out. "I didn't want the police chasing the wrong man."

"But they weren't chasing the wrong man, Tony," Harrison countered. "They were chasing you."

"I was only trying to bring you to justice, Bryden. Which should have been done years ago."

"Forgive me if I fail to see you as some kind of brave hero nobly fighting to restore the memory of his father. You have murdered two completely innocent men. You would have killed Inspector Turner as well, if I hadn't stopped you."

"Actually, I only killed that idiot servant who came crashing into the room as I was going out Lady Pembroke's window. I didn't mean to kill him, but he gave me no choice. As far as I'm concerned, you're the one responsible for his death, not me. As for Turner, I was trying to make absolutely sure that you would be found guilty of murder. That's what you deserve."

"What about Lord Haywood? You shot him dead on the steps of Lord Chadwick's house. Did he give you no choice, either?"

"I'm afraid I can't take credit for that one. I had been planning to break into Lord Chadwick's that night, but as I arrived, you were already stumbling out of the house with the lovely Miss Kent shielding you. You killed him."

Harrison frowned. If Tony didn't shoot Lord Haywood that night, then who the hell did?

"I must admit, I had been looking forward to the spectacle of your trial and hanging," Tony continued. "It would have been good to see you paraded before a judge and forced to fight for your life. I was most disappointed when that idiot Turner decided to release you. But I now realize this is a far more fitting way to bring the mystery of the Dark Shadow to an end."

"Don't you think people are going to wonder who murdered me? Inspector Turner is certain to have a few questions regarding my sudden demise."

"But you're not going to be murdered, Harry.

You're going to shoot yourself, just the way your father did."

"And why would I do that? If I am, as you say, the Dark Shadow, and I've just been released from prison because there was insufficient evidence against me, what could possibly make me want to kill myself? Somehow I don't think Inspector Turner will believe that I was suddenly overcome with remorse."

"You're going to kill yourself for the same reason your father ended his life, Harry. Because your mind is going and you can't bear to suffer the indignities of madness, at which point you won't be capable of killing yourself."

Harrison was very careful to keep his expression utterly calm. He had told no one about his fear that his mind was eroding. "But my mind isn't going, Tony," he countered.

"Perhaps not." Tony shrugged. "But every servant in your household is well aware that you suffer the same debilitating headaches that plagued your father. One need only look at your receipts for laudanum to see how regularly you dose yourself to alleviate the pain. When the police interview me, I will tell them how much you suffered, and attest to your growing forgetfulness. I will cite all the appointments we made where you never appeared, describe your inability to find everyday objects, and how you fought to recall the names of people familiar to you. Thanks to me, your mental deterioration is also well known amongst the members of your club, who have been most distressed to hear of it. Given the mental illness suffered by both your parents, however, everyone understands it was only a matter of time before you fell victim to the same disorder. It seems that very often these things are passed on from one generation to the next."

Harrison regarded him incredulously. A painful

throbbing began to beat at the front of his skull, warning that a headache was looming. *Easy,* he told himself, fighting it. He took a slow, deep breath, trying to release the tightly wound knot of rage and disbelief that was pushing him toward the precipice of helpless pain.

"Are you saying that all those times you claimed we had arranged to meet, or talked about people I supposedly knew, but couldn't recall—that they were lies?"

"Some things you actually did forget, and others I made up," Tony replied easily. "I knew you feared turning into your father more than anything. As my suspicions of you grew I played upon that fear, realizing that at some point it might prove useful to me."

Harrison didn't know whether to be enraged or relieved. The possibility that his mind was not deteriorating to the extent he had thought was almost too incredible to be believed. Could it be that he was not doomed to end up like his father after all?

Of course if Tony managed to put a bullet through his head, his mental health would scarcely matter.

"A bit bittersweet, to learn that you aren't nearly as senile as you thought just before your life comes to an end," Tony reflected. "At least you won't have to think about it for too long. Now if you don't mind, I'd like you to move over to that chair and sit down," he ordered, gesturing with his pistol. "I believe we'll set this up so it seems you were sitting contemplating putting a bullet in your head for a while before you actually found the courage to do it."

Harrison remained where he was. "No."

Tony sighed. "Really, Harry, this isn't the time to start imagining some scene where you bravely wrestle your way free. I'm not about to roll around with you on the floor the way we did at Lord Pembroke's. We both know that if you had a weapon you would have shown it to me by now, so really you only have two choices:

Get shot now while you are standing, or get shot in the chair where you can be sitting comfortably. If I were you, I would choose sitting in the chair. At least then you won't have far to fall. Also, it would be a shame to spill blood all over this handsome carpet. It would make such an awful mess for poor old Telford to clean up."

"I don't think I'll get shot at all, Tony. Not tonight."

Tony regarded him with amusement. "I apologize, Harry, if you have a better time in mind. Unfortunately, this is the only night I can spare for killing you."

"You might think differently if you turn around."

"Don't insult me, Harry. I'm not so stupid that you can distract me with an idiotic trick. Now move over to the chair before I—"

"Drop your weapon," commanded a sober voice behind him. "Now."

Harrison watched with grim satisfaction as Tony's eyes widened with surprise.

"Well, well," Tony murmured, his gaze never leaving Harrison. "It seems this moment has to be shared, after all." He raised his gun.

Harrison hurled himself against Tony and grabbed his arm, knocking him to the floor as the pistol exploded. A deafening blast tore through the room. The throbbing in Harrison's head exploded into a thousand fiery pieces, making him feel sick. Still gripping the gun, he smashed Tony's hand hard against the floor, forcing him to release it.

"Don't move!" snarled Lewis, who had risen from the steamer trunk in which he had been hiding and now had his pistol aimed at Tony's temple. "Or I'll blow your bloody head off."

"And if for some reason he misses," Simon added, emerging from the heavily carved wardrobe at the other end of the chamber, "I promise you I won't."

"Neither will I," said Jamie, stepping out from behind the drapes.

"By the toes of Saint Andrew, just what kind of a
fool's lock have ye got here?" demanded Oliver, heaving
the bedroom door open with a bang. "Ye'd think in a
great house like this, they'd put in somethin' a wee bit
stronger," he muttered, offended by how little resistance
the mechanism had given him. "Are ye nae afraid of
thieves breakin' in, lad?"

Wincing against the pain in his head, Harrison
pulled himself to his feet.

"You're under arrest." Lewis spoke the words
slowly, savoring the pleasure of finally uttering them to
the right man. "And if you do anything to try to escape,
or even anything that just manages to annoy me, I
promise you I won't hesitate to shoot you. I may just
shoot you anyway, just to alleviate some of the discomfort you've caused me with that bullet you put in my
leg. Take him to Newgate," he commanded to the half
dozen young police constables who had crowded into
the room. "But first put him in shackles, and for God's
sake make sure someone is watching him every minute."

"You have to arrest him, too," protested Tony as
two policemen hauled him to his feet. "He's the Dark
Shadow—the one who stole all those jewels years ago!"

"That's enough of yer blather," scolded Oliver impatiently. "As if anyone would listen to the likes of a
spineless cur like you!"

"It's true!" Tony insisted, fighting to keep from being led out the door. "Bryden broke into Lord Chadwick's home—just ask her," he shouted furiously as
Charlotte limped into the room. "She was with him that
night—she knows!"

"If you're suggesting anything even remotely offen-
sive about my sister, I'd suggest you keep your mouth
shut." Simon's tone was deceptively mild.

"That's good advice," Jamie added, wrapping a protective arm around Charlotte.

Harrison stared at her, ignoring Tony and his accusations. He had not seen her since she had visited him at Newgate. No one had told him that she was here, anxiously waiting to see what would happen as he used himself as bait to trap the Dark Shadow. He could see that despite the warmth of the night she was shivering.

"Bryden is the Dark Shadow—you heard him admit it!" Tony raged to Lewis, his face nearly crimson with frustration and fury. "You have to arrest him as well!"

Constable Wilkins regarded Lewis uncertainly. "Sir?"

"Wilkins, take this piece of scum out of here," Lewis commanded brusquely. He did not spare a glance to Harrison as he finished, "I believe Lord Bryden has endured quite enough of his ranting and foul behavior for one night."

"Yes, sir. All right then, let's go!" Constable Wilkins commanded, ushering Tony and the other police officers out of Harrison's bedchamber.

"You have to arrest him, too!" Tony insisted as he was being dragged down the corridor. "You can't let him get away!"

"'Tis a shame," mused Oliver, shaking his head. "Sometimes anger's more hurtful than the wrong that's caused it." He cast a meaningful glance at Harrison.

Harrison stood, waiting. The pounding pain at the front of his head had abated a little. If he could just stay very still, and very quiet, he just might be able to keep it from blooming into full-fledged agony.

Unfortunately, he did not think that Inspector Turner was about to dismiss what he had just learned during his conversation with Tony.

All he wanted in that moment was to go to Charlotte. He wanted to take her in his arms and pull her tight against him, to make her feel warm and protected and safe, if only for a moment. He wanted to close his eyes and lose himself to her, to feel her softness pressing against him, the gentle flutter of her heart beating against his chest, the summery fragrance of her intoxicating his senses. He wanted to escape everything that had gnawed at his life and his soul for sixteen years—all the pain and lies and deception, to which he could now add the guilt of having destroyed the innocent and admirably determined Inspector Winters and his family. All this he wanted, with such intensity he did not think he could bear it.

Instead he stood unmoving, watching in silence as Inspector Turner rifled through his valises and retrieved the stolen pieces of jewelry Tony had concealed in them.

Lewis stuffed the precious stones and jewelry into his pockets, aware that there was more wealth lumped into his rumpled coat than he had any hope of earning during the entirety of his career. Once he was certain he had retrieved all of the stolen evidence, he stood and regarded Harrison soberly.

"It seems, Lord Bryden, that I am indebted to you for my life. And I am deeply grateful." He paused. "Unfortunately, there is still a question which I must put to you."

So this is how it must end. Harrison fought hard not to let his despair permeate the grim calm he was trying to maintain. He could not blame Inspector Turner for insisting upon the truth. After all, that was his job. And more, Harrison understood that solving a case and putting every last detail to rest was also his passion. Even so, he could not help but resent him, just a little. It was hard to accept that he simply could not escape the mistakes of his past, however grave they might have seemed in the eyes of the law.

Especially when he had finally found Charlotte, who knew exactly how deeply flawed he was, and somehow cared for him anyway.

"Go ahead."

Lewis regarded Charlotte, Simon, Jamie, and Oliver uncertainly. "Perhaps you would give us a moment of privacy."

"Let them stay." Harrison's voice was rough.

He stared intently at Charlotte. He would keep no more secrets from her. He wanted her to know everything. He would not have her banished from the room as if she could not be trusted with whatever he was about to reveal. She was part of him now. She had helped him when he needed it most. She had trusted him when she had little reason to do so. She had been strong and determined for him when he had felt weary and defeated. And in doing so, she had cleaved her soul to his. She had a right to know the truth, however dark and ugly it might be.

And so he stated quietly, "I would prefer to have Miss Kent and her family with me."

Lewis hesitated. He wished Harrison had elected to meet with him alone. At least if they spoke privately, whatever was revealed was just between the two of them. Lewis could then consider what action he should take—if any. He clenched his jaw, frustrated and bewildered by his uncharacteristic reluctance to pursue the case of the Dark Shadow to its logical, inevitable conclusion.

"Lord Bryden, I apologize for asking you this, but based upon everything I must consider in this case, I'm afraid I have no choice." He paused, wishing that he did not have to go further. Finally, he forced himself to ask: "Did you shoot Lord Haywood to death on the night of Lord and Lady Chadwick's dinner party?"

Harrison shook his head. "No, Inspector Turner. I give you my solemn word that I did not."

Lewis stared at him, trying to ferret beneath any layers of artifice or lies or false protestations of innocence, so that he might know the truth.

Harrison met his gaze evenly. He had no idea whether he came across as truthful or not. All he knew was that Turner had the power to put him in prison or let him go free.

Were he to base his decision upon the surfeit of evidence against Harrison, and the fact that Tony had confirmed it was Harrison who had escaped Lord Chadwick's house with Charlotte that night, he really had only one choice.

"Lord Bryden couldn't have killed Lord Haywood," Charlotte blurted out suddenly. "He had only a hairbrush in his pocket."

Lewis turned and regarded her curiously. "A hairbrush?"

"Yes. I made him take Lady Chadwick's hairbrush, so he could put it in his pocket and pretend it was a pistol so he could use me as a hostage." Her words were threaded with desperation as she continued, "I thought it very poor planning on his part that he didn't carry a pistol with him, but it also confirmed my conviction that he didn't intend to hurt anyone—and he didn't. Instead he tried to shield me when Lord Haywood shot at us."

"The lad's from the old school, like me." Oliver winked at Harrison with approval. "There's nae honor in wavin' a gun about, threatenin' to put a hole in someone just for a few quid. Ye dinna burn down yer barn to get rid o' the mice, an' ye dinna blast a pistol when a nice wee dirk will do just as well. Too much noise an' smoke, an' how can ye get away quiet?"

Lewis frowned, confused. "Forgive me, Lord Bryden, but if you didn't shoot Lord Haywood, then who did?"

"I don't know," Harrison replied honestly. "I thought the Dark Shadow might have been there amongst the crowd and done it, perhaps because he didn't want me to be killed by anyone other than him. But after hearing Tony deny it, I'm not so sure."

"Maybe Lord Haywood had an enemy amidst the crowd," suggested Simon. "Someone who took advantage of the moment and shot him, knowing that the deed would be attributed to the Dark Shadow."

"Or maybe one of the men in the crowd shot him accidentally, in the excitement of the moment," Jamie reflected. "And then was so horrified by what he had done, he didn't own up to it."

"It would be most unusual for Lord Haywood to be shot accidentally while he was standing on the steps of Lord Chadwick's home, in quite the opposite direction of the Dark Shadow," Lewis pointed out. "Someone would have to be an incredibly bad shot."

"Aye, ye're probably right," Oliver said. "But either way, ye must agree that the lad here couldna have shot his lordship with nae but a wee hairbrush. I can swear that's all the lad had in his pockets—I was there when we laid him on a bed an' peeled off his togs—"

Lewis held up his hand, silencing Oliver before the old man managed to say something more that might incriminate Charlotte's family. He turned to Harrison. "Thank you, Lord Bryden, for your assistance in helping the police to apprehend a dangerous criminal tonight. I will be sure to make it clear in my report that your role in helping the police to apprehend the Dark Shadow was both extraordinary and vital."

He was letting him go, Harrison realized, astonished. All Turner had wanted to know was whether or not Harrison had murdered Lord Haywood. Now that he was satisfied that he hadn't, Turner was choosing to close the door upon the crimes of Harrison's past.

A glorious relief began to spread within him, all but obliterating the pain still pulsing in his head.

"Thank you, Inspector Turner."

Lewis nodded, then turned to Charlotte. "Forgive me, Miss Kent, but there is one more thing I would like to ask."

Charlotte regarded him uncertainly. "Yes?"

He shifted uncomfortably on his feet, unsure just exactly how to pose his question. He wished he had his walking stick to lean on, or fiddle with, or give him something to look at other than the scuffed toes of his leather shoes. "It is a matter regarding Miss Clarke, who resides in your house of refuge." He paused to clear his throat.

Alarm flared within Charlotte. "Has Annie done something wrong, Inspector?"

"No, no, nothing like that," he quickly assured her. "As you know, Miss Clarke came to see me the other day. We just took a walk together," he hastily added, lest she think that something inappropriate had transpired between them. "And I believe we passed a very pleasant hour in each other's company." He stopped, suddenly embarrassed.

Understanding began to dawn on Charlotte. "I believe Annie also enjoyed her walk with you, Inspector," she said, trying to ease his discomfiture.

A flicker of hope lit his gaze. "Well, as Miss Clarke is residing with you, I believe that makes you a guardian of sorts."

Actually Lewis wasn't entirely sure that was true, since it seemed that all those living at Miss Kent's house of refuge were there of their own accord, and therefore could come and go as they pleased. Nevertheless, he was anxious to show Annie that he wanted to give her the same deference he would any proper young unmarried woman. To do that, he had to treat her rather unconventional living situation as if it were conventional, which meant according Miss Kent the role of guardian and chaperone.

"What I'm trying to say, Miss Kent, is that I would like your permission to call upon Miss Clarke—providing she is willing to see me, of course."

"Here now, just what do ye mean by 'call upon'?" demanded Oliver sternly. "Annie's a good lass who's tryin' to make somethin' better of herself, an' I'll nae have ye comin' around to trifle with her feelings. If ye do, inspector be damned, bad leg or no, I promise ye'll know the heel of my boot right up yer bloody—"

"I believe Inspector Turner's intentions are honorable, Oliver," Charlotte interrupted quickly. She regarded Lewis sympathetically. "Aren't they, Inspector?"

"Yes," Lewis assured her. "Very."

Oliver raised a suspicious white brow, unconvinced. "Fine, then," he relented. "Ye can call upon her. But know that me, Eunice, and Doreen will always be about, makin' sure ye do nae to damage the lass's reputation."

Lewis nodded. It pleased him to know that Annie had the ornery old man watching out for her. It made him feel better that others were at least trying to protect her from scum when Lewis wasn't around.

As for Black Jimmy, Lewis was going to use every resource available to him to find the bastard. And when he did, he would make damn sure the cowardly piece of dung understood that beating women was not acceptable.

"Thank you, Oliver. And thank you to all of you," he added, addressing the rest of them, "for helping me to capture the Dark Shadow."

" 'Twas nothin', laddie," scoffed Oliver modestly. "If

ye're needin' help again, just let me know. There's a few things I could teach those green peelers of yours—like how to get through a locked door without breakin' it down, for instance. I'm proud to say there's nae a lock in London I canna crack—"

"I must be going," Lewis interrupted, desperate to leave before Oliver again revealed something he didn't want to know.

Oliver blinked, disappointed. "Very well, lad. We can talk about it more when ye come to see our Annie."

"That would be fine," Lewis said. "Good night."

"I'll see you out," Harrison offered. He had sent his mother and all his servants, including Telford, to stay at Charlotte's family home for safety that evening.

"That's all right, I'll do it," Oliver offered cheerfully. "Did ye know, lad, if I hadna been a thief, I think I'd have been a detective," he began conversationally as he led Lewis into the corridor. "So if ye're ever thinkin' ye need a wee bit o' help . . ."

Harrison stared at Charlotte in silence.

"I'm famished," declared Simon suddenly, motioning to Jamie. "Let's go down to the kitchen and see if we can find something to eat."

"Excellent idea," Jamie agreed. "All the while I was behind those curtains I was wishing I'd had the foresight to ask Eunice to pack some of her oatcakes and ginger biscuits for me."

Harrison remained where he was until they were gone.

And then he crossed the room in three strides and took Charlotte in his arms, pulling her tight against him as he crushed his mouth to hers. He kissed her thoroughly, desperately, warming her with his strength and touch, trying to make her understand what he did not think he could ever put into words. *I love you,* he declared silently, pouring the depths of his emotion into the urgency of his kiss, the tender caress of his hands upon her shoulders and back and hips, the hardness of his body as he enclosed her in the heat of his embrace. Finally he tore his mouth away and regarded her seriously.

"Where's Flynn?"

"He's still with my father." Charlotte held fast to him, drawing strength from his protective hold. "I received the money you arranged for me from your barrister. My father had said he would come for the money tomorrow. Simon, Jamie, and Oliver are going to stay with me at the house while we wait for him to appear. We just have to pray that he honors his word and brings Flynn with him."

"We're not waiting, Charlotte," Harrison decided. "I'm not leaving Flynn in the company of that bastard one second longer than necessary. Your brothers and I are going to find him tonight if we have to search every inch of St. Giles, and we're going to bring Flynn home."

"I'm going, too."

"No."

"I have to go with you, Harrison," she countered. "I'm the only one who knows what my father looks like."

"Once we find out where the man who goes by Boney Buchan is, I'm sure I'll be able to figure out which one is him." Harrison's voice was filled with barely contained fury. "I don't want you there when I do."

"But if my father sees three strange men approaching, he'll think it's a trap and run away—or worse, do something to hurt Flynn. You don't know him as I do, Harrison. You don't know what he's capable of."

"I've seen what he did to your face the other night, Charlotte," he countered. "I've seen what he did to your leg. I believe I know exactly what he's capable of. And

I'm going to make goddamn sure he never comes anywhere near you, or Flynn, or anyone else in your family
ever again."

"You have to let me go with you," Charlotte insisted. "He's my father, Harrison, and Flynn is my responsibility. I believe Flynn's best chance of being
returned safely to me is if my father sees that I am there
to bring him his money. That's what he has demanded,
and that is what he is expecting. If I'm not there, he will
be furious. And when he is angry he is capable of terrible things."

Harrison regarded her helplessly. He didn't want
Charlotte to go with him. He wanted her somewhere
safe until he and her brothers had confronted Boney
Buchan and brought Flynn home. He did not want her
exposed to any more violence or threats or abuse by her
father, or anyone else, for that matter.

Nor did he want her to witness the thrashing Harrison planned to give the old bastard, to ensure that he
never harassed Charlotte again.

He regarded her seriously, about to tell her that a
criminal-infested sewer like St. Giles was no place for a
woman like her. But she returned his gaze with the same
extraordinary determination that she had shown him on
the night they met. She had refused to abandon him
then, and she was refusing to abandon him now, or
Flynn, or Oliver and her brothers. That was the way it
was with Charlotte, he realized. Within her slender,
feminine, unassuming frame beat the heart and soul of a
fighter. She didn't give a damn if she was a woman, or
that she limped, or was supposedly weaker than most of
the world around her. Charlotte had endured a childhood of unspeakable deprivation and abuse. Instead of
being defeated by it, she had become strong and determined and relentless. He could see fear glimmering in
the soft jade and gold of her eyes, but not for an instant

did he think that fear was for herself. Her fear was for Flynn, and Oliver, and Simon, and Jamie.

And maybe even for him, although he would have liked to think that she had enough faith in him to believe he could handle himself against a common brute like Boney Buchan.

"If I say you can't come, will you listen to me and stay put?"

"No," Charlotte promptly returned. "But I'd much prefer to go with you instead of wandering about St. Giles on my own. I don't usually go there at night, and I always take Oliver with me."

Harrison sighed. "Very well then. But you are to remain in the carriage with Oliver—is that clear?"

Charlotte looped her arms around his neck and pressed her lips to his, kissing him with fervent tenderness. He growled and pulled her closer, his tongue sweeping into the moist dark heat of her mouth, his body instantly hardening beneath the sensual spell of her scent and softness and touch.

"I'll just go tell Oliver, Jamie, and Simon that we're leaving," Charlotte murmured, breaking the kiss suddenly and limping toward the door.

Harrison groaned and fought to overcome the desire now surging through him.

And then shook his head in exasperation as he realized she had not given him an answer to his ultimatum.

Chapter Sixteen

"For Christ's sake, Sal, would ye quit that noise?" grumbled Archie, his tongue thick with gin. He turned over on the creaking bed and smacked her hard on the rump.

"It ain't me," Sal protested, her words equally slurred. "Must be the lad." She buried her face further into the stale dampness of her pillow and resumed snoring.

"Quit yet racket, ye scraggy whelp, or I'll crack yer napper," Archie snarled.

"It ain't me," Flynn returned from where he lay bound upon the floor. "Someone's bangin' on the door."

"What the hell—" Archie sat up and ground his fists into his eyes, trying to clear his head. "Who the Christ is it?" he shouted furiously.

"It's me." A woman's voice, soft and tentative. "I've brought your money."

Archie stopped pummeling his eyeballs and blinked, confused. "Lottie?"

"Let me in," Charlotte urged. "Hurry."

"Open the door, quick," Sal hissed, elbowing

Archie in the ribs. "Before someone grabs her an' nicks the whack."

"I'm goin'," Archie snapped, heaving his legs over the edge of the bed. Staggering through the leaden gloom, he banged into the edge of the table. Cursing, he stumbled to the door and twisted the lock, struggling to remember when exactly he had told Lottie where he lived.

The door smashed against him, knocking him back. Powerful hands wrapped around his neck and jerked him off his feet, cutting off both air and sound.

"Good evening," drawled Harrison. "Boney Buchan, I presume?"

Struggling wildly, Archie clawed at Harrison's hands.

"I'll take that as a yes." Harrison heaved him hard against the wall while still gripping him by the throat.

"Leave 'im be!" Sal shrieked, clamoring from the bed. She grabbed an empty gin bottle off the floor and raised it over her head. "Set 'im down or I'll smash yer friggin' napper!"

"That won't be necessary, madam," Simon assured her, entering the room and pointing his pistol at her. "Why don't you just put down your bottle, light that lamp over there, and sit down, and this will all go much faster."

"Your friend is perfectly all right," added Jamie reassuringly, barely casting a glance at Archie as he entered. "I'm studying to be a doctor—I know for a fact that you don't need to start worrying until his eyes pop from his skull."

"Oliver! Miss Kent!" Flynn exclaimed as they entered the room. "What are ye doin' here?"

"Lookin' for ye, lad," Oliver told him, squinting against the thin veil of light coming from the lamp Sal had lit. "An' 'tis quite the time we've had of it, too."

"Are you all right, Flynn?" demanded Charlotte anxiously as she limped over to where he was lying on the floor. "Did they hurt you?"

"I'm fine, Miss Kent—just a bit stiff an' hungry is all." Flynn closed his eyes and inhaled her summery clean fragrance, letting it wash through him.

"Sweet Saint Columba!" Oliver swore, seeing that Flynn's ankles and wrists were bound. "What kind of devil are ye," he demanded fiercely, turning to Sal, "that ye'd bind a wee lad so tight even while he was tryin' to sleep?"

"We had to bind him so he wouldn't run off," Sal retorted, defensive. "If he tried to run off, Archie would've beaten him. Better to bind 'im tight and let 'im lie still."

Oliver shook his head in disgust as he saw where the bindings had bitten into the tender skin at Flynn's wrists and ankles. "Here, lad, hold steady," he said gruffly, sawing through the rope with his dirk. "I'll have this off soon."

"I'm sorry, Flynn." Tears welled in Charlotte's eyes as she gently stroked his bruised face. "I'm so terribly sorry."

"Weren't yer fault, Miss Kent," Flynn assured her, troubled by her stricken expression. "This old shanker's gone off his head." His arms free, he sat up and cast a look of pure loathing at Archie while Oliver cut the rope binding his ankles. "The old soaker thinks he's yer da."

"He does, does he?" Having strangled most of the fight out of Archie, Harrison eased his grip a little, still holding him pinned against the wall. "That's where he and I have a difference of opinion."

Archie coughed and gasped, fighting to replenish his lungs.

"He *is* her da," Sal insisted, feeling bolder now that she sensed the men around her did not intend to actually kill either her or Archie. "He quiffed some doxy up in Scotland."

"If I were you I'd hold my tongue," Jamie warned, fighting to keep his own temper in check.

"It's true," Archie managed, his voice a defiant rasp. "Looked after her from the time she was a squallin' bairn, an' now that's she's flush in the pocket all I asks is that she spare a few quid for her poor ol' da—an' what's she do? Sends you bell swaggers over to baste me."

"I told ye so." Flynn shook his head in disbelief. "Gone completely off his pate."

"You never looked after me." Charlotte's voice was low and raw as she held fast to Flynn. "You only used me—just like you use everybody."

"Used you?" Archie regarded her incredulously. "Ye was nothin' but a scraggy wee lass, always sick, an' afraid of yer own shadow. How the devil was I to use ye?"

"You made me go out and steal before I was five years old," Charlotte answered. "You turned me into a pickpocket and a thief, and if you didn't think whatever I managed to nick was valuable enough, you beat me."

"I was only tryin' to teach ye how to survive," Archie protested. He looked at Oliver, sensing the old Scotsman might understand better than any of the other men in the room. "We had nothin'—not even a spare coin to pay for a wee drop of medicine when Lottie needed it, an' she was sick all the time. I knew she'd have to learn a trade right quick if we was to keep a roof over our heads, so I figured she'd better learn the only thing I knew, which was fleecin'. That way if anythin' happened to me, I knew she'd be able to get on all right."

"You made me steal because it meant there was more for you to drink." Anger was pulsing through Charlotte now, anger and a powerful resentment. "That's all you really cared about. You didn't care whether I had food to eat or clothes to wear—it was always just about you. I was a burden to you, nothing more. And when it became apparent that I was not going to be the clever little shaver you had hoped, you decided the only way to make any decent money off me was to turn me into a whore. But then one night you heaved me into a table and broke my leg, leaving me with this—" She gestured furiously at her injured leg. "And suddenly I was a cripple, and no longer able to become the little child-whore you had hoped I would be."

"I never wanted ye to whore, Lottie," Archie protested, feeling Harrison's grip tighten. "I just didna know what else was to be done with ye. If ye didna have me around, ye needed somethin' ye could do all right to make a coin or two. Lots of lasses do it," he added defensively to Harrison. "It puts bread in their mouth an' a roof over their head—that's all I wanted for my Lottie."

"Your concern for her welfare is most touching." It was only by the most vigorous self-control that Harrison was able to keep from strangling him.

"I saved her life!" Archie mewled, cowering. "Surely I deserve somethin' for that!"

"You never saved my life," Charlotte retorted. "You never cared what happened to me."

"That ain't true! Who do ye think it was shot that gotch-gutted nob the night ye was taken by the Dark Shadow? Me!"

She regarded him incredulously.

"Aye—an' a good thing I did, too, what with the way he was wavin' his pistol about. I knew he had just as good a chance of puttin' a hole in my Lottie as he did the Shadow," he continued desperately, talking to Harrison now, "an' since the Shadow weren't man enough to take care of 'im, I did. She'd 'ave snuffed it for sure but for me, and that's the honest truth."

There was some truth to what Boney Buchan was saying, Harrison realized reluctantly. Lord Haywood had already shot Harrison once. If Harrison had shifted even slightly, the next shot might have hit Charlotte instead. Apparently her father had been astute enough to realize that.

"Even if you did shoot Lord Haywood, you were only doing it because you wanted to blackmail Charlotte," he pointed out. "You saw her as an easy source of money, and you didn't want anything to interfere with that."

"That ain't true!" Archie objected vehemently. "I ain't sayin' I'm above givin' her a clout or two," he conceded, realizing Harrison obviously knew about the beatings he had inflicted, "but when it comes to her very life, that's different. She's my lass, after all. A man's got to protect 'is own—an' that's what I did. I protected her."

"If you were so concerned for my welfare, then why did you let me be abducted?" demanded Charlotte, unconvinced. "You saw a dangerous thief taking me hostage. Why not shoot him, too?"

"He wasna dangerous," Archie scoffed. "I seen 'im wrap himself around ye the minute that jingle-brains come runnin' out o' the house—that's when I knew he'd nae let ye come to harm. Whatever he was about, my Lottie could handle herself against the likes of him." He regarded her steadily, his eyes filled with something akin to pride. "I also knew ye'd be more like to take 'im home an' fix 'im up than turn 'im over to the peelers—an' I was right. Ye may have lived with nobs for years, but ye ain't forgotten yer roots. Doesna matter what fancy airs ye get for yerself—deep down ye're Lottie Buchan from Devil's Den, an' that's who ye'll always be."

Charlotte stared at him, a storm of emotions roiling within her.

For as long as she could remember, she had despised and feared her father. She had hated him for his violence and his cruelty, and feared him because he controlled her life. Even after they were separated by their arrests, his power over her continued. The ugly memories of her childhood and the possibility that he might one day find her had haunted her into adulthood, leaving her timorous and afraid. And then there was the constant, unforgiving reality of her leg, which never let her forget her life as Lottie Buchan.

Yet somehow, as he stood cowering beneath Harrison's grip, desperately defending himself as a simple but caring father who only wanted to teach his daughter to survive, her fear and hate begin to crumble beneath the weight of overwhelming weariness. She no longer had any desire to sustain her anger toward Boney Buchan, despite everything he had done. Her father believed he had taught her to survive. Maybe he had. He also believed he had saved her life. Perhaps there was a grain of truth to that as well, although it pained her deeply to think Lord Haywood had inadvertently died because of her. His flawed attempt to protect her did not change the fact that her father was an abusive, selfish brute. But it did intimate that somewhere, deep within the recesses of his selfish soul, there was a kernel of something good.

She hoped so.

"I don't want to ever see you again," she said quietly. "If you ever try to come near me or any one of my family or friends again, I promise you I will go straight to the police and post such an enormous reward for your capture that every whore, thief, street urchin, and coster in all of London will be fighting amongst themselves to turn you in. Even Sal here will be quick to turn stag on you and become rich," she predicted, noting how Sal's eyes had rounded at the talk of a big reward.

"Ye'd nae send me back to prison, Lottie." Archie stared at her in disbelief. "I'm yer father!"

"No." Her voice was hollow. "You're not."

"Ye canna change what God planned," he challenged, growing angry. "God gave ye to me."

"And then he took me away from you and gave me to Lord and Lady Redmond." She clenched her fists, willing herself to be strong as she stood before him. Her voice was small but steady as she finished, "And they loved me and helped me to overcome everything you did to me."

"Why, ye ungrateful wee bitch—"

"Quiet!" barked Oliver, outraged. "Mind yer scabby tongue or I'll twist it from yer head!"

"Good-bye." Holding fast to Flynn, Charlotte limped across the gloomy chamber to the door, with Oliver following protectively behind her.

"Ye canna change what ye are, Lottie!" Archie shouted, furious. "Ye've my blood runnin' through those coddled veins—nothin' will ever change that! Ye'll always be a beggar an' a thief, do ye hear? Always!"

"I think we've heard enough from you." Harrison tightened his grip on Archie's throat, cutting off any possibility of further speech. "And now I'd like to add my piece. You're going to leave London today, and you're not going to return. You've been given eight hundred pounds. That should be more than enough to get you and your friend Sal here decent lodgings in almost any town you could think of. If you're smart, you'll invest the money in a business—I'd suggest something along the lines of a tavern or an inn, given your obvious expertise in drinking and sleeping. I don't really give a damn, as long as you stay the hell away from Charlotte. Which I'm sure you will do, if you at all value your life. Because if you ever go near her or her family again, I promise you I won't bother with the police. I'll find you myself." His voice was deadly soft. "And when I do, I'll make you wish you had listened to my very reasonable suggestions. Do you understand?"

Archie nodded furiously, his face crimson from lack of air.

"Good." Abruptly, Harrison released him.

"Archie—are ye all right?" cried Sal, flying over to him as he gasped and choked.

"He's fine," Jamie assured her. "His eyes hardly swelled at all." He sounded disappointed.

"All he needs is a bit of fresh air," Simon advised, following Harrison and Jamie out the door. "I think the seaside might make a nice change for both of you, actually. I understand it's very pleasant this time of year."

"Come here, Archie, let me hold ye," said Sal, pulling him against her bountiful form. "Are ye all right?"

"Get the hell away from me!" Archie snapped, incensed that he had been so thoroughly humiliated in front of her and Charlotte.

"Can I get ye somethin'?"

"Get me a goddamn drink," he ordered, staggering over to the bed. "An' then get yer things. We're leavin'."

She splashed some gin into a dirty glass and handed it to him. "Where are we goin'?"

"Any place that's the hell away from here," he muttered before downing his drink.

"Where?" she persisted, frowning. Sal knew Archie was in a bad way, but that didn't mean she was willing to go traipsing all over England with him, not knowing when he might just tire of her and toss her out. At least in London she had friends, sort of. She had places where she could go. She knew her way about. "If we're leavin' London, I got a right to know where we're goin'," she insisted, unmoved by his glower.

"I ain't sure," Archie grumbled. "Maybe north.

Maybe south. Maybe to the seaside. I've got a few quid—let's get to the train station an' decide."

She shook her head. "Ye know I've always gone with what ye wanted, Archie—an' maybe this time I will too. But first I want to know just what it is ye want. That ain't too much to ask, especially now that ye're flush in the pocket. I need to know what my stake in it is."

Christ, he thought, first he's nearly strangled to death and then he's being henpecked. Eight hundred pounds, he thought morosely, staring at his empty glass. It wasn't so bad. A man could go far on eight hundred pounds—especially if he didn't piss it all away on gin and gambling. No, he'd have to be smart. Maybe he would buy some kind of business—one where he could be the boss, and work only as hard as he liked. A tavern might be good, with a few rooms upstairs, for those that needed a bed for the night. If he made it friendly and relatively clean, and didn't water down the ale too much, he might do all right. It was definitely a possibility. Still, he didn't think he could manage it by himself. He knew more about drinking gin than pouring it, and he didn't know the first bloody thing about cooking or laundry or keeping a place nice enough that people might actually want to spend some money there.

He looked around the filthy, shabby room, then glanced uncertainly at Sal. She wasn't much at cooking or cleaning. Still, she was strong for a woman and not all that bad to look at. Besides, he'd grown used to having her around, nagging and all. He sighed and wiped his mouth on his sleeve.

"Tell me somethin', Sal—if I bought us a wee pub, do ye think ye could learn to cook?"

Chapter Seventeen

...AN' THEN THE LASS TAKES FLYNN HERE AN' WALKS
out as strong an' swack as ye please, leavin' old Boney
Buchan stewin' in his filthy blather." Oliver cast Charlotte a loving smile. "He'll nae be botherin' ye again,
lass—unless he wants to feel the edge o' my dirk slicin'
clean across his skinny, scabbit throat."

"Here now, that's nae way to be speakin' in front of
the lassies," objected Eunice sternly as she passed around
a plate of shortbread.

"Ye'll be giving them bad dreams," Doreen agreed as
she helped Haydon and Genevieve's butler and house-
keeper, Beaton and Lizzie, serve tea to Charlotte's family.

Oliver frowned, perplexed. "Why in the name o'
Saint Columba would that give 'em bad dreams? I said
I'd cut his throat—that should make them feel safe."

"You don't talk about cuttin' throats in front of
young ladies," Lizzie explained, heaping generous measures of sugar and milk into each of the cups. "Best to say
you'll send any rogues off with the whack of a broom,
which is what I'll do if that cur comes 'round here, an'
let that be that."

"I like it when you talk about using your dirk to protect us, Oliver," Annabelle assured him.

"It always makes us feel much better to know that you're ready to use it," Grace added, smiling.

"There, ye see?" Oliver demanded cheerfully. "The lassies know I'm ready to give a bastin' to any miserable swine who'd dare frighten them or trifle with their feelings." He raised a meaningful brow at Harrison.

"Forgive me, sir," said Lady Bryden, confused, "but what, exactly, is a basting?"

"A beatin'," Oliver explained succinctly. "An' dinna be fooled by these old hands—I can still knock a rogue's teeth clean from his head with one blow, leavin' them chewin' on the ground."

"Really?" Lady Bryden blinked, clearly impressed. "How extraordinary. Perhaps, sir, you might be willing to give a few lessons in fisticuffs to my Harry. He's such a quiet, gentle boy; I worry that some day he might have need to defend himself."

"Well, now, I suppose there's a thing or two I could teach the lad," Oliver returned amiably. "Although I dinna believe ye need worry. I've seen the lad stand his ground, an' he fared well enough. Of course the scraggy old toast he faced was half his size and twice his age!" He barked with laughter.

"Harry, have you been fighting?" Lady Bryden regarded Harrison with disapproval.

"I had no choice—the fellow was bothering Charlotte," Harrison explained.

"Oh, well, in that case, good for you." His mother smiled, pleased that her son was protective of his new friend.

"I'm terribly grateful to you, Oliver, for always taking such wonderful care of all the children." Genevieve wrapped her arm tighter around Charlotte. Her daughter seemed thin and pale and exhausted, which was troubling. Genevieve did not know whether Charlotte's condition could be attributed to the events of the last few weeks, or whether the tremendous stress of trying to run a refuge house in one of the less desirable areas of London had taken an unacceptable toll upon her. "It has given Haydon and me a great deal of comfort to know that you, Eunice, and Doreen have watched over Charlotte so closely since she decided to come to London and set up her refuge house."

"We realize that all three of you have been instrumental in helping her to get it established," Haydon added, wanting to be sure that the three elderly servants understood just how much they were appreciated. A quick glance at Genevieve's worried face had told him his wife had decided it would be best to take Charlotte home to Inveraray to rest for a while. Given everything Charlotte had been through recently, Haydon found himself in complete agreement.

" 'Twas nothin'," said Oliver modestly.

"The lass does most of the work," Doreen added, sensing that Genevieve and Haydon were having second thoughts about Charlotte's venture.

"Aye, we help keep things sailin' smooth—that's all," Eunice declared. " 'Tis always a fine day when we can seat a few hungry souls 'round a table an' give 'em a hot meal and a bed."

"Eunice makes prime treacle scones," Flynn said enthusiastically. "I was thinkin' of 'em night an' day while I was waitin' for a chance to escape that soddin' old shanker."

"Were ye now?" Eunice's plump face shone with pleasure. "Well, lad, it just so happens I'm fixin' treacle scones tonight, along with anythin' else ye please, to celebrate yer comin' home. What do ye fancy?"

"Anythin' but haggis," Flynn said, wrinkling his

nose. "Maybe some of yer brown beef stew with pota-
toes an' peas."

"Brown beef stew it is, with cranachan for dessert."

"That sounds splendid, Eunice." Simon's mouth began to water at the thought of one of Eunice's wonderful meals. "May I come over for dinner? I'm starving."

"I'd like to come too," Jamie swiftly added.

"Well, o' course, lads, there's room for both of ye.
Maybe ye'd all like to come—I'm sure Annie, Ruby, an'
Violet will have a fine time hearin' all about how ye
trapped the Dark Shadow an' gave Boney Buchan his
due last night."

"That's very kind of you, Eunice, but I think we
will wait for another night," Genevieve said. "I believe
Charlotte is tired, and needs to have an evening of quiet
rest."

"I'm fine," Charlotte assured her. "You're all welcome to come over if you wish."

She did not want to prevent her family from getting
together for dinner and celebrating. It was clear they
were excited and wanted more time to talk and laugh
and enjoy each other's company. She wished she felt
more like celebrating herself. She thought she should
have felt elated, for having just rescued Flynn and standing her ground against her father for the first time in her
life.

Instead she felt empty and strangely fragile.

"Can I come, too?" demanded a low, faintly teasing
voice from the doorway.

Charlotte looked up to see her beloved older
brother Jack leaning carelessly against the entrance to
the drawing room. A shaky smile spread across her face.

"Jack! When did you get here?" squealed
Annabelle, jumping up to kiss him.

"Why didn't you send us word that you were coming?" asked Genevieve, also rising to hug him.

The room dissolved into a whirl of excited questions as his family crowded around to welcome him home. Only Charlotte remained where she was, her hands clutching the wrinkled skirts of her gown. Jack studied her intently as he hugged each member of his family, assessing every detail of her, from the paleness of her skin to the bruised crescents of sleeplessness beneath her eyes. His gaze moved swiftly to Harrison and Lady Bryden, who were the only people in the room he did not know. Lady Bryden returned his gaze with warm curiosity, obviously enjoying the commotion his family was making around him as she waited for him to be introduced to her. The man seated beside her was harder to read. His expression seemed friendly enough, but his dark eyes were shadowed.

"Lady Bryden and Lord Bryden, permit me to introduce my son, Jack Kent," said Haydon. "Jack, this is Lord Bryden and his mother, Lady Bryden."

Feeling slightly wary, as he always did in the company of aristocratic strangers, Jack gave them a small, stiff bow.

"I'm delighted to meet you, young man," said Lady Bryden, smiling. "I assume from the bronze of your skin that you have been abroad?"

"Yes."

"Our Jack loves the sea," Oliver explained proudly. "Canna keep the lad in one place more than a week or two—he's always off on a ship to India or China or some such wild place. The need to wander is in his bones."

"Really? How fascinating," enthused Lady Bryden. "You must come over for dinner one night and tell us all about your travels. I'm sure my Harry would love to hear about all the places you have been, wouldn't you, Harry?"

"It would be an honor to have all of Charlotte's

family dine with us in our home." Harrison met Jack's penetrating gaze with affected calm.

He had understood the moment Charlotte's eyes fell upon her brother that the two of them shared a uniquely powerful bond. He had been able to feel it pulsing between them across the room, even as Jack stood and accepted the affection and good wishes of the rest of his family. Although he had yet to go to her, Harrison could also feel a shield of protectiveness emanating from Jack toward Charlotte.

It was clear that if this handsome young man suspected for an instant that Harrison had trifled with Charlotte, he would take great pleasure in beating Harrison to a pulp.

"You gave me quite a scare, Charlotte," Jack said, kneeling before her once everyone else had had a chance to hug him. He gently covered her hands with his, stopping her from clutching her skirts. "We were docked in Italy when one of my men told me they had seen an English newspaper which said you had been kidnapped."

" 'Twas nothin', lad," Oliver scoffed. "I kept the lass safe, an' then we took the Dark Shadow here home an' Eunice an' Doreen stitched him up and then we helped find the real tooler who's been goin' about London thievin' and murderin'. 'Tis all over an' done with now—but we're pleased to see ye've made the trip to London, all the same."

Jack glowered at Harrison. All that he had absorbed from what Oliver had just said was that this bastard had taken Charlotte against her will.

"Jack," began Charlotte, sensing his outrage, "it isn't what you think."

"Is he the one who took you hostage?" Jack demanded. "The one they were talking about in the newspapers?"

"Actually, your sister insisted that I take her hostage," Harrison explained. "I tried my best to talk her out of it."

"That's true," Charlotte quickly agreed. "I knew Harrison was trapped, and the only way he could get past everyone was if he used me as a shield—"

"And you did that?" Jack rose to his feet, unable to believe that Charlotte was actually defending the spineless bastard. "You took a helpless girl who can barely walk and dragged her in front of you as a shield, just because she suggested it?"

"No, I listened to the suggestion of a young woman who is both intelligent and strong-willed, and we walked out together," Harrison countered evenly as he rose from his chair to face him. "And quite frankly, I find your description of Charlotte as a helpless girl who can barely walk utterly wrong. She is a remarkable woman who is capable of extraordinary things, and the fact that she endures a limp does not prohibit her from doing anything she sets her mind to."

"Well said, lad!" Oliver slapped his knee with approval. "I've thought the same thing myself about the lass for years."

"Sometimes ye have to make the best o' a bad bargain," observed Eunice philosophically. "An' that's what our Charlotte has done."

"Charlotte really has done some amazing things, lately, Jack," Annabelle chimed in. "She has done marvelous work at her refuge house, and has already helped a number of women and children."

"And she has attended dinner parties and balls and even spoken in public, appealing for donations," added Grace.

"She came up with a clever plan to trap the real Dark Shadow," continued Jamie proudly.

"And last night she faced her father after he tried to

blackmail her, and she told him if he ever bothered her again she'd go straight to the police." Simon beamed at Charlotte as he finished, "She was brilliant."

Jack stared at his sister in surprise. "You did all that?"

Charlotte nodded, watching as Jack's expression shifted from disbelief to a kind of painful regret.

"Well," he murmured, "I guess a lot of things have changed while I've been away." He cleared his throat, then glanced uncertainly at Harrison. "Forgive me." He turned abruptly and left the room.

"Jack!" Charlotte rose and followed him out of the drawing room, closing the doors behind her. "Wait!"

He stopped at the top of the stairs and faced her. "I'm sorry, Charlotte."

"For what?"

He shrugged his shoulders helplessly. "So much has happened to you—I should have been there for you. You were kidnapped, for God's sake—and then your father..." He shook his head. "I should have been with you, and I wasn't."

Charlotte reached out and gently took his hand, and together they sat down on the top step of the staircase.

"You have nothing to apologize for, Jack," she assured him gently, leaning against him the way she had from the time they were children. "I've always known you could never stay in Inverness and spend your life looking after me—I've never expected it—never wanted it. And as you can see, I've managed all right, with the help of the rest of the family. I'm not as helpless as you think I am." She paused a moment before quietly reflecting, "I'm a lot stronger than even I realized."

He regarded her uncertainly, trying to absorb all the changes he sensed in her. "What about that Bryden? Do you have feelings for him?"

She looked down, suddenly unable to meet his gaze. "Yes."

He stared at her in grim silence, fighting to sort out the maelstrom of feelings tearing through him. There was loss there, and an undeniable sadness. When had his shy, gentle little sister, who had always looked to him for comfort and protection, grown up into this beautiful, self-assured woman? A woman who now looked to another man to be her champion? He swallowed thickly.

"I don't need to ask if he has feelings about you. I could sense them the minute I walked into the room."

She raised her gaze, surprised. "You could?"

He nodded. "Is he going to marry you?"

"I don't know. Last night he met my real father, and..." She clutched the folds of her skirts again, unable to finish.

"And what?"

"It's one thing to know about a person's past, Jack—you know, to have been told about it and think, well, that was many years ago. But it's quite another to be actually faced with it. Last night Harrison saw the world I come from, and the father I come from—and it was awful. How can I expect an elegant, titled gentleman like Harrison to want a wife who comes from such a vile world? What would people say?"

"He would be bloody lucky to have you," Jack stated flatly, "and if he doesn't agree, I'll make him bloody sorry."

A helpless smile spread across her face. "Of course you would say that, Jack, and I love you dearly for it. But don't you see how impossible it is?"

Jack raked his hand through his hair, feeling hopelessly ill equipped to deal with his sister's heartache. "Listen to me, Charlotte. I don't know much about love, and even less about marriage. But I know what I've seen between Haydon and Genevieve. People have always talked about them, and it never seemed to bother them."

"It did bother them," Charlotte countered. "They just tried not to let us see it."

"But it never affected how they felt about each other," Jack amended. "It bothered them only because they were protective of us, and they didn't want people judging us for where we came from. If Bryden cares about you, what people say about you will make him angry, but it won't alter how he feels about you. He already knows where you came from, Charlotte." He hoped to hell he was right about what he thought he saw in Bryden's eyes as he finished, "And if what he just said to me in the drawing room is any indication, I'd say he understands how incredibly rare and special you are."

"Do you really think so?"

He shrugged his shoulders. "Let's find out." Before Charlotte could stop him he stood and jerked open the drawing room doors.

"My sister wants to speak with you, Bryden," he announced without preamble. "She's waiting for you at the top of the stairs."

"Why doesna she just come in here?" asked Eunice, bemused. "Me an' Doreen is servin' a lovely tea—"

"I'm thinkin' the lass wants to see the lad alone," Oliver speculated.

"Children and their games," said Lady Bryden, shaking her head with amusement. "Tell me, Lady Redmond, how do you manage to keep track of so many children?"

Genevieve smiled tenderly at Haydon. "I've had a lot of help."

"Excuse me." Harrison made his way across the drawing room and past Jack, who glowered at him warningly before closing the doors behind him.

Charlotte was seated at the top of the staircase, waiting for him. Her expression was grave. What had Jack said to her, Harrison wondered, that made her suddenly appear so unsure of him?

"May I sit down?" he asked.

"Yes."

He seated himself on the step beside her, not quite touching her. "What did you want to speak with me about?"

Charlotte regarded him miserably. She had not wanted to speak to him about anything—not this way, with him being forced to face her on the landing of the staircase and her entire family anxiously waiting for a report in the next room.

"It was Jack's idea that I should speak with you," she confessed. "He's just being protective of me. He always has been—much more so than Simon or Jamie, or even Haydon, for that matter."

"You are lucky to come from such a loving family, Charlotte. It is part of what has made you so incredibly strong."

She nodded and looked away, suddenly unable to bear the intensity of his gaze.

"There is something I have to tell you, Charlotte." His voice was low and edged with regret.

Whatever he was about to say, she could see he dreaded telling her. It was over, she realized, struggling to maintain some semblance of dignity as her heart began to tear in two. And what had she thought would happen? Had she honestly believed that Harrison would marry her? That he would merely overlook the sordidness of her past, especially after coming face to face with Boney Buchan?

"Ye canna change what ye are," her father had railed at her. *"Ye've my blood runnin' through those coddled veins."* At that moment, as Harrison stared at her with such sorrow, she realized that her father was right. She might

have been able to change the way she dressed and talked and acted, but nothing would ever change the blood that pulsed through her veins. In flesh and bone she was still Lottie Buchan from Devil's Den.

"I believe I may be suffering from the same illness that afflicted my father," Harrison confessed in a halting voice. "You have a right to know that, so I'm telling you now."

Charlotte regarded him in surprise. "What do you mean?"

"I suffer from the same excruciating headaches that plagued him for years. Sometimes I can fight them by lying perfectly still in a dark room for hours by myself, but often I have to resort to dosing myself with laudanum. It doesn't do much except dull the pain and make me sleepy, but even a restless sleep is preferable to just enduring the pain."

"Have you seen a doctor about them?"

He shook his head. "I don't need to. My father saw enough doctors for his headaches to cure me of any desire to go near them. I'm not about to ingest any of their insane concoctions, and I'm afraid subjecting myself to bleedings and blisterings, or letting them crack my head open, is out of the question."

"You must talk to Jamie, Harrison," Charlotte urged. "He isn't a doctor yet, but he is studying at Edinburgh University, which is reputed to be one of the finest medical schools in the world. He has access to some of the best doctors in Britain, and he may be able to find out about new treatments you could try. Jamie is quite brilliant when it comes to medicine—he's always at the top of his class—so I don't think he would recommend anything that didn't have any proven benefit."

"Perhaps," Harrison allowed, unconvinced. He hesitated a moment before reluctantly adding, "There is something more you need to know, Charlotte."

She waited, fighting the dread that now gripped her.

"A couple of years ago, I found myself starting to forget things. At first I dismissed it as nothing but the relentless advance of age, but as the incidents of forgetfulness began to occur more frequently, I feared I was suffering the same mental deterioration that afflicted my father."

Charlotte looked at him in surprise. "I've never noticed you to be forgetful, Harrison."

"I believe I have learned to hide it well. But last night Tony admitted that he had played upon my fear of becoming like my father. For nearly two years he pretended I was growing increasingly forgetful, knowing that at some point he would use this against me." He shook his head in frustration. "While I'm relieved to know that my mind may not be deteriorating to the extent I had thought, now I have no way of knowing how much of my forgetfulness is real, and how much of it was merely constructed by Tony."

"But that is good news," Charlotte pointed out. "Knowing how desperately Tony wanted to destroy you, it is quite possible that all of these incidents were nothing more than either normal forgetfulness or Tony's invention."

"Perhaps," Harrison allowed. "But without knowing, how can I move forward with my life?" He looked away, unable to meet her gaze as he ruefully finished, "How can I ask you to marry me, not knowing whether I am condemning you to endure the same hideous fate my mother was forced to suffer as she watched my father's mind break?"

Charlotte stared at him, speechless. "Is that your way of proposing to me?" she finally managed.

"It's my way of explaining to you why I can't propose to you."

"And where I came from or who my father was has nothing to do with it?"

He creased his brow in confusion. "What on earth does your father have to do with it?"

A guarded sense of wobbly joy began to spread through Charlotte. He didn't care. It was incredible to her, but there it was. He knew about her childhood and all the ugliness that went with it—he had even seen some of it firsthand. He understood that Boney Buchan's blood ran through her veins.

And he didn't care.

"Honestly, Harrison, there are times when I don't know whether to shake you or kiss you," she declared, exasperated.

Harrison frowned. "I don't think you understand—"

"I believe I understand perfectly," Charlotte countered. "You are reluctant to ask me to marry you because you are afraid that you might be condemning me to having to support you through an illness that you don't even know you have—is that more or less correct?"

"Yes, but—"

"So you are suggesting that instead of living our lives together and loving each other and finding happiness in however much time we have, it would be better for us to part and live the remainder of our lives alone. Is that right?"

"Not quite. You could marry someone else, Charlotte," he told her gruffly. "You could build a life with someone else."

"No, Harrison, I'm afraid I could not. Because I happen to love you. Intensely. You're the only man I ever have loved, and you're the only man I ever will love."

She slipped one hand into his and tenderly traced her fingers along the shadowed curve of his jaw as she continued, "I'm not afraid of helping you to endure your headaches. I know what pain is. I've lived with it almost my entire life, and if we can't find a cure for yours, then I'll learn everything I can about helping you to live with it. And I'm not afraid of facing an uncertain future with you. If you do suffer from whatever illness afflicted your father, I will stay with you and help you cope with it, just as your mother did for your father. Because that's what people who love each other do. They look at each other with all their faults and frailties, and they love each other in spite of them, and they help each other to bear whatever burdens their lives may hold. And I love you, Harrison. Completely."

A guarded sense of happiness began to filter through Harrison, like faint ribbons of sunlight streaking a leaden sky. She was right, he realized. It was foolish to assume only the worst would befall his mind, when he had just been given reason to think that it would not. No one could predict the future. Whatever was to happen, one thing was utterly clear. He loved Charlotte to the depths of his being.

And he could not bear to live another moment of his life without her.

His mind suddenly felt remarkably lucid as he wrapped his arms around her and drew her close.

"I love you, Charlotte," he said hoarsely, nuzzling the fragrant silk of her hair. "If you'll let me, I would be very honored to marry you and spend the rest of my life showing you just how much." He began to press a trail of silky kisses along the ivory length of her throat. "I do believe we should arrange for our wedding as quickly as possible, however," he murmured, brushing his lips against the pale swell above the neckline of her gown. "If it weren't for the fact that your entire family is anxiously waiting for us on the other side of those doors, I'd lay you down upon this very handsome carpet and start demonstrating just how much I love you right now."

"Here?" Charlotte gasped, pretending to be horrified.

"Shocking, isn't it?" His voice was low and lazy. "In the middle of the day, yet." He caressed the gentle curves of her and kissed her deeply, leaving no doubt that he wanted to do exactly as he said. Finally he groaned and pulled his lips from hers.

"At the risk of seeming a coward, I'm afraid we shall have to stop," he managed huskily.

"It's all right, Harrison." Charlotte's expression was teasing as she brushed a dark lock of hair off his forehead. "I won't let Jack hurt you."

"It isn't Jack I'm worried about," Harrison assured her, sounding insulted. He gave her a quick kiss on her cheek. "It's Oliver."

She laughed and threw her arms around him, feeling gloriously happy and strong and whole. His half-hearted attempt at propriety vanquished, Harrison decided to risk Oliver's vexation after all, and once again captured her mouth with his.

ABOUT THE AUTHOR

KARYN MONK has been writing since she was a girl. In university she discovered a love for history. After several years working in the highly charged world of advertising, she turned to writing historical romance. She is married to a wonderfully romantic husband, Philip, who she allows to believe is the model for her heroes.

Readers can find out more about Karyn at www.karynmonk.com